RANDOM HOUSE
LARGE PRINT

THE
LAST TIME
I LIED

THE LAST TIME I LIED

A NOVEL

RILEY SAGER

RANDOM HOUSE
LARGE PRINT

Published in the United States of America by Random House Large Print in association with Dutton, an imprint of Penguin Random House LLC, New York.

Cover design by Alex Merto
Cover photograph © Aaron Smith/Gallery Stock

The Library of Congress has established a Cataloging-in-Publication record for this title.

ISBN: 978-0-5256-3180-4

www.penguinrandomhouse.com/large-print-format-books

FIRST LARGE PRINT EDITION

Printed in the United States of America

10   9   8   7   6   5   4   3   2   1

This Large Print edition published in accord with the standards of the N.A.V.H.

To Mike, as always

THE
LAST TIME
I LIED

This is how it begins.

You wake to sunlight whispering through the trees just outside the window. It's a faint light, weak and gray at the edges. Dawn still shedding the skin of night. Yet it's bright enough to make you roll over and face the wall, the mattress creaking beneath you. Within that roll is a moment of disorientation, a split second when you don't know where you are. It happens sometimes after a deep, dreamless slumber. A temporary amnesia. You see the fine grains of the pine-plank wall, smell the traces of campfire smoke in your hair, and know exactly where you are.

Camp Nightingale.

You close your eyes and try to drop back into sleep, doing your best to ignore the nature noise rising from outside. It's a jarring, discordant sound—creatures of the night clashing with those of the day. You catch the drumroll of insects, the chirp of birds, a solitary loon letting out one last ghostly call that skates across the lake.

The racket of the outdoors temporarily masks the silence inside. But then a woodpecker's rat-a-tat-tat subsides into echo, and in that brief lull, you realize how quiet it is. How the only sound you're aware of is the steady rise and fall of your own sleep-heavy breathing.

Your eyes dart open again as you strain to hear something else—anything else—coming from inside the cabin.

There's nothing.

The woodpecker starts up again, and its rapid jackhammering tugs you away from the wall to face the rest of the cabin. It's a small space. Just enough room for two sets of bunk beds, a night table topped by a lantern, and four hickory trunks near the door for storage. Certainly tiny enough for you to be able to tell when it's empty, which it is.

You fling your gaze to the bunks across from you. The top one is neatly made, the sheets pulled taut. The bottom is the opposite—a tangle of blankets, something lumpy buried beneath them.

You check your watch in the early half-light. It's a few minutes past 5:00 a.m. Almost an hour until reveille. The revelation brings an undercurrent of panic that hums just beneath your skin, itchy and irritating.

Emergency scenarios trot through your brain. A sudden illness. A frantic call from home. You even try to tell yourself it's possible the girls had to leave so quickly they couldn't be bothered to wake you. Or maybe they tried but you couldn't be roused. Or maybe they did and you can't remember.

You kneel before the hickory trunks by the door, each one carved with names of campers past, and fling open all of them but yours. The inside of each satin-lined box is stuffed to the brim with clothes and magazines and simple camp crafts. Two of them hold cell phones, turned off, unused for days.

Only one of them took her phone.

You have no idea what that could mean.

The first—and only—logical place you think the girls can be is the latrine, a cedar-walled rectangle just beyond the cabins, planted right at the threshold of the forest. Maybe one of them had to go to the bathroom and the others went with her. It's happened before. You've taken part in similar treks. Huddled together, scurrying along a path lit by a single, shared flashlight.

Yet the perfectly made bed suggests a planned absence. An extended one. Or, worse, that no one had even slept in it the night before.

Still, you open the cabin door and take a nervous step outside. It's a gray, chilly morning, one that makes you hug yourself for warmth as you head to the latrine. Inside, you check every stall and shower. They're all empty. The shower walls are dry. So are the sinks.

Back outside, you pause halfway between the latrine and the cabins, your head cocked, straining to hear signs of the girls hidden among all the buzzing and chirping and water gently lapping the lakeshore fifty yards away.

There's nothing.

The camp itself is completely silent.

A sense of isolation drops onto your shoulders, and for a moment you wonder if the whole camp has cleared out, leaving only you behind. More horrible scenarios fill your thoughts. Cabins emptying in a frenzied, worried rush. You sleeping right through it.

You head back to the cabins, circling them quietly, listening for signs of life. There are twenty cabins in all, laid out in a tidy grid covering a patch of cleared forest. You wind your way around them, fully aware of how ridiculous you look. Dressed in nothing more than a tank top and a pair of boxer shorts, dead pine needles and pathway mulch sticking to your bare feet.

Each cabin is named after a tree. Yours is Dogwood. Next door is Maple. You check the names of each, trying to pick one the girls might have wandered into. You picture an impromptu sleepover. You begin to squint into windows and crack open unlocked doors, scanning the double-decker rows of sleeping girls for signs of additional campers. In one of the cabins—Blue Spruce—you startle a girl awake. She sits up in her bottom bunk, a gasp caught in her throat.

"Sorry," you whisper before closing the door. "Sorry, sorry."

You make your way to the other side of the camp, which normally bustles with activity from sunrise until twilight. Right now, though, sunrise is still just a promise, nothing but faint pinkness inching above the horizon. The only activity involves you marching toward the sturdy mess hall. In an hour or so, the scents of coffee and burnt bacon should be wafting from the building. At the moment, there's no smell of food, no noise.

You try the door. It's locked.

When you press your face to a window, all you see is a darkened dining room, chairs still stacked atop long rows of tables.

It's the same at the arts and crafts building next door.

Locked.

Dark.

This time, your window peek reveals a semicircle of easels bearing the half-painted canvases of yesterday's lesson. You had been working on a still life. A vase of wildflowers beside a bowl of oranges. Now you can't shake the feeling the lesson will never be completed, the flowers always half-painted, the bowls forever missing their fruit.

You back away from the building, rotating slowly, contemplating your next move. To your right is the gravel drive that leads out of camp, through the woods, to the main road. You head in the opposite direction, right into the center of camp, where a mammoth, log-frame building sits at the end of a circular drive.

The Lodge.

The place where you least expect to find the girls.

It's an unwieldy hybrid of a building. More mansion than cabin. A constant reminder to campers of their own, meager lodgings. Right now, it's silent. Also dark. The ever-brightening sunrise behind it casts the front of the building in shadow, and you can barely make out its beveled windows, its fieldstone foundation, its red door.

Part of you wants to run to that door and pound on it until Franny answers. She needs to know that three girls are gone. She's the camp director, after all. The girls are her responsibility.

You resist because there's a possibility you

could be wrong. That you overlooked some important place where the girls might have stashed themselves, as if this were all a game of hide-and-seek. Then there's the fact that you're reluctant to tell Franny until you absolutely must.

You've already disappointed her once. You don't want to do it again.

You're about to return to deserted Dogwood when something behind the Lodge catches your eye. A strip of orange light just beyond its sloped back lawn.

Lake Midnight, reflecting sky.

Please be there, **you think.** Please be safe. Please let me find you.

The girls aren't there, of course. There's no rational reason they would be. It feels like a bad dream. The kind you dread the most when you close your eyes at night. Only this night-mare has come true.

Maybe that's why you don't stop walk-ing once you reach the lake's edge. You keep going, into the lake itself, slick rocks beneath your feet. Soon the water is up to your ankles. When you start to shiver, you can't tell if it's from the coldness of the lake or the sense of fear that's gripped you since you first checked your watch.

You rotate in the water, examining your surroundings. Behind you is the Lodge, the side facing the lake brightened by the sunrise, its windows glowing pink. The lakeshore stretches away from you on both sides, a seemingly endless line of rocky coast and leaning trees. You cast your gaze outward, to the great expanse of lake. The water is mirror-smooth, its surface reflecting the slowly emerging clouds and a smattering of fading stars. It's also deep, even in the middle of a drought that's lowered the waterline, leaving a foot-long strip of sun-dried pebbles along the shore.

The brightening sky allows you to see the opposite shore, although it's just a dark streak faintly visible in the mist. All of it—the camp, the lake, the surrounding forest—is private property, owned by Franny's family, passed down through generations.

So much water. So much land.

So many places to disappear.

The girls could be anywhere. That's what you realize as you stand in the water, shivering harder. They're out there. Somewhere. And it could take days to find them. Or weeks. There's a chance they'll never be found.

The idea is too terrible to think about, even though it's the only thing you can think about. You imagine them stumbling through the thick woods, unmoored and directionless, wondering if the moss on the trees really does point north. You think of them hungry and scared and shivering. You picture them under the water, sinking into the muck, trying in vain to grasp their way to the surface.

You think of all these things and begin to scream.

PART ONE

TWO TRUTHS

1

I paint the girls in the same order.

Vivian first.

Then Natalie.

Allison is last, even though she was first to leave the cabin and therefore technically the first to disappear.

My paintings are typically large. Massive, really. As big as a barn door, Randall likes to say. Yet the girls are always small. Inconsequential marks on a canvas that's alarmingly wide.

Their arrival heralds the second stage of a painting, after I've laid down a background of earth and sky in hues with appropriately dark names. Spider black. Shadow gray. Blood red.

And midnight blue, of course. In my paintings, there's always a bit of midnight.

Then come the girls, sometimes clustered together, sometimes scattered to far-flung corners of the canvas. I put them in white dresses that flare at the hems, as if they're running from something. They're usually turned so all that can be seen of them is their hair trailing behind them as they flee. On the rare occasions when I do paint a glimpse of their faces, it's only the slimmest of profiles, nothing more than a single curved brushstroke.

I create the woods last, using a putty knife to slather paint onto the canvas in wide, unwieldy strokes. This process can take days, even weeks, me slightly dizzy from fumes as I glob on more paint, layer upon layer, keeping it thick.

I've heard Randall boast to potential buyers that my surfaces are like Van Gogh's, with paint cresting as high as an inch off the canvas. I prefer to think I paint like nature, where true smoothness is a myth, especially in the woods. The chipped ridges of tree bark. The speckle of moss on rock. Several autumns' worth of leaves coating the ground. That's the nature I try to capture with my scrapes and bumps and whorls of paint.

So I add more and more, each wall-size canvas slowly succumbing to the forest of my imagination. Thick. Forbidding. Crowded with danger. The trees loom, dark and menacing. Vines don't creep so much as coil, their loops tightening into choke holds. Underbrush covers the forest floor. Leaves blot out the sky.

I paint until there's not a bare patch left on the canvas and the girls have been consumed by the forest, buried among the trees and vines and leaves, rendered invisible. Only then do I know a painting is finished, using the tip of a brush handle to swirl my name into the lower right-hand corner.

Emma Davis.

That same name, in that same borderline-illegible script, now graces a wall of the gallery, greeting visitors as they pass through the hulking sliding doors of this former warehouse in the Meatpacking District. Every other wall is filled with paintings. **My** paintings. Twenty-seven of them.

My first gallery show.

Randall has gone all out for the opening party, turning the place into a sort of urban forest. There are rust-colored walls and birch trees cut from a forest in New Jersey arranged in tasteful clumps. Ethereal house music throbs discreetly in the background. The lighting suggests October even though it's a week until St. Patrick's Day and outside the streets are piled with dirty slush.

The gallery is packed, though. I'll give Randall that. Collectors, critics, and lookyloos elbow for space in front of the canvases, champagne glasses in hand, reaching every so often for the mushroom-and-goat-cheese croquettes that float by. Already I've been introduced to dozens of people whose names I've instantly forgotten. People of importance. Important enough for Randall to whisper who they are in my ear as I shake their hands.

"From the **Times**," he says of a woman dressed

head to toe in shades of purple. Of a man in an impeccably tailored suit and bright red sneakers, he simply whispers, "Christie's."

"Very impressive work," Mr. Christie's says, giving me a crooked smile. "They're so bold."

There's surprise in his voice, as if women are somehow incapable of boldness. Or maybe his surprise stems from the fact that, in person, I'm anything but bold. Compared with other outsize personalities in the art world, I'm positively demure. No all-purple ensemble or flashy footwear for me. Tonight's little black dress and black pumps with a kitten heel are as fancy as I get. Most days I dress in the same combination of khakis and paint-specked T-shirts. My only jewelry is the silver charm bracelet always wrapped around my left wrist. Hanging from it are three charms—tiny birds made of brushed pewter.

I once told Randall I dress so plainly because I want my paintings to stand out and not the other way around. In truth, boldness in one's personality and appearance seems futile to me.

Vivian was bold in every way.

It didn't keep her from disappearing.

During these meet and greets, I smile as wide as instructed, accept compliments, coyly defer the inevitable questions about what I plan to do next.

Once Randall has exhausted his supply of strangers to introduce, I hang back from the crowd, willing myself not to check each painting for the telltale red sticker signaling it's been sold. Instead, I nurse a glass of champagne in a corner, the branch of a recently deforested birch tapping against my shoulder as I look around the room for people I actually know. There are many, which makes me grateful, even though it's strange seeing them together in the same place. High school friends mingling with coworkers from the ad agency, fellow painters standing next to relatives who took the train in from Connecticut.

All of them, save for a single cousin, are men.

That's not entirely an accident.

I perk up once Marc arrives fashionably late, sporting a proud grin as he surveys the scene. Although he claims to loathe the art world, Marc fits in perfectly. Bearded with adorably mussed hair. A plaid sport coat thrown over his worn Mickey Mouse T-shirt. Red sneakers that make Mr. Christie's do a disappointed double take. Passing through the crowd, Marc snags a glass of champagne and one of the croquettes, which he pops into his mouth and chews thoughtfully.

"The cheese saves it," he informs me. "But those watery mushrooms are a major infraction."

"I haven't tried one yet," I say. "Too nervous."

Marc puts a hand on my shoulder, steadying me. Just like he used to do when we lived together during art school. Every person, especially artists, needs a calming influence. For me, that person is Marc Stewart. My voice of reason. My best friend.

My probable husband if not for the fact that we both like men.

I'm drawn to the romantically unattainable. Again, not a coincidence.

"You're allowed to enjoy this, you know," he says.

"I know."

"And you can be proud of yourself. There's no need to feel guilty. Artists are supposed to be inspired by life experiences. That's what creativity is all about."

Marc's talking about the girls, of course. Buried inside every painting. Other than me, only he knows about their existence. The only thing I haven't told him is why, fifteen years later, I continue to make them vanish over and over.

That's one thing he's better off not knowing.

I never intended to paint this way. In art school, I was drawn to simplicity in both color and form. Andy Warhol's soup cans. Jasper Johns's flags. Piet Mondrian's bold squares and rigid black lines. Then came an assignment to paint a portrait of someone I knew who had died.

I chose the girls.

I painted Vivian first, because she burned brightest in my memory. That blond hair right out of a shampoo ad. Those incongruously dark eyes that looked black in the right light. The pert nose sprayed with freckles brought out by the sun. I put her in a white dress with an elaborate Victorian collar fanning around her swanlike neck and gave her the same enigmatic smile she displayed on her way out of the cabin.

You're too young for this, Em.

Natalie came next. High forehead. Square chin. Hair pulled tight in a ponytail. Her white dress got a dainty lace collar that downplayed her thick neck and broad shoulders.

Finally, there was Allison, with her wholesome look. Apple cheeks and slender nose. Brows two shades darker than her flaxen hair, so thin and perfect they looked like they had been drawn on with brown pencil. I painted an Elizabethan ruff around her neck, frilly and regal.

Yet there was something wrong with the finished painting. Something that gnawed at me until the night before the project was due, when I awoke at 2:00 a.m. and saw the three of them staring at me from across the room.

Seeing them. That was the problem.

I crept out of bed and approached the canvas. I grabbed a brush, dabbed it in some brown paint, and smeared a line over their eyes. A tree branch, blinding them. More branches followed. Then plants and vines and whole trees, all of them gliding off the brush onto the canvas, as if sprouting there. By dawn, most of the canvas had been besieged by forest. All that remained of Vivian, Natalie, and Allison were shreds of their white dresses, patches of skin, locks of hair.

That became No. 1. The first in my forest series. The only one where even a fraction of the girls is visible. That piece, which got the highest grade in the class after I explained its meaning to my instructor, is absent from the gallery show. It hangs in my loft, not for sale.

Most of the others are here, though, with each painting taking up a full wall of the multichambered gallery. Seeing them together like this, with their gnarled branches and vibrant leaves, makes me realize how obsessive the whole endeavor is. Knowing I've spent years painting the same subject unnerves me.

"I **am** proud," I tell Marc before taking a sip of champagne.

He downs his glass in one gulp and grabs a fresh one. "Then what's up? You seem **vexed**."

He says it with a reedy British accent, a dead-on impersonation of Vincent Price in that campy horror movie neither of us can remember the name of. All we know is that we were stoned when we watched it on TV one night, and the line made us howl with laughter. We say it to each other far too often.

"It's just weird. All of **this**." I use my champagne flute to gesture at the paintings dominating the walls, the people lined up in front of them, Randall kissing both cheeks of a svelte European couple who just walked through the door. "I never expected any of this."

I'm not being humble. It's the truth. If I had expected a gallery show, I would have actually named my work. Instead, I simply numbered them in the order they were painted. No. 1 through No. 33.

Randall, the gallery, this surreal opening reception—all of it is a happy accident. The product of being in the right place at the right time. That right place, incidentally, was Marc's bistro in the West Village. At the time, I was in my fourth year of being the in-house artist at an ad agency. It was neither enjoyable nor fulfilling, but it paid the rent on a crumbling loft big enough to fit my forest canvases. After an overhead pipe leaked into the bistro, Marc needed something to temporarily mask a wall's worth of water damage. I loaned him No. 8 because it was the biggest and able to cover the most square footage.

That right time was a week later, when the owner of a small gallery a few blocks away popped into Marc's place for lunch. He saw the painting, was suitably intrigued, and asked Marc about the artist.

That led to one of my paintings—No. 7—being displayed in the gallery. It sold within a week. The owner asked for more. I gave him three. One of the paintings—lucky No. 13—caught the eye of a young art lover who posted a picture of it on Instagram. That picture was noticed by her employer, a television actress known for setting trends. She bought the painting and hung it in her dining room, showing it off during a dinner party for a small group of friends. One of those friends, an editor at **Vogue**, told his cousin, the owner of a larger, more prestigious gallery. That cousin is Randall, who currently roams the gallery, coiling his arms around every guest he sees.

What none of them knows—not Randall, not the actress, not even Marc—is that those thirty-three canvases are the only things I've painted outside my duties at the ad agency. There are no fresh ideas percolating in this artist's brain, no inspiration sparking me into productivity. I've attempted other things, of course, more from a nagging sense of responsibility than actual desire. But I'm never able to move beyond those initial, halfhearted efforts. I return to the girls every damn time.

I know I can't keep painting them, losing them in the woods again and again. To that end, I've vowed not to paint another. There won't be a No. 34 or a No. 46 or, God forbid, a No. 112.

That's why I don't answer when everyone asks me what I'm working on next. I have no answer to give. My future is quite literally a blank canvas, waiting for me to fill it. The only thing I've painted in the past six months is my studio, using a roller to convert it from daffodil yellow to robin's-egg blue.

If there's anything vexing me, it's that. I'm a one-hit wonder. A bold lady painter whose life's work is on these walls.

As a result, I feel helpless when Marc leaves my side to chat up a handsome cater waiter, giving Randall the perfect moment to clutch my wrist and drag me to a slender woman studying No. 30, my largest work to date. Although I can't see the woman's face, I know she's important. Everyone else I've met tonight has been guided to me instead of the other way around.

"Here she is, darling," Randall announces. "The artist herself."

The woman whirls around, fixing me with a friendly, green-eyed gaze I haven't seen in fifteen years. It's a look you easily remember. The kind of gaze that, when aimed at you, makes you feel like the most important person in the world.

"Hello, Emma," she says.

I freeze, not sure what else to do. I have no idea how she'll act. Or what she'll say. Or even why she's here. I had assumed Francesca Harris-White wanted nothing to do with me.

Yet she smiles warmly before pulling me close until our cheeks touch. A semi-embrace that Randall witnesses with palpable jealousy.

"You already know each other?"

"Yes," I say, still stunned by her presence.

"It was ages ago. Emma was a mere slip of a girl. And I couldn't be more proud of the woman she's become."

She gives me another look. **The** look. And although that sense of surprise hasn't left me, I realize how happy I am to see her. I didn't think such a thing was possible.

"Thank you, Mrs. Harris-White," I tell her. "That's very kind of you to say."

She mock frowns. "What's with this 'Mrs. Harris-White' nonsense? It's Franny. Always Franny."

I remember that, too. Her standing before us in her khaki shorts and blue polo shirt, her bulky hiking boots making her feet look comically large. **Call me Franny. I insist upon it. Here in the great outdoors, we're all equals.**

It didn't last. Afterward, when what happened was in newspapers across the country, it was her full, formal name that was used. Francesca Harris-White. Only daughter of real estate magnate Theodore Harris. Sole grandchild of lumber baron Buchanan Harris. Much-younger widow of tobacco heir Douglas White. Net worth estimated to be almost a billion, most of it old money stretching back to the Gilded Age.

Now she stands before me, seemingly untouched by time, even though she must be in her late seventies. She wears her age well. Her skin is tan and radiant. Her sleeveless blue dress emphasizes her trim figure. Her hair, a shade balanced between blond and gray, has been pulled back in a chignon, showing off a single strand of pearls around her neck.

She turns to the painting again, her gaze scanning its formidable width. It's one of my darker works—all blacks, deep blues, and mud browns. The canvas dwarfs her, making it look as though she's actually standing in a forest, the trees about to overtake her.

"It's really quite marvelous," she says. "All of them are."

There's a catch in her voice. Something tremulous and uncertain, as if she can somehow glimpse the girls in their white dresses beneath the painted thicket.

"I must confess that I came here under false pretenses," she says, still staring at the painting, seemingly unable to look away. "I'm here for the art, of course. But also for something else. I have what you might call an interesting proposition."

At last, she turns away from the painting, fixing those green eyes on me. "I'd love to discuss it with you, when you have the time."

I shoot a glance to Randall, who stands behind Franny at a discreet distance. He mouths the word every artist longs to hear: **commission.**

The idea prompts me to immediately say, "Of course." Under any other circumstance, I already would have declined.

"Then join me for lunch tomorrow. Let's say twelve thirty? At my place? It will give us a chance to catch up."

I find myself nodding, even though I'm not entirely sure what's happening. Franny's unexpected appearance. Her even more unexpected invitation to lunch. The scary-yet-tantalizing prospect of being commissioned to paint something for her. It's another surreal touch to an already strange evening.

"Of course," I say again, lacking the wherewithal to utter anything else.

Franny beams. "Wonderful."

She presses a card into my hand. Navy print on heavy white vellum. Simple but elegant. It bears her name, a phone number, and a Park Avenue address. Before leaving, she pulls me into another half hug. Then she turns to Randall and gestures toward No. 30.

"I'll take it," she says.

2

Franny's building is easy to find. It's the one that bears her family's name.

The Harris.

Much like its residents, the Harris is steadfastly inconspicuous. No Dakota-like dormers and gables here. Just understated architecture rising high over Park Avenue. Above the doorway is the Harris family crest carved in marble. It depicts two tall pines crossed together to form an **X**, surrounded by an ivy laurel. Appropriate, considering the family's initial fortune came from the culling of such trees.

The inside of the Harris is as somber and hushed as a cathedral. And I'm the sinner tiptoeing inside. An impostor. Someone who doesn't belong. Yet the doorman smiles and greets me by name, as if I've lived here for years.

The warm welcome continues when I'm directed to the elevator. Standing inside is another familiar face from Camp Nightingale.

"Lottie?" I say.

Unlike Franny, she's changed quite a bit in the past fifteen years. Older, of course. More sophisticated. The shorts and plaid shirt I last saw her wearing have been replaced with a charcoal pantsuit over a crisp white blouse. Her hair, once long and the color of mahogany, is now jet-black and cut into a sleek bob that frames her pale face. But the smile is the same. It has a warm, friendly glow that's just as vibrant now as it was at Camp Nightingale.

"Emma," she says, pulling me into a hug. "My God, it's nice to see you again."

I hug her back. "You too, Lottie. I wondered if you still worked for Franny."

"She couldn't get rid of me if she tried. Not that she'd ever want to."

Indeed, the two of them were rarely seen apart. Franny the master of the camp, and Lottie the devoted assistant. Together they ruled not with an iron fist but with a velvet glove, their benevolent patience never strained, even when surprised by a latecomer like myself. I can still picture the moment I met Lottie. The unhurried way she emerged from the Lodge after my parents and I arrived hours later than expected. She greeted us with a smile, a wave, and a sincere **Welcome to Camp Nightingale**.

Now she ushers me into the elevator and presses the top button. As we're whisked upward, she says,

"You and Franny will be lunching in the greenhouse. Just wait until you see it."

I nod, feigning excitement. Lottie sees right through me. She eyes me from head to toe, taking in my stiff-backed posture, my tapping foot, the uncontrollable wavering of my plastered-on smile.

"Don't be nervous," she says. "Franny's forgiven you a hundred times over."

I wish I could believe that. Even though Franny was nothing but friendly to me at the gallery, a gnawing doubt persists. I can't shake the feeling that this is more than just a friendly visit.

The elevator doors open, and I find myself looking at the entrance foyer to Franny's penthouse. To my surprise, the wall directly facing the elevator already bears the painting she had purchased the night before. No little red sticker or weeks of waiting for Francesca Harris-White. Randall must have been up all night organizing its shipment from the gallery to here.

"It's a beautiful piece," Lottie says of No. 30. "I can see why Franny was taken with it."

I wonder if Franny would still be taken if she knew the girls were secreted within the painting, hiding there, waiting to be found. I then wonder how the girls themselves would feel about taking up residence in Franny's penthouse. Allison and Natalie likely wouldn't care. But Vivian? She'd fucking love it.

"I plan on taking an afternoon off to visit the gallery and see what else you've painted," Lottie says. "I'm so proud of you, Emma. We all are."

She leads me down a short hallway to the left, past a formal dining room and through a sunken sitting room. "Here we are. The greenhouse."

The word doesn't begin to do the room justice. It's a greenhouse in the same way Grand Central is a train station. Both are so ornate it defies easy description.

Franny's greenhouse is in reality a two-story conservatory built on what was once the penthouse terrace. Panes of heavy glass rise from floor to vaulted ceiling, some still bearing triangles of snow in their exterior corners. Contained within this fanciful structure is a miniature forest. There are squat pines, flowering cherry trees, and rosebushes aflame with red blooms. Slick moss and tendrils of ivy cover the ground. There's even a babbling brook, which flows over a creek bed stippled with rocks. In the center of this fairy-tale forest is a redbrick patio. That's where I find Franny, seated at a wrought-iron table already set for lunch.

"Here she is," Lottie announces. "And probably famished. Which means I better start serving."

Franny greets me with another semi-embrace. "How wonderful to see you again, Emma. And dressed so beautifully, too."

Since I had no idea what to wear, I put on the nicest thing I own—a printed Diane von Furstenberg wrap dress my parents gave me for Christmas. It turns out I shouldn't have worried about being underdressed. Next to Franny's outfit of black pants and white button-down, I feel the opposite. Stiff, formal, and agonizingly nervous about why I've been summoned here.

"What do you think of my little greenhouse?" Franny asks.

I take another look around, spying details previously missed. The statue of an angel half-consumed by ivy. The daffodils sprouting beside the creek. "It's marvelous," I say. "Too beautiful for words."

"It's my tiny oasis in the big city. I decided years ago that if I couldn't live outdoors, then I'd have to bring the outdoors inside to live with me."

"So that's why you bought my biggest painting," I say.

"Exactly. Looking at it feels like standing before a dark woods, and I must decide if I should venture forth into it. The answer, of course, is yes."

That would be my answer, too. But unlike Franny, I'd go only because I know the girls are waiting for me just beyond the tree line.

Lunch is trout almondine and arugula salad, washed down with a crisp Riesling. The first glass of wine calms my nerves. The second lets me lower my guard. By the third, when Franny asks me about my job, my personal life, my family, I answer honestly—hate it, still single, parents retired to Boca Raton.

"Everything was delicious," I say when we finish a dessert of lemon tart so tasty I'm tempted to lick the plate.

"I'm so pleased," Franny says. "The trout came from Lake Midnight, you know."

The mention of the lake startles me. Franny notices my surprise and says, "We can still think fondly of a place where bad things have occurred. At least, I can. And I do."

It's understandable that Franny feels this way in spite of everything that happened. It is, after all, her family's property. Four thousand acres of wilderness at the southern base of the Adirondacks, all preserved by her grandfather after he spent a lifetime deforesting land five times that size. I suppose Buchanan Harris thought saving those four thousand acres made up for it. Perhaps it did, even though that preservation also came at a cost to the environment. Disappointed he couldn't find a tract of land that contained a large body of water, Franny's grandfather decided to create one himself. He dammed the tributary of a nearby river, slamming the gates shut with the push of a button at the stroke of midnight on a rainy New Year's Eve in 1902. Within days, what was once a quiet valley became a lake.

The story of Lake Midnight. It was told to every new arrival at Camp Nightingale.

"It hasn't changed one bit," Franny continues. "The Lodge is still there, of course. My home away from home. I was just there this past week-end, which is how I happened upon the trout. I caught them myself. The boys hate that I go so often. Especially when it's just Lottie and myself. Theo worries that there's no one around to help if something terrible befalls us."

Hearing about Franny's sons gives me another uneasy jolt.

Theodore and Chester Harris-White. Such un-bearably WASPish names. Like their mother, they prefer their nicknames—Theo and Chet. The youngest, Chet, is hazy in my memory. He was just a boy when I was at Camp Nightingale, no more than ten. The product of a surprise, late-in-life adoption. I can't recall ever speaking to him, although I must have at some point. I simply re-member getting occasional glimpses of him run-ning barefoot down the Lodge's sloped back lawn to the edge of the lake.

Theo was also adopted. Years before Chet.

I remember a lot about him. Maybe too much.

"How are they?" I ask, even though I have no right to know. I do it only because Franny gives me an expectant look, clearly waiting for me to inquire about them.

"They're both well. Theo is spending the year in Africa, working with Doctors Without Borders. Chet will be getting his master's from Yale in the spring. He's engaged to a lovely girl." She pauses, allowing the information to settle over me. The silence speaks volumes. It tells me that her family is thriving, in spite of what I did to them. "I thought you might already know all this. I've heard the Camp Nightingale grapevine is still fully intact."

"I'm not really in touch with anyone from there anymore," I admit.

Not that the girls I knew at camp didn't try. When Facebook became the rage, I received friend requests from several former campers. I ignored them all, seeing no point in staying in touch. We had nothing in common other than spending two weeks in the same place at the same unfortunate time. That didn't stop me from being included in a Facebook group of Camp Nightingale alumni. I muted all posts years ago.

"Perhaps we can change that," Franny says.

"How?"

"I suppose it's time I reveal why I've asked you here today," she says, adding a tactful "Although I do enjoy your company very much."

"I'll admit I'm curious," I say, which is the understatement of the year.

"I'm going to reopen Camp Nightingale," Franny announces.

"Are you sure that's a good idea?"

The words tumble forth, unplanned. They contain a derisive edge. Cold and almost cruel.

"I'm sorry," I say. "That came out wrong."

Franny reaches across the table, gives my hand a squeeze, and says, "Don't feel bad at all. You're not the first person to have that reaction. And even I can admit it's not the most logical idea. But I feel like it's the right time. The camp has been quiet long enough."

Fifteen years. That's how long it's been. It feels like a lifetime ago. It also feels like yesterday.

The camp closed early that summer, shutting down after only two weeks and throwing lots of families' schedules into chaos. It couldn't be helped. Not after what happened. My parents vacillated between sympathy and annoyance after they picked me up a day later than everyone else. Last to arrive, last to leave. I remember sitting in our Volvo, staring out the back window as the camp receded. Even at thirteen, I knew it would never reopen.

A different camp could have survived the scrutiny. But Camp Nightingale wasn't just any summer camp. It was **the** summer camp if you lived in Manhattan and had a bit of money. The place where generations of young women from well-to-do families spent their summers swimming, sailing, gossiping. My mother went there. So did my aunt. At my school, it was known as Camp Rich Bitch. We said it with scorn, trying to hide both our jealousy and our disappointment that our parents couldn't quite afford to send us there. Except, in my case, for one summer.

The same summer that shattered the camp's reputation.

The people involved were all notable enough to keep the story in the news for the rest of the summer and into the fall. Natalie, the daughter of the city's top orthopedic surgeon. Allison, the child of a prominent Broadway actress. And Vivian, the senator's daughter, whose name often appeared in the newspaper with the word **troubled** in close proximity.

The press mostly left me alone. Compared with the others, I was a nobody. Just the daughter of a neglectful investment banker father and a high-functioning alcoholic mother. A gangly thirteen-year-old whose grandmother had recently died, leaving her with enough money to spend six weeks at one of the nation's most exclusive summer camps.

It was Franny who ultimately received the bulk of the media's scorn. Francesca Harris-White, the rich girl who had always befuddled the society columns with her refusal to play the game. Marrying a contemporary of her father at twenty-one. Burying him before she turned thirty. Adopting a child at forty, then another at fifty.

The coverage was brutal. Articles about how Lake Midnight was an unsafe place for a summer camp, especially considering that her husband had drowned there the year before Camp Nightingale opened. Claims that the camp was understaffed and unsupervised. Think pieces blaming Franny for standing by her son when suspicion swirled around him. Some even insinuated there might be something sinister about Camp Nightingale, about Franny, about her family.

I probably had something to do with that.

Scratch that. I know I did.

Yet Franny shows no ill will as she sits in her faux forest, outlining her vision for the new Camp Nightingale.

"It won't be the same, of course," she says. "It can't be. Although fifteen years is a long enough time, what happened will always be like a shadow hanging over the camp. That's why I'm going to do things differently this time. I've set up a charitable trust. No one will have to pay a penny to stay there. The camp will be completely free and merit-based, serving girls from around the tri-state area."

"That's very generous," I say.

"I don't want anyone's money. I certainly don't need it. All I need is to see the place filled again with girls enjoying the outdoors. And I'd truly love it if you would join me."

I gulp. Me? Spend the summer at Camp Nightingale? This is far different from the commission offer I had expected to receive. It's so outlandish I start to think I've misheard her.

"It's not that strange of an idea," Franny says. "I want the camp to have a strong arts component. Yes, the girls there will swim and hike and do all the usual camp activities. But I also want them to learn about writing, photography, painting."

"You want me to teach them to paint?"

"Of course," Franny says. "But you'll also have plenty of time to work on your own. There's no better inspiration than nature."

I still don't get why Franny wants me, of all people, to be there. I should be the last person she wants around. She senses my hesitation, of course. It's impossible not to, considering how I sit stiff-backed in my chair, fiddling with the napkin in my lap, twisting it into a coiled knot.

"I understand your trepidation," she says. "I'd feel the same way if our roles were reversed. But I don't blame you for what happened, Emma. You were young and confused, and the situation was horrible for everyone. I firmly believe in letting bygones be bygones. And it's my great wish to have some former campers there. To show everyone that it's a safe, happy place again. Rebecca Schoenfeld has agreed to do it."

Becca Schoenfeld. Notable photojournalist. Her image of two young Syrian refugees holding hands while covered in blood made front pages around the world. But more important for Franny's purposes, Becca's also a veteran of Camp Nightingale's final summer.

She noticeably wasn't one of the girls who sought me out on Facebook. Not that I expected her to. Becca was a mystery to me. Not standoffish, necessarily. Aloof. She was quiet, often alone, content to view the world through the lens of the camera that always hung around her neck, even when she was waist-deep in the lake.

I imagine her sitting at this very table, that same camera dangling from its canvas strap as Franny convinces her to return to Camp Nightingale. Knowing that she's agreed changes things. It makes Franny's idea seem less like a folly and more like something that could actually happen. Although not with me.

"It's an awfully big commitment," I say.

"You'll be compensated financially, of course."

"It's not that," I say, still twisting the napkin so hard it's starting to look like rope. "I'm not sure I can go back there again. Not after what happened."

"Maybe that's precisely why you **should** go back," Franny says. "I was afraid to return, too. I avoided it for two years. I thought I'd find nothing there but darkness and bad memories. That wasn't the case. It was as beautiful as ever. Nature heals, Emma. I firmly believe that."

I say nothing. It's hard to speak when Franny's green-eyed gaze is fixed on me, intense and compassionate and, yes, a little bit needy.

"Tell me you'll at least give it some thought," she says.

"I will," I tell her. "I'll think about it."

3

I don't think about it.

I obsess.

Franny's offer dominates my thoughts for the rest of the day. But it's not the kind of thinking she was hoping for. Instead of pondering how wonderful it might be to go back to Camp Nightingale, I think of all the reasons I shouldn't return. Crushing guilt I haven't been able to shake in fifteen years. Plain old anxiety. All of them continue to flutter through my thoughts when I meet Marc for dinner at his bistro.

"I think you should go," he says as he pushes a plate of ratatouille in front of me. It's my favorite dish on the menu, steaming and ripe with the scent of tomatoes and **herbs de Provence**. Normally, I'd already be digging in. But Franny's proposal has sapped my appetite. Marc senses this and slides a large wineglass next to the plate, filled almost to the rim with pinot noir. "It might do you some good."

"My therapist would beg to differ."

"I doubt that. It's a textbook case of closure."

God knows, I haven't had much of that. There were memorial services for all three girls, staggered over a six-month period, depending on when their families gave up hope. Allison's was first. All song and drama. Then Natalie's, always in the middle, her service a quiet, family-only affair. Vivian's was the last, on a bitterly cold January morning. Hers was the only one I attended. My parents told me I couldn't go, but I went anyway, ditching school to slide into the last pew of the packed church, far away from Vivian's weeping parents. There were so many senators and congressmen present that it felt like watching C-SPAN.

The service didn't help. Neither did reading about Allison's and Natalie's services online. Mostly because there was the chance, however slim, that they could still be alive. It doesn't matter that the state of New York declared all of them legally dead after three years. Until their bodies are found, there's no way of knowing.

"I'm not sure closure is the issue," I say.

"Then what **is** the issue, Em?"

"It's the place where three people vanished into thin air. **That's** the issue."

"Understood," Marc says. "But there's something else going on. Something you're not telling me."

"Fine." I sigh into my ratatouille, steam skirting across the table. "I haven't painted a thing in the past six months."

A stricken look crosses Marc's face, like he doesn't quite believe me. "Are you serious?"

"Deadly."

"So you're stuck," he says.

"It's more than that."

I admit everything. How I can't seem to paint anything but the girls. How I refuse to continue down that path of obliterating their white-frocked forms with trees and vines. How day after day I stare at the giant canvas in my loft, trying to summon the will to create something new.

"Okay, so you're obsessed."

"Bingo," I say, reaching for the wine and taking a hearty gulp.

"I don't want to seem insensitive," Marc says. "And I certainly don't want to belittle your emotions. You feel what you feel, and I get that. What I don't understand is why, after all this time, what happened at that camp still haunts you so much. Those girls were practically strangers."

My therapist has said the same thing. As if I don't know how weird it is to be so affected by something that happened fifteen years ago and fixated on girls I knew for only two weeks.

"They were **friends**," I say. "And I feel bad about what happened to them."

"Bad or guilty?"

"Both."

I was the last person to see them alive. I could have stopped them from doing whatever the hell it was they had planned to do. Or I could have told Franny or a counselor as soon as they left. Instead, I went back to sleep. Now I still sometimes hear Vivian's parting words in my dreams.

You're too young for this, Em.

"And you're afraid that being back there again will make you feel even worse," Marc says.

Rather than answer, I reach for the glass, the wine catching my wobbly reflection. I stare at myself, shocked by how strange I appear. Do I really look that sad? I must, because Marc's tone softens as he says, "It's natural to be afraid. Friends of yours died."

"Vanished," I say.

"But they **are** dead, Emma. You know that, right? The worst thing that could happen has already taken place."

"There's something worse than death."

"Such as?"

"Not knowing," I say. "Which is why I'm only able to paint those girls. And I can't keep doing that, Marc. I need to move on."

There's more to it than that. Although he knows the basics of what took place, there's still plenty I haven't told Marc. Things that happened at Camp Nightingale. Things that happened afterward. The real reason I always wear the charm bracelet, the birds clinking each time I move my left arm. To admit them out loud would mean that they're true. And I don't want to confront that truth.

Some would say I've been lying to Marc. To everyone, really. But after my time at Camp Nightingale, I vowed never to lie again.

Omission. That's my tactic. A different sin entirely.

"This is all the more reason for you to go." Marc reaches across the table and clasps my hands. His palms are calloused, his fingers lined with scars. The hands of a lifelong cook. "Maybe being there again is all you need to start painting something different. You know the old saying—sometimes the only way out is through."

After dinner, I return to my loft and stand before a blank canvas. Its emptiness taunts me, as it's done for weeks. A wide expanse of nothing daring me to fill it.

I grab a palette, well-worn and rainbow-hued. I smear some paint onto it, dab it with the tip of a brush, and will myself to paint something. Anything but the girls. I touch the brush to the canvas, bristles gliding, trailing color.

But then I take a step back and stare at the brush-stroke, studying it. It's yellow. Slightly curved. Like an **S** that's been squished. It is, I realize, a length of Vivian's hair, the blond streak doing a little flip as she retreats. There's nothing else it could be.

I grab a nearby rag that reeks of turpentine and swipe it over the yellow paint until it's just a faint smudge marring the canvas. Tears spring from my eyes as I realize the only thing I've painted in weeks is this indistinct smear.

It's pathetic. **I'm** pathetic.

I wipe my eyes, noticing something on the edge of my vision. Near the window. A movement. A flash.

Blond hair. Pale skin.

Vivian.

I yelp and drop the rag, the fingers of my right hand grasping at the bracelet around my left. I give it a twist, the birds taking flight as I whirl around to face her.

Only it's not Vivian I see.

It's me, reflected in the window. In the night-darkened glass, I look startled, weak, and, above all else, shaken.

Shaken that the girls are always in my thoughts and on my canvases, even though it makes no sense. That after fifteen long years, I know as much about what happened now as I did the night they left the cabin. That in the days following the disappearance, I only made things worse. For Franny. For her family. For myself.

I could finally change that. Just one small hint

about what happened could make a difference. It won't erase my sins. But there is a chance it could make them more bearable.

I turn away from the window, grab my phone, and dial the number printed so elegantly on the calling card Franny gave me last night. The call goes straight to voicemail and a recording of Lottie suggesting I leave a message.

"This is Emma Davis. I've given more thought about Franny's offer to spend the summer at Camp Nightingale." I pause, not quite believing what I'm about to say next. "And my answer is yes. I'll do it."

I hang up before I can change my mind. Even so, I'm struck with the urge to call again and take it all back. My finger twitches against the phone's screen, itching to do just that. Instead, I call Marc.

"I'm going back to Camp Nightingale," I announce before he can say hello.

"I'm glad to hear my pep talk worked," Marc says. "Closure is a good thing, Em."

"I want to try to find them."

There's silence on Marc's end. I picture him blinking a few times while running a hand through his hair—his normal reaction to something he can't quite comprehend. Eventually, he says, "I know I encouraged you to go, Em, but this doesn't sound like the best idea."

"Bad idea or not, that's why I'm going."

"But try to think clearly here. What do you rationally expect to find?"

"I don't know," I say. "Probably nothing."

I certainly don't expect to uncover Vivian, Natalie, and Allison. They literally vanished without a trace, which makes it hard to know where to start looking for them. Then there's the sheer size of the place. While Camp Nightingale may be small, much more land surrounds it. More than six square miles of forest. If several hundred searchers couldn't find them fifteen years ago, I'm not going to find them now.

"But what if one of them left something behind?" I say. "Something hinting at where they were going or what they were up to."

"And what if there is?" Marc asks. "It still won't bring them back."

"I understand that."

"Which begs another question: Why do you need this so much?"

I pause, thinking of a way to explain the unexplainable. It's not easy, especially when Marc doesn't know the full story. I settle on saying, "Have you ever regretted something days, weeks, even years after you've done it?"

"Sure," Marc says. "I think everyone has at least one big regret."

"What happened at that camp is mine. For fifteen years, I've waited for a clue. Just some small thing hinting at what happened to them. Now I have a chance to go back there and look for myself. Likely the last chance I'll get to try to find some answers. If I turn that down, I worry it will just become another thing to regret."

Marc sighs, which means I've convinced him. "Just promise me you won't do something stupid," he says.

"Like what?"

"Like put yourself in danger."

"It's a summer camp," I say. "It's not like I'm infiltrating the mob. I'm simply going to go, look around, maybe ask a few questions. And when those six weeks are over, perhaps I'll have some idea of what happened to them. Even if I don't, maybe being there again is all I need to start painting something different. You said it yourself—sometimes the only way out is through."

"Fine," Marc says with another sigh. "Plan your camping trip. Try to get some answers. Come back ready to paint."

As we say our good-nights, I get a glimpse of my first painting of the girls. No. 1, offering its scant views of Vivian, Natalie, and Allison. I approach it, looking for flashes of hair, bits of dress.

Even though a branch covers their eyes, I know they're staring back at me. It's as if they've understood all along that I'd one day return to Camp Nightingale. Only I can't tell if they're urging me to go or begging me to stay away.

FIFTEEN YEARS AGO

"Wake up, sunshine."

It was just past eight when my mother crept into my bedroom, her eyes already glazed from her morning Bloody Mary. Her lips were curled into the same smile she always wore when she was about to do something momentous. I called it her Mother of the Year smile. Seeing it never failed to make me nervous, mostly because there was usually a gaping chasm between her intentions and the end result. On that morning, I tightened into a ball beneath the covers, bracing myself for hours of forced mother-daughter bonding.

"You all ready to go?" she said.

"Go where?"

My mother stared at me, her hand fumbling with the collar of her chiffon robe. "Camp, of course."

"What camp?"

"**Summer** camp," my mother said, stressing the first word, letting me know that wherever I was headed, it was going to be for more than just a day or two.

I sat up, flinging aside the covers. "You never told me about any camp."

"I did, Emma. I told you weeks ago. It's the same place me and your aunt Julie went. Jesus, don't tell me you forgot."

"I didn't forget."

Being told I was going to be ripped away from my friends for the entire summer was something I would have remembered. It was more likely my mother had only thought about telling me. In her world, thinking about something was close enough to doing it. Yet knowing that didn't lessen the feeling of being ambushed. It reminded me of those extreme interventions in which parents hired rehab centers to abduct their junkie children.

"Then I'm telling you now," my mother said. "Where's your suitcase? We need to be on the road in an hour."

"An **hour**?" My stomach clenched as I thought of all my summer plans being snatched away from me. No lazing around with Heather and Marissa. No secret, unchaperoned train ride to Coney Island like we had planned in study hall. No flirting with Nolan Cunningham from next door, who wasn't quite as cute as Justin Timberlake but still had the same swaggering confidence. Plus, he was finally starting to notice me, now that my braces had come off. "Where are we going?"

"Camp Nightingale."

Camp Rich Bitch. Talk about a surprise on top of a surprise.

That changed things.

For two years I had begged my parents to send me, only to be told no. Now, after having given up hope, I was suddenly going. In an hour. That totally explained the Mother of the Year smile. For once, it was justified.

Still, I refused to show my mother how pleased I was. Doing that would have only encouraged her, subjecting me to more attempts at making up for lost time. High tea at the Plaza. A shopping spree at Saks. Anything to make her feel better about having zero interest in me for the first twelve years of my life.

"I'm not going," I announced as I laid back down and pulled the covers over my head.

My mother ignored me as she started to root through my closet, her voice muffled. "You'll love it there. It'll be a summer you'll remember for the rest of your life."

Under the covers, an anticipatory shiver ran through me. Camp Nightingale. Six weeks of swimming and reading and hiking. Six weeks away from this stuffy apartment and my mother's disinterest and my father's eye rolls when she poured herself a third glass of Chardonnay. Heather and Marissa were going to be so jealous. After pretending to be pissed at me for abandoning them the whole summer, of course.

"Whatever," I say, following it up with an indignant huff. "I'll go, even though I don't want to."

It was a lie.

My first in a summer filled with them.

4

The drive to Camp Nightingale takes up most of the afternoon. Almost five hours when counting in rest stops. Most of it a straight shot north along truck-clogged I-87.

The length of the trip is something I'd forgotten from my first visit, when I had spent the drive huddled in the back seat while my parents blamed each other for not telling me I was going to camp. This time, I'm once again in the back, although the driver of the private town car Franny hired for me hardly says a word. But my nervousness is the same. That butterfly-trapped-in-the-chest feeling. Back then, it was because I didn't quite know what the camp would be like.

Now I know exactly where I'm going.

And who I'll see while I'm there.

In the months leading to my departure, I didn't have time to be nervous. I was too consumed with applying for a temporary leave of absence from the ad agency and finding someone to sublet the loft while I'm gone. The leave was approved, and

I eventually found an artist acquaintance to stay in the loft. She paints trippy starscapes with wax melted in scalding-hot aluminum pots. I've seen her at work, each colorful pot bubbling like a witch's cauldron. I hope she doesn't burn the place down.

While all that was taking place, I received weekly emails from Lottie that filled in various details of my stay. The debut summer of the new Camp Nightingale planned to have roughly fifty-five campers, five counselors, and five specialized instructors made up of camp alumni. Just like in the past, none of the cabins had electricity. The camp was monitoring the threats of Zika, West Nile, and other mosquito-borne illnesses. I should remember to pack accordingly.

I took that last note to heart. When I was thirteen, the sudden notice about going to camp delayed our departure for hours. First there was the matter of finding my suitcase, which ended up being in the back of the hall closet, behind the vacuum cleaner. Then came the arduous task of packing, with me not knowing what to bring and my lack of preparation necessitating a trip to Nordstrom's to pick up the things I lacked. This time around, I went overboard in the sporting goods store, snapping up items with the whirlwind intensity of a romantic comedy heroine in a shopping montage. Much of it was necessary. Several pairs of shorts. Heavy-duty socks and a sturdy pair of hiking boots. An LED flashlight with a wrist strap. Some of it was not, such as the waterproof case that fits over my iPhone like a condom.

Then there was the matter of my parents. Neglectful as they were when I was growing up, I knew they wouldn't like the idea of my returning to Camp Nightingale. So I didn't tell them. I simply called to say I'd be away for six weeks and that they should contact Marc in case of an emergency. My father half listened. My mother simply told me to have "such a wonderful time," her words slurred from cocktail hour.

Now there's nothing left for me to do but quell my growing anxiety by sorting through all the things I thought I'd need to help my search. There's a map of Lake Midnight and the surrounding area; a satellite view of the same thing, courtesy of Google Maps; and a stack of old newspaper articles about the disappearance collected from the library and printed off the internet. I even brought along a dog-eared Nancy Drew paperback—**The Bungalow Mystery**—for inspiration.

I examine the map and satellite view first. From above, the lake resembles a giant comma that's been tipped over. More than two miles from end to end, with a width ranging from a half mile to five hundred yards. The narrowest area is the eastern point, the location of the dam Buchanan Harris used to create the lake on that cold and rainy stroke of midnight. From there the lake flows west, skirting the edge of a mountain, following the path of the valley it replaced.

Camp Nightingale sits to the south, nestled in the middle of the lake's gentle exterior curve. On the map, it's just a tiny black square, unlabeled, as if fifteen years of disuse had left it unworthy of mention.

The satellite view offers more detail, all of it colored grainy shades of green by the library printer that spat it out. The camp itself is a rectangle of fern green, speckled with buildings in variations of brown. The Lodge is clearly visible, as are the cabins, latrine, and other buildings. I can even see the dock jutting out over the water, the white specks of two motorboats moored to its sides. A gray line of road leads out of camp to the south, eventually connecting with a county road two miles away.

One theory about the girls' disappearance is that they walked to the main road and hitched a ride. To Canada. To New England. To unmarked graves when they climbed into the cab of a deranged trucker.

Yet no one reported seeing three teenage girls on the highway's edge in the middle of the night, even after their disappearance became national news. No one anonymously confessed to giving them a ride. No traces of their DNA were ever found inside the rigs of drivers arrested for violent crimes. Plus, all their belongings were left behind, tucked safely inside their hickory trunks. Clothes.

Cash. Brightly colored Nokia cell phones just like the ones my parents said I was too young and irresponsible to own.

I don't think they planned to be gone for very long. Certainly not forever.

I put away the map and tackle the newspaper clippings and internet articles, none of which offer anything new. The details of the disappearance are as vague now as they were fifteen years ago. Vivian, Natalie, and Allison vanished in the early-morning hours of July 5. They were reported missing by yours truly a little before 6:00 a.m. A camp-wide search that morning turned up nothing. By the afternoon, the camp's director, Francesca Harris-White, had contacted the New York State Police, and an official search began. Because of the girls' high-profile parents—Vivian's, especially—the Secret Service and the FBI joined the fray. Search parties of federal agents, state troopers, and local volunteers scoured the woods. Helicopters skimmed the treetops. Bloodhounds primed with scents from clothes the girls had left behind sniffed a trail around camp and back again, their keen sense of smell leading them in frustrating circles. Little was found. No footprints leading into the forest. No wispy strands of hair snagged on low-hanging branches.

Another team of searchers headed to the water, even though they were stymied by the lake itself. It was too deep to dredge, too filled with downed trees and other underwater remnants of its days as a valley to dive safely. All they could do was crisscross Lake Midnight in police rescue boats, knowing there was nothing left to rescue. If the girls were in the lake, surely only corpses would be found. The boats returned empty-handed, as everyone suspected they would.

The only trace of the girls anyone ever found was a sweatshirt.

Vivian's sweatshirt, to be precise. White with **Princeton** spelled out in orange across the chest. I'd seen her wear it to the campfire a few nights before the disappearance, which is how I was able to identify it as belonging to her.

It was found the morning after the disappearance, sitting on the forest floor two miles away, almost directly across the lake from Camp Nightingale. The volunteer searcher who discovered the sweatshirt—a local retiree and grandfather of six with no earthly reason to lie—said it was neatly folded into a square, like the sweaters you see on display at the Gap. A lab analysis of the sweatshirt found skin cells that matched Vivian's DNA. What it didn't find were any rips, tears, or traces of blood suggesting she had been attacked. It was simply discarded, apparently by Vivian on her way to whatever fate befell her.

But here's the weird part.

Vivian wasn't wearing the sweatshirt when I saw her leave the cabin.

In the days after the disappearance, various investigators repeatedly asked me if I was sure it wasn't tied around her waist or thrown over her shoulders, sleeves knotted in true Princeton preppy fashion.

It wasn't.

I'm certain of it.

Still, authorities treated that sweatshirt like a beacon, following it into the hills. The search of the lake was called off as everyone took to the forest, searching it in vain. No one—least of all me—had an inkling as to why the girls would have marched miles away from camp. But nothing about the disappearance made sense. It was one of those rare instances that defied all known logic and reason.

The only person ever considered a suspect was Franny's oldest son, Theo Harris-White. Nothing came of it. No traces of him were discovered on Vivian's sweatshirt. Nothing incriminating was found in his possession. He even had an alibi—he spent the night with Chet, teaching his younger brother how to play chess into the wee hours of the morning. With no evidence that a crime had actually taken place, Theo wasn't charged. Which meant he also wasn't officially exonerated. Even now, a Google search of Theo's name brings up true-crime websites that suggest he killed the girls and managed to get away with it.

The hunt for the girls didn't officially end so

much as it lost steam. The search parties fruitlessly continued for another few weeks, their numbers dwindling day by day until they eventually dried up. News coverage of the disappearance also evaporated as reporters moved on to newer, flashier stories.

Filling that void were darker theories. Ones found in the deepest corners of Reddit and conspiracy websites. Rumors swirl that the girls had been murdered by a savage madman who lived in the woods. That they had been abducted—either by humans or aliens, depending on which website you read. That something even more mystically sinister happened to them. Witches. Werewolves. Spontaneous cellular disintegration.

Not even former campers are immune from the rumors, which I learn when I open Facebook on my phone and finally unmute the posts from Camp Nightingale alumni. The first thing I see is a photo posted an hour ago by Casey Anderson, a short, red-haired counselor I had met on my first morning at camp. She was also, incidentally, the first Camp Nightingale veteran to seek me out on Facebook. Although I genuinely liked her, that friend request went ignored with all the others. Now I stare at a photo she took of the cabins with Lake Midnight glistening in the background.

Back again, she wrote. **Feels like old times.**

The picture had already received fifty likes and several responses.

Erica Hammond: Have a great summer!

Lena Gallagher: Awwww. Brings back memories.

Felecia Wellington: I can't believe you went back there. Franny could offer me a million dollars and I still wouldn't go.

Casey Anderson: Which is probably why Franny didn't ask you. I'm happy to be here.

Maggie Collins: Agreed! That place always freaked me out.

Hope Levin Smith: I'm with Felecia. This is a bad, bad idea.

Casey Anderson: Why?

Hope Levin Smith: Because that place and its lake are messed up! We've all heard the legend. We all know there's a ring of truth to it.

Lena Gallagher: OMG, that legend! Scared me so much back then.

Hope Levin Smith: You had every right to be scared.

Casey Anderson: You're all being ridiculous.

Hope Levin Smith: Casey, you're the one who talked about it the most! You can't call it bullshit now that you're back there.

Felecia Wellington: Don't forget we all know what happened to Viv, Ally, and Natalie wasn't an accident. You said so yourself.

Brooke Tiffany Sample: Who else is going to be there this summer?

Casey Anderson: Of people you know, me, Becca Schoenfeld, and Emma Davis.

Brooke Tiffany Sample: Emma?!? Holy fuck!

Maggie Collins: After all that shit she said about Theo?

Hope Levin Smith: Wow.

Lena Gallagher: That's, um, interesting.

Felecia Wellington: I'd love to know how that happened. Watch your back, Casey. LOL

Casey Anderson: Be nice. I'm excited to see her.

Erica Hammond: Who's Emma Davis?

I close Facebook and turn off my phone, unable to stomach reading another word of gossip and crackpot theories. Other than Casey, I can't recall meeting any of those women while at camp. Nor have I heard the stories that the lake is cursed or haunted. It's bullshit. All of it.

Only one of the responses is the absolute truth. What happened to Vivian, Natalie, and Allison wasn't an accident.

I know because I'm the one who caused it.

Although their eventual fate remains a mystery, I'm certain that what happened to those girls is all my fault.

5

I bolt from my slumped position in the back seat when the rounded peaks of the Adirondacks push over the horizon. The sight of them sets my heart racing ever-so-slightly—a soft hum in my chest that I try to ignore. It gets worse once the driver turns off the highway and announces, "Almost there, Miss Davis."

Immediately, the car starts to bump down a gravel road. Both sides of the road are lined with forest that seems to get thicker and darker the deeper we go. Gnarled limbs stretch overhead, reaching for one another, branches intertwined. Towering pines diffuse the sun. The underbrush is a tangle of leaves, stems, thorns. It is, I realize, like one of my paintings come to life.

Soon we're at the wrought-iron gate that serves as the only way into Camp Nightingale. It's wide-open—an invitation to enter. But the gate and its surroundings are anything but inviting. Flanking the road are four-foot-high stone walls that stretch into the woods. An ornate archway, also wrought iron, curves over the road, giving the impression that we're about to enter a cemetery.

The camp reveals itself in increments. Structures slide into view as if pushed there by stagehands. All of them are remnants from when the land was a private retreat for the Harris family, now repurposed for camp use. The arts and crafts building, low-slung and quaint, used to be a horse stable. All white paint and gingerbread trim. A flower bed sits in front of it, bright with crocuses and tiger lilies. Next is the mess hall. Less pretty. More utilitarian. A former hay barn turned into a cafeteria. A side door gapes open as workers haul in cases of food from an idling delivery truck.

In the distance to my right are the cabins, barely visible through the trees. Nothing but edges of moss-stippled roof and slivers of pine siding. I catch glimpses of girls settling in. Bare legs. Slender arms. Glistening hair.

At first glance, the camp looks the same as it did when I left it all those years ago. It's a weird sensation, like I've been shuttled back in time. One foot in the present, another planted in the past. Yet something about the place feels slightly off. An air of neglect hangs over everything like cobwebs. And the longer I'm here, the more I become aware of what has changed in the past fifteen years. The tennis court and archery range both now sit in a startling state of disuse. Spiky weeds burst through the court's surface in jagged lines. The grass in the archery range is knee-high, dotted on the far end with rotting hay bales that had once held targets.

Atop the otherwise immaculate arts and crafts building, a handyman nails shingles to the roof. He stills his hammer as the town car passes, peering down at me, his face round and reddened. I stare back, suddenly recognizing him from my first visit. I remember seeing him quite a bit around camp, constantly tinkering and fixing. He was younger then, of course. Better looking. Possessed a brooding intensity that intimidated some, intrigued others.

I'd grab his tool any day, Vivian once said at lunch, prompting eye rolls from the rest of us.

I wave to him, wondering if he also recognizes the older me. He returns his gaze to a shingle, raises his hammer, pounds it into place.

By then the town car is whipping around the circular drive in front of the Lodge. Franny's home away from home, as she calls it, although it's more home than most people will ever lay claim to. But that's been its purpose ever since it was built by her grandfather on the shore of the lake he also created. A summer house for a family that chose nature over Newport. Like most old structures, there's a heaviness to the Lodge, a somberness. I think of all the years it's witnessed. All those seasons and storms and secrets.

"We've arrived," the driver says as he stops the car in front of the Lodge's red front door. "I'll get your bags from the trunk."

I exit the car, legs stiff and back aching, and I'm immediately engulfed by fresh air. It's a smell I'd forgotten. Clean and pine-scented. So different from the city's fumes. It sparks a hundred memories I'd also forgotten. Simple ones of walking through the woods behind Vivian or sitting alone with my toes in the lake, contemplating everything and nothing all at once. The scent beckons me, pulling me forward. I start walking, unsure of where I'm headed.

"I'll be right back," I tell the driver, who's busily unloading my suitcase and box of painting supplies. "I need to stretch my legs."

I keep walking, around the Lodge to the grassy slope behind it. There I see what the fresh air has led me to.

Lake Midnight.

It's larger than I remember. In my memory, it had become similar to the Central Park Reservoir. Something contained. Something that could be controlled. In reality, it's a vast, sparkling presence that dominates the landscape. The trees lining its bank lean slightly toward it, branches bending over the water.

I start down the sloping lawn, continuing until I reach the tidy dock that juts over the water. Two motorboats are moored to it. On the shore nearby are two racks upon which upside-down canoes have been stacked like firewood.

I walk the length of the dock, my footfalls slipping through cracks in the planks and echoing off the water. At its edge, I stop to look across the lake to the far shore a half mile away. The forest there is thicker—a dense wall of foliage shimmering in the sunlight, at once inviting and forbidding.

I'm still staring at the far shore when someone approaches. I hear the swish of sneakers in grass, followed by their thunk against the planks of the dock. Before I can turn around, a voice rises behind me like a bird chirp catching the breeze.

"There you are!"

The voice belongs to a twentysomething woman who rushes down the dock. Behind her, still on land, is a man roughly the same age. Both are young and tan and fit. If it wasn't for their official Camp Nightingale polos, they could easily be mistaken for J.Crew models. They have that same outdoorsy, sun-kissed glow.

"Emma, right?" the woman says. "Hooray! You're here!"

I reach out to shake her hand but wind up getting pulled into an enthusiastically tight embrace. No Franny-like half hugs with this girl.

"It's so nice to meet you," she says, breaking the embrace, slightly out of breath from the exertion of it all. "I'm Mindy. Chet's fiancée."

She gestures to the man on shore, and it takes

me a moment to realize she's referring to Chester, Franny's younger son. He's grown into a handsome man, lean and lithe and tall. So tall that he towers over both Mindy and me, stooping in a slightly self-conscious way. It's a far cry from the short, skinny kid I had seen flitting around camp. Yet hints of that boyishness remain. In the sandy hair that flops over his face, covering one eye. In the shy smile that flickers across his lips as he calls out, "Hey there."

"I was just getting reacquainted with the lake," I say, when I'm not really sure that's the case. I can't shake the sense it was the other way around and Lake Midnight was getting reacquainted with me.

"Of course you were," Mindy says, politely ignoring how unusual it was for me to immediately roam to the water's edge. "It's nice, right? Although the weather isn't doing it any favors. It hasn't rained in weeks, and the lake is looking a little ragged, if you ask me."

It's only after she's pointed it out that I notice the telltale signs of drought around the lake. The plants on its bank bear several inches of browned stem—areas that had once been submerged. There was a drought happening the first time I was here, too. It didn't rain once in two weeks. I remember climbing into a canoe, leaving sneaker prints in a strip of sunbaked earth between the bank of the lake and the water itself.

I'm eyeing a similar thirsty patch of land when Mindy grabs my hand and leads me off the dock.

"We're thrilled to have you back, Emma," she says. "Franny especially. This summer is going to be awesome. I just know it."

Back on shore, I go to Chet and shake his hand.

"Emma Davis," I say. "You probably don't remember me."

It's wishful thinking. A hope that he remembers nothing about me. But the brow over Chet's only visible eye lifts slightly. "Oh, I remember you well," he says, not elaborating.

"Before you get settled in, Franny needs to see you," Mindy says.

"About what?"

"There's a slight problem with the rooming situation. But don't worry. Franny's going to sort it all out."

Leaving Chet behind, she loops an arm through mine, guiding me up the slope and into the Lodge. It's the first time I've ever been inside, and I'm surprised to see it's not at all what I was expecting. As a girl on the outside looking in, I had pictured something from **Architectural Digest**. The kind of tastefully rustic retreat where movie stars spend Christmas in Aspen.

The Lodge isn't like that. It's musty and dim, the air inside tinged with a century's worth of wood-fed blazes in the fireplace. The entrance hall we stand in leads to a general living area stuffed with worn furniture. Covering the walls are antlers, animal skins, and, oddly, an assortment of antique weapons. Rifles. Bowie knives with thick blades. A spear.

"Everything's so old, right?" Mindy says. "I'm all for antiques, but some of this stuff is ancient. The first time Chet brought me here, it felt like sleeping in a museum. I'm still not used to it. But if it takes spending a summer working at a camp to impress my future mother-in-law, then so be it."

She's clearly a talker. Exhausting but also potentially useful. When we pass a small office on the left, I pause and ask, "What's in there?"

"The study."

I crane my neck to peek into the room. One wall is filled with framed photos. Another contains a bookshelf. As we pass, I glimpse the corner of a desk, a rotary telephone, a Tiffany lampshade.

"I use the electrical outlet in there to charge my phone," Mindy says. "You're welcome to do the same. Just don't let Franny catch you. She wants all of us to disconnect and commune with nature or whatever."

"How's service up here?"

Mindy makes a dramatic gagging sound. "Horrible. Like, one bar most of the time. I honestly don't know how these girls are going to cope."

"The campers can't use their phones?"

"They can until their batteries run out. No electricity in the cabins, remember? Franny's orders."

To my right, a staircase rises to the second floor, the steps tiny and impossibly narrow. Under the stairs sits a door intended to blend into the wall. The only things giving it away are a brass doorknob and an old-fashioned keyhole.

"And what's that?" I ask.

"The basement," Mindy says. "I've never been down there. It's probably nothing but old furniture and cobwebs."

We move on, Mindy playing tour guide, giving a running commentary about various family heirlooms. A portrait of Buchanan Harris that, I swear, might have been painted by John Singer Sargent, elicits a solemn "That's worth a fortune."

Soon we're at the back deck, which spans the entire width of the Lodge. Wooden boxes crammed with flowers line the twig-work railing. Scattered around the deck are several small tables and the obligatory Adirondack chairs, all painted as red as the front door. Two of the chairs are occupied by Franny and Lottie.

Both are dressed in the same khaki shorts and camp polo ensemble as Chet and Mindy. Franny surveys Lake Midnight from the heightened view provided by the deck. Lottie, meanwhile, taps the screen of an iPad, looking up when Mindy and I step outside.

"Emma," she says, her face brightening as she pulls me into what feels like my fifth hug of the day. "You have no idea how nice it is to see you back here."

"It is," Franny agrees. "It's wonderful."

Unlike Lottie, she doesn't get up from her chair to greet me. I'm surprised, until I notice her wan and tired appearance. It's the first time I've seen her since our lunch meeting months ago, and the change is startling. I had assumed being back at her beloved Lake Midnight would make her robust and hearty. Instead, it's the opposite. She looks, for lack of a better word, old.

Franny catches me staring and says, "There's worry in your eyes, my dear. Don't think I can't see it. But fear not. I'm just tired from all this activity. I'd forgotten how exhausting the first day of camp can be. Not a moment to spare, it seems. I'll be right as rain tomorrow."

"You need to rest," Lottie says.

"And that's what I'm doing," Franny replies, somewhat testily.

I clear my throat. "You needed to see me about something?"

"Yes. I'm afraid there's a bit of a problem."

Franny frowns slightly. It's an echo of the half frown she gave me upon my first arrival at camp, when the family Volvo finally pulled up to the Lodge at the cusp of eleven. Franny greeted us with the same expression I see now. **I wasn't ex-**

pecting you, she said. **When you didn't arrive with the others, I thought you had canceled.**

"A problem?" I say, trepidation thickening my voice.

"That sounds so dramatic, doesn't it?" Franny says. "I suppose it's more of a complication."

"About what?"

"Where to put you."

"Oh," I say, which I'm sure is what I said when Franny told me something similar fifteen years ago.

Back then, my lateness was to blame. They had already gotten all the girls settled into their cabins, grouped together that morning by age. Since there was no more room available with girls my own age, I was forced to bunk with ones who were several years older. That's how I ended up with Vivian, Natalie, and Allison, intimidated by their additional years of life experience, their acne-free complexions, their fully formed bodies.

Now Franny tells me it's the opposite problem.

"My intention was to give the instructors some privacy. Let you have a nice cabin all to yourselves. But there was a bit of a mix-up with planning, and we find ourselves with more girls than we initially expected."

"Fifteen more," Lottie says, unprompted.

"Which means all our instructors will have to share lodgings with some of the campers."

"Why can't the instructors bunk together?"

"I asked her the same thing, Emma," Lottie says.

"That's a fine idea in theory," Franny tells us. "But there are five of you and only four bunks in each cabin. One person would have to bunk with the campers anyway. Which wouldn't be remotely fair to that single person."

"Couldn't we stay in the Lodge instead?"

"The Lodge is for family only," Mindy pipes up from the corner of railing where she's been watching our conversation. She gives her ring finger a wiggle, drawing attention to the fat engagement ring circling it. The message isn't subtle, but it's clear. She's one of them. I'm not.

"What Mindy means," Franny says, "is that although I'd be thrilled to have all of you stay here with us, there simply isn't enough room. This house can be deceiving. From the outside, it looks plenty big. But the reality is that there aren't enough bedrooms to spare. Especially for all five instructors. And you know I can't play favorites. I do apologize."

"It's fine," I say, when in fact it isn't. I'm a twenty-eight-year-old woman being forced to spend the next six weeks living with strangers half my age. Definitely not what I signed up for. But there appears to be no way around it.

"It's not fine," Franny says. "It's an awkward situation, and I'm so sorry to be putting you into it. I wouldn't blame you one bit if you decided to get back in the car and demand to be driven directly home."

I'd be tempted to do just that if I had a home to return to. But the artist subletting the loft is probably moving in at this very minute, everything booked and paid for until the middle of August. It is what it is, as Marc likes to say.

"Can I at least choose my cabin?"

"Most of the campers are settling in now, but I think we can accommodate your request. What did you have in mind?"

I touch my charm bracelet, giving it a quick twirl. "I want to stay in Dogwood."

The same cabin I stayed in fifteen years ago.

Although Franny says nothing, I know what she's thinking. Her expression shifts as quickly as the sunlight glinting off the lake, revealing confusion, then understanding, then, finally, pride.

"Are you certain you want to do that?"

I'm not even sure I want to be here at all. Yet I give a firm nod, trying to convince not only Franny but also myself. At least Franny buys it, because she turns to Lottie and says, "Please arrange it so that Emma can stay in Dogwood." To me, she says, "You're either very brave or very foolish, Emma. I can't decide which one it is."

I can't, either. I suppose that, just by being here, I'm a little bit of both.

FIFTEEN YEARS AGO

As the sound of my parents' Volvo faded into the creaking, chirping night, I learned two things—that Francesca Harris-White was rich beyond words, and that she had the stare of a movie star.

The rich part was only mildly intimidating. Obscene wealth was on display everywhere in our Upper West Side neighborhood. But Franny's stare? That stopped me cold.

It was intense. Those green eyes of hers latched on to me like twin spotlights, illuminating me, studying me. Yet hers wasn't a cruel stare. There was warmth in her gaze. A gentle curiosity. I couldn't remember the last time my parents looked at me that way, and it made me all too happy to stand completely still and let her take me in.

"I must admit, dear, I have absolutely no idea where to put you," Franny said, breaking her stare to turn to Lottie, who stood directly behind her. "Is there any room left in a cabin reserved for our junior campers?"

"They're all full," Lottie replied. "Three campers and one counselor in each. The only open spot is in a senior cabin. We could move one of the counselors there, but that might not go over too well. It will also leave a junior cabin unsupervised."

"Which I'm reluctant to do," Franny said. "What's the open cabin?"

"Dogwood."

Franny turned that green-eyed gaze back to me, smiling. "Then Dogwood it shall be. Lottie, be a dear and fetch Theo to take Miss Davis's bags."

Lottie vanished into the massive house behind us. A minute later, a young man emerged. Dressed in baggy shorts and a tight T-shirt, he had sleepy eyes and tousled brown hair. On his feet were flip-flops that clapped against the ground as he approached.

"Theo, this is Emma Davis, our latecomer," Franny told him. "She's headed to Dogwood."

Now it was my turn to stare, for Theo was unlike any boy I had ever seen. Not cute, like Nolan Cunningham. Handsome. With wide brown eyes, a prominent nose, a slightly crooked smile that slanted when he said, "Hey, latecomer. Welcome to Camp Nightingale. Let's get you to your cabin."

Franny bid me good-night as I followed Theo deeper into the camp, my heart beating so hard I feared he could hear it. I knew part of it was apprehension about being in an unknown place with unknown people. But another reason for my madly thrumming heart was Theo himself. I couldn't take my eyes off him as he walked a few paces ahead of me. I studied him the same way Franny had studied me, my gaze locked on his tall frame, the long, steady stride of his legs, the spread of his back and shoulders under his threadbare shirt. His biceps bulged as he carried my suitcase. No boy I knew had arms like that.

It didn't hurt that he was friendly, calling over his shoulder to ask me where I was from, what music I liked, if I had been to camp before. My answers were weak, barely audible over my pounding heart. My nervousness clearly showed, for when we reached the cabin, Theo turned and said, "Don't be nervous. You'll love it here."

He rapped on the door, prompting a response from inside. "Who is it?"

"Theo. Are you awake and decent?"

"Awake, yes," the same voice replied. "Decent, never."

Theo handed me the suitcase and gave an encouraging nod. "Go on in. And remember, their bark is worse than their bite."

He walked away, flip-flops clopping, as I turned the doorknob and stepped inside. The cabin's interior was dim, lit only by a lantern placed beside a window opposite the door. In that golden half-light, I saw two sets of bunk beds and three girls occupying them.

"I'm Vivian," announced the one sprawled on the top bunk to my right. She gestured to the bunk directly across from her. "That's Allison. Below is Natalie."

"Hi," I said, clutching my suitcase just inside the cabin, too frightened to enter farther.

"Your trunk is by the door," said the girl identified as Natalie, all wide cheeks and formidable chin. "You can put your clothes there."

"Thanks."

I opened the hickory trunk and started transferring all my frantically purchased clothes into it. Everything except my nightgown, which I kept out before sliding the suitcase under the bed.

Vivian slipped from the top bunk in a cropped T-shirt and a pair of panties, her exposure making me even more self-conscious as I stripped off my clothes under the protection of the nightgown.

"You're a little young. Are you sure you're supposed to be here?" She turned to the others in the cabin, both still ensconced in their bunks. "Isn't there a cabin for babies we can send her to?"

"I'm thirteen," I said. "Clearly not a baby."

Vivian terrified and dazzled me in equal measure. All three of them did. They seemed like women. I was just a girl. A skinny, scabby-kneed twerp with a flat chest.

"Is this your first night away from home?" asked Allison. She was thin and pretty, with hair the color of honey .

"No," I said, when it was, other than a handful of sleepovers at the apartments of friends who lived mere blocks away, which wasn't quite the same thing.

"You're not going to cry, are you?" Vivian said. "All newbies cry their first night. It's so fucking predictable."

Her casual use of the f-word made me freeze. It was different from when Heather or Marissa used it during desperate attempts to sound grown-up and cool. The word easily rolled off Vivian's tongue, making it clear she said it quite a lot. It told me these girls were older, wiser, and tougher. In order to survive, I had to be just like them. There was no other choice.

I closed the lid of my trunk and faced Vivian head on. "If I cry, it's because I've been put in here with you bitches."

A moment passed in which no one said anything. It wasn't long, yet time seemed to slow, feeling like minutes as I wondered if they were amused or angry, and if I truly would end up crying, which, quite honestly, is what I had felt like doing since the moment my parents sped away from camp in a cloud of gravel dust. Then I noticed Natalie and Allison with blankets pulled to their noses, trying to hide the fact that they were giggling. Vivian grinned and shook her head, as if I had just paid them the highest compliment.

"Well played, kid."

"Don't call me kid," I said, feigning toughness

despite the fact that I still wanted to cry, only this time with relief. "My name is Emma."

Vivian reached out and tousled my hair. "Well, Em, welcome to Camp Nightingale. You ready to help us rule this place?"

"Sure," I said, not quite believing that someone so effortlessly cool was paying attention to me. At school, I spent my days blending in with Heather and Marissa, all but ignored by the older girls. But there was Vivian, staring me down, asking me to join her clique.

"Awesome," she replied. "Because tomorrow, we kick ass."

6

From the outside, Dogwood looks exactly the way I left it. Same rough brown walls. Same green-shingled roof speckled with pinecones. Same tidy sign announcing its name. I had expected it to be different somehow. Older. Decrepit. A firm reminder that I'm fifteen years and worlds away from the weeping girl who last set eyes upon the place.

Yet, it feels like no time has passed between then and now. That the last decade and a half of my life was nothing but a dream. It's a disorienting feeling. And slightly scary. But I continue to stare at the cabin, gripped not by fear but by something else. Something sharper.

Curiosity.

I **want** to go inside, look around, see what memories it dredges up. That's why I'm here, after all. Yet when I twist the doorknob, I realize my hand is shaking. I don't know what I'm expecting. Ghosts, I suppose.

Instead, I find three different girls, all of them

very much alive as they lounge on their respective bunks. They look up at me, surprised by my sudden intrusion.

"Hi," I say.

My voice is meek, almost apologetic, as if I'm sorry to be invading their space, dragging my suitcase behind me. I haven't been alone with a group of teenage girls since, well, not long after my first time at Camp Nightingale. After what happened here, I gravitated to boys. Shy, nerdy ones. Math whizzes, sci-fi geeks, and drama club members quakingly emerging from the closet. They became my tribe. They still are. I'm comfortable in their presence.

Yes, boys can break your heart and betray you, but not in the same stinging way girls can.

I clear my throat. "I'm Emma."

"Hi, Emma. I'm Sasha."

This is spoken by the youngest, a girl of about thirteen who's perched on the top bunk to my left, her skinny legs dangling. She's got a friendly face—huge smile, rounded cheeks, bright eyes made even more prominent by a pair of red-framed glasses. I find myself relaxing in her presence. At least one of them seems nice.

"Nice to meet you, Sasha."

"I'm Krystal," says the girl sprawled on the bunk below her. "Spelled with a **K**."

A few years older and several pounds heavier than Sasha, she's practically hidden inside an oversize hoodie and baggie shorts. White socks with blue stripes circling the cuff have been pulled up to her knees. On the bed next to her is a ragged-looking teddy bear. In her lap sits a comic book. Captain America.

"Krystal with a **K**. Got it."

I turn to the other girl in the room, who lies on her side on the top bunk, elbow bent, head propped up. She appraises me in silence, her almond-shaped eyes flashing a combination of disdain and curiosity. A diamond stud adorns her nose. She looks to be about sixteen and, like most girls her age, thoroughly unimpressed with everything.

"Miranda," she says. "I took the top bunk. Hope you don't mind."

"Bottom bunk is fine," I say as I hoist my suitcase onto the bed, the mattress springs sighing under its weight.

Miranda climbs down from the bunk and stretches, her arms and legs enviably thin. She's knotted her camp-mandated polo shirt at her midriff, revealing her taut stomach. Another diamond stud rests in her navel. She keeps stretching, although it's more of a silent declaration. She's an alpha female. Marking her territory. Making it abundantly clear she's the hottest in the room. An old Vivian trick.

I feel exactly like I did the first time I set foot inside this cabin. Naïve. Tremulous. Unsure of what to do next as the girls stare at me expectantly.

Well, Sasha and Krystal do. Miranda climbs back to her top bunk and spreads herself across the bed with a dramatic sigh.

"They did tell you I'd be staying here, right?" I say.

"They said someone else would be here," Krystal informs me. "But they didn't say who it was."

Miranda's voice floats from above. "Or how old you are."

"Sorry to disappoint you," I say.

"Are you our camp counselor?" Sasha asks.

"More like babysitter," Krystal adds.

Miranda does her one better. "More like warden."

"I'm an artist," I tell them. "I'm here to teach you how to paint."

"What if we don't want to paint?" Sasha says.

"You don't have to, if you don't want to."

"I like to draw." This comes from Krystal, already leaning off the bed to reach beneath it, where several tattered notebooks sit. She pulls one from the pile and opens it up. "See?"

On the page is a sketch of a superhero. A woman with fiery eyes and the bulging muscles of a weight lifter. Her uniform is dark blue and skintight, with a green skull emblazoned across the chest. The skull's eyes glow red.

"You did this?" I say, sincerely impressed. "It's really good."

And it is. The hero's face is perfect. She's been

given a square jaw, a sharp nose, eyes that blaze with defiance. Her hair flows off her head in dark tendrils. With a few strokes of her pencil, Krystal had conveyed this woman's strength, courage, and determination.

"Her name is Skull Crusher. She can kill a man with her bare hands."

"I wouldn't want it any other way," I say. "Since you're already an artist, I'll let you draw while the others paint."

Krystal accepts the deal with a smile. "Cool."

She and Sasha continue to stare as I unpack, waiting for me to say more. Feeling extremely awkward, I ask, "So why did you want to come to camp?"

"My guidance counselor at school suggested it," Sasha says. "She said it would be a good learning experience for me, seeing how I'm inquisitive."

"Oh?" I say. "About what?"

"Um, everything."

"I see."

"My dad wanted me to come," Krystal says. "It was either this or get a job flipping burgers somewhere."

"I think you made the right choice."

"I didn't want to come," Miranda says. "My grandmother forced me to. She said I'd only get in trouble if I stayed home this summer."

I look up at her. "And would you?"

Miranda shrugs. "Probably."

"Listen," I say, "whether you want to be here or not, I need to be clear about something. I'm not here to be your den mother. Or babysitter." I flick my gaze up at Miranda. "Or warden. I don't want to cramp your style."

All of them groan.

"What, don't kids say that anymore?"

"No," Krystal says emphatically.

"Definitely not," Sasha adds.

"Well, whatever the current equivalent of that is, it's not why I'm here. I'm here to help you learn, if you want. Or, if you'd like, we can just talk. Basically, think of me as your big sister for the summer. I just want you to enjoy yourselves."

"I have a question," Sasha says. "Are there bears here?"

"I guess so," I reply. "But they're more afraid of us than we are of them."

"I did some research before I left home and read that that's not true."

"It's probably not," I say. "But it's nice to imagine, don't you think?"

"What about snakes?"

"What about them?"

"How many do you think are in the woods? And how many of those are venomous?"

I look at Sasha, intimidated by her curiosity. What a delightfully strange girl, with her thick-framed glasses perched on her tiny nose, her eyes wide behind their immaculate lenses.

"I honestly don't know," I say. "But I don't think we need to worry too much about snakes."

Sasha pushes her glasses higher up the bridge of her nose. "So, we should be more worried about sinkholes? I read that hundreds of thousands of years ago, this whole area was covered by glaciers that left ice deep inside the earth. And that ice eventually melted and ate away at the sandstone, forming deep caves. And sometimes those caves collapse, leaving giant craters. And if you're standing above one when it collapses, you'll fall so deep into the earth that no one will ever find you."

She finally stops, slightly out of breath.

"I think we'll be okay," I say. "Honestly, the only thing you need to worry about is poison ivy."

"And getting lost in the woods," Sasha says. "According to Wikipedia, it's very common. People disappear all the time."

I nod. Finally, a fact I can confirm.

And one that I can't forget.

7

When it's time for dinner, I stay behind, using the excuse that I have to unpack and change into my shorts and camp polo. The truth is that I want to be alone with Dogwood, just for a moment.

I stand in the middle of the cabin, rotating slowly, taking it all in. It feels different from fifteen years ago. Smaller and tighter. Like the cramped sleeping car where Marc and I once spent a red-eye train ride from Paris to Nice. But the cabin's differences are outweighed by its similarities. It has the same smell. Pine and musty earth and the faintest trace of woodsmoke. The third floorboard from the door still creaks. The trim around the only window still bears its faded-blue paint job. A touch of whimsy I noticed even during my first stay here.

Memories of the girls' voices return to me, like an echo of an echo. Random snippets I had completely forgotten until now. Allison mock-singing "I Feel Pretty" while flouncing around in her too-big polo shirt. Natalie sitting on the edge of the bottom bunk, her legs spackled with calamine lotion.

These mosquitoes are, like, obsessed with me, she said. **There's something about my blood that attracts them.**

I don't think that's how it works, I said.

Then why are they biting me and not the rest of you?

It's your sweat, Vivian announced. **Bugs love it. So slather on that Teen Spirit, girls.**

My phone squawks deep inside my pocket, snapping me out of my self-indulgent, admittedly morbid reverie. I dig out the phone and see that Marc's attempting to FaceTime. With only one bar of signal, I have doubts it's going to work.

"Hey, Veronica Mars," he says once I answer. "How's the sleuthing going?"

"I'm just starting." I sit on the edge of my bed, holding out my arm so my entire face fits into the frame. "I can't talk very long. The signal here is terrible."

Marc gives me his dramatic pouting face in return. He's in the kitchen of his bistro, the glossy, stainless-steel door of the walk-in freezer behind him.

"How's Camp Crystal Lake?"

"Devoid of masked killers," I say.

"That's a plus, I suppose."

"But I'm rooming with three teenage girls."

"Definitely not in your wheelhouse," Marc says. "What are they like?"

"I would describe them as sassy, but that term is probably out-of-date."

"**Sassy** never goes out of style. It's like blue jeans. Or vodka. Is that a bunk bed?"

"It is indeed," I say. "It's about as comfortable as it looks."

Marc's expression changes from pouting to horrified. "Oh dear. I apologize for convincing you to go back there."

"You didn't convince me," I say. "You just nudged me a little closer."

"I wouldn't have nudged if I'd known bunk beds would be involved." His image sputters a moment. When he moves his head, an afterimage follows in a stream of pixels.

"You're breaking up," I say, when in reality it's me. The signal has dropped from one bar to none. On the screen, Marc's face is frozen, nothing but an abstract blur. Yet I can still hear him. His voice cuts in and out, letting me catch only every other word.

"You . . . out . . . bored . . . okay?"

The phone gives up the ghost, and the call dies. My screen goes blank. Replacing Marc's face is my own reflection. I stare at it, shocked at how tired I look. Worse than tired. Haggard. No wonder Miranda made that crack about my age. I look positively ancient compared with them.

It makes me wonder what the other girls of Dogwood would look like today. Allison would probably still be cute and petite like her mother, who I saw a few years ago in a revival of **Sweeney Todd**. I spent the whole show wondering how much she thought of her daughter, if there's a picture of Allison in her dressing room, if seeing it made her sad.

I suspect Natalie would have remained physically formidable, thanks to sports in college.

And Vivian? I'm certain she'd be the same. Slim. Stylish. A beauty that bordered on haughtiness. I imagine her taking one look at present-day me and saying, **We need to talk about your hair. And your wardrobe.**

I shove the phone back in my pocket and open my suitcase. Quickly, I change into a pair of shorts and one of the official camp polos that arrived in the mail two weeks ago. The rest go into my assigned trunk by the door. It's the same trunk from my previous stay here. I can tell from the grayish stain that mars the satin lining.

I close the trunk and run my hands across the lid, feeling the bumps and grooves of all the names that have been carved into the hickory. Another memory prods my thoughts. Me on my first morning at camp, kneeling before this very trunk with a dull pocketknife in my hand.

Carve your name, Allison urged.

Every girl does it, Natalie added. **It's tradition.**

I followed that tradition and carved my name. Two letters in all caps white against the dark wood.

EM

Vivian stood behind me as I did it, her voice soft and encouraging in my ear. **Make your mark. Let future generations know you were here. That you existed.**

I look to the other side of the cabin, at the two trunks resting by the door. Natalie's and Allison's. Their names have faded with time, barely distinguishable from all the others carved around them. I then move to the trunk next to mine. Vivian's. She had carved her name in the center of the lid, larger than all the others.

VIV

I crack open her trunk, even though I know it's Miranda's now and that inside aren't Vivian's clothes and crafts and bottle of Obsession she swore covered the scent of bug spray. In their place are Miranda's clothes—an assortment of too-tight shorts and lacy bras and panties utterly inappropriate for camp. In a corner sits a surprisingly high stack of paperbacks. **Gone Girl, Rosemary's Baby**, a few Agatha Christie mysteries.

But the lining inside the lid is the same. Burgundy satin. Just like mine. The only difference, other than the gray stain, is a six-inch tear in the fabric. It sits on the left side of the lid, running vertically, the edges feathery.

Vivian's hiding place, used to store the pendant necklace she took off only when she slept. A heart-shaped locket hung from it. Gold with a small emerald inlaid in its center.

I know of the hiding place only because I saw Vivian use it on the first full day of camp. I was at my own trunk, searching for my toothbrush, when she knelt in front of hers. She unclasped the necklace and held it for a moment in her cupped hands.

That's pretty, I said. **An heirloom?**

It belonged to my sister.

Belonged?

She died.

Sorry. Apprehension fluttered in my chest. I'd never met someone with a dead sibling before and didn't know how to act. **I didn't mean to bring it up.**

You didn't, Vivian said. **I did. And it's healthy to talk about it. That's what my therapist says.**

I felt another flutter. A dead sister **and** therapy? At that moment, Vivian was the most exotic creature I had ever met.

How'd she die?

She drowned.

Oh, I said, too surprised to say more.

Vivian didn't say anything else, either. She simply poked her fingers through the tear in the lining and let the necklace slither out of view behind it.

Now I stare at the slash in the fabric, fingering my own piece of jewelry. Unlike Vivian's necklace, I never remove the charm bracelet. Not to sleep. Not to shower. Not even when painting. The wear and tear shows. Each tiny bird has scratches in the pewter that stand out like scars. Dots of dried paint mar their beaks.

I pry my right hand away from the bracelet and plunge it through the tear in the lining. Fabric tickles my wrist as I stretch my fingers and feel around the inside of the lid. I'm not expecting to find anything. Certainly not the necklace, which Vivian had been wearing when she left the cabin for the very last time. I do it because once I check, I'll know there's no trace of Vivian left there.

Only there is.

Something is inside the lid, sitting at the bottom, wedged between wood and fabric. A piece of paper, folded in half. I run a finger along the crease, feeling its length. Then I pinch the edge between my thumb and forefinger and slide it from the lining.

Age has given the paper a yellowish tint—a sickly shade that reminds me of dried egg yolk. The page crackles when I unfold it, revealing an even older-looking photograph nestled in its crease.

I study the photo first. It's surprisingly old. Something more likely to be found in a museum than in a camp cabin. Sepia-toned and worn along the edges, it depicts a young woman in a plain dress. She sits before a bare wall, turned at an angle that shows off long, dark hair cascading down her back and out of frame.

Clutched in the woman's hands is a large silver hairbrush, which she holds to her chest like a prized possession. I find the gesture oddly endearing, although one could also assume it's vanity that makes her grip the brush so tightly. That she spends her days running it through that absurdly long hair, breaking up the tangles, smoothing the strands. But the woman's expression makes me assume that's not the case. Although she looks to be in repose, her face is anything but peaceful. Her lips are pressed together, forming a flat line. Her face is pinched. Her eyes, wild and dark, convey sadness, loneliness, and something else. An emotion I know well.

Distress.

I stare into those eyes, finding them disturbingly familiar. I've seen that same expression in my own eyes. Not long after I left Camp Nightingale for what I had thought was the last time.

I flip over the photo and see a name scrawled on its back in faded ink.

Eleanor Auburn.

Several questions settle uneasily onto my shoulders. Who is this woman? When was this picture taken? And, above all else, where did Vivian get it, and why was it hidden in her trunk?

The contents of the unfolded page don't provide any answers. Instead, I see a drawing crudely scratched onto a ruled piece of paper torn from some sort of notebook. The focal point of the drawing is a blob that resembles a paisley, strange and formless. Surrounding it are hundreds of dark slashes, each dashed off in strokes so quick and forceful my painting hand aches just from looking at them. Beneath the paisley, tucked among the slashes, are several shapes. Messy ones. Not quite circles, not quite squares. Off to their left is another circle-square. Bigger than the others.

I realize what it is and gasp.

For reasons I can't begin to understand, Vivian drew Camp Nightingale.

The paisley is Lake Midnight, dominating the landscape, demanding attention. The slashes are an abstract version of the woods surrounding it. The series of shapes are the cabins. I count twenty of them, just like in real life. The big splotch, of course, is the Lodge, commanding the southern shore of the lake.

Vivian had drawn another cabin-size shape on the other side of the lake, almost directly across from camp. It sits next to the water, all alone. Only there aren't any structures on the other side of the lake. At least, none that I'm aware of.

Just like the photo, the sketch defies explanation. I try to think of a logical reason why Vivian drew it but come up empty. She had gone here three summers in a row. Surely there was no need for her to draw a map of the camp to find her way around.

Because that is indeed what it looks like. A map. Not just of camp but of the entire lake. It reminds me of the satellite view I studied on the ride here. All of Lake Midnight in one handy image.

I bring the page closer to my face, zeroing in not on the camp but on the area on the other side of the lake. A short distance behind the mystery structure is something barely distinguishable from the slashes that surround it.

An **X**.

Small but noticeable, it sits near a cluster of ragged triangles that resemble tiny mountains drawn by a kindergartener. Vivian had used extra force when drawing it. The lines push into the paper, creating two crisscrossed indentations.

That means it was important to her.

That something of interest was located there.

I fold the photograph inside the map and secure them both inside my own hickory trunk. It strikes me that if Vivian had taken such great care to hide them, then I should do the same thing.

It was, after all, her secret.

And I've become very good at keeping them.

FIFTEEN YEARS AGO

"There's one thing you need to know about this place," Vivian said. "Never arrive to anything on time. Either be there first or get there last."

"Even meals?" I asked.

"**Especially** meals. You won't believe how crazy some of these bitches get around food."

It was my first morning at camp, and Vivian and I had just left the latrine on the way to the mess hall. Although the mealtime bell rang fifteen minutes earlier, Vivian showed no sign of hurry. Her pace bordered on lackadaisical as she looped her arm through mine, forcing me to slow as well.

When we eventually did reach the mess hall, I noticed a girl with frizzy hair standing outside the arts and crafts building with a camera around her neck. She noticed us, too, because something flickered in her eyes. Recognition, maybe. Or worry. It lasted only a second before she raised her camera and aimed it our way, the blue-black lens following us as we entered the mess hall.

"Who was that taking our picture?" I asked.

"Becca?" Vivian said. "Don't mind her. She's a nobody."

Taking my hand, she pulled me toward the front of the room, where a handful of kitchen workers in hairnets stood before steaming trays of food. Because we were among the last to arrive, there was no wait. Vivian was right, not that I ever doubted her.

The only person later than us was a smiling red-headed counselor with the name **Casey** stitched onto her camp polo. She was short—practically my height—and had a pear-shaped frame made more pronounced by the large pockets of her cargo shorts.

"Well, if it isn't Vivian Hawthorne," she said. "You told me last summer that you were done with this place. Couldn't stay away?"

"And miss out on a chance to torment you for another summer?" Vivian said as she grabbed two bananas, placing one of them on my tray. "No way."

"And here I thought I was going to have it easy this year." The counselor gave me an appraising look. She seemed surprised—not to mention a little confused—to see me by Vivian's side. "You're new, right?"

Vivian ordered two bowls of clumpy oatmeal, again giving one to me. "Emma, this is Casey. Former camper, current counselor, forever bane of my existence. Casey, meet Emma."

I lifted my tray up and down in a weak approximation of a wave. "Nice to meet you."

"She's my protégé," Vivian said.

"That's a scary thought." Casey turned to me again and put a hand on my shoulder. "Come see me if she starts to corrupt you too much. I'm in Birch."

She passed us on her way to a decanter of coffee and the platter of doughnuts next to it. Before leaving the food line, I also ordered what I really wanted for breakfast—toast and a plate of bacon. Vivian eyed the extra side dishes but said nothing.

We then made our way through the clanging, slurping girls huddled at tables in configurations familiar from my school's cafeteria. Younger girls on one side. Older ones on the other. And at that moment, I wasn't adhering to my socially acceptable pack. A few girls my age took notice and watched with envy as Vivian led me to the side of the mess hall populated by older girls. She waved to some and ignored others before sitting me down with Allison and Natalie.

I had been awake when the two of them left the cabin to head to the latrine. Although they invited me to join them, I stayed behind, waiting for Vivian to rise. She was the only one I wanted showing me the ropes. While Allison and Natalie seemed nice, they reminded me too much of girls I knew at school. Slightly older versions of Heather and Marissa.

Vivian was different. I'd never met anyone so unfiltered. To a shy girl like me, her attention was as warm and welcome as the sun.

"Morning, bitches," she said to the others. "Sleep well?"

"The usual," Allison said as she picked at a bowl of fruit salad. "You, Emma?"

"Great," I said.

It was a lie. The cabin was too stuffy, too quiet. I missed air-conditioning and the sounds of Manhattan—all those irritated car horns and wailing sirens in the distance. At Camp Nightingale, there was nothing but bug noise and the lake lapping against the shore. I assumed I'd get used to it.

"Thank God you don't snore, Em," Vivian said. "We had a snorer last year. Sounded like a dying cow."

"It wasn't that bad," said Natalie. On her tray sat two servings of bacon and the syrupy remains of flapjacks. She bit into a bacon slice, chewing and talking at the same time. "You're just being mean because you don't like her anymore."

Already, I had noticed the weird dynamic between the three of them. Vivian was the ringleader. Obviously. Natalie, athletic and a little bit gruff, was the resistance. Pretty, subdued Allison was the peacekeeper, a role she assumed that very morning.

"Tell us about yourself, Emma," she said. "You don't go to our school, right?"

"Of course she doesn't," Vivian replied. "We'd know if she did. Half our school goes here."

"I go to Douglas Academy," I said.

Allison stabbed a chunk of melon, lifted it to her lips, put it back down. "Do you like it there?"

"It's nice, I guess. For an all-girls school."

"Ours is, too," Vivian said. "And I'd honestly kill to spend a summer away from some of these sluts."

"Why?" Natalie asked. "You pretend half of them don't exist when we're here."

"Just like I'm pretending right now that you're not stuffing your face with bacon," Vivian shot back. "Keep eating like that and next year it'll be fat camp for you."

Natalie sighed and dropped the half-eaten bacon onto her plate. "You want any, Allison?"

Allison shook her head and pushed away her barely touched bowl of fruit. "I'm stuffed."

"I was just joking," Vivian said, looking genuinely remorseful. "I'm sorry, Nat. Really. You look . . . fine."

She smiled then, the word lingering like the insult it really was.

I spent the rest of the meal eyeing Vivian's plate, taking a bite of oatmeal only when she did, trying to make the portions match up exactly. I didn't touch the banana until she did. When she left half of it on her tray, I did the same. The bacon and toast remained untouched.

I told myself it would be worth it.

Vivian, Natalie, and Allison left the mess hall before me, preparing for an advanced archery lesson. Senior campers only. I was scheduled to take part in an activity with girls my own age. I assumed I'd find them boring. That's what one night in Dogwood had already done to me.

On my way there, I passed the girl with the camera. She veered into my path, halting me.

"What are you doing?"

"Warning you," she said. "About Vivian."

"What do you mean?"

"Don't be fooled. She'll turn on you eventually."

I took a step toward her, trying to match the same toughness I had summoned the previous night. "How so?"

Although the girl with the camera smiled, there was no humor there. It was a bitter grin. On the cusp of curdling into a sneer.

"You'll find out," she said.

8

Arriving at the mess hall for dinner, I find Franny standing at the head of the room, already halfway through her welcome speech. She appears more robust than before. It's clear she's in her element, dressed for the great outdoors before a packed room of girls while extolling the virtues of camp life. She sweeps her gaze across the room as she speaks, making momentary eye contact with each and every girl, silently welcoming them. When she spots me by the door, her eyes crinkle ever so slightly. An almost-wink.

The speech sounds just like the one I heard fifteen years ago. For all I know, it could be exactly the same, summoned from Franny's memory after all these years. She's already recited the part about how the lake was formed by her grandfather on that long-ago New Year's Eve and is now delving into the history of the camp itself.

"For years, this land served as a private retreat for my family. As a child, I spent every summer—and quite a few winters, springs, and falls—exploring the thousands of acres my family was fortunate enough to own. When my parents passed away, it was left to me. So, in 1973, I decided to turn the Harris family retreat into a camp for girls. Camp Nightingale opened a year later, where it welcomed generations of young women."

She pauses. Just long enough for her to take a breath. But contained in that brief silence are years of omitted history. About my friends, the camp's shame, its subsequent closure.

"Today, the camp welcomes all of you," Franny says. "Camp Nightingale isn't about cliques or popularity contests or feeling superior. It's about you. All of you. Giving each and every one of you an experience to cherish long after the summer is over. So if you need anything at all, don't hesitate to ask Lottie, my sons, or Mindy, the newest member of our family."

She gestures to her left, where Chet stands against the wall, pretending not to notice the adoring gazes of half the girls in the room. Next to him, Mindy smiles and gives a beauty-pageant wave. I scan the room, looking for Theo. There's no sign of him, which is both a disappointment and a relief.

Franny clasps her hands together and bows her head, signaling that the speech is over. But I know it's not. There's still one part left, completely scripted but performed with the polish of a career politician.

"Oh, one last thing," Franny says, pretending to think of it just now. "I don't want to hear a single one of you call me Mrs. Harris-White. Call me Franny. I insist upon it. Here in the great out-doors, we're all equals."

From her spot along the wall, Mindy starts clapping. Chet does, too, albeit with more reluctance. Soon the whole room is applauding as Franny, their benefactor, takes another quick bow. Then she's off, skirting out of the mess hall via a side door opened by Lottie.

I make my way to the food stations, where a small crew of white-uniformed cooks dish out greasy hamburgers, fries, and coleslaw so runny that milky liquid sloshes around the bottom of the plate.

Rather than join Sasha, Krystal, and Miranda, who are surrounded on all sides by other campers, I head to a table near the door where eight women are seated. Five of them are young, definitely college age. The camp counselors. The other three range in age from midthirties to pushing sixty. My fellow instructors. Minus Rebecca Schoenfeld.

I recognize only one—Casey Anderson. Little about her has changed between then and now. She's still got that pear-shaped frame and red hair that grazes her shoulder when she tilts her head in sympathy upon seeing me again. She even gives me a hug and says, "It's good to see you back here, Emma."

The other instructors nod hello. The counselors merely stare. All of them, I realize, know not only who I am but also what happened while I was here.

Casey introduces me to the other instructors. Teaching creative writing is Roberta Wright-Smith, who attended Camp Nightingale for three summers, beginning with its inaugural season. She's plump and jolly and peers at me through a pair of glasses perched on her nose. Paige McAdams, who went here in the late eighties, is gray-haired and willowy, with bony fingers that clasp my hand too hard when she shakes it. She's here to teach pottery, which explains her grip.

Casey informs me she's been assigned to that catchall camp staple of arts and crafts. She's an eighth-grade English teacher during the school year, available to help out here because her two kids are away at their own camp and it's her first summer alone since she divorced her husband.

Divorce, it turns out, is a dominant theme among the other instructors. Casey wanted to escape six weeks alone in an empty house. Paige needed a place to go until her soon-to-be ex-husband moves out of their Brooklyn apartment. And Roberta, a creative-writing professor at Syracuse, wanted to go somewhere quiet after recently parting ways with her poet girlfriend. I'm the only one, it seems, who doesn't have a former spouse or partner to blame for being here. I'm not sure if that's liberating or merely pathetic.

I suppose I have more in common with the counselors, those college juniors who've yet to be touched by life's disappointments. They're all pretty and bland and basically interchangeable. Hair pulled into ponytails. Pink lip gloss. Their exfoliated faces glisten. They are, I realize, exactly the kind of girls who would have attended Camp Nightingale had it been open during their adolescence.

"Who else is psyched about the summer?" one of them says. I think her name is Kim. Or maybe it's Danica. Each of their names left my memory five seconds after I was introduced to them. "I definitely am."

"But don't you think it's weird?" Casey says. "I mean, I'm happy to help out for the summer, but I don't understand Franny's decision to open the camp again after all these years."

"I don't think it's necessarily weird," I say. "Surprising, maybe."

"I vote for weird," Paige says. "I mean, why now?"

"Why not now?"

This comes from Mindy, who's swooped up to the table without notice. I find her standing behind me, arms crossed. Although it's unclear how much she's heard, it was enough to make the edges of her plastered-on smile twitch.

"Does Franny need a reason for doing a good deed?" she says, directing the comment to Roberta,

Paige, Casey, and me. "I didn't know it was wrong to try to give a new generation of girls the same experiences the four of you had."

If this is an attempt to sound like Franny, she's failing miserably. Franny's speeches might be scripted, but the emotion behind them is real. You believe every word she says. Mindy's tone is different. It comes off so sweetly sanctimonious that I can't help but say, "I wouldn't wish my experience here on anyone."

Mindy gives a sad shake of her head. Clearly, I've let her down. Holding her hand to her heart, she says, "I expected more from you, Emma. Franny showed a great deal of courage inviting you back here."

"And Emma showed courage by agreeing to come," Casey says, leaping to my defense.

"She did," Mindy replies. "Which is why I thought she'd show a little bit more Camp Nightingale spirit."

I roll my eyes so hard the sockets hurt. "Really?"

"Fine." Mindy plops into an empty chair and lets out a sigh that reminds me of air hissing from a punctured tire. "I've been told by Lottie that we need to make a cabin check schedule for the summer."

Ah, cabin check. The nightly examination of all the cabins by counselors to make sure everyone is present, accounted for, and staying out of trouble. Naturally, it had been the highlight of Vivian's day.

"Each night, we need two people to check on the cabins that don't have counselors or instructors staying in them," Mindy says. "Who wants to volunteer first? And where's Rebecca?"

"Sleeping, I think," Casey says. "I saw her earlier, and she said she needed a nap or the jet lag was going to kill her. She was on assignment in London and came straight here from the airport."

"I guess we'll have to pencil her in later," Mindy says. "Who wants to do it tonight?"

As the others wrangle over the schedule, I see the mess hall's double doors open and watch as Rebecca Schoenfeld steps inside. Unlike Casey, she's changed quite a bit. Gone are the braces and the adolescent pudge. She's become harder, compact, with a worldly style. Her hair, once a frizzy mass kept in place with a scrunchie, is now sleek and short. She's accented her shorts-and-polo ensemble with a brightly colored scarf. Beneath it hangs her camera, which sways as she walks. Her movements are another change. Instead of the shuffling teenager I remember, she walks with swift precision—a woman on a mission. She crosses the mess hall to the food station and grabs an apple. She takes a bite on her way out, stopping only when she spots me on the other side of the room.

The look she gives me is unreadable. I can't tell

if she's surprised, happy, or confused by my presence. After another sharp bite of apple, she turns and exits the mess hall.

"I need to go," I say.

Mindy emits another deflated-tire sigh. "What about cabin check?"

"Sign me up for whenever."

I leave the table, abandoning my tray, the food barely touched. Outside the mess hall, I search in every direction for signs of Becca. But she's nowhere to be found. The areas in front of both the mess hall and the arts and crafts building next door are empty. In the distance, I see Franny slowly making her way to the Lodge with Lottie by her side. Beyond the Lodge, on the patch of grass that leads down to the lake, I spot the maintenance man who was fixing the roof when I arrived. He pushes a wheelbarrow toward a rickety toolshed situated on the edge of the lawn. Lots of activity. None of it from Becca.

I start to head back to the cabins when someone says my name.

"Emma?"

I freeze, knowing exactly who the voice belongs to.

Theo Harris-White.

He calls to me from the open door of the arts and crafts building. Like Franny's speech, nothing about his voice has changed. Hearing it sends more memories shooting into me. They hurt. Like a quiver of arrows to the gut.

Seeing Theo for the very first time, shyly shaking his hand, trying not to notice how his T-shirt swelled across his chest, confused about why the sight made me feel so warm inside.

Theo waist-deep in the lake, skin sun-kissed and blazing, me cradled in his arms, practically trembling from his touch as he lowers me in the water until I'm floating.

Vivian nudging me toward the extra-wide crack in the latrine's exterior wall. Through the gap escaped the sound of a running shower and Theo absently humming a Green Day song. **Go on,** Vivian whispered. **Take a look. He'll never know.**

"Emma," he says again, this time without the questioning inflection. He knows it's me.

I turn around slowly, unsure what to expect. Part of me wants him to be ruddy and balding, the march toward middle age leaving him thick around the waist. Another part of me wants him to look exactly the same.

The reality is somewhere in between. He's aged, of course. No longer the strapping nineteen-year-old I remember him being. That youthful glow has dimmed into something darker, more intense. Yet he wears the years well. Too well, to be honest. There's more bulk than before, but it's all muscle. The flecks of gray in his dark hair and five o'clock shadow suit him. So does the slight weathering of his face. When he smiles at me, a few faint wrinkles crepe the skin around his mouth and eyes. I hate that it only makes him look more attractive.

"Hi."

It's not much of a greeting, but it's the best I can manage. Especially while I'm being blindsided by another memory. One that eclipses the others.

Theo standing in front of the Lodge, looking exhausted and disheveled after a day spent searching the woods. Me rushing at him, crying as I pound his chest and scream, **Where are they? What did you do to them?**

Until today, it was the last thing I ever said to him.

Now that he's right here in front of me again, I expect him to be angry or bitter about what I'd accused him of doing all those years ago. It makes me want to flee the same way Becca had left the mess hall, only faster. But I stay completely still as Theo steps forward and, shockingly, gives me a hug. I pull away after only a second, afraid touching him for too long will prompt even more memories.

Theo takes a step back, looks at me, shakes his head. "I can't believe you're really here. My mother told me you were coming, but I just didn't think it would happen."

"Here I am."

"And it looks like life is treating you well. You look great."

He's being kind. I saw my reflection in the blank screen of my phone. I know how I look.

"So do you," I say.

"I hear you're a painter now. Mom told me she bought one of your works. I haven't had a chance to see it yet. I just got back from Africa two days ago."

"Franny mentioned that. You're a doctor?"

Theo gives a little shrug, scratches his beard. "Yeah. A pediatrician. I've spent the past year working with Doctors Without Borders. But for the next six weeks, I've been demoted to camp nurse."

"I guess that makes me the camp painter," I say.

"Speaking of which, I was just working on your studio for the summer." Theo jerks his head toward the arts and crafts building. "Care to take a peek?"

"Now?" I say, surprised by his casual willingness to remain alone with me.

"No time like the present," Theo says, head cocked, his face poised somewhere between curiosity and confusion. It is, I realize, the same look Franny gave me earlier on the Lodge's back deck.

"Sure," I say. "Lead the way."

I follow him inside, finding myself in the middle of an airy, open room. The walls have been painted a cheerful sky blue. The carpet and baseboard are as green as grass. The three support columns that rise from the floor to the ceiling in equal intervals have been painted to resemble trees. The areas where they meet on the ceiling contain fake branches that drip with paper leaves. It's like stepping into a picture book—happy and bright.

To our left is a little photo studio for Becca, complete with brand-new digital cameras, charging stations, and a handful of sleek computers used for processing pictures. The center of the room is an elaborate crafts station, full of circular tables, cubbyholes, and cabinets filled with string, beads, leather bands the color of saddles. I spot several dozen laptops for Roberta's writing classes and a pair of pottery wheels for Paige.

"I'm impressed," I say. "Franny did a great job fixing this place up."

"This is all Mindy's handiwork, actually," Theo tells me. "She's really thrown herself into reopening the camp."

"I'm not surprised. She's certainly—"

"Enthusiastic?"

"I was going to say 'overwhelming,' but that works, too."

Theo leads me to the far end of the room, where a semicircle of easels has been set up. Along one wall is a shelf holding tubes of oil paints and brushes clustered in mason jars. Clean palettes hang next to windows that let in natural light.

I roam the area, fingers trailing over a blank canvas leaning on one of the easels. At the shelf of paints, I see a hundred different colors, all arranged by hue. Lavender and chartreuse, cherry red and royal blue.

"I put your supplies over there," Theo says, gesturing to the box I brought with me. "I figured you'd want to unpack them yourself."

Honestly, there's no need. Everything I could possibly want is already here. Yet I go to the box anyway and start pulling out my personal supplies. The well-worn brushes. The squished tubes of paint. The palette so thoroughly speckled with color that it resembles a Pollock painting.

Theo stands on the other side of the box, watching me unpack. Fading light from the window falls across his face, highlighting something that's definitely different from fifteen years ago. Something I didn't notice until just now.

A scar.

Located on his left cheek, it's an inch-long line that slants toward his mouth. It's a single shade lighter than the rest of his face, which is why I had missed it earlier. But now that I know it's there, I can't stop looking at it. I'm about to ask Theo how he got it when he checks his watch and says, "I need to go help Chet with the campfire. Will I see you there?"

"Of course," I say. "I never turn down an opportunity to have s'mores."

"Good. That you're coming, I mean." Theo's departure is hesitant. A slow amble to the door.

When he reaches it, he turns around and says, "Hey, Emma."

I look up from my supplies, the suddenly serious tone of his voice worrying me. I suspect he's about to mention the last time we saw each other. He's certainly thinking about it. The tension between us is like a fraying rope, pulled taut, ready to snap.

Theo opens his mouth, reconsiders what he's about to say, closes it again. When he finally does speak, sincerity tinges his voice. "I'm glad you're here. I know it isn't easy. But it means a lot to my mother. It means a lot to me, too."

Then he's gone, leaving me alone to wonder what, exactly, he meant by that. Does it mean a lot to him because it pleases Franny? Or does it mean my presence reminds him of happier times before the camp shuttered in disgrace?

Ultimately, I decide it's neither of those things.

In truth, I think it means he forgives me.

Now all I need is to somehow find a way to forgive myself.

9

Apparently to Mindy, **whenever** meant **tonight**, because after the campfire I find myself on cabin-check duty. While not thrilled, I'm at least pleased to have Casey as my co-checker. Together we go from cabin to cabin, peeking inside to do a head count and ask if any of the campers need anything.

It's strange being on the other side of things. Especially with Casey in tow. When I was a camper here, she'd give a single rap on the door before throwing it open, trying to catch us in the act of some imagined misbehavior. We greeted her with wide-eyed innocence, lashes fluttering. Now I'm the one getting those looks—a surreal turn of events that makes me feel partly jealous of their mischievous youth, partly annoyed by it.

In two of the cabins, I find girls balled up in their bunks, crying from homesickness. While Vivian was wrong about all newbies crying their first night, a small few truly do. I spend a few minutes with each one, telling them that while camp may seem scary now, they'll soon grow to love it and will never want to go back home.

I hope it's the truth.

I never got the chance to find out.

After the cabins have all been checked, Casey and I walk to the patch of grass behind the latrine. It's dark back here, made even more oppressive by the forest that begins a yard or so away. Shadows crowd the trees, broken only by fireflies dancing among the leaves. The utility light affixed to the latrine's corner swarms with bugs.

Casey pulls a cigarette from a battered pack hidden in her cargo shorts and lights up. "I can't believe I'm sneaking cigarettes. I feel like I'm fourteen again."

"Better this than face the wrath of Mindy."

"Want to know a secret?" Casey says. "Her real name is Melinda. She goes by Mindy to be more like Franny."

"I get the feeling Franny doesn't like her very much."

"I can see why. She's the kind of girl I went out of my way to avoid in high school." Casey blows out a stream of smoke and watches it languidly float in the night air. "Honestly, though, it's probably for the best that she's here. Without her, it would be open season on poor Chet. These girls would eat him alive."

"But they're all so young."

"I'm a teacher," Casey says. "Trust me, girls that age are just as full of raging hormones as boys. Remember how you were back then. I saw the way you fawned over Theo. Not that I blamed you. He was a fine-looking young man."

"Have you seen him now?"

Casey gives a slow, knowing nod. "Why is it that men only look better with age? It's completely unfair."

"But he's still just as friendly," I say. "I didn't expect that."

"Because of what you said last time you were here?"

"And because of what people are saying now. I saw some of the responses to your Facebook post. They were pretty brutal."

"Ignore them." Casey gives her hand a casual flip, as if brushing away the smoke still spouting from her cigarette. "Most of those women are just adult versions of the bitchy teenagers they were when they went here."

"A few of them mentioned that this place gave them the creeps," I say. "Something about a legend."

"It's just a silly campfire tale."

"So you've heard it?"

"I've **told** it," Casey says. "That doesn't mean I think the story is true. I can't believe you never heard it."

"I guess I wasn't here long enough."

Casey looks at me, the cigarette held between her lips, its trail of smoke making her squint.

"The story is that there was a village here," she says. "Before the lake was made. Some will say it was full of deaf people. I heard it was a leper colony."

"A leper colony? Was an ancient Indian burial ground too much of a cliché?"

"I didn't make up the story," Casey snaps. "Now, do you want to hear it or not?"

I do, no matter how ridiculous it seems. So I nod for her to continue.

"Deaf village and leper colony aside, the rest of the story is the same," Casey says. "It's that Franny's grandfather saw this valley and decided on the spot it was where he was going to create his lake. But there was one problem. The village sat right in the middle of it. When Buchanan Harris approached the villagers and offered to buy their land, they refused. They were a small, tight-knit community, ostracized by the rest of the world. This was their home, and they weren't going to sell it. This made Mr. Harris angry. He was a man accustomed to getting what he wanted. So when he increased his offer and the villagers again refused, he bought all the land surrounding them instead. Then he built his dam and flooded the valley at the stroke of midnight, knowing the water would wash away the village and that everyone who lived there would drown."

She lowers her voice, speaking slowly. Full storyteller mode.

"The village is still there, deep below Lake Midnight. And the people who drowned now haunt the woods and the lake. They appear at midnight, rising from the water and roaming the forest. Anyone unlucky enough to encounter them gets dragged into the lake and pulled to the bottom, where they quickly drown. Then they become one of the ghosts, cursed to search the woods for all eternity looking for more victims."

I give her an incredulous look. "And that's what people think happened to Vivian, Natalie, and Allison?"

"No one truly believes that," Casey says. "But bad things have happened here, with no explanation. Franny's husband, for example. He was a champion swimmer. Almost made it to the Olympics. Yet he drowned. I heard that Franny's grandmother—the first wife of Buchanan Harris—also drowned here. So when Vivian and the others disappeared, some people said it was the ghosts of Lake Midnight. Or else the survivors."

"Survivors?"

"It's been said that a handful of villagers escaped the rising waters and fled into the hills. There they stayed, living off the land, rebuilding the village in a remote section of the woods where no one could find them. The whole time, they held a grudge against the Harris family, passing it on to their ancestors. Those ancestors are still there, hidden somewhere in the woods. And on nights when the moon is full, they sneak down to the land that used to belong to them and exact their revenge. Vivian, Natalie, and Allison were just three of their victims."

It turns out that Casey's an expert tale-spinner, for as she finishes, I feel a chill in the air. A light frisson that makes me look to the woods behind her, half expecting to see either a ghostly figure or mutant forest-dweller emerging from the tree line.

"What do you really think happened to them?" I say.

"I think they got lost in the woods. Vivian was always wandering off." Casey drops her cigarette and grinds it out with the toe of her sneaker. "Which is why I've always felt partly responsible for what happened. I was a camp counselor. It was my job to make sure all of you were safe. And I regret not paying more attention to you and what was going on in that cabin."

I stare at her, surprised. "Were there things going on I didn't know about?"

"I don't know," Casey says as she fumbles in her pocket for another cigarette. "Maybe."

"Like what? You were friends with Vivian. Surely you noticed something."

"I wouldn't say the two of us were friends. I was a senior camper her first summer and then came back to work as a counselor the two years after that. She was always a troublemaker, but charming enough to get away with it."

Oh, I know that all too well. Vivian excelled at charm. That and lying were her two greatest skills.

"But something about her seemed off that last summer," Casey continues. "Not majorly different. Nothing that someone who only knew her casually would notice. But she wasn't the same. She seemed distracted."

I think of the strange map Vivian had drawn and the even stranger photo of the woman with long hair.

"By what?"

Casey shrugs and looks away again as she irritably puffs out more smoke. "I don't know, Emma. Like I said, we weren't that close."

"But you noticed things."

"**Little** things," Casey says. "I noticed her walking alone around camp a few times. Which never happened the previous summers. Vivian was always surrounded by people. And maybe she just wanted to be left alone. Or maybe . . ."

Her voice trails off as she takes one last draw of her cigarette.

"Maybe what?"

"She was up to no good," Casey says. "On the second day of camp, I caught her trying to sneak into the Lodge. She was hanging around the steps on the back deck, ready to run inside. She said she was looking for Franny, but I didn't buy it."

"Why would she want to break into the Lodge?"

Casey shrugs again. The gesture contains a note of annoyance, almost as if she wishes she'd never brought up the topic of Vivian. "Your guess is as good as mine," she says.

My final stop on cabin check is Dogwood, where I find all three girls on their beds, phones in hand, faces awash in the ice-blue light of their screens. Sasha is already under the covers, her glasses perched on the tip of her nose as she plays Candy Crush or some similarly frustrating time-waste of a game. A cacophony of chirps and beeps erupts from her phone.

In the bunk below her, Krystal has changed into baggy sweats. The matted teddy bear sits in the crook of her arm as she watches a Marvel movie on her phone, the soundtrack leaking out of her ear-buds, tinny and shrill. I can hear blips of gunfire and the telltale crunch of fist hitting skull.

On the other side of the cabin, Miranda re-clines on the top bunk, now dressed in a tight tank top and black shorts so small they barely qualify to be called that. She holds her phone close to her face, doing a faux pout as she takes several pictures.

"You shouldn't be using your phones," I say, even though I was guilty of doing the same thing earlier. "Save your batteries."

Krystal tugs off her earbuds. "What else are we going to do?"

"We could, you know, talk," I suggest. "You may find it hard to believe, but people actually did that before everyone spent all their time squinting at screens."

"I saw you talking to Theo after dinner," Miranda says, her voice wavering between innocence and accusation. "Is he, like, your boyfriend?"

"No. He's a—"

I truly don't know what to call Theo. Several different labels apply.

My friend? Not necessarily.

One of my first crushes? Probably.

The person I accused of doing something horrible to Vivian, Natalie, and Allison?

Definitely.

"He's an acquaintance," I say.

"Do you have a boyfriend?" Sasha asks.

"Not at the moment."

I have plenty of friends who are boys, most of them gay or too socially awkward to consider a romantic relationship. When I do date someone, it's not for very long. A lot of men like the idea of being in a relationship with an artist, but few actually get used to the reality of the situation. The odd hours, the self-doubt and stained hands that stink of oil paint more often than not. The last guy I dated—a dorky-cute accountant at a rival ad agency—managed to put up with it for four months before breaking things off.

Lately, my romantic life has consisted of occasional dalliances with a French sculptor when he happens to be in the city on business. We meet for drinks, conversation, sex made more passionate by how infrequent it is.

"Then how do you know Theo?" Krystal says.

"From when I was a camper here."

Miranda latches on to this news like a shark biting into a baby seal. A wicked grin widens across her face, and her eyes light up. It reminds me so much of Vivian that it causes a strange ache in my heart.

"So you were at Camp Nightingale before?" she says. "Must have been a long time ago."

Rather than be offended, I smile, impressed by the stealthiness of her insult. She's a sly one. Vivian would have loved her.

"It was," I say.

"Did you like it here?" Sasha says as bombastic music rises from her phone and exploding candy pieces reflect off the lenses of her glasses.

"At first. Then not so much."

"Why did you come back?" Krystal asks.

"To make sure you girls have a better time than I did."

"What happened?" Miranda says. "Something horrible?"

She leans forward, her phone temporarily discarded as she waits for my answer. It gives me an idea.

"Phones off," I say. "I mean it."

All three of them groan. Miranda's is the most dramatic as she, like the others, switches off her phone. I sit cross-legged on the floor, my back pressed against the edge of my bunk. I pat the spaces on either side of me until the girls do the same.

"What are we doing?" Sasha asks.

"Playing a game. It's called Two Truths and a Lie. You say three things about yourself. Two of them must be true. One is false. The rest of us have to guess the lie."

We played it a lot during my brief time in Dogwood, including the night of my arrival. The four of us were laying on our bunks in the darkness of the cabin, listening to nature's chorus of crickets and bullfrogs outside the window, when Vivian suddenly said, **Two Truths and a Lie, ladies. I'll start.**

She began to utter three statements, either assuming we already knew how the game was played or just not caring if we didn't.

One: I once met the president. His palm was sweaty. Two: My parents were going to get a

**divorce but then decided not to when my dad
got elected. Three: Once, on vacation in Aus-
tralia, I got pooped on by a koala.**

Three, Natalie said. **You used it last year.**

No, I didn't.

You totally did, Allison said. **You told us the
koala peed on you.**

That's how it went every night. The four of us
in the dark, sharing things we'd never reveal in
the light of day. Constructing our lies so they'd
sound real. It's how I learned that Natalie once
kissed a field hockey teammate and that Allison
tried to sabotage a matinee of **Les Misérables** by
spilling grape juice on her mother's costume five
minutes before curtain.

The game was Vivian's favorite. She said you
could learn more about a person from their lies
than their truths. At the time, I didn't believe her.
I do now.

"I'll start," Miranda says. "Number one: I once
made out with an altar boy in the confessional
during Christmas mass. Number two: I read a
hundred books a year, mostly mysteries. Number
three: I once threw up after riding the Cyclone at
Coney Island."

"The second one," Krystal says.

"Definitely," Sasha adds.

Miranda pretends to be annoyed, even though
I can tell she's secretly pleased with herself. "Just

because I'm smoking hot doesn't make me illiterate. Hot girls read."

"Then what's the lie?" Sasha says.

"I'm not telling." Miranda gives us an impish grin. "Let's just say I've never been to Coney Island, but I go to mass all the time."

Krystal goes next, telling us that her favorite superhero is Spider-Man; that her middle name is also Crystal, although spelled with a **C**; and that she, too, threw up after riding the Cyclone.

"Second one," we all say in unison.

"Was it that obvious?"

"I'm sorry," Miranda says, "but Krystal Crystal? No parent would be that cruel."

When it's time for her turn, Sasha nervously pushes her glasses higher onto her nose and wrinkles her brow in concentration. Clearly, she's not used to lying.

"Um, my favorite food is pizza," she says. "That's number one. Number two: My favorite animal is the pygmy hippopotamus. Three: I don't think I can do this. Lying's wrong, you guys."

"It's okay," I tell her. "Your honesty is noble."

"She's lying," Miranda says. "Right, Sasha? The third one is the lie?"

Sasha shrugs broadly, feigning innocence. "I don't know. You'll have to wait and see."

"Your turn, Emma," Krystal says. "Two truths and one lie."

I take a deep breath, stalling. Even though I knew this was coming, I can't think of suitable things to say. There's so much I could reveal about myself. So little I actually want to have exposed.

"One: My favorite color is periwinkle blue," I announce. "Two: I have been to the Louvre. Twice."

"You still need to give us a third one," Miranda says.

I stall some more, mulling the possibilities in my head, ultimately settling on something perched between fiction and fact.

"During the summer of my thirteenth year, I did something terrible."

"Totally the last one," Miranda says to nods of agreement from the others. "I mean, if you truly had done something terrible, you're not going to admit it during a game."

I smile, pretending that they're right. What none of them understand is that the point of the game isn't to fool others with a lie.

The goal is to trick them by telling the truth.

FIFTEEN YEARS AGO

My second night at Camp Nightingale was as sleepless as the first. Possibly worse. No electricity in the cabin meant no air-conditioning, no fan, nothing to act as a shield against the late June heat. I awoke before dawn, sweaty and uncomfortable, a patch of warm moisture between my legs. When I dipped an index finger into my underwear to investigate, it came back stained with blood.

I was seized with panic, unsure what to do. I knew about menstruation, of course. The girls in my class had been given "the talk" the year before, much to the relief of my mother, who was spared such awkwardness. We were told why it would happen. We were told how it would happen. But my gym teacher—kindly, clueless Miss Baxter— had neglected to tell us what to do **when** it happened.

Ignorant and fearful, I crawled out of bed and awkwardly climbed the ladder to the bunk above mine, afraid to part my legs too much. Rather than ascend one foot at a time, I gripped the ladder's sides and lifted both feet up each rung in quick, bunk-shaking hops. By the time I reached the top, Vivian was already half-awake. Her eyes fluttered beneath a swath of blond hair that covered her face like a veil.

"What the hell are you doing?"

"I'm bleeding," I whispered.

"What?"

"I'm **bleeding**," I said again, stressing the second word as much as I could.

"Then go get a Band-Aid."

"It's between my legs."

Vivian's eyes opened fully as she swiped the hair from her face. "You mean—"

I nodded.

"Is this your first time?"

"Yes."

"Fuck." She sighed, partly out of annoyance and partly out of pity. "Come on. There are tampons in the latrine."

I followed Vivian outside, waddling like a duck down the mulch-covered path. At one point, she glanced back at me and said, "Quit walking like that. You look like an idiot."

Inside the latrine, Vivian hit the light switch by the door and led me to the nearest stall. Along the way, she grabbed a tampon from the dispenser attached to the wall. I sequestered myself inside the stall, Vivian whispering instructions from the other side of the door.

"I think I did it right," I whispered back. "I'm not sure."

"You'd know if you did it wrong."

I remained in the stall, humiliated, humbled, and not sure how to feel. Womanhood had officially arrived. The thought filled me with sadness. And fear. I began to cry all the tears I had managed to hold back the night before. I couldn't help it.

Vivian, of course, heard me and said, "Are you crying?"

"No."

"You totally are. I'm coming in."

Before I could protest, she was in the stall, closing the door behind her and nudging me aside with her hips so she could join me on the toilet seat.

"Come on," she said. "It's not that bad."

"How would you know? You're only, like, three years older than me."

"Which is a lifetime. Trust me. Just ask your older sister."

"I'm an only child."

"That's a shame," Vivian said. "Big sisters are awesome. At least mine was."

"I always wanted a sister," I said. "One who could teach me things."

"Like how to shove cotton up your twat each month?"

I laughed then, in spite of my fear and discomfort. In fact, I laughed so hard I momentarily forgot about both.

"That's better," Vivian said. "No more crying. I forbid it. And since I've already gone above and beyond the call of duty here, I am offering up my services as surrogate big sister. For the next six weeks, you can talk to me about any damn thing you want."

"Like boys?"

"Oh, I happen to have lots of experience in that area." She let out a rueful chuckle. "Trust me, Em, they're more trouble than they're worth."

"How much experience?"

"If you're asking if I've had sex, the answer's yes."

I shrank away from her, suddenly intimidated. I'd never met a girl who'd done **it** before.

"You look scandalized," Vivian said.

"But you're only sixteen."

"Which is old enough."

"Did you like it?"

Vivian flashed a wicked grin. "Loved it."

"And did you love him?"

"Sometimes it's not about love," she said. "Sometimes it's just about seeing someone and wanting him."

I thought of Theo just then. How handsome he was, with muscles in all the right places. How looking at him made me feel deliciously unbalanced. Only in that cramped stall with Vivian did

I understand that I had experienced the first flush of desire.

The realization almost made me start to cry again. The only thing that stopped me was the sound of the latrine door squeaking open, followed by the slap of flip-flops on the tile floor. Vivian peeked through the crack in the stall door. She turned back to me with wide eyes and mouthed two words: **Holy shit.**

Who is it? I mouthed back.

Vivian answered in an excited whisper, "Theo!"

Water began to blast inside a shower stall. The one in the far corner of the latrine. I started to feel dizzy as my brain filled with the same stew of emotions I had felt the night before. Warmth. Happiness. Shame. I was in the same room with a boy who was showering!

No, not a boy. A man.

And not just any man. Theo Harris-White.

"What do we do?" I whispered to Vivian.

She didn't answer. Instead, she moved. Out of the stall. Toward the door. Dragging me with her, the two of us incapable of making a silent retreat. Vivian giggled madly. I tripped and slammed a shoulder into the paper towel dispenser.

"Halt!" Theo called from the shower stall. "Who goes there?"

Vivian and I exchanged looks. I'm certain mine was deer-in-headlights panicked. Hers was delighted.

"It's **Vivian**," she said coyly, drawing out the end of her name into an extra syllable.

"Hey, Viv."

Theo said it so casually that jealousy bloomed in my chest. How lucky Vivian was. To be known by Theo. To be greeted with such easy familiarity. Vivian noticed the envy in my eyes and added, "Emma's here, too."

"Emma who?"

"Emma Davis. She's new."

"Oh, that Emma. Cool, fashionably late Emma."

I let out a squeak, shocked and elated that Theo knew who I was. That he remembered leading me to Dogwood in the dark of night. That he had noticed me.

Vivian elbowed me in the ribs, prompting me to meekly reply, "Hi, Theo."

"Why are you two up so early?" he asked.

I froze, one hand latched on to Vivian's wrist, silently begging her not to tell him the truth. I wasn't sure if a thirteen-year-old girl could die of embarrassment, but I certainly didn't want to find out.

"Um, going to the bathroom," she replied. "The real question is why you're here. Isn't there a shower in the Lodge?"

"The water pressure there sucks," Theo said. "Those pipes are ancient. Which is why I haul ass out of bed extra early and shower here before any of you girls can stumble in."

"We were here first," Vivian said.

"And I'd be grateful if you'd finally leave so I can shower in peace."

Vivian looked down at me, smirking, and whispered, "He means jerk off."

It was so dirty and inappropriate that a laugh burst out of me. Theo heard it, of course, and said, "I mean it, guys. I can't stay in here all day."

"Fine," Vivian called back. "We're gone."

We departed in a torrent of giggles, me still clutching Vivian's wrist, the two of us twirling each other in the predawn. We spun until I grew dizzy and everything—the camp, the latrine, Vivian's face—became a glorious, happy blur.

10

It takes me hours to fall asleep. The silence is once again too oppressive for my Manhattanite ears. When I finally do manage to drift off, my sleep is stormy with bad dreams. In one of them—the most vivid—I see the long-haired woman from the photo found in Vivian's trunk. I stare into those distressed eyes until it dawns on me that it's not a picture I'm looking at but a mirror.

I'm the woman in the photograph. It's **my** absurdly long hair trailing to the floor, **my** dark-cloud eyes staring back at me.

The realization jolts me from sleep. I sit up, my breath heavy and my skin coated in a thin sheen of sweat. I'm also struck by the need to pee, which tugs me reluctantly from bed. Careful not to wake the others, I fumble in the darkness for my flashlight and those newly purchased boots, which I stuff my bare feet into once I'm outside. The flashlight remains off as I indulge myself with a view of the darkened sky above. I'd forgotten how different night is here. Clearer than in the city. Unmarred by light pollution and constant air traffic, the sky spreads out like a vast canvas painted midnight blue and studded with stars. The moon sits low on the horizon, already dipping into the forest to the west. It's such a beautiful sight that I get the urge to paint it. Which, I suppose, is progress.

Inside the latrine, I hit the light switch by the door. Fluorescent bulbs overhead hum to life as I head to the nearest stall. The same stall, coincidently, where Vivian led me on that fraught, frightening night.

To this day, it amazes me how I entered the latrine that night feeling one thing and left feeling the complete opposite. Going in, I was terrified by the ways my body could betray me. I departed riding a wave of laughter, still clutching Vivian. I remember how happy I was in that moment. How **alive** I had felt.

The memory of that time makes me sigh as I prepare to leave the stall. I'm stopped by the sound of the latrine door being opened. At first, I think it might again be Theo. A sad, silly thought, when you get right down to it. But it's not entirely out of the realm of possibility, seeing how we're both back here after all this time.

Instead, when I peek through the crack in the stall door, I see a girl. Long, bare limbs. A flash of blond hair. She stands at the row of sinks along the wall, checking her features in the mirror. I check them, too, shifting slightly in the stall to get a better view of her reflection. I spot dark eyes, a perky nose, a chin that tapers to a point.

A gasp leaps from my throat as I push out of the stall, calling her name.

"Vivian?"

I know I'm wrong even before the girl at the sink spins around, startled. Her hair's not as blond as I had thought. Her skin is more tanned. When she fully faces me, I see the diamond stud in her nose, winking at me.

"Who the hell is Vivian?" Miranda asks.

"No one," I start to say, stopping myself mid-lie. "A camper I knew."

"Well you scared the shit out of me."

I have no doubt. I scared myself as well. When I look down at my hands, I see I'm clutching the charm bracelet, the birds rattling. I force myself to let go.

"I'm sorry," I tell Miranda. "I'm confused. And tired."

"Can't sleep?"

I shake my head. "You?"

"Same."

She says it with forced casualness, which instantly tips me off that it's a lie. I'm good at that kind of thing. I was trained by the best.

"Is everything okay?"

Miranda gives me a nod that soon veers into a slow shake of her head. The movement highlights the redness of her eyes and the faint shimmering lines that run down her cheeks. Tears, recently dried.

"What happened?"

"I was just dumped," she says. "Which is a first, by the way. I do the dumping. Always."

I go to the sink next to her and turn on the tap. The water rushing from the faucet is blessedly cold. I run a paper towel under the stream and press it to my cheeks and neck. The feeling is delicious—crisp water against my skin evaporating in the heat, the vanished droplets leaving pinpricks in their wake.

Miranda watches me, silently seeking comfort. It occurs to me that's also part of my job. One I'm woefully unprepared for. Yet I know about heartbreak. All too well.

"You want to talk about it?"

"No," Miranda says, but then adds, "It's not like we were serious. We'd only dated for, like, a month. And I get it. I'm gone for six weeks. He wants to have fun this summer."

"But . . ."

"But he dumped me by text. What kind of jack-ass does that?"

"One who clearly doesn't deserve you," I say.

"But I really liked him." More tears glisten at the edges of her eyes. She refuses to let them fall, instead using a fist to wipe them away. "It's usually the other way around. Normally I couldn't care less about guys who really like me. But he was different. You must think I'm, like, such a baby."

"I think you're hurt," I tell her. "But you'll feel better sooner than you think. By the time you get back from camp, he'll be with some—"

"Skank," Miranda says.

"Exactly. He'll be with some skank, and you'll wonder why you even liked him in the first place."

"And he'll regret dumping me." Miranda checks her reflection in the mirror, smiling at what she sees. "Because I'm going to look so hot with my camp tan."

"That's the spirit," I say. "Now, go back to the cabin. I'll be there in a minute."

Miranda heads to the door, giving me a wiggle-finger wave as she goes. Once she's gone, I stay behind to splash more cold water on my face and compose myself. I can't believe I'd momentarily thought she was Vivian. Not a road I want to go down again. Those days are over. No thanks to this place and all these memories that keep returning like a bad habit.

When I step outside, even the sky is familiar—a shade of grayish blue that I've used often in my paintings. Muted and melancholy and just the tiniest bit hopeful. It was that same color when Vivian and I bolted from the latrine in the wee hours of the morning, laughing with abandon, the rest of camp sleepy and silent. It had felt like we were the only people on earth.

But there had been a third person also awake, as Vivian soon reminded me.

Come here, she whispered, standing by the latrine, her elbow bent against its cedar wall. **There's something I** know **you'll want to see.**

With a grin, she gestured to two planks in the latrine's exterior wall. One was slightly crooked, leaving a crack big enough for light to trickle through it. Occasionally, the light would blink out a moment, blocked by someone on the other side of the wall.

That someone was Theo. Still in the shower. I heard the rush of water and his faint humming of a Green Day tune.

How do you know about this? I asked.

Vivian grinned from ear to ear. **Found it last year. No one knows about it but me.**

And you want me to spy on Theo?

No, Vivian replied. **I** dare **you to spy on him.**

But it's wrong.

Go on. Take a look. He'll never know.

I swallowed hard, my throat suddenly parched. I edged closer to the wall, wanting to get a better look, ashamed by that want. Even more shameful was my need to please Vivian.

It's fine, Vivian whispered. **When you get an opportunity to look, you're a fool not to take it.**

So I looked. Even though I knew it was wrong. I leaned in and placed an eye to the crack in the wall, at first seeing nothing but steam and the water-specked shower wall. Then Theo appeared. Skin slick. Body smooth in some places, matted with dark hair in others. It was the most beautiful, frightening thing I had ever seen.

I didn't watch him for very long. After a few seconds, the wrongness of the situation crashed over me and I turned away, red-faced and dizzy. Vivian stood behind me, shaking her head in such a way that I couldn't tell if she thought I had looked too much or not enough.

Well, how was it? she asked as we headed back to the cabin.

Gross, I said.

Right. She bumped my hip with hers. **Totally gross.**

I'm halfway to the cabins when a strange, sudden noise gets my attention. It's a rustling sound. Like someone walking through the grass to my left.

My thoughts turn instantly to Casey's story about the victims of Lake Midnight. When something appears on the edge of my vision, I think for a split second it's one of the ghosts, ready to drag me to a watery grave. Or one of the rumored survivors' grandsons wielding an ax. I switch on the flashlight and swing it toward the noise.

It turns out to be a fox slinking toward the forest. Something is in its mouth—an unknown creature, now dead. All I can make out is blood-slicked fur. The fox pauses in the flashlight's glare, its body coiled, eyes glowing greenish white as it stares at me, deciding if I'm a threat. I'm not. Even the fox can see that. It trots on, unconcerned, a dead limb of whatever's in its mouth flopping as it vanishes into the forest.

I, too, resume walking, feeling a little bit frightened and a lot foolish. The mood persists as I reach Dogwood. Because that's when I notice something out of the ordinary as I reach for the doorknob.

A light. Tiny and red. Flaring like the tip of a cigarette.

It glows from the back wall of the cabin in front of ours. Red Oak, I think. Or maybe Sycamore. I aim the flashlight at it and see a black rectangle tucked into the nook where the two sides of the roof connect. A slim cord drips down the wall to the ground.

A surveillance camera. The kind you see in the corners of convenience stores.

I turn off the flashlight and stare at the camera's lens, which shimmers slightly in the darkness. I don't move a muscle.

The red light snaps off.

I wait five seconds before waving the flashlight over my head.

The red light flicks on again, triggered by the motion. I assume it does this every time someone enters or exits the cabin.

I have no idea how long the camera's been doing this. Or why it's there. Or if there are others scattered throughout camp. All I know is that Franny or Theo or someone involved with Camp Nightingale decided it was a good idea to keep an eye on the cabin.

The irony of the situation unsettles me.

Fifteen years later, I'm the one being watched.

11

Inside, I'm unable to go back to sleep. I change into my bathing suit and a brightly patterned silk robe bought during a long-ago trip to Cozumel. I then grab a towel from my trunk and slip quietly out of the cabin. On my way out the door, I will myself not to look at the camera. I don't want to see its red light switch on. Nor do I want to face the lens' prying eye. I walk past it quickly, face averted, pretending I don't know it's there, just in case someone is watching.

As I make my way to the lake, I sneak glances at the other cabins, checking for cameras on those as well. I don't see any. Nor do I see any on the handful of light poles that dully illuminate the pathway into the heart of the camp. Or in the trees.

I try not to let that worry me.

At the edge of Lake Midnight, I place the towel on the cracked dirt of the shore, drop the robe, and step gingerly into the water. The lake is cold, bracing. Not at all like the heated pool at the local Y where I swim each morning. Lake Midnight is murkier. Although the water's only up to my knees, my bare feet look blurred and slightly greenish. When I scoop some into my cupped hands, I see swirling specks of feathery algae.

Steeling myself with a deep breath, I dive under, kicking hard, arms extended in front of me. I emerge only when my chest starts to tighten, lungs swelling. I then start to cut my way across the lake. Strands of mist hover just above the surface, breaking apart when I burst through them. In the water, yellow perch flee my path, startled.

I stop once I reach the middle of the lake— probably a quarter mile from shore. I have no idea how deep the water is here. Maybe thirty feet. Maybe a hundred. I think about how everything below me used to be dry land. A valley filled with trees and rocks and animals. All of it is still down there. The trees rotted by water. The stones fuzzy with algae. The animals stripped of their flesh by fish, now nothing but bones.

Not a comforting thought.

I think of the story Casey told me. The village still at the bottom of the lake, its skeletal inhabitants tucked in their beds.

That's even less comforting.

Paddling in place, I turn back toward camp. At this hour, it's quiet and still, bathed in pinkish light from the rising sun that peeks above the mountains to the east. The only activity I see is a solitary figure standing at the dock's edge, watching me.

Even from this distance, I know the figure is Becca Schoenfeld. I see the splash of color from the scarf circling her neck and can make out the shape of her camera as she lifts it to her face.

Becca remains on the dock as I swim back to shore, her camera poised. I try not to feel self-conscious as the staccato clicks of the shutter echo across the water. Instead, I swim harder, increasing my strokes. If Becca's going to watch, then I'll give her something worth watching.

That's another, different lesson I learned in this lake.

I get to my feet a few yards from shore and wade the rest of the way. Becca has left the dock and is now directly in front of me, gesturing for me to stop. I indulge her, standing shin-deep in the water as she clicks off a few more shots.

"Sorry," she says once she's finished. "The light was so perfect, I couldn't resist. Such a beautiful sunrise."

She holds the camera in front of me as I dry off, scrolling through the photos. Of the last one, she says, "This one's the keeper."

In the picture, I've risen from the lake, water streaming down my body, backlit by the sunrise. I think Becca was going for something fierce and empowering. A woman emerging victorious from the surf, now determined to conquer land. But instead of fierce, I simply look lost. As if I've just woken up in the water, confused by how I'd gotten there. It makes me feel so self-conscious that I quickly reach for my robe and wrap it tight around me.

"Please delete that."

"But it looks great."

"Fine," I say. "Just promise me it won't end up on the cover of **National Geographic**."

We settle onto the grass and stare out at the water, which reflects the pinkish-orange sky so perfectly it's hard to tell which is which. At least Becca was right about that. The sunrise is indeed beautiful.

"So you're an artist," she says. "I read about your gallery show."

"And I've seen your photographs."

Having stated the obvious, we settle into an awkward silence. I pretend to adjust the sleeves of my robe. Becca fiddles with her camera strap. We both keep an eye on the sunrise, which has now gained a few streaks of gold.

"I can't believe I'm back here," Becca eventually says. "I can't believe **you're** back here."

"You and me both."

"Listen, I'm sorry for acting weird yesterday. I saw you in the mess hall and momentarily freaked out. I don't know why."

"I do," I say. "Seeing me brought back a hundred

different memories. Some of which you weren't prepared to face."

"Exactly."

"It happens all the time to me," I admit. "Almost nonstop. Everywhere I look, a memory seems to be lurking."

"I'm assuming Franny lured you back," Becca says.

I nod, even though it's not entirely the truth.

"I volunteered," Becca says. "I mean, I already knew Franny was going to ask. She somehow managed to track me down during one of my rare returns to New York and invited me to lunch. As soon as she started talking about Camp Nightingale, I knew what she had planned. So I jumped at the chance."

"I took a little more convincing."

"Not me. For the past three years, I've been living out of a suitcase. Staying in one place for six weeks definitely had its appeal." Becca stretches out on the grass, as if to prove how relaxed she truly is. "I don't even mind that I'm bunking with three teenagers. It's worth it if I can get a camera into their hands and possibly inspire them. Plus, this feels like a vacation after some of the horrible shit I've seen."

She lifts her chin to the sunrise and closes her eyes. In that light clenching of her eyelids, I can see that she, too, is haunted by the unknown. The only difference between us is that she's returned to Camp Nightingale to forget. I'm here to remember.

"Yesterday, when I saw you in the mess hall, I wanted to ask you something."

"Let me guess," Becca says. "It's about that summer."

I give a curt nod. "Do you remember much?"

"About the summer or the . . . ?"

She doesn't finish her sentence. It's almost like she's afraid to utter that final word. I'm not.

"The disappearance," I say. "Did you notice anything strange the night before it happened? Or maybe the morning I realized they were gone?"

A memory arrives. A bad one. Me at the lake, telling Franny that the girls were missing as other campers gathered around. Becca stood in the crowd, watching it all unfold through her camera, the shutter clicking away.

"I remember you," she says. "How frantic and scared you were."

"Other than that, you don't recall anything out of the ordinary?"

"Nope." The word comes out too fast and pitched too high. Like a chirp. "Nothing."

"And how well did you know the girls in my cabin?"

"Allison, Natalie, and Vivian?"

"Yeah," I say. "You had all spent the previous summer here. I thought you might have known them."

"I didn't. Not really."

"Not even Vivian?" I think of Becca's warning my first morning at camp. **Don't be fooled. She'll turn on you eventually.** "I thought the two of you might have been friends."

"I mean, I knew her," Becca says. "Everyone here knew Vivian. And everyone had an opinion."

"What was the general consensus?"

"Honestly? That she was kind of a bitch."

I flinch at her tone. It's so surprisingly harsh that no other reaction is appropriate. Becca sees it happen and says, "I'm sorry. That was cruel."

"It was," I say, my voice quiet.

I expect Becca to backtrack a bit or maybe offer a better apology. Instead, she doubles down. Squaring her shoulders, she flashes me a hard look and says, "Come on, Emma. You don't need to pretend around me. Vivian doesn't automatically become a good person just because of what happened to her. I mean, you of all people should know that."

She stands and brushes dirt from her shorts. Then she walks away, slowly, silently, not looking back. I remain where I am, contemplating the two truths Becca just revealed to me.

The first is that she's right. Vivian wasn't a good person. Vanishing into thin air doesn't change that.

The second is that Becca remembers much more than she'd like to admit.

The beach at Camp Nightingale—a combination of sand and pebbles strewn along a patch of Lake Midnight decades earlier—felt as uncomfortable as it looked. Not even spreading two towels on top of each other could completely dull the prodding of the stones below. Still, I grinned and tried to bear it as I watched waves of campers tiptoe into the water.

Although all four of us had changed into our bathing suits, only Natalie and Allison joined the others in the lake. Natalie swam like the natural athlete she was, using hard, long strokes to easily make it to the string of foam buoys marking the area no one was allowed to swim past. Allison was more of a show-off, somersaulting in the water like a synchronized swimmer.

I remained on shore, nervous in my modest one-piece swimsuit. Vivian sat behind me, coating my shoulders with Coppertone, its coconut scent sickeningly sweet.

"It's criminal how pretty you are," she said.

"I don't feel pretty."

"But you are," Vivian said. "Hasn't your mother ever told you that?"

"My mother gives me as little attention as possible. Same thing with my dad."

Vivian clucked with sympathy. "That sounds just like my parents. I'm surprised I didn't die of neglect as a newborn. But my sister and I learned how to fend for ourselves. She's the one who made me realize how pretty I was. Now I'll do the same for you."

"I'm far from pretty."

"You **are**," Vivian insisted. "And in a year or two, you'll be gorgeous. I can tell. Do you have a boyfriend back home?"

I shook my head, knowing how I was all but invisible to the boys in my neighborhood. I was among the last of the late bloomers. Flat as cardboard. No one paid attention to cardboard.

"That'll change," Vivian said. "You'll snag yourself a hottie like Theo."

She gestured to the lifeguard stand a few feet away, where Theo sat in red swim trunks, the whistle roped around his neck nestled in his chest hair. Every time I looked at him, which was often, I tried not to think about that morning at the latrine. Watching him. Wanting him. Instead, it was all I could think about.

"Why aren't you in the water?" he called down to us.

"No reason," Vivian said.

"I don't know how to swim," I said.

A grin spread across Theo's face. "That's quite a coincidence. One of my goals today is to teach someone."

He hopped down from the lifeguard stand and, before I could protest, took my hand and led me to the water. I paused when my feet touched the mossy rocks at the lake's edge. They were slick, which made me worry that I'd slip and plunge under. The dirty look of the water only heightened my anxiety. Bits of brown stuff floated just below the surface. When some touched my ankle, I recoiled.

Theo tightened his grip around my hand. "Relax. A little algae never hurt anyone."

He guided me deeper into the lake, the water rising against me in increments. To my knees. Then to my thighs. Soon I was up to my waist, the chill of the water leaving me momentarily breathless. Or maybe it wasn't the water. Maybe it was the way Theo's broad shoulders glowed in the late June sun. Or the way his crooked smile widened when I took another, unprompted step deeper into the water.

"Awesome, Em," he said. "You're doing great. But you need to relax more. The water is your friend. Let it hold you up."

Without warning, he slid behind me and scooped me up in his arms. One wrapped around my back. The other slid behind my knees. The areas where his skin touched mine became instantly hot, as if electricity coursed through them.

"Close your eyes," he said.

I closed them as he lowered me into the lake until I couldn't tell the difference between his arms and the water. When I opened my eyes, I saw him standing next to me, arms crossed. I was on my own, letting the water hold me up.

Theo grinned, his eyes sparkling. "You, my dear, are floating."

Just then, noise rippled across the lake. Splashing. Urgent and panicked. A couple of girls in the deep end began to shriek, their arms flapping against the water like ducks unable to take flight. Beyond them, I saw a pair of hands rising and falling from the lake's surface, waving frantically, water flinging off the fingertips. A face poked out of the drink, gasped, slipped back under.

Vivian.

Theo left my side and surged toward her. Without him near me, I sank into the water, dropping until I hit the lake bed. I began to paddle, guided by instinct more than anything else, clawing at the water until my nose and mouth broke the surface. I continued to paddle and kick until, lo and behold, I was swimming.

I kept at it, looking across the water first to Vivian, still flailing, and then to Natalie and Allison, who bobbed in place, frozen with fear, their faces suddenly pale. I watched them watch Theo as he reached Vivian and clamped an arm around her waist. He swam to shore that way, not stopping until both of their backs were on the pebble-specked beach.

Vivian coughed once, and a bubble of lake water spurted from her throat. Tears streamed down her crimson cheeks.

"I-I don't know what happened," she said, gasping. "I went under and couldn't come up. I thought I was going to die."

"You would have if I hadn't been here," Theo said, anger peeking through his exhaustion. "Jesus, Viv, I thought you could swim."

Vivian sat up and shook her head, still crying. "I thought I'd try after watching you teach Emma. You made it look so easy."

Standing a few yards away from them was Becca. Her camera hung from her neck even though she was wearing a bathing suit. She clicked off a picture of Vivian sprawled on shore. Then she turned to the lake, picking me out of the crowd of still-stunned campers paddling in the water. She smiled and mouthed four words, each of them silent but unmistakable.

I told you so.

12

I remain on the beach until reveille blasts from the ancient speaker atop the mess hall. The music rushes past me and across the lake, its sound skimming the water on its way to the far shore. The first full day of camp has begun.

Again.

Rather than battle a horde of teenage girls for space in the latrine, I shuffle to the mess hall, shy in my damp robe and clacking flip-flops. It's mostly empty, thank God. Nobody but me and the kitchen workers. One of them—a guy with dark hair and a patchy goatee—checks me out for half a second before turning away.

I ignore him and grab a doughnut, a banana, and a cup of coffee. The banana is consumed quickly. The doughnut not so much. Each bite brings a flash of Vivian squinting, her lips pursed. Her disapproving look. I set down the doughnut, sigh, pick it up, and shove what's left into my mouth. I wash it down with the coffee, pleased with my fifteen-years-too-late defiance.

My walk back to Dogwood is spent swimming against the tide of campers making their way to the mess hall. All of them are freshly scrubbed, trailing scents behind them. Baby powder. Noxzema. Shampoo that smells like strawberries.

One scent cuts through the others. Something thick and flowery. Perfume.

But not just any old perfume.

Obsession.

Vivian wore it, spritzing it on her neck and wrists twice a day. Once in the morning. Once in the afternoon. The scent used to fill the cabin, lingering there long after she had departed.

Now I get that same feeling. Like she's just been here, leaving only her scent behind. I spin among the stream of girls, searching for her in the departing crowd, knowing she's not there but looking anyway. I reach for my bracelet and tap a pewter beak. Just in case.

The girls surge forward, taking the perfume scent with them. Left behind is a clammy sensation on the back of my neck. It makes me shiver as I stop into Dogwood to grab my clothes for the day. I sniff the air for traces of perfume, detecting nothing but the tang of someone's deodorant.

In the latrine, I spot Miranda, Krystal, and Sasha amid the morning stragglers at the sinks. Miranda stares in the mirror, fussing with her hair. Beside her, Sasha says, "Can we go now? I'm **starving**."

"Just a second." Miranda gives her hair one last flip. "There. Now we may go."

I give them a wave on my way to the shower stalls, all but one of which are in use. The empty stall is the last one in the row. Like the others, it's a cubicle of cedar walls and a door of smoked glass. A pinpoint of white light glows in the center of that door. Behind me, a similar light peeks through a crack in the cedar wall.

Alarm flares in my chest, calming a second later once I understand what's happening. The white glow is sunlight. Its source is a minuscule crack in the shower wall. The same crack I peered through to spy on Theo fifteen years ago.

I let out a breath, feeling both foolish for not realizing it sooner and relieved that it's not something worse, like another camera. One is enough to make me seriously paranoid. So much so that I consider waiting for another stall to open up. I decide against it for the simple reason that I'm already inside this one with the water running. And thanks to a morning of heavy use, it's not getting any warmer.

Besides, Vivian was the only person who knew about that crack. She told me so herself.

So I stay where I am, showering as fast as possible. I give my hair a quick shampoo and an even quicker rinse, closing my eyes as the soapy water cascades down my face. I enjoy that moment of temporary blindness. It allows me to pretend, just for a moment, that I'm thirteen again and experiencing Camp Nightingale for the very first time. That Vivian, Natalie, and Allison are safe within the confines of Dogwood. That the events of fifteen years ago never happened.

It's a nice feeling. One that makes me want to linger under the shower's spray. But the water keeps getting colder, turning from lukewarm to the wrong side of chilly. In a minute or two, it'll be as cold as Lake Midnight.

I finish rinsing my hair and open my eyes.

The point of light on the door is gone.

I spin around, frantically checking the shower wall behind me. No light peeks through the crack. It's gone, eclipsed by something outside.

No, not something.

Someone.

Right on the other side of the wall.

Watching me.

I yelp and rush to the door, fumbling for my towel and robe in the process. By the time I'm pushing my way out of the stall, the light has reappeared, both through the wall and onto the door as it swings open. Whoever was there is now gone.

That doesn't stop me from yanking on my robe and clutching it tight around me. I rush through the now-empty latrine, bursting through the door with the hope of catching whoever had been watching me.

No one is outside. The entire vicinity is deserted. The closest people I see are two campers more than a hundred yards away. Late for breakfast, they hurry to the mess hall, ponytails bobbing.

I'm the only one here.

Just to be safe, I do a quick, awkward circle around the building, seeing nothing. By the time I'm back at the latrine door, I start to wonder if I'm mistaken and that what I saw was merely someone leaning against the building, obliviously covering the crack in the wall.

Yet that explanation doesn't quite make sense. If it had been unintentional, then the person responsible wouldn't have left the moment I realized they were there. They would be here still, no doubt wondering why I've rushed outside dripping wet, soap remnants sticky on my skin.

So I think of other possibilities. A low-flying bird swooping past the latrine. Or maybe those late-for-breakfast campers rushing by. There's even a chance it might not have been anything at all. I try to estimate how long the light through the crack was blocked. Not long. A fraction of a second at most. My eyes had been closed a lot longer than that. When I opened them again, it would have taken a second or two for them to adjust to the dimness of the shower stall. Maybe that's all it was—my vision catching up to reality.

By the time I'm back at Dogwood, I've concluded that's what it was. A trick of the light. A brief optical illusion.

At least that's what I force myself to believe.

Lying to myself.

It's the only falsehood I allow.

The first painting lesson of the summer is held outside, away from the arts and crafts building and its crowd of campers. Despite reassuring myself that it never happened, I remain shaken by my experience in the shower. Paranoia clings to me like cold sweat, making me hyperalert to even the briefest of glances.

When Sasha suggests we paint the lake, I embrace the idea. It temporarily soothes my anxiety while giving the dozen girls who arrived for the lesson something better to paint than the still life I had planned.

Now they stand at their easels, which have been carried to the lawn behind the Lodge, facing the lake. Palettes in hand, all of them contemplate their blank canvases, slightly nervous, fingers absently fiddling with the brushes poking from their cargo shorts. I'm nervous, too, and not just from the stress of the morning. The way the girls stare at me, seeking guidance, is intimidating. Marc was right. This is definitely not in my wheelhouse.

It helps slightly that the girls from Dogwood are here, including Krystal with her promised sketchpad and a set of charcoal pencils. They're familiar enough to give me a boost of confidence before I begin.

"The assignment this morning is to paint what you see," I announce. "Just look out at the lake and paint it as only you see it. Use whatever colors you want. Use any techniques you want. This isn't school. You won't be graded. The only person you need to please is you."

As the girls paint, I walk behind them, checking their progress. Watching them paint calms me. Some—such as Sasha and her meticulously clean lines—even show promise. Others, like Miranda's defiantly blue brushstrokes, do not. But at least they're painting, which is more than I've done for the past six months.

When I reach Krystal, I see that she's sketched a superhero in tight spandex and a flowing cape standing before an easel. The hero's face is my own. Her muscular body most definitely is not.

"I think I'm going to name her Monet," Krystal says. "Painter by day, crime fighter by night."

"What's her superpower?"

"I haven't decided yet."

"I'm sure you'll think of something."

Class ends when a bell clangs from the mess hall, signaling lunchtime. The girls put down their brushes and scurry off, leaving me alone to gather up their canvases and easels. I move the canvases first, carrying them back to the arts and crafts building two by two so as not to smudge the still-wet paint. Then I return for the easels, finding them already in the process of being collected.

The gatherer is the maintenance man I saw fixing the roof of the arts and crafts building when I arrived. He's come from the toolshed on the edge of the lawn. Its door sits open, offering a glimpse of a lawn mower, a handsaw, chains hanging on the wall.

"I figured you could use some help," he says.

His voice is gruff, thickened by a trace of Maine accent.

"Thanks." I hold out my hand. "I'm Emma, by the way."

Instead of shaking my hand, the man nods and says, "I know."

He doesn't tell me how he knows this. He doesn't need to. He was here fifteen years ago. He knows the score.

"You were here before, right?" I say. "I recognized you when I arrived."

The man folds another easel, drops it onto a growing pile of them. "Yep."

"What did you do in the time the camp was closed?"

"I don't work for the camp. I work for the family. Doesn't matter if the camp is open or closed, I'm still here."

"I see."

Not wanting to feel useless, I collapse the last

remaining easel and hand it to him. He adds it to the stack and scoops up all of them at once, carrying six under each arm. Impressive, considering I could have only managed one or two.

"Can I help carry some of those?" I say.

"I got 'em."

I step out of his way, revealing several splotches of paint that mar the grass. White and cerulean and a few dots of crimson that unnervingly resemble drops of blood. The maintenance man sees them and grunts his disapproval.

"Your girls made a mess," he says.

"It happens when you're painting. You should see my studio,"

I give him a smile, hoping it will appease him. When it doesn't, I remove the rag hanging from my back pocket and dab at the grass. "This should do the trick," I say, even though it does the opposite, spreading the paint in widening smears.

The man grunts again and says, "Mrs. Harris-White doesn't like messes."

Then he's off, carting away the easels as if they weigh nothing at all. I remain where I am, attempting a few more futile dabs at the grass. When that doesn't work, I simply pluck the blades from the parched earth and toss them into the air. They catch the dull breeze and scatter, rolling on the wind and out over the lake.

13

Before heading to lunch, I return to the arts and crafts building to root through Casey's supplies. I don't find what I'm looking for among the bins of wood glue and colored markers, so I head to Paige's pottery station. A dime-size chunk of wet clay sits on one of the pottery wheels. Perfect for what I have planned.

"Shouldn't you be at lunch?"

I whirl around to see Mindy in the doorway, her arms crossed, head tilted. She gives me a too-big smile as she steps inside. Pretend friendliness.

I smile, too. Pretending right back. "I had some things to finish up in here."

"You do pottery as well?"

"I was just admiring what you've done to the place," I say, curling my fingers around the bit of clay to hide it from her. I'd rather not explain to Mindy what I intend to do with it. She's suspicious enough as it is. "It looks incredible."

Mindy nods her thanks. "It was a lot of work and a lot of money."

"It really shows."

The extra compliment works. Mindy's gritted-teeth smile melts into something that almost resembles a human expression. "Thanks," she says. "And I'm sorry for acting so suspicious. I'm just on high alert now that camp's in full swing."

"No worries. I get it."

"Everything needs to go as smooth as possible," Mindy adds. "Which is why you should probably get to the mess hall now. If campers don't see you there, they'll think they can start skipping lunch, too. We lead by example, Emma."

First, I got a warning from the groundskeeper. Now here's one from Mindy. And it definitely is a warning. I'm supposed to tread lightly and not make any messes. In short, do the opposite of what I did last time I was here.

"Sure," I say. "Going there now."

It's a lie. But a justifiable one.

Instead of heading to the mess hall, I make my way to the latrine. A few stragglers mill about the front door, waiting for friends to accompany them to lunch. After they're all gone, I head to the side of the building, seeking out the crack on the exterior wall. Once I find it, I stuff a bit of clay between the two planks, covering the crack.

The irony of the act isn't lost on me. Fifteen years ago, I'd peered through this very crack, watching Theo without his knowledge or consent. While I'd like to blame that on youth and naïveté, I can't. I was thirteen. Old enough to know that spying on Theo was wrong. Yet I did it anyway.

Now no one can look inside. One act of atonement down. Many more to go.

When I finally do reach the mess hall, I find Theo waiting for me outside, a wicker basket at his feet. It's an unexpected sight. One that makes me irrationally think the mere memory of my long-ago transgression summoned his appearance. That after all these years, he somehow found out I had watched him. I stop a few steps short of him, bracing for confrontation. Instead, Theo announces, "I'm going on a picnic. And I thought you might like to come along."

"What's the occasion?"

He nods toward the mess hall doors. "Does one need a special occasion to skip the horror of whatever's being served in there?"

He says it with his brows arched, aiming for levity. But the same tension from last night is still present. Theo feels it, too. I can see it in the apprehensive twitch at the corners of his smile. A knot of guilt twists in my chest. Now there's no doubt he's forgiven me. What I don't understand is why.

Still, a picnic lunch does sound appealing. Especially because Mindy wouldn't like the idea one bit.

"Count me in," I say. "My taste buds thank you."

Theo lifts the basket and leads me away from the mess hall. Rather than go to the sloped lawn behind the Lodge, where I assumed we'd head, he instead guides me past the cabins and latrine and into the woods.

"Where are you taking me?"

Theo grins back at me before entering the forest. "Someplace special."

Although there's no path for us to follow, he walks with purpose, as if he knows exactly where he's going. I trail behind him, stepping over downed branches and crunching through fallen leaves. The idea of being led into the woods by Theo would have made my thirteen-year-old heart sing. Even now my pulse quickens a bit as I ponder the strange possibility that Theo might be interested in me. Young Emma would certainly think he was. Cynical, adult me highly doubts it. He couldn't. Not after everything I've done. Yet here we are, whisking through the forest.

Eventually, we come to a small clearing so unexpected that I force myself to blink just to make sure it's real. The area is a small circle cleared of dead leaves and underbrush. In its place is a patch of soft grass punctuated in spots by clusters of wildflowers. A halo of sunlight pours through the gap in the trees, catching the pollen drifting in the air and making it look as though a light snow is falling. A round table sits in the middle of the clearing, similar to the one where Franny and I had lunch in her fantastical greenhouse. And just like at that months-ago meal, Franny is present, already seated at the table with a napkin across her lap.

"There you are," she says with a warm smile. "Just in time, too. I'm positively famished."

"Hi," I say, hoping I don't sound as surprised as I feel. More heat spreads across my cheeks—a combination of disappointment that this picnic isn't some romantic gesture on Theo's part and embarrassment that I ever thought it might be. I feel something else, too. Apprehension. Franny's surprise appearance tells me that this isn't an impromptu picnic. Something else is going on.

Not helping is the presence of six marble statues arranged on the outskirts of the space, almost tucked into the trees, like silent witnesses. Each statue is of a woman in artful stages of half-dress. They're frozen in unnatural poses, their arms raised, hands open, as if waiting for small birds to perch on their delicate fingers. Others carry baskets overflowing with grapes, ripe apples, sheaths of wheat.

"Welcome to the sculpture garden," Franny says. "One of my grandfather's more fanciful ideas."

"It's lovely," I say, even though the opposite is true. While beautiful from a distance, the clearing gives off a creepier vibe once I'm seated in its center. The statues bear the scars of years spent exposed to the elements. The folds of their togas are crusted with dirt. Some have cracks running up their sides and chips in their otherwise flawless skin. One statue's face is stained by moss. All have blank eyes. It's as if they've been blinded. Punished for seeing something they shouldn't have.

"You don't need to be polite," Theo says as he places the picnic basket on the table and starts to unpack it. "It's creepy as hell. At least, I think so. I hated coming here as a kid."

"I'll admit it's not to everyone's taste," Franny says. "But my grandfather was proud of it. And so it must remain."

She gives a helpless shrug, drawing my attention to the statue directly behind her. Its face is exquisite, with fine-boned features and a daintily elegant chin. Yet whoever sculpted it had added an extra layer of emotion to the statue's face. Its lifeless eyes are wider than they should be and sit beneath a pair of dramatically arched brows. Its rosebud lips are parted ever-so-slightly, either in ecstasy or in surprise. I suspect it's the latter. The statue looks, for lack of a better word, startled.

"Lunch is served," Theo announces, snapping my attention from the statue to the table. A plate bearing an open-faced sandwich of smoked salmon heaped with crème fraîche, capers, and dill now sits in front of me. Definitely not what the others are currently being served in the mess hall. When Theo pours me a glass of prosecco, I take an extra-long sip in an effort to calm my nerves.

"Now that we're all cozy," Franny says, "I think it's time to reveal why we've brought you here under such mysterious circumstances. I thought it might be a good idea to have our conversation in relative privacy."

"Conversation?"

"Yes," Franny says. "There's an important matter Theo and I would like to discuss with you."

"Oh?" I say it while cutting into my sandwich, pretending to be calm when I'm anything but. Apprehension clings to my insides. "What is it?"

"The camera outside your cabin," Franny says.

I freeze, a forkful of smoked salmon poised halfway to my mouth.

"We know you've seen it," Theo says. "We watched the footage this morning."

"To be completely frank, we were hoping it wouldn't be noticed," Franny adds. "But now that it has, I do hope you'll give us the chance to explain why it's there."

I set my fork on my plate. Any appetite I might have had is gone. "I'd certainly appreciate one. I didn't see any others around the camp."

"That's because it's the only one, dear," Franny says.

"How long has it been there?"

"Since last evening," Theo says. "Ben installed it during the campfire."

At first, the name is unfamiliar to me. Then I

remember the groundskeeper. No wonder he was acting so strangely when gathering up those easels.

"Why did he put it there?"

"To keep an eye on Dogwood, of course," Franny says.

Since we're on the topic of surveillance, I'm tempted to tell her that someone might have watched me take a shower this morning. I don't because I'm not entirely sure there was. It would also require me to reveal just how I know about the crack in the shower wall. That's a conversation I'd like to avoid at all costs.

Instead, I say, "That doesn't answer my question."

But it does, actually. Only the answer is an unspoken one, left for me to infer on my own. The camera is trained on Dogwood because I'm staying there. That's why it was installed last night. They didn't know it was the cabin I'd be occupying until after I'd arrived.

Franny looks at me from across the table, her head tilted, concern glowing in her green eyes. "You're upset. And probably offended. I can't say I blame you. We should have told you immediately."

The slight throb of a headache presses against my temples. I chalk it up to confusion and too much hastily swallowed prosecco on an empty stomach. But Franny is right. I **am** upset and offended.

"You still haven't told me why it's there," I say. "Are you spying on me?"

"That's putting it a bit harshly. **Spying.**" Franny smacks her lips in distaste, as if just saying the word has soured her tongue. She takes a tiny sip of prosecco to wash it away. "I like to think it's there for your own protection."

"From what?"

"Yourself."

It's Theo who answers. Hearing it from him forces a huff of surprise from my lungs.

"Back when I was getting ready to reopen the camp, we did background checks on everyone staying here for the summer," Franny says, exhibiting more gentleness than her son. "I didn't think it was necessary, but my lawyers insisted on it. Instructors. Kitchen staff. Even the campers. We found nothing to be concerned about. Except with you."

"I don't understand," I say, when really I do. I know what's coming next.

A pained expression crosses Franny's face. It strikes me as exaggerated and not entirely sincere. Like she wants me to know just how much it hurts to utter whatever she's about to say.

"We know, Emma," she tells me. "We know what happened to you after you left Camp Nightingale."

14

I don't talk about it.

Not even with Marc.

The only other people who know what happened are my parents, who are all too happy to avoid discussing those horrible six months when I was fourteen.

I was still in school when it began. A gangly freshman desperately trying to fit in with all the other prep school girls. It wasn't easy. Not after what had happened that summer. Everyone knew about the disappearance at Camp Nightingale, giving me the kind of notoriety no one wanted anything to do with. My friends started pulling away from me. Even Heather and Marissa. My life became a form of solitary confinement. Weekends spent in my room. Cafeteria lunches consumed alone.

Just when it seemed like things couldn't get any worse, I saw the girls and everything truly went to hell.

It was during a class trip to the Metropolitan

Museum of Art. A hundred schoolgirls tittering through the halls in a parade of plaid skirts and haughty insecurity. I had broken off from the group in the wing of nineteenth-century European paintings, roaming the labyrinth of galleries, dazzled by all the Gauguins and Renoirs and Cézannes.

One of the galleries was empty, save for three girls standing in front of a work by Gustave Courbet. **Young Ladies of the Village.** A massive landscape painted mostly in greens and golds and populated by four women. Three of them appear to be in their late teens. The young ladies of the title, casually elegant with their afternoon dresses, bonnets, and parasols. The other girl is younger. A peasant. Barefoot, kerchief on her head, apron around her waist.

I stared, but not at the painting. I was more interested in the girls studying it. They wore white dresses. Plain and subdued. They stood straight-backed and completely still, as poised as the young women Courbet had created. It was almost as if they had just emerged from the painting itself and were now curious to see how it looked without them.

It's beautiful, one of the girls said. **Don't you think so, Em?**

She didn't turn around. She didn't need to. I knew in my bones that it was Vivian, just as I knew the other two were Natalie and Allison. I didn't care if it was actually them or their ghosts or figments of my imagination. Their presence was enough to terrify me.

You seem surprised, Vivian said. **Guess you never pegged us as art lovers.**

I couldn't summon the nerve to reply. Fear had silenced me. It took all the strength I could muster to take a step backward, trying to put some distance between us. Once I managed that first tiny step, others followed in quick succession. My legs propelled me out of the gallery, saddle shoes tapping loudly against the parquet floor. Once I was safely out, I risked a glance behind me.

Vivian, Natalie, and Allison were still there, only now they were facing me. Before I could run away completely, Vivian winked and said, **See you soon.**

And I did. A few days later during a matinee of **Jersey Boys** my mother dragged me to during one of her rare instances of attentiveness. When she ducked out a minute before intermission to secure a prime spot at the lobby bar, Vivian took her place. The house lights rose, and there she was, once again in the white dress.

This show sucks, she said.

I didn't dare look at her. I stayed frozen in my seat, eyes fixed to the distant stage in front of me. Vivian remained where she was, a white blur on the edge of my vision.

You're not real. My voice was a murmur,

pitched low so that no one else could hear it. **You don't exist.**

Come on, Em. You and I both know you don't believe that.

Why are you doing this?

Doing what?

Haunting me.

You know exactly why.

Vivian didn't sound angry when she said it. There was no accusation in her voice. If anything, she sounded sad. So desperately sad that a sob rose in my throat. I croaked it out through trembling lips, tears stinging the corners of my eyes.

Spare me the tears, Vivian said. **We both know they're not real.**

Then she was gone. I waited a full five minutes before summoning the courage to leave my seat and go to the ladies' room. I spent the second act hiding in a stall. After the show, I told my mother I wasn't feeling well. She was too buzzed on over-priced vodka tonics to realize I was lying.

The girls appeared frequently after that. I saw Natalie standing on the opposite side of the street as I walked to school. Allison stared at me across the cafeteria one day at lunch. All three roamed the lingerie department at Macy's as I tried to pick out a bra to accommodate my suddenly blossoming frame. I never said a word about it to anyone. I feared that no one would believe me.

It could have gone on like that for months if I

hadn't woken up one night to find Vivian sitting on the edge of my bed.

I'm curious, Em, she said. **Did you really think you could get away with it?**

I woke my parents with my screaming. They burst into my room to find me cowering under the covers, completely alone. I spent the rest of the night explaining that I kept seeing the girls, that they were haunting me, that I feared they wanted to do me harm. I talked for hours, most of what I said incoherent even to myself. My parents dismissed it as a vividly bad dream. I knew otherwise.

After that, I refused to leave the apartment. I skipped school. Feigned illness. Spent three days locked in my room, unwilling to shower or let a toothbrush touch my filmed-over teeth. My parents had no choice but to take me to a psychiatrist, who declared that the sightings of the girls were in fact hallucinations.

I was officially diagnosed with schizophreniform disorder, a kissing cousin to schizophrenia itself. The doctor made it clear that what happened at Camp Nightingale didn't cause the disorder. That particular chemical imbalance had always been there, lightly percolating in the recesses of my brain. All the girls' disappearance did was set it free like lava bursting forth from a long-dormant volcano.

The doctor also stressed that schizophreniform disorder was mostly temporary. He said those who suffered from it usually got better with the right treatment. Which is how I came to spend six months in a mental-health facility that specialized in treating teenage girls.

The place was clean, comfortable, professional. There was no raving insanity on display. No **Girl, Interrupted**–style drama. It was just a bunch of girls my age trying their best to get better. And I did, thanks to a combination of therapy, medication, and old-fashioned patience.

That hospital was where I first started painting. Art therapy, it was called. They set me down in front of a blank canvas, stuck a brush in my hand, and told me to paint my feelings. I sliced the canvas with a streak of blue. The instructor, a spindly woman with gray hair and a gentle demeanor, took the canvas away, replaced it with a fresh one, and said, **Paint what you see, Emma.**

I painted the girls.

Vivian, Natalie, Allison.

In that order.

It was far different from my later efforts. Rough and childish and awful. The girls in the painting bore no resemblance to their real-life counterparts. They were black squiggles protruding from triangular dresses. But I knew who they were, which was enough to help me heal.

Six months later, I was released, although I still had to take an antipsychotic and go to therapy once a week. The meds lasted another five years. The therapy continues to this day. It helps, although not as much as the sessions at the mental hospital with the kind, infinitely patient Dr. Shively. On my last day there, she presented me with a charm bracelet. Dangling from it were three delicate birds.

Consider it a talisman, she said as she clasped it around my wrist. **Never underestimate the power of positive thinking. If you ever experience another hallucination, I want you to touch this bracelet and tell yourself that what you're seeing isn't real, that it has no power over you, that you're stronger than everyone realizes.**

Instead of returning to my old prep school, my parents sent me to the nearest public one. I made friends. I got serious about art. I started to thrive.

I never saw the girls again.

Except in my paintings.

I had thought that information was private. That it was my secret to bear. Yet somehow Franny was able to find out. I'm not surprised. I suppose her kind of money can open a lot of doors. Now she and Theo stare at me, curiosity dancing in their eyes, likely wondering if I'm capable of snapping at any moment.

"It was a long time ago," I say.

"Of course it was," Theo says.

Franny adds, "The last thing we want is for you

to feel ostracized or punished in any way. Which is why we should have told you about the camera in the first place."

I have no idea what they want me to say. That all is forgiven? That it's perfectly acceptable to be spied on because of something I experienced when I was still in high school?

"I understand," I say, my voice clipped. "It's better to be safe than sorry. After all, we don't want another mess on our hands, do we?"

I excuse myself from the table and make my escape between two of the statues. Both seem to stare at me as I depart, their blank eyes seeing nothing but knowing everything.

Theo follows me into the woods. His footsteps shush through the underbrush behind me, faster than my own, more familiar with the terrain. I quicken my pace, despite already knowing he'll catch up to me. I just want to make him work for it. I veer left without warning, trying to outmaneuver him. Cutting across untrampled forest floor. When Theo follows suit, I do it again, this time zigging farther to the left.

He calls out to me. "Emma, don't be mad."

I make another sharp veer, heading off in a new direction. This time, my right foot gets caught on a tree root curving out of the ground. I trip and take a series of increasingly faltering steps, trying to right myself before succumbing to the inevitable fall.

The only thing I end up hurting is my pride. I land on my hands and knees, the blow cushioned by the leaves coating the soft, mossy earth. Getting to my feet, I see I'm in another clearing. One not as neatly maintained as the sculpture garden. It's darker, wilder, on the cusp of again becoming one with the forest.

I rotate slowly, looking around, trying to get my bearings.

That's when I notice the sundial.

It sits in the center of the clearing—a copper circle atop a tilted column of marble. Time has turned the copper a light blue, which makes the Roman numerals and compass rose etched into the surface stand out even more. The center of the dial bears a motto, written in Latin.

Omnes vulnerant; ultima necat.

I remember the phrase from high school Latin class, although not because I excelled at the language. In fact, I was terrible at it. I remember only because it sent a chill through me when I first learned what it meant.

All hours wound; the last one kills.

I touch the sundial, running my fingers over the words as Theo finally catches up to me. He emerges through the trees, slightly out of breath, his hair mussed by the chase.

"I don't want to talk to you," I say.

"Listen, you have every right to be angry. We should have just told you what we were doing. We completely handled it the wrong way."

"That we can agree on."

"I just want to know that you're better," he says. "As your friend."

"I'm one hundred percent fine."

"Then I'm sorry, okay? So is my mother."

The apology, more forced than sincere, angers me all over again. "If you don't trust me, then why did you invite me back here?"

"Because my mother wanted you here," Theo says. "We just didn't know what to expect. Fifteen years have passed, Emma. People change. And we had no idea what you'd be like, especially considering what happened the last time you were here. It was a matter of safety, not trust."

"Safety? What do you think I'm going to do to these girls?"

"Maybe the same thing you said I did to Vivian, Allison, and Natalie."

I stumble backward, gripping the sundial for support, the copper cold and smooth beneath my fingers.

"It's because of that, isn't it?" I say. "The camera. Digging up my health records. It's because I accused you of hurting them all those years ago."

Theo runs a hand through his hair, exasperated. "That couldn't be further from the truth. But since you brought it up, I have to say it was a lousy thing you did back then."

"It was," I admit. "And I've spent years beating myself up over it. But I was young and confused and scared."

"You think I wasn't?" Theo shoots back. "You should have seen the way the police grilled me. We had cops, state troopers, the fucking FBI coming to the Lodge, demanding that I tell them the truth. They made me take a lie-detector test. They made Chet do it, too. A ten-year-old kid hooked up to a polygraph. He cried for an entire week after that. And all because of what you accused me of doing."

His face has gone red, making the pale slash of scar on his cheek stand out. He's mad now, piling it on to make it clear how much I had wronged him.

"I didn't know any better," I say.

"There's more to it than that," Theo says. "We were friends, Em. Why did you think I had anything to do with what happened to them?"

I stare at him, dumbfounded. The fact that he has to ask why I accused him makes my anger flare up once again. He might not have caused Vivian and the others to vanish, but he's certainly not completely innocent. Neither of us are.

"You know exactly why," I say.

Then I'm off again, leaving Theo alone in the clearing. After a few wrong turns and another stumble-inducing sneak attack by exposed tree roots, I find my way back to camp. I march to the cabins, seething all the way. I'm mad at Franny. Even more mad at Theo. Yet the bulk of my anger is reserved for myself for thinking that returning here was a good idea.

Back at Dogwood, I throw open the door. Inside, something springs from the floor, taking flight. I see dark shapes at the window, hear the flap of wings.

Birds.

Three of them.

Crows. I can tell by their jet-black feathers.

They fly in a frenzied group, smacking against the ceiling, squawking. One of them swoops toward me. Clawed feet skim my hair. Another heads straight for my face. Black eyes staring. Sharp beak gaping.

I drop to the floor and cover my head. The crows keep flapping. Keep squawking. Keep slamming themselves against the cabin walls. I stretch across the floor, reaching for the door, opening it wide. The movement sends the birds in the opposite direction. Toward the window, where they strike glass in a series of sickening thuds.

I crawl toward them, my right hand over my eyes, my left one slicing the air to shoo them the other way. The bracelet slides up and down my wrist. Three more birds in motion. It does the trick. One crow spies the open door and darts through it, followed immediately by another.

The third bird lets out one last squawk, its feathers brushing the ceiling. Then it, too, is gone, leaving the cabin suddenly silent.

I remain on the floor, catching my breath and calming down. I look around the cabin, making sure there's not another bird inside waiting to attack. Not that attacking was their goal. They were just trapped and scared. I assume they came in through the window, curious and hungry. Once inside, they didn't know how to get back out, so they panicked.

It makes sense. I've been there.

But then I remember the birds thudding against the glass. Such a dreadful sound. I sit up and look to the window.

It was closed the entire time.

15

It takes me ten minutes to gather all the feathers the crows have left behind. More than a dozen littered the floor, with more scattered along Miranda's and Sasha's bunks. At least there were no bird droppings to go along with the feathers. I consider that a win.

While cleaning, I try to think of ways the birds could have gotten inside even though the window was closed. Two possibilities come to mind. The first is that they came in through a hole in the roof, one tucked in a corner where it's hard to spot. The second, more logical reason is that one of the girls left the door open and the birds flew in. Someone else came along and shut the door, not realizing they were trapping birds inside Dogwood.

But as I carry the handful of feathers behind the cabin, a third possibility enters my head—that someone caught the birds and released them inside on purpose. There were three of them, after all, echoing the number of charms on my bracelet, which are themselves symbols.

I shake my head while scattering the feathers. No, that can't be the reason. Like the idea of being spied on in the shower, it's too sinister to think about. Besides, who would do such a thing? And why? Just like that shadow in the shower stall, I tell myself the most innocent explanation is also the most logical.

Yet once I'm back inside the cabin, I can't shake the idea that something's not quite right here. Between the camera, the shadow at the shower stall, and the birds, I've been on edge all day. So much so that I feel the need to get out of the cabin for a little bit. Maybe go for a hike. A little exercise might be just the thing to sweep away the weird thoughts I'm having.

I throw open my hickory trunk, looking for my hiking boots. The first thing I see is the folded piece of paper Vivian had hidden in her own trunk. My hands tremble when I pick it up. I tell myself it's residual stress from everything else that's happened today. But I know the truth.

That page makes me nervous. As does the photograph that once again slides from its fold.

I stare at the woman in the picture, getting another shudder of familiarity when I look into her eyes. It makes me wonder what the woman—this Eleanor Auburn—was thinking when the photograph was taken. Did she fear that she was going insane? Was she seeing something that wasn't really there?

Setting the picture aside, I make another examination of the map Vivian had drawn. I scan the entire page. The camp. The lake. The crudely drawn forest on the far shore. Yet my gaze lingers on the small **X** that's left two deep grooves in the paper. Vivian did that for a reason. It means something is located there.

There's no way to know for certain until I go there myself.

Which is exactly what I intend to do. Heading across the lake will both get me out of the cabin and let me start the search for more information in earnest. Like killing two birds with one stone, which I realize is a bad metaphor when I spot a stray feather peeking out from behind my trunk.

I begin to gather supplies and stuff them into my backpack. Sunblock and hand sanitizer. My phone. A water bottle. The map also goes into the backpack, which I zip shut as I leave the cabin. On my way out, I give the camera a defiant stare, hoping both Theo and Franny will see it later.

Before departing camp, I stop by the mess hall to fill up my water bottle and grab a banana and granola bar in case I get hungry. Two women and a man are outside. Kitchen workers spending the lull between lunch and dinner smoking in the shade of the overhanging roof. One of the women gives a disinterested wave. The man beside her is the same guy with the goatee who briefly checked me out this morning. The tag affixed to his apron strap says his name is Marvin.

Now Marvin stares past me to the lake in the distance. Afternoon swimming lessons are taking place, the shore and water dotted with young women in bathing suits of varying degrees of modesty. He catches me watching him and displays a grin so slimy it makes me want to reach for the hand sanitizer in my backpack.

"It's not illegal to look," he says.

With that, Marvin jumps to the top of my list of suspected Peeping Toms. In truth, he's the only suspect. A weak one at that. Marvin was working in the mess hall before I left for my shower. While there's a chance he followed me there, I doubt he could have done it without anyone else noticing.

Besides, it's possible no one was watching me.

Maybe.

"It might not be illegal, **Marvin**." I put extra emphasis on his name, making sure he understands that I know it. "But those girls are young enough to be your daughters."

Marvin drops his cigarette, stubs it out, goes back inside. The women begin to chuckle. One of them nods my way. A silent thank-you.

I continue toward the lake, my backpack slung over my shoulder. I spot Miranda lingering by the lifeguard station in a bikini designed to expose the maximum amount of skin while still being legal.

The lifeguard for the afternoon is Chet, which explains Miranda's presence there. He's undeniably handsome up there on his perch, with his Ray-Bans and whistle. Miranda stares up at him, laughing too loudly at something he's just said, a finger twirling in her hair while she uses her big toe to trace a circle in the sand. Apparently she's already gotten over the texter who broke her heart. She just better hope Mindy doesn't see her. I suspect flirting with Chet is definitely not a display of Camp Nightingale spirit.

Nearby, Sasha and Krystal share a large beach blanket. They sprawl across it, still in shorts and camp polos, listlessly flipping through a stack of comic books. I walk over to them, my shadow falling across the blanket.

"Did one of you leave the cabin door open?"

"No," Sasha says. "It lets in bugs, which cause disease."

"Not even for a little bit?"

"We didn't," Krystal replies. "Why?"

Now that the cabin's been cleared of feathers, I see no reason to tell them about the birds. It would only make Sasha more worried. I opt for a change of subject. "Why aren't you swimming?"

"Don't want to," Krystal says.

"Don't know how," Sasha says.

"I can teach you sometime, if you want."

Sasha wrinkles her nose, her glasses rising and falling. "In that dirty water? No thank you."

"Where are you going?" Krystal asks, eyeing my backpack.

"Canoe trip."

"Alone?" Sasha says.

"That's the plan."

"Are you sure that's a good idea? Each year, an average of eighty-seven people die in canoe and kayak accidents. I looked it up."

"I'm a good swimmer. I think I'll be okay."

"It's probably safer if someone is with you."

Next to her, Krystal slaps her comic book shut and sighs. "What Miss Wikipedia here is trying to say is that we want to come along. We're bored, and we've never been canoeing."

"Yeah," Sasha says. "That's what I meant."

"That's not a good idea. It's a long trip. And there'll be hiking involved."

"I've never hiked, either," Krystal says. "Please, can we come?"

Sasha bats her eyes at me, the lashes fluttering behind her glasses. "Pretty please?"

My plan was to cross the lake, find the spot marked on Vivian's map, and proceed from there. Sasha and Krystal will only slow me down. Nevertheless, a sense of duty tugs at me. Franny told me the purpose of reopening Camp Nightingale was to give the campers new experiences. That remains true, even if I'm currently pissed at Franny.

"Fine," I tell them. "Put on life vests and help me with the canoe."

The girls do as they're told, grabbing dirty life vests that hang from the sides of the canoe racks. They slip them on and help me lift a canoe off one of the racks. It's heavier than it looks and so unwieldy that we come close to dropping it. We remain a sorry sight as we awkwardly carry the canoe to the lake's edge, Krystal holding up the front and me taking the rear. Sasha is in the middle, hidden beneath the overturned boat, just a pair of knobby legs shuffling toward the water.

Our struggle is enough to tear Miranda's attention away from Chet. She trots over to us and says, "Where are you going?"

"Canoeing," Sasha says.

"And hiking," I add, hoping they'll be dissuaded by the fact that there's more to this trip than just paddling across the lake.

Instead, Miranda frowns. "Without me?"

"Do you want to come along?"

"Not really, but . . ."

Her voice trails off, the sentence unfinished but its meaning perfectly clear. She doesn't want to be the only one left behind. I know the feeling.

"Go get changed," I tell her. "We'll wait for you."

Another person means another canoe. So while Miranda runs back to the cabin to fetch shorts and a pair of sneakers, Krystal, Sasha, and I wrangle a second canoe to the water's edge. When Miranda returns, we climb in, she and Krystal in one canoe,

Sasha and me in the other. Using oars, we push off and start to drift out onto the lake.

The bulk of the rowing in my boat falls to me. I sit in the back, paddling on alternating sides of the canoe. Sasha sits up front, her own paddle across her lap, dipping it into the water whenever I need to straighten things out.

"How deep do you think it is here?" she says.

"Pretty deep in parts."

"A hundred feet?"

"Maybe."

Sasha's eyes widen behind her glasses as her free hand unconsciously clasps her life vest. "You're a good swimmer, though, right?"

"I am," I say. "Although not as good as some people I know."

It takes us a half hour to cross the lake. We slow when the water's surface is darkened by tall pines along the shoreline, their reflections jagged and unwelcoming. Just beneath the surface are the remnants of trees submerged when the valley was flooded. Stripped of leaves and whitewashed by time, their branches seem to be grasping for fresh air that's just beyond their reach. It's a discomfiting sight. All those blanched limbs tangled together as mud-brown fish slip between them. Because the lake's been lowered by drought, the farthest-reaching branches scrape the bottoms of the canoes, sounding like fingernails trying to scratch their way out of a coffin.

More trees jut out of the lake in front of us. Although to call them trees isn't entirely accurate. They're more like ghosts of trees. Bare and sun-bleached. Trapped in a limbo between water and land. Gone are their bark, their leaves, their limbs. They've been reduced to sad, brittle sticks.

After passing through the graveyard of trees, we come to the shore itself. Instead of the welcoming flatness Camp Nightingale was built upon, the landscape rises sharply—an ascent that eventually leads to the rounded peaks in the distance. The trees here tower over the water. Pines, mostly, their limbs connecting to form a pale green wall that undulates in the slight breeze coming off the lake.

To our right, a heap of boulders sits partway out of the water. They look out of place, like they had rolled down the mountain one by one, eventually accumulating there. Beyond them is a cliff where the land has been chipped away by the elements. Small, tenacious vines cling to the cliff wall, and mineral deposits stripe the exposed rock. Trees line the ridge atop the cliff, some leaning forward, as if they're about to jump.

"I see something," Miranda says, pointing to a ragged-looking structure sitting farther down the shore.

I see it, too. It's a gazebo. Rather, it used to be. Now it's a leaning structure of splintered wood slowly being overtaken by weeds. Its floorboards sag. Its roof sits slightly askew. While I'm not certain, I think it might be the cabin-like structure marked on Vivian's map.

I start to row toward it. Miranda follows suit. On shore, we step out of the canoes, paddles clattering, life vests discarded. Then we drag the boats farther onto land to reduce the potential of them drifting away without us. I grab my backpack and pull out the map.

"What's that?" Sasha asks.

"A map."

"What does it lead to?"

"I don't know yet."

I frown at the woods before us. It's dense, dark, all silence and shadows. Now that we're on the other side of the lake, I have no idea how to proceed. Vivian's map is short on details, and the accuracy of what she did draw is questionable at best.

I run my finger from the spot that probably-is-but-might-not-be the gazebo to the ragged triangles nearby. I assume those are rocks. Which means we need to make our way northeast until we reach them. After that, it looks to be a short walk north until I find the **X**.

Our route now set, I open the compass app downloaded to my phone the morning I left for camp, rotating until it points northeast. Then I snag a handful of wildflowers and, with Miranda, Sasha, and Krystal in tow, march into the forest.

"Let's go," Vivian said.

"Go where?"

I was curled up in my bunk, reading the dog-eared copy of **The Lovely Bones** I had brought with me to camp. Looking up from the book, I saw Vivian standing by the cabin door. She had tied a red handkerchief around her neck. Allison's floppy straw hat sat atop her head.

"On an adventure," she said. "To search for buried treasure."

I closed my book and crawled out of bed. As if there was any doubt I wouldn't. In the short time that I'd been there, it was already clear that what Vivian wanted, she got.

"Allison's going to need her hat, though," I told her. "You know how she is about UV rays."

"Allison's not coming. Neither is Natalie. It's just you and me, kid."

She didn't bother to tell me where, exactly, we were going. I simply let her lead the way. First to the canoes near the dock, then across Lake Midnight itself, me struggling with my oar the entire way.

"I'm going to take a wild guess and say you've never been in a canoe before," Vivian said.

"I've been in a rowboat," I told her. "Does that count?"

"Depends. Was it on a lake?"

"The pond in Central Park. I went there once with Heather and Marissa."

I almost told her how we jostled the boat so much that Heather fell in, but then I remembered about Vivian's sister and how she had drowned. Vivian never told me where it happened. Or how. Or even when. But I didn't want to bring it up, even in an innocent, roundabout way. I stayed quiet until we came ashore alongside a grassy area aflame with tiger lilies.

Vivian picked enough lilies to make a bouquet. When we entered the woods, she began to pluck their petals and drop them to the ground.

"Always leave a trail of bread crumbs," she said. "So you know how to find your way back. Franny taught me that my first summer here. I think she was afraid I'd get lost."

"Why?"

"Because I wandered off too much."

That didn't surprise me. Vivian's personality was too big to fit inside the tidy confines of camp life. All those tennis lessons and crafting sessions. I'd started to notice how she greeted each one with a bored sigh.

She dropped another petal, and I turned around

to look at the long line of them stretching away from us, marking our progress. It was a comforting sight. Like tiny, tangerine-colored footprints we had left behind that would eventually guide us home.

"Two Truths and a Lie," Vivian said as she plucked off another petal and let it flutter to the ground. "I'll go first. One: A guy once flashed me in the subway. Two: I have a flask of whiskey hidden under my mattress. Three: I don't know how to swim."

"The second one," I said. "I'd have noticed if you were secretly drinking."

I thought of my mother and how she smelled when she greeted me after school. The spearmint gum she chewed did little to hide her wine breath. Even if it had, I was already an expert at noticing the slight dimness in her eyes whenever she drank too much.

"Aren't you the observant one," Vivian said. "That's why I thought you'd like to see this."

We had come to a large oak tree, its sturdy branches spread wide to create a canopy over the surrounding ground. An **X** had been carved into the bark, as big and bold as the way Vivian marked the lid of her trunk back in Dogwood. At the base of the tree sat a pile of leaves that camouflaged something beneath it.

Vivian pushed the leaves out of the way, exposing an old and rotting wooden box. Time had stripped the veneer from the lid, which allowed water and sunlight to do their damage, staining the wood in some spots, bleaching it in others. As a result, the box had become a patchwork of colors.

"It's cool, right?" Vivian said. "It's, like, ancient."

I ran a finger over the lid, feeling a series of groves in the wood. At first I thought it was just another product of age and the elements. But when I looked closer, I noticed two faint letters etched into the wood. They were so worn by exposure that it was hard to make them out. Only when I leaned in close, the odor of mold and wood rot filling my nostrils, could I read them.

CC

"Where did you find it?"

"Washed up on the shore last summer."

"While you were wandering off?"

Vivian smirked, pleased with herself. "Of course. God knows how long it was there. I brought it here for safekeeping. Go ahead and open it."

I lifted the lid, the wood so soft and waterlogged I feared it might disintegrate in my hands. The inside of the box was lined with a fabric that might have once been green velvet. I couldn't quite tell because the fabric was in tatters—nothing but dark, leathery strips.

Inside the box lay several pairs of scissors. Antique ones with ornate circles for finger holes and thin blades tapered like stork legs. I suspected the scissors were made of silver, although they'd been tarnished the same color as motor oil. The screws that held them together were swirled with rust. When I picked up a pair and tried to pry them open, they wouldn't budge. Age and disrepair had rendered them useless.

"Who do you think they belonged to?"

"A hospital or something. There's a name on the bottom." Vivian took the box and shut the lid, holding it closed. When she flipped it over, the scissors inside rattled together. It sounded like broken glass. "See?"

Engraved on the bottom of the box, in tiny letters dulled by time, were four words: **Property of Peaceful Valley.**

"I wonder how it got here."

Vivian shrugged. "Tossed into the lake, probably. Decades ago."

"Have you asked Franny about it?"

"No way. I want to keep it a secret. No one else knows about it but me. And now you."

"Why are you showing me this?"

I looked down at the box, a lock of hair falling over my face. Vivian leaned forward and tucked it behind my ear.

"I'm your big sister for the summer, remember?" she said. "This is what big sisters do. We share things. Things no one else knows."

16

I take the lead in the woods, trying to walk in a straight line, my eyes constantly flicking to the wavering compass for guidance. When I'm not looking at the app, I'm studying our surroundings, seeking out places in the brush where someone could be hiding. Although we're far from camp, the feeling of being watched stays with me. Every thicket gets a second, suspicious glance. I mistrust each shadow that stretches across the forest floor. Whenever a bird screeches in the trees, I fight the urge to duck.

Get a grip, Em, I tell myself. **The four of you are all alone out here.**

I can't decide if that makes me feel better or worse.

If the girls notice my jumpiness, they don't say anything. Krystal and Sasha walk behind me. Every so often, Sasha calls out the names of trees she recognizes.

"Sugar maple. American beech. White pine. Birch."

Behind them is Miranda, who peels off petals from the flowers I'd picked and drops them to the ground at regular intervals.

"Why do I have to do this again?" she asks.

"Always leave a trail of bread crumbs," I tell her. "It'll help us find our way back."

"From **where**?" Krystal says.

"I'll know it when I find it."

The ground slants upward as we walk, slightly at first, the incline hidden under a sheet of amber leaves that fell the previous autumn. We're aware of the rising land only from the warm ache in our legs and the growing heaviness of our breath. But soon the landscape becomes more obviously steep. A sharp, steady rise that can't be avoided. We press on, shoulders hunched, legs bent. Along the way we pass whippet-thin saplings, grabbing them for support, hauling ourselves higher.

"I want to go back," Krystal says, huffing out the words.

"Me, too," Sasha says.

"I told you there would be hiking," I remind them. "Hey, let's play another game. Instead of Two Truths and a Lie, let's just do truth. Tell me, in all honesty, what you'd like to be doing twenty years from now."

I look over my shoulder to Sasha, who's quickly losing steam. "You start. Any ideas about what you want to be doing?"

"Plenty," she says with a nudge of her glasses. "A

professor. A scientist. Maybe an astronaut, unless everyone's already colonizing on Mars. I like to have options."

"And what about you, Krystal?"

She doesn't need to think about it. The answer is obvious to all.

"Working for Marvel. Hopefully illustrating my own superhero series. Someone cool that I came up with."

"Why do you like comic books so much?" Sasha asks.

"I dunno. I guess because most of the superheroes start off as regular people just like us. Nerdy and awkward."

"Speak for yourself," Miranda chimes in.

"Just like everyone **but** you," Krystal says, placating her. "But something happens that makes these average people realize they're stronger than they thought. Then they believe they can do anything. And what they choose to do is help people."

"I prefer regular books," Miranda says. "You know, without pictures."

She's passed Krystal and Sasha on the way up the incline and now walks beside me, the only one of us not fazed by the climb.

"Ever think about becoming a writer?" I ask her. "Since you like to read so much."

"I'm going to be a police detective like my uncle," she says. "Why write about crimes when you can solve them in real life?"

"Um, that's called a superhero," Krystal says with no small amount of satisfaction.

Miranda forges ahead to where the incline finally levels off into less wearying terrain, waiting impatiently for the rest of us. Once there, we pause to catch our breath and take in the scenery. On our right, slivers of blue sky peek through the trees. I move instinctively toward them, following the light, emerging from the trees onto a thin strip of craggy ground. Beyond it, the land drops away, and for a dizzying, disoriented moment, I think I'm about to drop with it. I wrap an arm around the nearest tree, steadying myself, my eyes aimed at my feet to make sure I remain on solid ground.

When the girls reach my side, one of them—I think it's Miranda—whistles with appreciation.

"**Day-um**," Krystal says, stretching the word into two syllables. She sounds beyond impressed. Awed.

I lift my eyes to the horizon, seeing what they see. I realize we're atop the ridge I'd spotted from the canoe, overlooking the stone-walled cliff. The view it affords us is stunning. Lake Midnight spreads out below us, the water dappled with sunlight. From this height, I can see the full shape of the shoreline curving inward, the spot in the distance where it narrows toward the dam.

Across from us, hazy in the distance, sits Camp Nightingale. It looks so small from here. A miniature. Something placed in the center of a model railroad.

I dig the map from my pocket and give it a quick peek. Vivian drew nothing to indicate the cliff where we now stand. From what I can gather from her crude markings, we're close to the raggedly triangular rocks. Sure enough, when I turn away from the water and point north, I get a glimpse of rocks through the thick forest.

I'm getting closer. To what, I still have no clue.

The rocks on Vivian's map differ greatly from the ones I see in person. These are boulders. Dozens of them. Massive ones that only get larger as we approach, their weight palpable, so heavy and unwieldy it's a wonder the earth can support them. They sit in a line running up a sharp rise similar to the one we've just climbed.

The girls spread out among them, scaling the boulders like kids in a playground.

"I bet these rocks used to be part of the mountain's peak," Sasha says as she clambers up a boulder twice her height. "They froze and broke apart, then glaciers took them down the hill. Now they're here."

Explanation aside, the boulders still unsettle me. They make me think of the rumored survivors of Lake Midnight's creation. I picture them when the moon is full, creeping around these very boulders at night, searching for new victims. To push away the unease, I check both the compass and the map, making sure this is where we should be. It is.

"Hey, girls," I call out. "We should keep moving."

I squeeze between two boulders and edge around another. That's when I get a view of another rock farther up the incline. One bigger than the others. A monolith.

Nearly two stories tall, it rises from the ground like an enormous tombstone. The side facing me is mostly flat. A sheer wall of rock. A large fissure runs diagonally through it, widening at the top. A tree grows inside the crack, its roots curling along the rock face, seeking soil. Standing beside the tree, looking up into its branches, is Sasha.

Krystal is up there, too. She takes a step toward the boulder's edge and peers down at me. "Hey," she says.

"What are you doing up there?"

"Exploring," Sasha says.

"I'd prefer it if you stayed on the ground," I say. "Where's Miranda?"

"Right here."

Miranda's voice emanates from the northwestern side of the giant rock. It sounds watery, akin to an echo. I follow it as Sasha and Krystal scramble down the boulder's opposite side. I work my way around it, seeing another large crack in the rock's side. This one runs in a straight line, widening at the bottom. It opens up completely about a foot from the ground, creating a hole large enough for a person to crawl into.

Or, in Miranda's case, crawl out of. She climbs to her feet, circles of mud dotting her knees and elbows. "I wanted to see what was in there."

"Bears or snakes, probably," Sasha says.

"Exactly," I say. "So no more exploring. Understood?"

"Yes, ma'am," Krystal says.

"We understand," Sasha adds.

Miranda stands with her hand on her hip, annoyed. "Isn't that why we're out here?"

I say nothing. I'm too busy looking past her, my head tilted, eyes narrowed in curiosity. In the distance behind her are what appear to be ruins. I can make out a crumbled stone wall and one jagged wooden beam pointing skyward.

I start to creep toward it, the girls behind me. When I get closer, I see that it's the remains of what might have been a barn or farmhouse. The walls are mostly now a pile of rocks, but enough are intact to be able to make out the building's rectangular foundation. Inside are several pines that have sprouted from what's left of the building's roof and floor.

In much better shape is a nearby root cellar built into the slope of the land. There's no roof—just a slightly rounded mound of earth. A fieldstone wall forms the front. In the center is a wooden door, shut tight, its rusted slide bolt firmly in place.

"Creepy," says Sasha.

"Cool," says Miranda.

"Both," says Krystal. "It looks like something from **Lord of the Rings**."

But I'm thinking of another, more ominous tale. One about a flooded valley, a clan of survivors hiding in the woods, a thirst for revenge. Maybe a small seed of truth lies in the legend Casey told me. Because someone used to live in these hills. The foundation and root cellar make that abundantly clear. And although there's no evidence showing it was the same people from Casey's story, my skin nonetheless starts to tickle. Goose bumps, running up my arm.

"We should—"

Go. That's what I intended to say. But I'm stopped by the sight of a large oak sitting fifty yards away. The tree is large, its thick branches spread wide. In its trunk is a familiar letter.

X

Immediately, I know it's not the same tree Vivian led me to fifteen years ago. I would have remembered the crumbled foundation and creepy-cool root cellar. No, this is a different tree and a different **X**. Yet I get the feeling both letters were carved by the same hand.

"Stay here," I tell the girls. "I'll be right back."

"Can we look inside that hobbit house?" Miranda asks.

"No. Don't go anywhere."

They mill about the crumbled foundation while I dash to the tree and search around its trunk. I take a step, and the ground beneath me thumps. A muffled, hollow sound.

Something is down there.

I drop to my knees and start scraping away years' worth of weeds and dead leaves until I reach soil. I swipe my hands back and forth, clearing the dirt. Something brown and moist appears.

Wood. A pine plank dyed brown from more than a decade underground. I sweep away more dirt before burrowing my fingers into the soil underneath it, prying the plank loose. Its bottom is coated with mold, mud, a few bugs that scurry away. Beneath the plank someone has dug a hole the size of a shoe box. Inside the hole is a yellow grocery bag wrapped tightly around a rectangular object.

I unfurl the bag and reach into it, feeling more plastic. A freezer bag. The kind that can be zipped shut. Through the clear plastic, I see a splash of green, the stubble of leather, the edges of pages kept dry by the double layers of protection.

A book. Auspiciously fancy.

I peer inside the yellow grocery bag, checking for anything else that might be inside. There's just a second freezer bag, empty and crumpled, and a single strand of hair. I set it on the ground and carefully open the other bag, letting the book slip out of it. It's floppy in my hands, made pliant by fifteen seasons of being frozen and thawed and frozen again. Yet I'm able to peel back the cover to the first page, where I see the chaotic swirl of someone's handwriting.

Vivian's handwriting, to be exact.

"What are you doing over there?" Miranda calls.

I slam the book shut and shove it into my backpack, hoping my body shields the action from the girls' view.

"Nothing," I reply. "It's not what I was looking for. Let's head back."

I place the now-empty bags back in the hole and cover it with the plank. I kick some dirt and leaves over the wood, more out of respect for Vivian than caution. I want to keep her secret safe. Because whatever's inside this book, Vivian thought it important enough to hide it here, on the other side of the lake, as far away from prying-eyes and Camp Nightingale as possible.

"Two Truths and a Lie," Vivian said as we rowed back to camp. "Your turn."

I dipped my paddle into the lake, arms straining to push it through the resistant water. Vivian wasn't only older than me; she was also stronger. Each stroke of her oar forced me to paddle even harder just to keep up. Which I couldn't. As a result, our canoe curved through the water instead of cutting straight across it.

"Do we have to do this right now?" I asked through labored breaths.

"We don't **have** to," Vivian said. "Just like I don't **have** to tell Allison and Natalie you were too chickenshit to play today, even though I probably will."

I believed her, which is why I opted to play. I didn't really care what Allison and Natalie thought of me. Vivian's opinion was the only one that mattered. And the last thing I wanted was for her to think I was chickenshit about anything.

"One: My mother once got so drunk that she

passed out in our building's elevator," I said. "Two: I've never kissed a boy. Three: I think Theo is the most handsome man I've ever seen."

"You're **cheating**," Vivian said, her voice sing-songy. "None of those are a lie."

She was almost right. My mother had passed out **waiting** for our building's elevator. I had found her facedown in the hallway, snoring lightly, a small puddle of her drool seeping into the carpet.

"But I'll allow it," Vivian said as she pulled her oar from the water and set it aside. "Just this once. Mostly because of your incorrect guess during my turn."

"I don't think so," I said. "I totally know you don't have a flask. Besides, I saw that you can't swim."

"Guess again."

Vivian stood suddenly, the canoe rocking as she shed her clothes. There was no bathing suit underneath. Just matching pearl-colored bra and panties, silky and shiny in the afternoon glare. Before I could utter a word of protest, she dove into the lake, making the canoe pitch so sharply I thought I was going to tumble in as well. I yelped, grabbed the sides of the boat, waited for it to stop rocking.

It was only then that I noticed Vivian slicing the water like a knife through butter. Her strokes were quick, powerful, elegant. Tanned back flattening as her arms swept out in front of her before arcing to her sides. Feet flicking in short, strong kicks. Hair billowing like cream in coffee behind her. A mermaid.

When she finally came up for air, she was ten feet from the canoe.

"Wait," I said. "You really can swim?"

She grinned. Her smile was slanted, sly, colored pink by her lip gloss.

"Duh," she said.

"But the other day—"

I stopped talking as Vivian ducked below the surface again, emerging with a mouthful of water that she squirted through pursed lips, like a fountain.

"You told Theo you didn't know how," I said.

"You can't believe everything I tell you, Em."

I thought about the drama of that day on the beach. The panic. The splashing. Vivian's wide-eyed terror as she flailed. I remembered Becca, her camera trained on the chaos, yet her attention aimed at me.

I told you so.

"I thought you were drowning," I said. "We all did. Why would you lie about something like that?"

"Why not?"

"Because it wasn't one of your stupid games!"

Vivian sighed and began the swim back to the canoe. "Everything is a game, Em. Whether you know it or not. Which means that sometimes a lie is more than just a lie. Sometimes it's the only way to win."

17

The dinner hour is torture, and not just because of the food, which is predictably awful. Runny sloppy joes and french fries. Despite having consumed next to nothing all day, I can only stomach the fries, which glisten with grease. Right now, my main concern is getting back to Dogwood and learning what's in the book Vivian had buried. And that requires privacy, which is in short supply.

Skipping dinner to read it would only make the girls more suspicious than they already are. On the canoe trip back across the lake, they bombarded me with questions about the map, the rocks, our purpose for roaming so far from camp. My vague, mumbled answers did little to appease them. So I force myself to suffer through dinner, delaying the reading of the book until the girls are at the campfire.

I take my tray to what's already become known as the adults' table. It's a full house tonight, with every counselor and instructor present, including Becca. She sits at a slight remove from the others, her eyes glued to her phone. I get the feeling she thinks there's nothing left to say to me. I think otherwise.

I head to the opposite end of the table, where Casey is listening to the counselors play a game of Do, Dump, or Marry. I remember it well, having played it fifteen years ago with Vivian, Natalie, and Allison. Only Vivian had given it a more brutal name—Fuck, Marry, Kill.

As the counselors choose between the men at Camp Nightingale, I sneak a glance at Casey, as if to say, **Isn't this such a silly, sexist game?** Yet I suspect Casey is mulling the choices, just like I secretly am.

"I'd do Chet, dump the janitor, and marry Theo," the counselor named Kim or Danica announces.

"I think he's technically a maintenance man," another one says.

"Groundskeeper," Casey tells them. "He's worked for the family for years. He's kind of creepy but also kind of hot. He'd be my Do."

Both counselors look scandalized, their mouths forming twin ovals of shock. "Over Chet and Theo?"

"I'm being realistic here. There's no way Mindy's going to let Chet out of her sight." Casey nudges me with an elbow. "And Emma's already got her hooks into Theo."

"Definitely not," I say. "He's all yours, ladies."

"But the rumor is the two of you had a picnic lunch in the woods."

Across the table, Becca looks up, clearly surprised. She stares at me a second too long before returning her gaze to her phone.

"We were just catching up," I say. "It's been years since we last saw each other."

"Of course," Casey says before leaning closer and whispering, "You can tell me all the sordid details later tonight."

On the other side of the mess hall, I see Mindy enter and make a beeline for our table. She's smiling, which doesn't necessarily mean good news. I've come to realize Mindy's the kind of girl who wields a smile like a scythe.

"Hi, Emma," she says without a hint of friendliness. "Next time you decide to vanish for an entire afternoon, I'd appreciate it if you told someone. Franny would, too. She was distressed to hear that you left with a group of campers without telling anyone where you were going."

"I didn't know that was a requirement."

"It's not," Mindy says. "But it certainly would have been a courtesy."

"I went canoeing with the girls from my cabin. In case you're keeping a record of my whereabouts."

I assume Mindy knows about the camera. And everything else, for that matter. Especially when she says, "It's just very noticeable when a group of campers goes missing. As you well know."

She stands there, pleased with herself, her next move predicated on how I react. I know because it's right out of the Vivian playbook. I opt for a curveball.

"Sit with us," I say, my voice chirpy, so unlike my natural tone. "Have some fries. They're **so** good."

I hold out a fry, the end sagging, its tip dripping grease. Mindy stares at it with thinly veiled repulsion. I suspect she hasn't consumed a trans fat since junior high.

"No, thanks. I have to get back to the Lodge."

"Not even one fry?" I say. "If it's calories you're worried about, don't be. You look . . . fine."

Later in the night, I wait until the girls leave for the campfire before reclining in my bunk with the meager collection of snacks from my backpack. Gnawing absently on the granola bar, I open the book Vivian had left behind.

On the first page, I see a date written in her hand.

The first day of camp. Fifteen years ago.

This is a diary.

Vivian's diary.

I suck in a breath, exhale it back out, and begin to read.

June 22,

Well, here I am, back at Camp Nightmare for another six weeks. I can't say I'm thrilled to be back, unlike The Senator and Mrs. Senator, who were ECSTATIC when I told them I wanted to spend the summer here and not slutting my way through Europe with Brittney, Patricia, and Kelly. If they only knew that I would absolutely love to be in Amsterdam with those bitches, sucking face with some stubbled douchebag wannabe deejay just for the weed.

Everyone seems to think I adore this place. That couldn't be further from the truth. It creeps me out. It has ever since I first got here. There's something not right about it.

But here is where I need to be. Just for one more summer. As they say in those shitty movies The Senator likes to watch, I've got unfinished business. But will I finish it? That's the big question hanging over this whole summer. Before I left, I asked it to Katherine's stupid Magic 8 Ball that she loved so much. All signs pointed to yes.

In the meantime, tomorrow I'll get the pleasure of hearing F give that goddamn speech for the umpteenth time. It's so pathetic how she goes out of her way trying to sound folksy when the rest of us know she's worth a billion dollars. You are not fucking fooling us! At least, not for long.

Nat and Ali are here, of course. Fourth camper to be announced. I hope that bottom bunk stays empty. It'll make things easier for all of us, but mostly me. If not, I'll settle for Theodore. I'd sleep on top of him any damn day of the week. My God, he's looking fine. Don't get me wrong, he's always looked fine. But I'm talking FINE. Worthy even of a dozen lame exclamation points.

!!!!!!!!!!!!!

Pull it together, Viv. Don't get distracted by all that fineness. You're on a mission. Theo isn't part of it. Unless he needs to be. Sweet Jesus Lord I hope he needs to be.

Update: It's after dinner. No fourth camper has arrived. Fingers crossed she never does.

Update #2: The fourth camper just came in. A new girl. Time to either terrorize her or befriend her. I haven't decided which one it'll be.

June 23,

Today I showed New Girl the ropes. Someone had to. This place is not for the faint of heart.

New Girl has a name, by the way. It's Emma. Cute, right? And she is. So young and innocent and shaky. Like a newborn kitten. She reminds me of when I was that age, mostly because, underneath that My Little Pony exterior, I think she might actually be a bitch in training. She stood up to me last night, which took major ovaries. I was duly impressed. No one has stood up to me since Katherine died. I missed that feeling of being put in my place. It's tough being the only alpha female in the pack.

But, like Theo's divine handsomeness, I can't let New Girl distract me too much. Mission first. Friendship second. You-know-who learned that the hard way.

At least I got to roam a little bit after

archery. I scoped out all the places I haven't looked yet, including the Big L. I almost made it inside before Casey caught me sniffing around the place. With any other counselor, I would have tried to sneak in anyway. But not her. She's weirdly devoted to this place. I mean, a former camper coming back as a counselor for two summers in a row? I can't think of anything more pathetic.

My guess is she's obsessed with Theo. It's obvious she's got the hots for him. She throws herself at him every chance she can get. Last year she caught me flirting with Theo and got all huffy, like she fucking owned him or something. Ever since, she's been dying to get me kicked out. Hence the extra attention I receive during cabin check.

Like I said—pathetic.

June 24,

On her second night at camp, poor Emma had her VERY. FIRST. PERIOD. She woke me up last night with blood on her fingers like Carrie White. I felt so bad for her. I remember my first period. It was awful. I swear, the only thing that kept me sane was Katherine, who'd been through it all by that point. And where was Mrs. Senator, you ask? Gone, of course. Oblivious. She didn't even know I was menstruating until the maid told her six months later.

So I did for Em what Kath did for me. Which means, in Carrie terms, I'm Sue Snell in this scenario. Wait, I guess that actually makes me the gym teacher. No, I refuse to be that bore. I'm sticking with Sue.

She survived.

June 26,

I almost drowned this afternoon.

Well, pretended to drown, which isn't quite the same thing. It wasn't planned. I just spontaneously decided to do it. Still, I deserve an Oscar for that performance. Or at least a Golden Globe. Best Performance of Drowning by a Regional Champion in the 100-Meter Butterfly. The gulping-down-lake-water part sucked, though. There's probably some creepy water-borne microbe swimming in my stomach as I write this. But it was worth it. I got the reaction I was looking for.

While I'm on the subject of drowning, let's talk about Franny's husband for a sec. Don't you think it's strange that a dude who almost made it to the Olympics drowned? I sure as fuck do.

June 28,
Holy shit holy shit holy shit.
I made it into the Big L. At last! I went during lunch when I knew all the campers and counselors would be in the mess hall and F and her entourage would be dining on the back deck. That gave me enough time to slip in through the front door without anyone noticing. And wow, was it worth the wait. I knew F was hiding something in there. And, sure enough, she was. Several somethings. I managed to steal one before Lottie caught me in the study. She acted all cool about it, but I think she was seriously pissed to find me there. And now I'm freaking out because she's going to tell F. I just know it.
Not fucking good, diary.

My reading is interrupted by a sudden, startling rap on the cabin door. I'd fallen so far down the rabbit hole of Vivian's thoughts that the real world melted away, unnoticed. Now it's back, making me look up from the page and call out in a trembling voice, "Who is it?"

"Emma, it's Chet. Is everything okay?"

I slam the diary shut, stuff it under my pillow, and take a quick, calming breath before saying, "Yeah, I'm fine."

The door opens a crack, and Chet peers inside, his hair a swoosh over his eyes. He pushes it away and says, "Can I come in?"

"Make yourself at home."

He steps inside and takes a seat on my hickory trunk, his long legs extended, arms crossed. Although he and Theo aren't biologically related, the two nevertheless share some traits. Both have the height and physique that makes everything they wear seem perfectly tailored. Both move with athletic grace. And both radiate that laid-back, carefree vibe that comes from being to the manor born. Or, in their case, adopted.

"I noticed you weren't at the campfire," Chet says. "I wondered if something was wrong. You know, after what happened at lunch."

"Which one of them sent you? Your mother or your brother?"

"Neither, actually. I came on my own. I wanted to clear up a few things. About the camera and why my mother invited you back here. Both were my idea."

I sit up in surprise. Yesterday, I had wondered if Chet even remembered who I was. Clearly, he did.

"I had assumed both were Franny's idea."

"Technically, they were. But I'm the one who instigated them." Chet gives me a grin. It's a great smile. Another thing he and his brother have in common. "The camera was just a precaution. Theo and my mother had nothing to do with it. I thought it would be a good idea to monitor your cabin. Not that I expect anything bad to happen. But it doesn't hurt to be prepared in case it does."

It's a polite way of saying that he, too, knows about my fragile mental state after my first stay here. At this rate, it'll be common knowledge among every camper and kitchen worker by the end of the week.

"Please don't be offended," Chet says. "I understand why you felt unfairly targeted, and I'm sorry. We all are. And if you want it taken down, I'll get Ben to do it first thing tomorrow morning."

I'm tempted to demand that it be dismantled right this instant. But, oddly, I also understand the need for caution. After what happened in the shower this morning—or, more accurately, what **might** have happened—it's not a bad idea to monitor the camp.

"It can stay," I tell him. "For now. And only if you tell me why it was your idea to invite me back here."

"Because of what you said back then," Chet says. "About Theo."

There's no need for him to elaborate. I know he's referring to how I told police Theo had something to do with the girls' disappearance and never took it back. Both are actions I've come to regret. The former because of why I blamed him. The latter because it would mean admitting to all that I'm a liar.

Two truths I'm not yet ready to face.

"I can't change what I did back then," I say. "All I can do is tell you that I regret it and that I'm sorry."

Chet raises a hand to stop me. "Getting an apology isn't why I told my mother she should invite you back here. I did it because your presence says more than any apology ever could."

So that's why Franny was so eager to have me return to Camp Nightingale. She had pitched it as a way to show that the camp was a safe, happy place again. In truth, my being here is a silent retraction of what I said about Theo fifteen years ago.

"Because I'm here again, it means I think Theo is innocent," I say.

"Exactly," Chet says. "But it's more than that. It's an opportunity for closure."

"That's why I decided to come."

"Actually, I was talking about Theo. I thought having you here would be a chance to make amends. That it would do him some good. God knows, he needs it."

"Why?" It's the only thing I can think to say. Theo is handsome, wealthy, and successful. What else could he possibly need?

"Theo's not as put together as he looks," Chet says. "He had a rough time after what happened here. Not that I can blame him. The police kept questioning him. Vivian's father said some awful stuff about him, as did the press. And Theo couldn't take it. Dropped out of school. Went heavy on the drugs and alcohol. Rock bottom came on the Fourth of July. A year after the disappearance. Theo went to a party in Newport, got lit, borrowed someone's Ferrari, and smashed it into a tree a mile down the road."

I shudder, recalling the scar on Theo's cheek.

"It's a miracle he survived," Chet continues. "Theo got lucky, I guess. But the thing is, I'm pretty sure he didn't plan to survive that crash. He's never come out and admitted he was trying to kill himself, but that's my theory. For months he had certainly acted like someone with a death wish. Things got better after that. My mother made sure of it. Theo spent six months in rehab, went back to Harvard, finally became a doctor, although two years later than he had planned. Because everything eventually went back to normal, none of us talk about that time. I guess my mother and Theo think I was too young to remember. But

I do. It's hard to forget watching your only brother go through something like that."

He stops talking, takes a deep breath, lets out a long, sad sigh.

"I'm so sorry," I say, even though it's meaning-less. It doesn't change what happened. It can't erase the pale line that now runs down Theo's cheek.

"I don't know why you accused him," Chet says. "I don't need to know. What matters is that you don't believe it now; otherwise you wouldn't be here. I don't want you to feel bad."

But I feel worse than bad. Truly villainous. I can't even will myself to look at Chet. Instead, I stare at the floor, mute and guilt-ridden.

"Don't beat yourself up over it," Chet says as he stands to leave. "That's the last thing any of us want. It's time to let go of the past. That's why you're here. It's why we're all here. And I hope it'll do everyone some good."

18

I wait a full five minutes after Chet leaves before diving back into Vivian's diary. It stays under my pillow as I count the seconds. I'm not worried about him returning to interrupt me once again. It's more of a moment to decompress after what he said about Theo. Even though he told me not to beat myself up, I can't help it.

Theo spent six months in rehab. Probably at the same time I was being treated for my own problems. Our first years after Camp Nightingale were almost identical. The only difference was the demons we faced.

Mine looked like Vivian.

Theo's looked like me.

Again, I know I can't repair the damage I've caused him. That opportunity passed fifteen years ago. But I can prevent further damage if I find out more about what happened to Vivian, Natalie, and Allison. He'll no longer have suspicion trailing after him like a shadow.

He'll be free.

And if it happens to him, it could also happen to me.

When the five minutes have elapsed, I remove Vivian's diary from under my pillow, flip to where I had left off, and dive in once more.

June 29,

It turns out I was right. Lottie told F, who pulled me aside after lunch and basically went apeshit on me. She threatened to call The Senator, as if he'd fucking care. She also said I needed to respect personal boundaries. I felt like telling her to shove those personal boundaries up her dusty twat. I didn't because I need to keep my head down. I can't rock that damn boat until it must be capsized.

So, to recap:

Bad news: She definitely suspects something.

Good news: I'm close to finding out her dirty little secret.

July 1,

I'm thinking about telling Emma. Someone needs to know in case something happens to me.

July 2,

Well, that sucked.

I decided not to tell Em the whole truth about what I'm doing. It's safer for her that way. Instead, I opted to hint at it by taking her to my secret stash in the woods. You guessed it, THE BOX. The thing that started this whole investigation when I found it last summer.

I thought showing it to Emma would spark her interest, just in case the Magic 8 Ball lied and all signs actually point to getting my sorry ass booted from camp. That way she can continue what I started, if she's so inclined. And I was right. It DID spark her interest. I saw it in her eyes as soon as she opened that box.

But then the bad stuff had to take place. Yep, I showed her that I could swim. I thought she should know, for several reasons. One: If, God forbid, my body washes up on the beach one morning, she'll be able to tell police that I'm an expert swimmer. Two: She needs to learn not to trust everything everyone tells her. Two Truths and a Lie isn't just a game. For most people, it's a lifestyle. Three: I'll need to break her heart eventually. Might as well put a crack in it now.

So now she's pissed at me. Rightly so. She spent the rest of the day ignoring me. And it hurt like a motherfucker. There's so much I want to tell her. That life is hard. That you need to punch it before it punches you.

I know she's hurt. I know she thinks she's the only one whose parents ignore her. But she should try being left behind in New York while The Senator and Mrs. Senator go off to DC two months after her sister dies! Now that's abandonment.

As for the fake drowning, I had to do it. Hopefully Em will only pout a day. I'll give her flowers tomorrow and she'll love me again.

July 3,

Fun fact: In the 1800s, women could be sent to asylums for these reasons:

Hysteria	Egotism
Immoral life	Nymphomania
Jealousy	Bad company
Masturbation	Novel reading (!)
Kicked in the head by a horse	

Other than the horse kicking, every single woman I've ever met could have been declared insane back then. Which is exactly how men wanted it. It's how they managed to keep women down. Don't like something they've said? Call them crazy and ship them off to the loony bin. Don't fuck their husbands enough? Commit them. Want to fuck them too much? Commit them. It's sick.

And don't you dare think things have changed much, diary. They haven't. The Senator was ready to have me locked up after Kath died. Like it was wrong of me to mourn her. Like grief was a mental illness.

Anyway, that's the lesson I learned today. Every woman is crazy. The ones who can't hide it well enough are shit out of luck.

150.97768 WEST
164

Update: And now I'm fucked. I forgot I left you out, dear diary. Came back from the campfire to find Natalie and Allison reading you. Which doesn't surprise me. They've been trying to get a peek at you all week. And now they have. I'm sure it was an eyeful. Thank God I didn't write that Natalie's gotten so thick in the thighs she looks like a lady wrestler or that Allison's so pasty she might as well be an albino. That would be AWFUL if they read that about themselves, right?

And while I'm tempted to leave you open to this page so they can do exactly that, I've decided it's best to hide you. You're no longer safe here, baby.

The less they know, the better.

Update #2: Welcome to your new home, little book. Hope you don't rot here. Drawing a map so I don't forget where you are.

July 4,
Can't write much. Rowing here already took half the morning. Rowing back will take even longer. F has probably noticed I'm gone. She's got spies everywhere. I'm certain she told Casey to double-check on me each night.

But that might not matter for much longer.

Because. I. Found. It.

That clichéd missing piece that ties everything together. Everything makes sense now. I know the truth. All I need to do is expose it.

But there's a hitch. After reading you, dear diary, Natalie and Allison want in on it. And I've decided I'm going to tell them everything. Because I can't do this without their help. I thought I could, but that's no longer an option.

Yes, I know I could just drop it, forget the whole thing, spend my summer, my year, the rest of my goddamned life pretending it never happened. A sane person would do that.

But here's the thing: some wrongs are so terrible that the people responsible must be held accountable. Call it justice. Call it revenge. Call it whatever. I don't give a fuck.

All I care about is this particular wrong. It can't be ignored. It must be righted.

And I'm the bitch that's going to do it.

I'm scared

19

That's it. The rest of the pages—more than two-thirds of the diary—are blank. I flip through them anyway, just in case I've missed something. I haven't. There's nothing.

I close the diary and exhale. Reading it has left me feeling the same way I did after each of Vivian's hallucinatory visits. Confused and light-headed, spent and frightened.

Vivian was looking for something, that much is clear. What it was—and what she eventually found—remain frustratingly out of reach. Honestly, the only thing I'm certain about is that the paper on which Vivian drew her map was torn from the journal. There's a page missing between her entry about its new location and the one she made on the Fourth of July. I remove the map from my backpack and hold it against the ragged remnants of the missing page. It's a match.

I reread the entire diary, studying each page, parsing every word, trying to make sense of it. Little does, least of all why Vivian, a person who rarely failed to say exactly what she was thinking and feeling, needed to keep some things secret. So I give it yet another read, this time from back to front, starting with Vivian's unsettling final entry.

I'm scared.

That one confounds me the most. Of all the myriad emotions Vivian displayed in the short time I knew her, fear wasn't one of them.

I flip to the previous page. That entry was made the morning of July 4, prompting two new questions: When did she write that final entry, and what was she afraid of?

I clutch the book, frustrated, aching for answers that refuse to reveal themselves. "What did you learn, Viv?" I murmur, as if she could somehow answer me.

Judging by the entry dates, I assume she buried the book sometime during the night of July 3. My guess is that she snuck out while the rest of us were asleep. Not unusual for her. She had also done it the night before.

I remember because I was still mad that she had lied to me about her swimming skills. I was especially livid about the reason she lied—because Theo had been paying too much attention to me. She saw me in his arms, whispering encouraging words as he taught me how to swim. And she couldn't stand it. So she faked drowning just to become the center of attention again.

I ignored her the rest of that canoe trip back to

camp. And the rest of the afternoon. And at dinner, where I took her advice and showed up so late I was last in line. I sat alone and picked at the dinnertime dregs—lukewarm meat loaf and mashed potatoes dried to a crust. At the campfire, I sat with girls my own age, who showed little interest in me. Afterward, I went to bed early, pretending to be asleep while the others played Two Truths and a Lie without me.

Later that night, I woke to find Vivian tiptoeing into the cabin. She tried to be sneaky about it, but the creak of the third floorboard from the door gave her away.

I sat up, bleary-eyed. **Where did you go?**

I had to pee, Vivian said. **Or is taking a piss something else you disapprove of?**

She said nothing else as she climbed up to her bunk. But in the morning, a handful of tiny flowers were sitting on my pillow, right beside my head. Forget-me-nots. Their petals were a delicate blue. In the center of each was a yellow starburst.

I later stored them in my hickory trunk, pressed inside my copy of **The Lovely Bones**. Although she never admitted to putting them there, I knew they were from Vivian. She had indeed given me flowers. And just as she thought, I loved her again.

I flip back to the page where Vivian had made that prediction, reading it feverishly, wondering again if my feelings had been that transparent. It's only after I reread the passage about her own parents that I get an answer—Vivian simply knew. Because she was just like me. Neglected and lonely. Basking in whatever scraps of attention she received. It's how she was able to foresee that a hastily picked bunch of forget-me-nots would be enough to appease me. Because it would have been enough for her, too.

More flipping. More pages. More questions.

I turn to the page with Vivian's musings about insanity. Of all the things she had written, this one shakes me to my core. Reading it feels as though she's speaking directly to me, as if she foresaw my slide into madness a year before it would happen.

But why did she seek out that information? And where?

I vividly remember the day she made that entry. Riding to town in the camp's mint-green Ford, squeezed tight between Vivian and Theo at the wheel. He drove one-handed, his legs spread wide so that his thigh kept bumping against mine. Each touch made my heart feel like a tiny bird trapped in a cage, fluttering against the gilded bars. I didn't mind at all when Vivian said she was going shopping and slipped away from us, leaving me alone with Theo.

I flip to the next page, where she had jotted down that strange set of numbers.

150.97768 WEST
164

At first, I think they might be coordinates on a map. But when I grab my phone and check the compass app, I discover that 150 degrees points southeast. Which means it's something else. Only Vivian knows for sure. But I'm certain she wrote down the numbers for a reason. Like everything else, I get the sense that she's urging me forward, step by step, to find out what she learned all those years ago.

I'm in the process of taking a picture of the numbers with my phone when the door to Dogwood opens and Miranda, Krystal, and Sasha burst inside. Their sudden presence sends me once again scrambling to close the book and shove it under my pillow. I'm not as quick this time around, allowing them to catch me in the act.

"What are you doing?" Sasha asks, eyeing first the corner of the book poking from beneath my pillow and then my phone, which remains clutched in my hand.

"Nothing."

"Right," Miranda says. "You're totally not acting like someone just caught looking at porn."

"It's not porn." I pause, trying to see if the girls believe me. It's clear they don't, so I tell them the truth, minus any context that would make them ask more questions. "I'm trying to decipher something. A code."

Miranda's face lights up at the idea of solving a mystery. "What kind of code?"

I glance at the picture on my phone, reading off the number. "What does 150.97768 WEST mean to you?"

"Easy," Miranda says. "It's the Dewey Decimal System. Some book has that call number."

"You positive?"

She gives me a disbelieving look. "Um, yeah. I've spent, like, half my life at the library."

The library. Maybe that's where Vivian went when she claimed to be shopping. While there, she found a book important enough to note its call number in her diary. It's clear she was looking for something. I even think she might have found it.

I recall her entry about getting somewhere she wasn't supposed to be. The Big L is the Lodge. F is Franny. Simple enough. But Vivian frustratingly failed to mention exactly what she found there and what she managed to steal.

Still, she wrote enough to thoroughly unnerve me. Thinking about Franny's reaction to her snooping sends a chill flapping through me. It doesn't sound like Franny at all, which makes me wonder if Vivian was being paranoid. It certainly seems that way, especially Vivian's line about wanting to tell me what she was doing in case something happened to her.

I'm close to finding out her dirty little secret.

It turns out something bad did happen, only there's no proof it had anything to do with Franny or a deep, dark secret. Yet some events are too con-

nected to be mere coincidence. This feels like one
of them.

I know the truth.

The idea that I might be closer to learning what
happened to the girls should excite me. Instead, a
hard ball of pain forms in the pit of my stomach.
Worry snowballing inside me. I assume Vivian
experienced this exact feeling when she scribbled
those last two words in her diary.

I'm scared.

So am I.

Because it's possible I've stumbled upon something sinister, even dangerous.

That after years of wondering, I'm on the cusp
of getting actual answers.

Above all, I'm scared that if I keep digging, I
might not like what I'll find.

20

That night, my dreams are haunted by Vivian.

It's not like the hallucinations of my youth. Never do I think she's really there, returned from the ether. There's a cinematic quality to them—like I'm seeing one of the film noirs my father still watches on Sunday afternoons. Vivian in expressionistic black and white. First running through a forest as wild as one of my paintings. Then on a barren island, holding a pair of scissors. Finally in a canoe, rowing mightily into a rolling fog bank that whooshes over her, swirling and hungry, ultimately consuming her.

I wake clutching my charm bracelet as reveille blasts through camp. To my utter surprise, I have slept through the night. My eyelids flutter, tentatively facing the light of morning. Even before they're fully open, I can make out something at Dogwood's sole window.

A shape, dark as a shadow.

A gasp catches in my throat, lodging there, momentarily blocking all breath as whoever's at the window flees. I can't tell who it is. All I see is a dark figure streaking away.

Only when it's gone do I swallow hard, suppressing the gasp, forcing it back down. I don't want to wake the girls. Nor do I want to scare them. When I notice Sasha squinting down at me from her upper bunk, I can tell she didn't see whoever was at the window. All she sees is me sitting up in bed, my face as white as my cotton pillowcase.

"I had a nightmare," I tell her.

"I read that bad dreams can be caused by eating before bed."

"Good to know," I say, although I'm pretty sure my dreams of Vivian were caused by her diary and not what little I ate last night.

As for what I saw at the window, I'm certain it wasn't a dream. Nor was it my imagination or a play of the light, like I tried to convince myself is what happened at the latrine. This time, there's no talking myself out of it, no matter how much I'd like to.

Someone was **there**.

I still feel their presence. A ghostly hum right outside the window. My pulse races, humming in response. It tells me that I wasn't mistaken about yesterday.

Someone had watched me in that shower.

Just like someone trapped those crows inside the cabin.

And now someone was just watching me sleep.

I shudder, horrified, my skin crawling. If the girls weren't here, I'd let out a scream, just because it might make me feel better. Instead, I slide out of bed and head to the door.

"Where are you going?" Sasha whispers.

"Latrine."

Another lie. Tossed off to keep Sasha calm. Unlike me with my still-furious pulse and continuing shudder as I bolt outside to see if I can spot whoever was at the window. But already dozens of girls are spilling out of their cabins, roused by reveille and groggily starting the day. All of them stop when they see me. They also stare, some with their heads tilted in curiosity, others with outright surprise. A few more campers join the fray, doing the same thing. As does Casey when she passes by with two fingers pressed to her lips, already craving that first cigarette.

That's when it dawns on me. They're not staring at me. Their gazes are fixed on the cabin behind me.

I turn around slowly, not sure if I want to see what the others do. Their expressions—a little fearful, a little stunned—tell me it's nothing good. But curiosity keeps me spinning until I'm facing the front of Dogwood.

The door has been smeared with paint. Red. Still wet. Sliding down the wood in rivulets that resemble streaks of blood.

The paint forms a word spelled out in all caps,

the letters large and bold and as piercing as a knife to the ribs.

LIAR

Franny again stands before a mess hall filled with campers, although this time it's to give a different kind of speech.

"To say I'm disappointed is an understatement," she says. "I'm devastated. Vandalism of any sort will not be tolerated at Camp Nightingale. Under normal circumstances, the culprit would be asked to leave immediately. But since you all have only been here a few days and may not yet understand the rules, whoever painted on the door of Dogwood will be allowed to stay if you come forward now. If you don't and are later caught, you'll be banned from this place for life. So, please, if any of you are responsible, speak up now, apologize, and we'll put the entire incident behind us."

Silence follows, broken by a few coughs and the occasional squeak of a cafeteria chair. No girls stand to confess. Not that I was expecting it. Most teenage girls would rather die than admit they did something wrong.

I should know.

I survey the crowd from my spot by the door. Most of the girls have their heads bowed in collective shame. The few who don't stare ahead with wide-eyed innocence, including Krystal and Sasha. Miranda is the only girl from Dogwood who seems pissed off by the incident. She sneaks glances at the girls around her, trying to find the guilty culprit.

Standing along the wall are Lottie, Theo, Chet, and Mindy. Mindy catches me looking and gives me a scowl. I have officially ruined her goal of things running smoothly.

"Well then," Franny says after a suitably unbearable length of time. "My disappointment only grows. After breakfast, all of you will return to your cabins. Morning classes are canceled while we sort everything out."

She makes her way out of the mess hall with the rest of the Lodge denizens in tow. When they pass, Lottie taps my shoulder and says, "Emma, please come with us."

I follow them to the arts and crafts building next door. Once everyone's inside, Lottie closes the door. I stand next to it, my body coiled, resisting the urge to sprint. Not just from the room but from the camp itself. My left hand started trembling the moment I saw the paint on the door, and it hasn't stopped since. The birds around my wrist rattle.

"Well, this is a fine mess," Franny says. "Emma, do you have any idea who could have done this?"

The obvious answer would be someone in this room. A major clue lies in the painted word

currently being scrubbed off Dogwood's door.
Other than Mindy, I've lied to all of them in the
past. About Theo. About what I accused him of
doing. And while none of them have called me a
liar to my face, I wouldn't be surprised if they all
felt that way in private. I wouldn't blame them,
either.

Yet my gut tells me none of them are responsible.
They're the ones who invited me back here, after
all. And petty vandalism seems beneath a member
of the Harris-White clan. If they wanted to be rid
of me, they'd just say so.

"I don't know." I debate telling them about the
person I saw at the window. Call it paranoia from
Vivian's diary rubbing off on me, but I'm not sure
I can trust anyone with the truth. Not until I get a
better grasp on what's going on. There's a chance
that, considering my history, no one will believe
it's happening at all unless I have more proof. "I
only knew about it once I left the cabin."

Franny turns to her younger son. "Chet, did you
check the camera?"

"Yeah," he says while swiping the hair from over
his eyes. "There's nothing. Which is a big red flag.
The slightest motion triggers that camera."

"But someone had to be outside that cabin," I
say. "That door didn't paint itself."

"Is the camera working now?" Franny asks,
keeping her tone calm to counter my growing
shrillness.

"Yes," Chet says. "Which means it either mal-
functioned overnight or someone tampered with
it. I imagine it wouldn't be too hard to climb up
there on a ladder and put tape over the sensor."

"Wouldn't there be video of that?" Theo says.

Chet answers with a shake of his head. "Not
necessarily. The camera is programmed to automatically turn on at nine p.m. and turn off at six
in the morning. Someone could have tampered
with it before nine and removed the tape right
at six."

Franny then fixes her green-eyed gaze on me.
Although current circumstances have dimmed it
slightly, I still feel trapped by her stare.

"Emma, have you told anyone else about the
camera?"

"No. But that doesn't mean people don't know
about it. If I noticed it, then others probably
did, too."

"Let's talk about the paint," Theo says. "If we
can figure out where it came from, maybe it'll give
us a better idea of who did it."

"Emma's the painter," Mindy pipes up. "She's
the one with the most access to it."

"Oil paint," I say, shooting her an angry look.
"And that's not what was on the door. It doesn't
run like that. If I had to guess, I'd say it was acrylic
paint."

"What's it used for?" Theo says.

I look to the center of the room, where Casey's

workstation sits. All those cabinets and cubby-holes, filled with supplies.

"Crafts," I say.

I edge around one of the circular crafting tables and head to the cabinet against the wall behind it. Flinging it open, I see rows of plastic paint bottles. They're translucent, giving a glimpse of the colors contained within them. All the bottles are full, save for one.

Basic red.

Sitting nearby is a trash can. I go to it and spot a medium-size paintbrush at the bottom. Red paint clings to the bristles, still wet.

"See?" I say. "Not my paint. Not my brush."

"So someone snuck in here early this morning and used the paint," Theo says.

"The door is locked overnight," Lottie replies. "At least, it's supposed to be. Maybe whoever was last to leave yesterday forgot to lock it."

"Or has a key," Chet adds.

Lottie shakes her head. "The only people with keys are me, Franny, and Ben."

"Neither Lottie nor I would do such a thing," Franny says. "And Ben was only just arriving when the paint was discovered."

"So that means the door was left unlocked," Theo says.

"Maybe not," Mindy says. "Yesterday, while everyone was going to lunch, I caught Emma snooping around the other workstations."

All eyes turn to me, and I wilt in the heat of their stares. I take a step back, bump into a plastic chair, drop into it. Mindy looks at me with a sad, scrunched face, as if to show how much making the accusation has pained her.

"You honestly think I'm the one who did this?" I say. "Why would I vandalize my own door?"

"Why have you done a lot of things?"

Although Mindy says it, I assume that question has occurred to everyone in the room at some point. They might not have spoken it aloud like Mindy, but it's been asked all the same. It's in every look of Franny's green eyes. It's in the red light of the camera that blinks on when I enter Dogwood.

I have every reason to believe they'd forgiven me. It doesn't mean any of them trust me.

Except for maybe Theo, who says, "If Emma says she didn't do it, then I believe her. What we should be doing is asking why someone would do this to her."

I know the answer. But like that unspoken question, it's one I can't say aloud. It's there all the same, visible in my still-shaking hands.

Because someone at camp knows.

That's why I was watched in the shower. Why those three birds were released into the cabin. Why someone was at the window and smeared paint across the door.

It was their way of telling me that they know.

Not what I did to Theo.

What I did to the girls.

The realization keeps me pinned to the flimsy chair, even after everyone starts to leave. Before exiting, Theo looks at me with concern, his cheeks flushed enough to make his scar stand out.

"Are you okay?" he says.

"No."

I picture Vivian, Natalie, and Allison as paint marks on one of my canvases, waiting for me to cover them up. One of the reasons I came back here is because I couldn't keep doing that. Because I thought that if I learned more about what happened to them, my conscience would be clean.

But now I can't foresee spending an entire six weeks here. Whoever's been watching me will continue to do so, stepping up the reminders bit by bit. Trapped birds and paint on the door, I fear, are only the beginning. If there are answers to be found, I have to do it quickly.

"I need to get out of here. Just for a little bit."

"Where do you want to go?" Theo says.

I think of Vivian's diary and the call letters of a book.

"Town," I say.

FIFTEEN YEARS AGO

The radio, like the rest of the truck, had seen better days. The little music that did fizz from the speakers sounded tinny and pockmarked with static. Not that it mattered. The only radio station Vivian and I could find played nothing but country music, the steel guitar and fiddle twang accompanying our journey out of Camp Nightingale.

"So why are we doing this again?" Theo asked as the truck passed under the camp's entrance arch.

"Because I'm in need of some hygiene products," Vivian said. "Personal, lady ones."

"That's more than I need to know." Theo shook his head, amused in spite of himself. "What about you, Em?"

"I'm just along for the ride."

And I was. Quite unexpectedly. I had been waiting for the others outside the mess hall, the pollen from Vivian's forget-me-nots still dusting my fingertips, when Natalie and Allison arrived.

"Vivian needs you," Allison said.

"Why?"

"She didn't say."

"Where is she?"

Natalie jerked her head toward the arts and crafts building on her way inside. "Over there."

That's where I found Vivian, Theo, and the mint-green pickup. Vivian was already inside, drumming her fingers against the sill of the open window. Theo leaned against the driver's-side door, his arms crossed.

"Hey there, latecomer," he said. "Hop in."

I squeezed between the two of them, their bodies warm against me as the truck bucked along the pothole-riddled road. Theo's legs continually bumped mine, as did his arm whenever he turned the steering wheel. Downy hairs from his forearm tickled my skin. The sensation made my stomach flutter and heart ache, as if they were being filled beyond capacity, becoming too large for my scrawny frame.

It stayed that way the entire drive into town, which had no discernible name but could have been any small town anywhere in the country. There was a main drag; quaint storefronts; red, white, and blue bunting on porches. We passed a town green with its generic war memorial and a sign promising a parade the next morning and fireworks at night.

Theo parked the truck, and Vivian and I quickly hopped out, stretching our legs, pretending the journey was uncomfortable, a burden. Better that than to have let Theo think I enjoyed his accidental touches.

Properly stretched, Vivian started to cross the street, heading toward an old-timey drugstore on the corner. "I'll see you losers in an hour," she said.

"An **hour**?" Theo said.

Vivian kept walking. "I plan to enjoy my freedom by going shopping. Maybe I'll buy myself something pretty. You and Emma go get lunch or something."

She strode into the pharmacy without another word. Through the window, I watched her pause at a rack of cheap sunglasses by the door and try on a pair shaped like hearts.

"Well, I guess it's just us," Theo said, turning my way. "You hungry?"

We walked to a diner that was as sleek and shiny as a bullet and settled into a booth by the window. Theo ordered a cheeseburger, fries, and a vanilla milk shake. I did the same, minus the milk shake, which Vivian never would have approved of in a million years. While we waited for the food, I stared out the window and watched cars lazily cruise up and down the street, their lowered windows revealing kids, dogs, harried mothers behind the wheel.

Even though he was across the table from me, I didn't want to look at Theo too much. Each time I did glance his way, I pictured him in the latrine shower, glistening and beautiful and oblivious to my prying gaze. The image brought a shameful warmth to my face, my stomach, between my legs. I wondered if Vivian knew that was going to happen when she urged me to peek between those ill-spaced cedar planks. I hoped not. Otherwise, it just seemed cruel.

And Vivian wasn't cruel, despite sometimes appearing that way. She was my friend. My summer-camp big sister. As I sat there with Theo, listening to oldies drift from a corner jukebox, I understood that the whole trip was Vivian's ruse to let me spend time alone with him. Another apology. One better than flowers.

"How are you liking Camp Nightingale?" Theo asked once the food had arrived.

"I love it," I said, taking a rabbitlike nibble on a french fry.

"My mother will be pleased to hear that."

"Do you like it there?"

Theo took a bite of burger, leaving a smudge of ketchup on the corner of his mouth. I resisted the urge to swipe it off with a flick of my finger. "I love it, too. Unfortunately, this looks like it'll be my last summer before internships take over my life. College certainly keeps you busy. Especially when you're premed."

"You're going to be a doctor?"

"That's the plan. A pediatrician."

"That's so noble," I said. "I think it's great you want to help people."

"And what do you want to be?"

"I think I want to be a painter."

I don't know why I said it. I certainly had no artistic ambitions I didn't quite know what to do with. It just sounded like the kind of profession Theo would want a woman to have. It was adult and sophisticated. Like something from a movie.

"Emma Davis, famous painter. That has a nice ring to it." Theo gave me a smile that made my legs quiver. "Maybe I'll come to one of your gallery openings."

Within seconds, I had my entire future mapped out. We'd keep in touch after the summer, exchanging letters that would become more meaningful as time passed. Love would eventually be declared. Plans would be made. We'd have sex for the first time on my eighteenth birthday, preferably in a candlelit room at some exotic locale. We'd stay devoted as I went to art school and he completed his residency. Then we'd marry and be the kind of couple other people envied.

As outlandish as it seemed, I told myself it could come true. I was mature for my age, or so I thought. Smart. Cool. Like Vivian. And I knew exactly what she would have done in that situation.

So when Theo attempted to take a sip of his

milk shake, I beat him to it, leaning in and sucking from his straw. The move was bold, so utterly unlike me. I blushed, my face turning the same shade of peachy pink as the lip gloss I left behind on Theo's straw.

Yet there was more boldness in store. The kind of thing I never would have attempted had I spent even a fraction of a second thinking about it. But I didn't think. I simply acted, closing my eyes and tilting my mouth toward Theo's, the vanilla taste on my tongue spreading to my lips as I kissed him. His breath was hot. His lips were cold. The warmth and chill merged into a sweet, fluttery sensation that filled my body.

I pulled away quickly, my eyes still closed. I didn't want to look at Theo. I didn't want to see his reaction and bring an end to the magic spell I was under. He ended it anyway, softly saying, "I'm flattered, Emma. I really am. But—"

"I was just kidding," I blurted out, my eyes still squeezed shut as my heart twisted inside my chest. "It was a joke. That's all."

Theo said nothing, which is why I leaned back in the booth, turning to the window before opening my eyes.

Vivian was on the other side of the glass, her presence an unwelcome surprise. She stood on the sidewalk, wearing the drugstore sunglasses. Heart-shaped frames. Dark lenses reflecting diner chrome. Although I couldn't see her eyes, the smile that played across her lips made it clear she had witnessed everything.

I couldn't tell if she was happy about what she saw or amused by it. Maybe it was both. Just like during her games of Two Truths and a Lie, it was sometimes hard to tell the difference.

21

My excuse for going into town was to fill a prescription for allergy medicine I'd forgotten to bring with me. Yet another lie. At this point, I've fallen off the truth wagon completely. But again, I consider it justified, especially because it gave me the chance to return to Dogwood and grab my backpack and Vivian's diary. By then the paint on the door had been completely wiped away. The only evidence it had been there at all was a swath of freshly cleaned wood and the nose-tickling smell of turpentine.

Now Theo and I ride in the same mint-green pickup that had whisked us out of camp fifteen years ago. Inside, all is silent, the radio apparently having died years ago. Theo drives with one hand on the steering wheel, his bent elbow jutting out the open window. My window is also rolled down. I stare at the woods as we leave Camp Nightingale, the trees a blur, light sparking through their branches.

I'm long past being mad at Theo about the

camera outside Dogwood. My silence stems not from anger but from guilt. It's the first time we've been alone together since I learned about his breakdown, and I'm not sure how to act. There's so much I want to ask. If he felt as lonely during his six months of rehab as I did in the mental hospital. If he thinks about me every time he sees his scar in the mirror. With questions like that, silence seems to be the best choice.

The truck hits a whopper of a pothole, and both of us bounce toward the center of the bench seat. When our legs touch, I quickly pull away, edging as far as the passenger door will allow.

"Sorry," I say.

More silence follows. Tense and thick with things unspoken. It becomes too much for Theo, for he suddenly says, "Can we start over?"

I wrinkle my brow, confused. "You mean go back to camp?"

"I mean go back to the beginning. Let's start fresh. Pretend it's fifteen years ago and you're just arriving at camp." Theo flashes the same crooked smile he gave when we first met. "Hi, I'm Theo."

Once again, I'm amazed by his forgiveness. Maybe all bitterness and anger left him the instant that car smashed into a tree. Whatever the reason, Theo's a better person than me. My default reaction to being hurt is to hurt right back, as he well knows.

"Feel free to play along," he urges.

I'd love nothing more than to erase much of what's happened between then and now. To rewind back to a time when Vivian, Natalie, and Allison still existed; Theo was still the dreamiest boy I'd ever seen; and I was a knock-kneed innocent nervous about camp. But the past clings to the present. All those mistakes and humiliations following us as we march inevitably forward. There's no ignoring them.

"Thank you for doing this," I say instead. "I know it's an inconvenience."

Theo keeps his eyes on the road, trying to hide how I've disappointed him yet again. "It's nothing. I needed to go into town anyway. Lottie gave me a list of things to pick up from the hardware store. And what Lottie demands, she gets. She's the one who really runs this place. Always has been."

When we reach town, I see it's more or less the same as I had left it, although some of the charm has been rubbed away. No patriotic bunting hangs from porch railings. A couple of empty storefronts mar the main drag, and the diner is gone, replaced by a Dunkin' Donuts. The drugstore remains, although it's now part of a chain, the name spelled out in red letters garishly placed against the building's original brick exterior.

"After this, I might make a quick stop at the library. I need a place with good Wi-Fi to catch up on work emails," I say, aiming for breeziness, as if the idea has just occurred to me.

I guess it works, because Theo doesn't question the idea. Instead, he says, "Sure, I'll meet you there in an hour."

He remains in the idling truck, watching. This gives me no choice but to keep up the ruse and hurry into the drugstore. Since I know it'll look suspicious on the return trip if I'm not carrying a bag from the place, I spend a few minutes browsing the shelves for something small to buy. I settle on a four-pack of disposable phone chargers. One for me and each girl in Dogwood. Franny will never know. Even if she does, I'm not sure I care.

At the cash register, I notice a rotating rack of sunglasses. The kind with a tilted mirror on top so customers can see how they look in the dime-store shades. I give it a spin, barely eyeing the knockoff Ray-Bans and cheap aviators when a familiar pair whirls by.

Red plastic.

Heart-shaped frames.

I snatch the sunglasses from the rack and turn them over in my hands, remembering the pair Vivian wore the entire ride back to camp that long-ago summer. I spent the whole drive wondering what she was thinking. Vivian said little during the return trip, preferring instead to stare out the open window as the breeze whipped her hair across her face.

I try on the sunglasses and lift my face to the rack's mirror, checking how they look. Vivian wore them better, that's for damn sure. On me, they're just silly. I look exactly like what I am—a woman approaching thirty in cheap shades made for someone half her age.

I toss the sunglasses onto the counter anyway. I pay with cash and stuff the disposable chargers into my backpack. The sunglasses are worn out of the store, slid high up my forehead to keep my hair in place. I think Vivian would approve.

Next, it's on to the library, which sits a block back from the main street. Inside, I pass the usual blond-wood tables and elderly patrons at desktop computers on my way to the reference desk. There a friendly librarian named Diana points me to the nonfiction section, and soon I'm scanning the stacks for 150.97768 WEST.

Astonishingly, it's still there, tucked tightly on a shelf of books about mental illness and its treatment. If the subject matter didn't already make me uneasy, the title certainly would.

Dark Ages: Women and Mental Illness in the 1800s by Amanda West.

The cover is stark. Black letters on a white background. Very seventies, which is when the book was printed. The publisher is a university press I've never heard of, which makes it even more baffling as to how or why Vivian learned of its existence.

I take the book to a secluded cubicle in the corner, pausing for a few steadying breaths before opening it. Vivian read this book. She held it in her hands. Mere days before she disappeared. Knowing this makes me want to put it back on the shelf, walk away, find Theo, and return to camp.

But I can't.

I need to open the book and see what Vivian saw.

So I fling it open, seeing on the first page a vintage photo of a young woman confined in a straitjacket. Her legs are nothing but skin covering bone, her cheeks are beyond gaunt, and her hair is wild. Yet her eyes blaze with defiance. As wide as half-dollars, they stare at the photographer as if willing him to look at her—really look—and understand her predicament.

It's a startling image. Like a kick in the stomach. A shocked huff of air lodges in my throat, making me cough.

Below the photo is a caption as sad as it is vague. **Unknown asylum patient, 1887.**

I turn the page, unable to gaze at the image any longer, just the latest person who could bear to look at this unnamed woman for only a brief amount of time. In my own way, I've also failed her.

Skimming through the book is an exercise in masochism. There are more photos, more infuriating captions. There are tales of women being committed because their husbands abused them, their families didn't want them, polite society didn't want to see them. There are accounts of beatings, of starvation, of cold baths and scrubbings with wire brushes on skin that hadn't seen daylight in months.

Each time I find myself gasping at a new horror, I realize how lucky I am. Had I been born a hundred years earlier, I would have become one of these women. Misunderstood and suffering. Hoping that someone would figure out why my mind betrayed me and thus be able to fix it. Most of these women never enjoyed such a fate. They suffered in sorrow and confusion until the end of their days, whereas my madness was temporary. It left me.

The shame is another story.

After a half hour of torturous skimming, I finally come to page 164. The one Vivian noted in her diary. It contains another photo, one that fills most of the page. Like the others in the book, it bears the same sepia-toned fuzziness of something taken a century ago. But unlike those images of anonymous girls imprisoned within asylum walls, this photograph shows a man standing in front of an ornate, Victorian structure.

The man is young, tall, thick of chest and stomach. He boasts an impeccably waxed mustache and a distinct darkness to his eyes. One hand grips the lapel of his morning coat. The other is slid into a vest pocket. Such a pompous pose.

The building behind him is three stories tall, made of brick, with dormer windows on the top floor and a chimneylike turret gracing the roof. The windows are tall and arched. A weathervane in the shape of a rooster rises from the turret's peaked roof. A less showy wing shoots off from the building's left side. It has only one floor, no windows, patchy grass instead of a lawn.

Even without that utilitarian wing, there's something off about the place. Brittle strands of dead ivy cling to a corner. Sunlight shining onto the windows have made them opaque. It reminds me of an Edward Hopper painting—**House by the Railroad**. The one that's rumored to have inspired the house from **Psycho**. All three structures project the same aura of homespun menace.

Beneath the photo is a caption—**Dr. Charles Cutler poses outside Peaceful Valley Asylum, circa 1898.**

The name summons a memory from fifteen years ago. Vivian and I alone in the woods, reading the tiny name engraved on the bottom of a rotting box.

Peaceful Valley.

I remember being curious about it. Clearly, Vivian was, too, for she came here looking for more information. And what she learned was that Peaceful Valley had been an insane asylum.

I wonder if that realization stunned her as much as it does me. I wonder if she also sat blinking in disbelief at the page in front of her, trying to wrap her head around how a box of scissors from an insane asylum ended up on the banks of Lake Midnight. I wonder if her heart raced as much as mine does. Or if her legs also suddenly started to twitch.

That sense of shock subsides when I look at the text on the page opposite the photo. Someone had drawn a pencil line beneath two paragraphs. Vivian, most likely. She was the kind of person who'd have no problem defacing a library book. Especially if she found something important.

> By the end of the nineteenth century, a growing divide had formed regarding the treatment of mentally ill women. In the nation's cities, asylums remained crowded with the poor and indigent, who, despite a growing call for reform, still lived in deplorable conditions and were subjected to harsh treatment from undertrained and underpaid staff. It was quite a different story for the wealthy, who turned to enterprising physicians opening small, for-profit asylums that operated without government control or assistance. These retreats, as they were commonly known, usually existed on country estates in areas remote enough for family members to send troubled relatives without fear of gossip or scandal. As a result, they paid handsomely to have these black sheep whisked away and cared for.

A few progressive doctors, appalled by the extreme difference in care between the rich and the poor, attempted to bridge the gap by opening the doors of their bucolic retreats to those less fortunate. For a time, Dr. Charles Cutler was a common sight in the asylums of New York and Boston, where he sought out patients in the most unfortunate of situations, became their legal guardian, and whisked them away to Peaceful Valley Asylum, a small retreat in upstate New York. According to the diary of a doctor at New York's notorious Blackwell's Island Asylum, Dr. Cutler intended to prove that a more genteel course of care could benefit all mentally ill women and not just the wealthy.

While I'm almost positive this is what Vivian was pointing to in her diary, I have no idea what it has to do with Franny. In all likelihood, it doesn't. So why was Vivian so convinced that it did?

There seems to be only one way to find out—I need to search the Lodge. Vivian discovered something in the study there before Lottie came in and disrupted her. Whatever she found led her here, to this same book in this same library.

Always leave a trail of bread crumbs. That's what Vivian told me. **So you know how to find your way back.**

Only I can't help but think that the trail she left for me won't be enough. I'll need a little help from a friend.

I grab my phone and immediately FaceTime Marc. He answers in a rush, his voice almost drowned out by the cacophony in his bistro's kitchen. Behind him, a line cook mans a skillet that sizzles and pops.

"It's a bad time, I know," I tell him.

"The lunch rush," Marc says. "I've got exactly one minute."

I dive right in. "Remember that reference librarian at the New York Public Library you used to date?"

"Billy? Of course. He was like a nerdy Matt Damon."

"Are the two of you still friendly?"

"Define friendly."

"Would he try to get a restraining order if he saw you again?"

"He follows me on Twitter," Marc says. "That's not a restraining order level of animosity."

"Do you think he'd help you do some research for your best friend in the entire world?"

"Possibly. What will we be researching?"

"Peaceful Valley Asylum."

Marc blinks a few times, no doubt wondering if he's heard me correctly. "I guess camp's not going so well."

I quickly tell him about Vivian, her diary of

cryptic clues, the fact that an insane asylum, of all things, might be involved. "I think Vivian might have found something before she disappeared, Marc. Something that someone else didn't want her to know."

"About an asylum?"

"Maybe," I say. "In order to be sure, I need to know more about that asylum."

Marc pulls his phone closer to his face until all I can see is one large, squinting eye. "Where are you?"

"The local library."

"Well, someone there is watching you." Marc moves the phone even closer. "A **hot** someone."

My eyes dart to the lower corner of my screen, where my own image rests in a tiny rectangle. A man stands roughly ten feet behind me, his arms folded across his chest.

Theo.

"I need to go," I tell Marc before ending the call. As his image cuts out, I get a one-second glimpse of his face, which is stony with concern. It's the opposite of Theo's expression. When I finally turn around to face him, his face is a placid surface, unreadable.

"Are you ready to go?" he says, his voice as blank as his features. "Or do you need more time?"

"Nope," I reply. "All done."

I gather my things, leaving the book where it is. Its contents are stamped on my memory.

On our way out of the library, I pull the sunglasses over my eyes, shielding them not only from the midafternoon glare but from Theo's inquisitive gaze. The expression on his face hasn't wavered once since he caught me talking to Marc. The least I can do is match him in opaqueness.

"Nice sunglasses," he says once we're in the truck.

"Thanks," I reply, even though it didn't sound like a compliment.

Then we're off, heading back to camp in a fresh cocoon of silence. I'm not sure what it means. Nothing good, I assume. Gregariousness is second nature to Theo. Or I could simply be projecting, letting Vivian's diary entries seep into my psyche and make me paranoid. Then again, considering what happened to her, Natalie, and Allison, maybe a little paranoia isn't such a bad thing.

It's only when the camp's gate slides into view that Theo says, "I need to ask you something. About that summer."

I already know he's going to bring up my false accusation against him. It's like barbed wire that's been stretched between us—invisible yet keenly felt whenever one of us nudges against it. Rather than respond, I roll down the window and turn my face toward the breeze, letting it tangle my hair just like Vivian's.

"It's about that day we drove into town," he continues.

I exhale into the rush of warm air hitting my face, relieved to not have to talk about why I had accused him. At least for now.

"What about it?"

"Well, we had lunch at that diner and—"

"I kissed you."

Theo chuckles at the memory. I don't. It's hard to laugh at one of the most humiliating moments of your adolescence.

"Yes, that. Were you lying then? About it being a joke?"

Rather than continue the lie, dragging it into a second decade, I say, "Why?"

"Because, at the time, I didn't think it was." Theo pauses, rubbing the salt-and-pepper stubble on his chin until he can summon the right words. "But I was flattered. And I want you to know that, had you been older, I probably would have kissed you back."

The same boldness I had felt in that diner returns out of nowhere. I think it might be the sunglasses. I feel different with them on. More direct. Less afraid.

I feel, I realize, like Vivian.

"And now?" I say.

Theo steers the truck to its spot behind the arts and crafts building. As it shudders to a stop, he says, "What about now?"

"I'm older. If I kissed you now, would you kiss me back?"

A grin spreads across Theo's face, and for a split second it's like we've been shuttled back in time, all those intervening years yet to be experienced. He's nineteen and the most handsome man I'd ever seen in my life. I'm thirteen and smitten, and every glimpse of him makes my heart explode into a flock of butterflies.

"You'll have to try it again sometime and see for yourself," he says.

I want to. Especially when he glances my way, a flirty glint in his eyes, that grin spreading wider until his lips part, practically begging to be kissed. It's enough to make me lean across the pickup's bench seat and do just that. Instead, I step out of the car and say, "That's probably not the best idea."

Theo—and the prospect of kissing him—is a distraction. And now that I'm inching closer to learning what Vivian was looking for, I can't be distracted.

Not by Theo.

Not by what I did to him.

And especially not by the lies both of us have told but aren't yet brave enough to admit.

22

That evening, the girls and I eat dinner at a picnic table outside the mess hall. The whole camp is still buzzing about the paint on the door. Liargate is what they're calling it, giving the incident the proper ring of scandal. I assume Casey, Becca, and the other instructors are also talking about it, which is why I'm fine with dining outdoors. I'm in no mood for their gossip.

"Where did you go this afternoon?" Sasha asks me.

"Into town."

"Why?"

"Why do you think?" Miranda snaps. "She did it to get away from this place."

Sasha swats at a fly buzzing around her tray of gray meat loaf and lumpy mashed potatoes. "Do you think one of the campers did it?"

"It sure wasn't one of the counselors," Krystal says.

"Some of the girls are saying you did it," Sasha tells me.

"Well, they're wrong," I say.

Across the picnic table, Miranda's face hardens. For a second, I think she's going to storm into the mess hall and punch the offending campers. She certainly looks ready for a fight.

"Why would Emma paint **liar** across our door?"

"Why would anyone do it?" Sasha asks.

Miranda answers before I get the chance, giving an answer far more pointed than mine. "Because some girls," she says, "are just basic bitches."

After dinner, I present them with their disposable chargers. "For emergencies only," I say, even though I know all that extended battery life will be wasted on Snapchat, Candy Crush, and Krystal's beloved superhero movies. Still, it puts the girls in a good mood as we head off to the nightly campfire. They deserve it after what they've endured today.

The fire pit is located on the outskirts of camp, as far away from the cabins as the property will allow. It sits in a round meadow that looks carved from the forest like a crop circle. In its center is the fire pit itself—a circle within the circle ringed by rocks hauled out of the woods and arranged there almost a century ago. The fire is already burning when we arrive, the engulfed logs placed in an upright triangle, like a teepee.

The four of us sit together on one of the sagging benches placed near the blaze. We roast marshmallows on twigs whittled to sharpness by Chet's

Swiss Army knife, the handles sticky, the tips crusted and charred.

"You went here when you were our age, right?" Sasha asks.

"I did."

"Did you have campfires?"

"Of course," I say, pulling a freshly roasted marshmallow off my stick and popping it into my mouth. Although the hot sugar burns my tongue, it's not an unwelcome sensation. It brings back memories, both good and bad.

During my first, tragedy-shortened time here, I loved the campfire. It was hot, powerful, just the right amount of intimidating. I loved feeling its heat on my skin and watching the way it glowed white in the center. The burning logs popped and sizzled, like something alive, fighting the flames until they finally collapsed in a pile of embers, sending tiny dots of fire swirling upward.

"Why didn't you like this place, again?" Miranda says.

"It's not the place I didn't like," I tell her. "It's what happened while I was here."

"Someone vandalized the cabin back then, too?"

"No," I say.

"Did you see ghosts?" Sasha asks, her eyes shiny and wide behind her glasses. "Because Lake Midnight is haunted, you know."

"Bullshit," Krystal says with a sniff.

"It's not. People really believe it," Sasha says.

"A lot of people. Especially once those girls vanished."

My body tenses. The girls. That's who she's referring to. Vivian and Natalie and Allison. I had hoped their disappearance would somehow elude this new group of campers.

"Disappeared from where?" Krystal says.

"Right here," Sasha replies. "It's why Camp Nightingale closed in the first place. Three campers snuck out of their cabin, got lost in the woods, and died or something. Now their spirits roam the forest. On nights when the moon is full, they can be seen walking among the trees, trying to find the way back to their cabin."

In truth, it was inevitable that the missing girls of Dogwood would pass into legend. They're now as much a part of Camp Nightingale lore as Buchanan Harris's flooded valley and the villagers caught in the water's path. I picture the current campers whispering about them at night, huddled under sleeping bags, nervous eyes flicking to the cabin window.

"That's not true," Krystal says. "It's just a dumbass story to frighten people from going into the woods. Like that stupid movie by the guy who made **The Sixth Sense**."

Miranda, not to be outdone, pulls out her phone and holds it to her ear, pretending to answer it.

"It's the creepy ghost girls calling," she announces to Sasha. "They said you're a terrible liar."

———

Later in the night, after the girls have gone to sleep, I remain awake in my bottom bunk, irritated and restless. The heat is partly to blame. It's a stifling, stuffy night made worse by a lack of airflow inside the cabin. I insisted on keeping the window closed and the door locked. After this morning, it felt like a necessary precaution.

That's the other reason I can't sleep. I'm worried that whoever is watching me will make a repeat appearance. And I worry more about what they plan to do next. So I keep my gaze trained on the window, staring out at heat lightning flashing in the distance. Each flash brightens the cabin in throbbing intervals—a strobe light painting the walls an incandescent white.

During one blinding burst, I see something at the window.

Perhaps.

Because the flash of lightning is so quick, I can't quite tell. All I get is the briefest of glimpses. Half a glimpse, really. Just enough to make me think once again that someone is there, standing completely still, peering into the cabin.

I want to be wrong. I want it to be just the jagged shadows of the trees outside. But when the lightning returns, arriving in a bright flash that lingers for seconds, I realize I'm right.

There **is** someone at the window.

A girl.

I can't see her face. The lightning backlights her, turning her into a silhouette. Yet there's something familiar about her. The slenderness of her neck and shoulders. The slick tumble of her hair. Her poise.

Vivian.

It's her. I'm sure of it.

Only it's not the Vivian who could exist today. It's the one I knew fifteen years ago, unchanged. The Vivian who haunted me in my youth, prompting me to bury her in my paintings time and time again. Same white dress. Same preternatural poise. Held in her fist is a bouquet of forget-me-nots, which she holds out formally, like a silent-film suitor.

My right hand flies first to my chest, feeling the frightened thrum of my heart. Then it drops to my left arm, seeking out the bracelet around my wrist. I give it a sharp tug.

"I know you're not real," I whisper.

I pull harder, the bracelet digging into my skin. The bird charms clatter together—a muted, clicking sound almost drowned out by my panicked whispers.

"You have no power over me."

More tugging. More clicking.

"I'm stronger than everyone realizes."

The bracelet breaks. I hear a snap of the clasp, followed by the sensation of the chain slithering off my wrist. I fumble for it, catching it in my palm, squeezing my fingers around it. At the window, lightning flashes again. A burst of blinding light that quickly fizzles into darkness. All I see outside are a smattering of trees and a sliver of lake in the distance. No one is at the window.

The sight should bring relief. But with the bracelet now a curl of chain in my fist, it brings only more fear.

That Vivian will come again. If not tonight, then soon.

I'm stronger than everyone realizes, I think, repeating it in my head like a mantra. **I'm stronger than everyone realizes. I'm strong. I'm—**

By the time I fall asleep—my heart hammering, body rigid, hand tight around my abused bracelet—the chant has mutated into something else. Less reassuring. More panicked. The words pinging against my skull.

I'm not going crazy. I'm not going crazy. I'm not going crazy.

In the morning, instead of reveille blaring from the speakers on the mess hall roof, I was yanked from sleep by "The Star-Spangled Banner," in honor of Independence Day. Vivian slept right through it. When I climbed to her bunk to wake her, she swatted my hand and said, "Go the fuck away."

I did, pretending not to feel hurt as I headed to the latrine to shower and brush my teeth. After that, it was on to the mess hall, where kitchen workers dished out a Fourth of July special: pancakes topped with stripes of blueberries, strawberries, and whipped cream. I was told they were called Freedom Flapjacks. I called them ridiculous.

Vivian didn't show up for breakfast, not even fashionably late. Her absence freed Natalie to get a second helping of pancakes, which she consumed with abandon, strawberry sauce staining the corner of her mouth like stage blood.

Allison, on the other hand, didn't budge from her routine. She put down her fork after taking three bites and said, "I'm so full. Why am I such a pig?"

"You can eat more," I urged. "I won't tell Viv."

She gave me a hard stare. "What makes you think Vivian has anything to do with what I eat?"

"I just thought—"

"That I'm like you and do everything she tells me to?"

I looked down at my plate, more ashamed than offended. I had downed two-thirds of the pancakes without a second thought. Yet I knew that if Vivian had been there, I would have consumed only as much as she did. One bite or one hundred, it didn't matter.

"Sorry," I said. "I don't do it on purpose. It's just that—"

Allison reached across the table and patted my hand. "It's okay. **I'm** sorry. Vivian's very persuasive."

"And a bitch," Natalie added as she slid one of Allison's untouched pancakes onto her own plate. "We get it."

"I mean, we're friends," Allison explained. "Best friends. The three of us. But there are times when she can be—"

"A **bitch**," Natalie said, more emphatically that time. "Viv knows that. Hell, she'd say it herself if she were here."

My mind flashed back to the previous day. Her witnessing my disastrous attempt to kiss Theo. The smirk playing across her lips afterward. She had yet to bring it up, which worried me. I had ex-

pected some mention during the campfire or right
before bed. Instead, there had been nothing, and
it made me think she was saving it for a later game
of Two Truths and a Lie, when it could inflict the
most emotional damage.

"Why do you put up with it?" I said.

Allison shrugged. "Why do you?"

"Because I like her."

But it was more than that. She was the older girl
who took me under her wing and shared her secrets. Plus, she was cool. And tough. And smarter
than I thought she let on. To me, that was something worth clinging to.

"We like her, too," Natalie said. "And Viv's been
through a lot, you know."

"But she's sometimes so mean to the two of you."

"That's just her way. We're used to it. We've
known her for years."

"All our lives," Natalie chimed in. "We knew
who she was and what she was like even before
we became friends. You know, same school, same
neighborhood."

Allison nodded. "We know how to handle her."

"What she means," Natalie said, "is that when
Vivian gets in a mood, it's best to stay out of her
way until it passes."

I spent the rest of the morning separated from the
others in Dogwood, thanks to another advanced

archery lesson. I was relegated to the arts and crafts building, where the camp's other thirteen-year-olds and I used leather presses to decorate rawhide bracelets. I would have preferred to shoot arrows.

After that it was lunch. That time, Natalie and Allison also didn't bother to show. Rather than eat alone, I declined the ham-and-Swiss sandwich on the menu and headed to Dogwood to look for them. To my surprise, I found them before I even reached the cabin. The roar of voices inside told me all three of them were there.

"Don't lecture us about secrets!" I heard Natalie yell. "Especially when you refuse to tell us where you were this morning."

"It doesn't matter where I went!" Vivian shouted back. "What matters is that you lied."

"We're **sorry**," Allison said with all the drama she could muster. "We told you a hundred times."

"That's not fucking good enough!"

I opened the door to see Natalie sitting shoulder to shoulder with Allison on the edge of her bunk. Vivian stood before them, her face flushed, hair stringy and unwashed. Natalie had her chest thrust forward, as if in the process of blocking a field hockey rival. Allison shrank into herself, her hair over her face, trying to hide what looked like tears. All three of them swiveled my way when I entered. The cabin plunged into silence.

"What's going on?" I asked.

"Nothing," Allison replied.

"Just bullshitting," Natalie said.

Only Vivian admitted the obvious truth. "Emma, we're in the middle of something. Shit needs to be sorted out. Come back later, okay?"

I backed out of the cabin, closing the door behind me and shutting out the raging storm taking place inside. Vivian was apparently having one of those moods Natalie and Allison had warned me about.

This time, they couldn't stay out of its path.

Not sure where else to go, I turned to head back to the center of camp. There was Lottie, standing right behind me. She wore a plaid shirt over a white tee. Her long hair was pulled back in a braid that ran down her back. Like me, she was close enough to hear the commotion coming from Dogwood, and her expression was one of curious surprise.

"Locked out?" she said.

"Sort of."

"They'll let you back in soon enough." Her gaze flicked from me to the cabin door and back again. "First time living with a group of girls?"

I nodded.

"It takes some getting used to. I was an only child, too, so coming here was a rude awakening."

"You were a camper here?"

"Yes, in my own special way," Lottie said. "But

what I learned is that each summer there's always
a fight or two in these cabins. It comes from being
shoved together in such close quarters."

"This one sounds pretty bad," I said, surprised
by how shaken seeing them fighting had left me. I
couldn't stop picturing Vivian's cheeks flaring red
or the tears glistening behind Allison's hair.

"Well, I know of a friendlier place we can go."

Lottie put a hand on my shoulder, steering me
away from the cabin and into the heart of camp.
To my surprise, we headed to the Lodge, skirting
the side of the building to the steps that led to
the back deck. At the top stood Franny, leaning
against the railing, her eyes aimed at the lake.

"Emma," she said. "What a pleasant surprise."

"There's some drama in Dogwood," Lottie explained.

Franny shook her head. "I'm not surprised."

"Do you want me to defuse it?"

"No," Franny said. "It'll pass. It always does."

She waved me to her side, and the two of us
stared at the water, Lake Midnight spread before
us in all its sun-dappled glory.

"Gorgeous view," she said. "Makes you feel a
little bit better, doesn't it? This place makes everything better. That's what my father used to say.
And he learned it from **his** father, so it must be
true."

I looked across the lake, finding it hard to believe the entire body of water hadn't existed a

hundred years earlier. Everything surrounding it—trees, rocks, the opposite shore shimmering in the distance—felt like it had always been there.

"Did your grandfather really make the lake?"

"He did indeed. He saw this land and knew what it needed—a lake. Because God had failed to put one here, he made it himself. One of the first people to do that, I might add." Franny inhaled deeply, as if trying to consume every scent, sight, and sensation the lake provided. "And now it's yours to enjoy any way you'd like. You do enjoy it here, don't you, Emma?"

I thought I did. I loved it here two days ago, before Vivian took me out in the canoe to her secret spot. Since then, my impression of the place had been chipped away by things I didn't quite understand. Vivian and her moods. Natalie and Allison's blind acceptance. Why the thought of Theo continued to make my knees weak even after I humiliated myself in front of him.

Unable to let Franny know any of this, I simply nodded.

"Wonderful," Franny said, beaming at my answer. "Now try to forget about the unpleasantness in your cabin. Don't let anything spoil this place for you. I certainly don't. I won't let it."

23

I wake with the dawn, my fingers still curled around the broken bracelet. Because I spent the night clenched with worry, my lower back and shoulders hurt, the pain there beating as steadily as a drum. I slide out of bed, shuffle to my trunk, and dig out my bathing suit, towel, trusty robe, and drugstore sunglasses. On my way out, I do a quick check of the door. Nothing new has been painted there. I'm grateful that, for now, seeing Vivian again is the worst of my worries.

After that, it's more shuffling to the latrine, where I change into the bathing suit, then to the lake and finally into the water, which is such a relief that I actually sigh once I'm fully submerged. My body seems to right itself. Muscles stretch. Limbs unfurl. The pain settles to a mild ache. Annoying but manageable.

Rather than full-out swim, I lean back in the water, floating the way Theo taught me. It's a hazy morning, the clouds as gray as my mood. I stare up at them, searching in vain for hints of sunrise.

A blush of pink. A yellow glow. Anything to take my mind off Vivian.

I shouldn't have been surprised by her appearance. Honestly, I should have expected it after three days of nonstop thinking about her. Now that I've seen her, I know she'll return. Yet another person watching me.

I take a deep breath and slip beneath the lake's surface. The colorless sky wobbles as water comes between us, rushing over my open eyes, distorting my vision. I sink deeper until I'm certain no one can see me. Not even Vivian.

I stay submerged for almost two full minutes. By then my lungs burn like wildfire and my limbs involuntarily scramble for the surface. When I emerge, I'm hit once again with the sensation of being watched from a distance. My muscles tighten. Bracing for Vivian.

On shore, someone sits near the water's edge, watching me. It's not Vivian, thank God. It's not even Becca.

It's Franny, sitting in the same grassy area Becca and I had occupied two mornings ago. She still wears her nightgown, a Navajo blanket wrapped around her shoulders. She waves to me as I swim back to shore.

"You're up early," she calls out. "I thought I was the only early riser around here."

I say nothing as I dry myself with the towel, put on the robe, and slip on the sunglasses. Although Franny appears happy to see me, the feeling isn't quite mutual. With Vivian now fresh in my thoughts, so, too, is her diary.

I'm close to finding out her dirty little secret.

That line, the appearance of the camera, and Franny's noticeable lack of support after Mindy accused me of vandalizing my own damn door have left me in a state of deep mistrust. I'm debating whether to walk away when Franny says, "I know you're still upset about yesterday. With good reason, I suppose. But I hope that doesn't mean you can't sit with an old woman looking for a little company."

She pats the grass next to her—a gesture that squeezes my heart a little. It makes me think I can forgive the camera and her failure to rush to my defense. As for Vivian's diary, I tell myself that she could have been lying about Franny keeping secrets. Being dramatic for drama's sake. It was, after all, her forte. Perhaps the diary was just another lie.

I end up brokering a compromise between my suspicious mind and my squishy heart. I sit beside Franny but refuse to engage her in conversation. Right now, it's the best I can do.

Franny seems to intuit my unspoken rules and doesn't press me for details about why I'm up so early. She simply talks.

"I have to say, Emma, I'm envious of your swimming ability. I used to spend so much time in that lake. As a girl, you couldn't get me to leave the water. From sunrise to dusk, I'd be out there paddling away. Not anymore, though. Not after what happened to Douglas."

She doesn't need to elaborate. It's clear she's referring to Douglas White. Her much-older husband. The man who died years before she adopted Theo and Chet. Another piece of Vivian's diary snakes into my thoughts.

Don't you think it's strange that a dude who almost made it to the Olympics drowned?

I push it away as Franny keeps talking.

"Now that my swimming days are over, I observe," she says. "Instead of being in the lake, I watch everything going on around it. Gives you a new perspective on things. For instance, this morning I've been keeping an eye on that hawk."

Franny leans back, putting her weight on one arm. The other emerges from her blanket and points to a hawk lazily circling over the lake.

"Looks like an osprey," she says. "I suspect he sees something he likes in the water. Once, years ago, two peregrine falcons made their nest right outside our living room window at the Harris. Chet was just a boy at the time. My word, was he fascinated by those birds. He'd stare out that window for hours, just watching, waiting for them to hatch. Soon enough, they did. Three eyesses. That's what falcon chicks are called. They were so small. Like squawking, wriggling cotton balls. Chet was overjoyed. As proud as if they were his own. It didn't last long. Nature can disappoint as easily as it entrances. This was no exception."

The osprey overhead suddenly dives toward the lake and, wings spread wide, slices its feet through the water. When it rises again, there's a fish gripped in its talons, unable to escape no matter how much it wriggles and flops. The osprey swoops away, heading to the far side of the lake, where it can eat in peace.

"Why did you reopen the camp?"

I blurt it out, surprising even myself. But Franny was expecting it. Or at least a question similar to it. She pauses long enough to take a breath before replying, "Because it was time, Emma. Fifteen years is too long for a place to stay empty."

"Then why didn't you do it sooner?"

"I didn't think I was ready, even though the camp was right here waiting for me."

"What convinced you that you were?"

This time, there's no pat answer at the ready. Franny thinks it over, her eyes on the lake, jaw working. Eventually, she says, "I'm about to tell you something, Emma. Something personal that very few people know. You must promise not to tell another soul."

"I promise," I say. "I won't say a word."

"Emma, I'm dying."

My heart feels squeezed again. Harder this time. Like it, too, has been scooped up by that osprey.

"Ovarian cancer," Franny says. "Stage four. The doctors gave me eight months. That was four months ago. I'm sure you can do the math."

"But there must be something you can do to fight it."

The implication is clear. She's worth millions. Certainly someone with that much money can seek out the best treatment. Yet Franny gives a sad shake of her head and says, "It's too late for all that fuss now. The cancer's spread too far. Any treatment would only be a way of delaying the inevitable."

I'm stunned by her calmness, her serene acceptance. I'm the exact opposite. My breath comes in short bursts. Tears burn the corners of my eyes, and I hold back a sniffle. Like Vivian, I now know one of Franny's secrets. Only it's not dirty. It's sad and makes me think of that sundial hidden away in the forest. That last hour truly does kill.

"I'm so sorry, Franny. Truly I am."

She pats my knee the way my grandmother used to. "Don't you dare feel sorry for me. I understand how fortunate I am. I've lived a long life, Emma. A good one. And that should be enough. It is, really. But there's one thing in my life that wasn't fortunate."

"What happened here," I say.

"It's troubled me more than I let Theo and Chet know," Franny says.

"What do you think happened to them? To Vivian and the others?"

"I don't know, Emma. I really don't."

"You must have some theory. Everyone else does."

"Theories don't matter," Franny says. "It's no good dwelling on what happened. What's done is done. Besides, I don't like being reminded of how much that disappearance cost me in so many ways."

That's a sentiment I can understand. Camp Nightingale was forced to close. Franny's reputation was sullied. The taint of suspicion never entirely left Theo. Then there was the matter of three separate lawsuits filed by Vivian's, Natalie's, and Allison's parents, accusing the camp of negligence. All three were settled immediately, for an undisclosed sum.

"I wanted to have one last summer of things being the way they used to be," she says. "That's why I reopened the camp. I thought if I could do that successfully, with a new mission, then it might ease the pain of what happened fifteen years ago. One last glorious summer here. And then I could die a content woman."

"That's a nice reason," I say.

"I think so," Franny replied. "And it would

certainly be a shame if something happened to spoil it."

The ache in my heart fades to numbness as yet another thing Vivian wrote in her diary commands my thoughts.

She definitely suspects something.

"I'm sure it won't." I try to sound chipper when I say it, hoping it hides the sudden unease overcoming me. "Everyone I've talked to is having a great time."

Franny tears her gaze away from the water and looks at me, her green eyes untouched by illness. They're watchful, probing, as if they can read my thoughts. "And what about you, Emma? Are you enjoying your time here?"

"I am," I say, unable to stare back. "Very much."

"Good," Franny says. "I'm so pleased."

Her voice contains not a hint of pleasure. It's as chilly as the slight breeze that gusts across the lake and ripples the water. I pull my robe tight around me, fending off the sudden cold, and look to the Lodge, where Lottie has emerged on the back deck.

"There you are," she calls down to Franny. "Is everything okay?"

"Everything's fine, Lottie. Emma and I are just chatting about camp."

"Don't be too long," Lottie says. "Your breakfast isn't getting any warmer."

"You should go," I tell Franny. "And I should probably wake the girls in Dogwood."

"But I haven't finished my story about Chet and the falcons," Franny says. "It ends not long after those birds emerged from their eggs. Chet was obsessed with them, as I've said. Spent all his free time watching them. I think he truly grew to love those birds. But then something happened that he wasn't prepared for. Those eyesses got hungry. So the mother falcon did what mother falcons are known to do. She fed them. Chet watched her leave her perch outside our window and fly into the sky, circling, until prey appeared. It was a pigeon. A poor, unsuspecting pigeon probably on its way to Central Park. That mama falcon swooped down and snatched it in midair. She brought it back to the nest by our window, and as Chet watched, she used that sharp, curved beak to tear that pigeon apart and feed it to her babies, piece by piece."

I shudder as she talks, picturing flapping wings and downy feathers floating in the air like snow.

"You can't blame that mother falcon," Franny says matter-of-factly. "She was simply doing what she needed to do. Taking care of her children. That was her job. But it broke Chet's heart. He watched those squawking little eyesses too closely, and they showed their true natures. Some of his innocence was taken away that day. Not much. Just the tiniest bit. But it was a part of him he would never be able to get back. And although we don't talk about those falcons, I'm certain that he'd say he regrets watching them closely. I think he'd say that he wished he hadn't looked so much."

Franny climbs to her feet, struggling slightly, the effort leaving her body quivering. The blanket slips, and I get a peek at her rail-thin arms. Pulling the blanket around herself, she says, "You have a good morning, Emma."

She shuffles away, leaving me alone to contemplate the story of Chet and the falcons. While it didn't sound like a lie, it also didn't quite have the ring of truth.

It might have been, I realize with another robe-tightening chill, a threat.

24

The morning painting class is spent in a state of distraction. The girls arrange their easels in a circle around the usual still-life fodder. Table. Vase. Flowers. I monitor their progress with disinterest, more concerned with the bracelet that's once again around my wrist. I'd managed to fix the clasp with some colored string from Casey's craft station—a stopgap measure I suspect won't last until the end of the day, let alone the rest of the summer. Not the way I'm constantly twisting it.

I'm made nervous by all the activity drifting through the building like a tide. Becca and her budding photographers marching in from the woods. Casey and her crafters stringing slim leather necklaces with beads. All these girls. All these prying eyes.

And one of them knows what I did fifteen years ago. A fact I'm sure I'll be reminded of sooner rather than later.

I give the bracelet another tug as I stand next to Miranda, examining her work in progress. When her gaze lingers on my wrist, I pull my hand away from the bracelet and look out the window.

From the arts and crafts building, I have an angled view of the Lodge, where various members of the Harris-White family come and go. I see Mindy and Chet bickering about something as they head to the mess hall, followed by Theo trotting past on a morning jog. A minute later I spot Lottie gingerly guiding Franny toward the lake.

Right now, the Lodge is empty.

Franny's story returns to me, whispering in my ear.

He watched them too closely, and they showed their true natures.

I know I should heed her warning. This won't end well. Even if I do get answers, there's no guarantee my conscience will rid itself of guilt. But I'll never know if I don't try. Not knowing is what brought me here. Not knowing is why I kept seeing Vivian all those years ago. It's why I saw her last night. This is my only chance.

"I need to take care of something," I tell the class. "I'll be right back. Keep painting."

Outside, I slip away to Dogwood and retrieve my phone and charger. I then make my way to the Lodge, moving at an awkward half run, torn between being inconspicuous and being speedy. In truth, I need to be both.

At the Lodge, I knock on the red front door, just in case someone returned during my jaunt to the cabin and back. When seconds tick by and no one answers, I give the doorknob a twist. It's unlocked. I check to see if anyone is nearby and possibly watching. No one is. Quickly, I tiptoe inside and close the door behind me. Then it's through the entrance hall and living room before veering left into the study.

The room is roughly the same size as Dogwood, with a desk in the center and floor-to-ceiling bookshelves where our bunk beds would be. The wall behind the desk is covered with framed photographs. There's an air of neglect about the place—like a museum that's not very good at upkeep. A thin layer of dust covers the Tiffany lampshade on the desk. There's a thicker coat of it on the rotary phone, which looks like it hasn't been touched in years.

I lower myself onto my hands and knees, searching the walls for an outlet. I find one behind the desk and plug in the phone charger. Then I stand in the middle of the study, wondering where to look first. It's hard to decide without Vivian's diary to guide me. I recall her writing about how she managed to sneak something out of the study, which means there could be multiple possible clues here.

I head to the bookshelf on my left, which holds dozens of thick, musty volumes about nature. Darwin's **On the Origin of Species**. Audubon's **Birds of America**. **Walden** by Thoreau. I grab a thick purple book and examine its cover. **Poisonous Plants of North America**. A quick flip through its pages reveals pictures of lacy white flowers, red berries, mushrooms colored a sickly green. I doubt these books are what Vivian was referring to.

I turn next to the desk, giving its phone, lamp, and blotter calendar a cursory glance before reaching for the three drawers stacked from floor to desktop. The first drawer is the usual menagerie of pen caps and paper clips. I close it and move to the middle one. Inside is a stack of folders. They bulge with documents, their edges brittle with age. I flip through them. Most appear to be receipts, financial statements, invoices for long-ago work on the property. None contain a hint of scandal. At least nothing that Vivian could suss out during a brief bit of snooping.

In the bottom drawer, I find a wooden box. It's just like the one Vivian showed me during our outing to the other side of the lake, only better preserved. Same size. Same surprising heft. Even the initials carved into the lid are the same.

CC

Charles Cutler.

The name slips into my head without warning or effort. One look at those initials and it's right there, summoned at will. I lift the box from its hiding place and carefully turn it over. On the bottom are four familiar words.

Property of Peaceful Valley.

I turn the box back over and open it, revealing a green velvet interior. Nestled inside are photographs.

Old ones.

Of women in gray with long hair draped down their backs.

Each one assumes the same pose as Eleanor Auburn, minus the clutched hairbrush.

This is where Vivian got that picture. I'm certain of it. It's merely one of what appears to be two dozen. I sort through them, unnerved by their uniformity. Same clothes. Same bare-wall background. Same eyes made dark by despair and hopelessness.

Just like the one of Eleanor, the back of each photo has been marked with a name.

Henrietta Golden. Lucille Tawny. Anya Flaxen.

These women were patients at Peaceful Valley. The unfortunates whom Charles Cutler rescued from squalid, crowded asylums and brought to Peaceful Valley. Only I have a gnawing suspicion his intentions weren't so noble. A chill settles over me, increasing with every name I read until I'm practically numb.

Auburn. Golden. Tawny. Flaxen.

Those aren't last names.

They're hair colors.

I'm struck by a dozen different thoughts, all clashing together in my brain. Scissors in that crumbling box. The broken-glass sound they made when Vivian turned it over. Watching Allison's mother in that guilt-inducing production of **Sweeney Todd**. A character sent to bedlam, at the mercy of wardens who sold their hair to wigmakers.

That's what Charles Cutler was doing. It explains these women's long locks and why their last names went unwritten, as if the only important aspect of their identity was the color of their hair.

It makes me wonder if any of them knew the purpose they served. That they weren't patients but commodities, ones who surely saw none of the money Charles Cutler received from wigmakers. The idea is so distractingly sad that I don't realize someone has entered the Lodge until a voice rings out from the entrance hall.

"Hello?"

I drop the photos back into the box and quickly replace the lid. The motion sets the charms on my bracelet clicking. I press my wrist against my stomach to silence them.

"Is someone in here?" the voice calls.

"I am," I say, hoping it will cover the sound of me closing the desk drawer. "Emma Davis."

Springing to my feet behind the desk, I find Lottie in the doorway. She's surprised to see me. The feeling is mutual.

"I'm charging my phone. Mindy told me I could do it here if I needed to."

"You're lucky Franny's not here to see you. She's a stickler about such things." Lottie sneaks a glance behind her, making sure Franny is indeed elsewhere. Then she creeps into the room with a conspiratorial gleam in her eyes. "It's a silly rule if you ask me. I warned her that girls are different now than they were back then. Always glued to their phones. But she insisted. You know how stubborn she can be."

Lottie joins me at the desk, and for a heart-stopping second, I think she knows what I've been doing. I brace myself for questions, perhaps a thinly veiled threat similar to the one Franny offered this morning. Instead, she focuses on the framed photographs cramming the wall behind the desk. They seem to have been placed there in no discernible order. Color photos mingle with black-and-white ones, forming a wall-size collage of images. I spot a grainy picture of an imposing man in front of what I presume to be Lake Midnight. A date has been hastily scrawled in the picture's lower right corner: 1903.

"That's Franny's grandfather," Lottie says. "Buchanan Harris himself."

He has a hugeness so many important men of

that age possessed. Big shoulders. Big belly. Big, ruddy cheeks. He looks like the kind of man who could make a fortune stripping the land of its trees and then spend that money creating a lake just for his personal enjoyment.

Lottie points to a birdlike woman also in the photo. She has big eyes and Kewpie doll lips and is dwarfed by her husband. "Franny's grandmother."

"I heard she drowned," I say.

"Childbirth," Lottie replies. "It was Franny's husband who drowned."

"How did it happen?"

"The drowning? That was before my time. What I heard is that Franny and Douglas went for a late-night swim together like they did every day. Nothing strange about that. Only on that particular night, Franny came back alone. She was hysterical. Carrying on about how Douglas went under and never came back up. That she searched and searched but couldn't find him. They all went out in boats to look for him. His body wasn't found until the next morning. Washed up on shore. The poor man. This place certainly has seen its fair share of tragedy."

Lottie moves on to another black-and-white one showing a young girl leaning against a tree, a pair of binoculars around her neck. Clearly Franny. Below it is another photo of her, also taken at the lake, rendered in the garish colors of Kodachrome. She's a few years older in this one, standing on the

Lodge's deck, her back turned to the water. Another girl stands beside her, smiling.

"There she is," Lottie says. "My mother."

I take a step closer to the photo, noticing the similarities between the woman posing with Franny and the one standing at my side. Same pale skin. Same Bette Davis eyebrows. Same heart-shaped faced that tapers to a pointed chin.

"Your mother knew Franny?"

"Oh, yes," Lottie says. "They grew up together. My grandmother was the personal secretary to Franny's mother. Before that, my great-grandfather was Buchanan Harris's right-hand man. In fact, he helped create Lake Midnight. When Franny turned eighteen, my mother became her secretary. When she passed away, Franny offered the job to me."

"Is this what you wanted to do?"

I'm aware of how rude the question sounds. Like I'm judging Lottie. In truth, I'm judging Franny for continuing the Harris tradition of using generations of the same family to make their own lives easier.

"Not exactly," Lottie says with unyielding tact. "I was going to be an actress. Which meant I was a waitress. When my mother died and Franny offered me the job, I almost turned it down. But then I came to my senses. I was in my thirties, barely scraping by. And the Harris-Whites have been so kind to me. I even think of them as family. I grew up with them. I've spent more time here at Lake Midnight than Theo and Chet combined. So I accepted Franny's offer and have been with them ever since."

There's so much more I want to ask. If she's happy doing the same thing her mother did. If the family treats her well. And, most important, if she knows why Franny keeps photos of asylum patients in her desk.

"I think I see Casey in this one," Lottie says farther down the wall, at a spot of pictures of Camp Nightingale during its prime. Groups of girls posing on the tennis court and lined up at the archery range, bows pulled back. "Right here. With Theo."

She points to a photo of the two of them swimming in the lake. Theo stands waist-deep in the water, the telltale lifeguard whistle around his neck. Cradled in his arms—in the exact way he cradled me during my swimming lesson—is Casey. She's slimmer in the picture, with a happy, youthful glow. I suspect it was taken when she was still a camper here.

Just above that picture is one of two girls in polo shirts. The sun is in their eyes, making them squint. The photographer's shadow stretches into the bottom of the frame, like an unnoticed ghost swooping down on them.

One of the girls in the photograph is Vivian.

The other is Rebecca Schoenfeld.

The realization stops my heart cold. Just for a second or so. In that pulseless moment, I stare at the two of them and their easy familiarity. Wide, unforced smiles. Skinny arms tossed over shoulders. Keds touching.

This isn't a photo of two girls who barely know each other.

It's a picture of friends.

"I should go," I say as I quickly gather my phone and charger. "You won't tell Franny about this, will you?"

Lottie shakes her head. "Some things Franny's better off not knowing."

She also starts to leave, skirting around the desk and giving me roughly two seconds to lift my phone and snap a picture of Vivian and Becca's photo. I then hurry out of the room, exiting the Lodge the same the way I came. At the front door, I literally bump into Theo, Chet, and Mindy. I bounce between the brothers. First Theo, then Chet, who grabs my arm to steady me.

"Whoa there," he says.

"Sorry," I say, holding up my phone. "I needed a charge."

I push past them into the heart of camp. The morning lessons have ended, and girls drift among their cabins, the mess hall, and the arts and crafts building. When I reach Dogwood, I find the girls inside, indulging in some reading time. A comic book for Krystal and an Agatha Christie paperback for Miranda. Sasha flips through a battered copy of **National Geographic**.

"Where did you go?" Krystal says. "You never came back."

"Sorry. I got tied up with something."

I kneel in front of my hickory trunk and run my hands over the lid, feeling the ridges of all the names that had been carved before mine.

"What are you doing?" Miranda asks.

"Looking for something."

"What?" Sasha says.

I lean to my right, my fingers tripping down the side of the trunk. That's where I find it. Five tiny letters scratched into the hickory, a mere inch from the floor.

becca

"A liar," I say.

Campfire. Fourth of July.

There was a charge in the air that night. A combination of heat, freedom, and the holiday. The campfire seemed higher, hotter. The girls surrounding it were louder and, I noticed, happier. Even my group of girls.

Whatever had caused the earlier drama in Dogwood was resolved by dinner. Vivian, Natalie, and Allison laughed and joked through the entire meal. Vivian said nothing when Natalie had an extra helping. Allison, astonishingly, cleaned her plate. I simply felt relieved that Franny was right. The storm had passed. Now they surrounded me beside the fire, basking in the orange warmth of the leaping flames.

"We're sorry about earlier," Vivian told me. "It was nothing."

"Nothing," echoed Allison.

"Nothing at all," added Natalie.

I nodded, not because I believed them but because I didn't care. All that mattered was that they were with me now, at the end of my lonely day.

"You're best friends," I said. "I understand."

The counselors handed out sparklers, which we lowered into the campfire until they ignited into starbursts. Sizzling. White-hot.

Allison climbed to her feet and sliced the sparkler through the air, forming letters, spelling her name. Vivian did the same, the letters massive, hovering there in streaks of sparks.

A distant boom drew our attention to the sky, where golden tendrils of fireworks trickled to nothingness. More replaced them, painting the night red then yellow then green. The fireworks promised in the nearby town, only we at Camp Nightingale could also see them. Allison stood on one of the benches to improve her view. I stayed on the ground, pleasantly surprised when Vivian embraced me from behind and whispered in my ear, "Awesome, right?"

Although it seemed as though she was talking about the fireworks, I knew she was actually referring to something else. Us. This place. This moment.

"I want you to always remember this," she said as another bloom of color streaked through the sky. "Promise me you will."

"Of course," I said.

"You've got to promise, Em. Promise me you'll never forget."

"I promise."

"That's my little sister."

She kissed the top of my head and let me go. I kept my eyes on the sky, enthralled by the colors, how they shimmered and blended before fading away. I tried counting the colors, losing track as explosion after explosion erupted in the distance. The big finish. All the colors commingling until the sky grew so bright I was forced to squint.

Then it was over. The colors vanished, replaced by black sky and pinpoint stars.

"So pretty," I said, turning around to see if Vivian agreed.

But there was no one behind me. Just a campfire slowly reducing itself to glowing embers.

Vivian was gone.

25

I skip the campfire again, using tiredness as an excuse. It's not entirely a lie. All this being watched and sneaking around have left me exhausted. So I slip into comfortable clothes—a T-shirt and a pair of plaid boxers worn as shorts—and sprawl out in my bottom bunk. I tell the girls to go have fun without me. When they leave Dogwood, I check my newly charged phone for an email from Marc regarding his research assignment. All I get is a text reading, Mr. Library is still adorbs! Why did I ever break up with him? xoxo

I text back, Stay focused.

A few minutes later, I'm back outside and heading to another cabin. Golden Oak. I wait by the door until a trio of campers scurry out, on their way to the campfire. Becca is the last to emerge. Her body goes rigid when she sees me. Already she knows something is amiss.

"Don't wait up. I'm right behind you," she tells her campers before turning to me and, in a far less friendly voice, says, "Need something, Emma?"

"The truth would be nice." I hold up my phone, revealing a photo of a photo. Her and Vivian, their arms entangled, inseparable. "You feel like sharing this time?"

Becca nods, her lips pursed, and retreats back into the cabin. When a minute passes and she doesn't emerge, I start to think that she simply intends to ignore me. But she comes out eventually with a leather satchel slung over her shoulder.

"Supplies," she says. "I think we're going to need them."

We cut through the cabins and head to the lake. It's the thick of twilight, the sky tilting ever closer from day to night. A few stars spark to life overhead, and the moon sits low in the sky on the other side of the lake, still on the rise.

Becca and I each take a seat on rocks near the water's edge, so close our knees practically touch. She opens the satchel, removing a bottle of whiskey and a large folder. She opens the bottle and takes a deep gulp before passing it to me. I do the same, wincing at the whiskey's sharp burn in the back of my throat. Becca takes the bottle from my hands and replaces it with the folder.

"What's this?"

"Memories," she says.

I open the folder, and a stack of photographs spills onto my lap. "You took these?"

"Fifteen years ago."

I sort through the photos, marveling at how

talented she was even at such a young age. The pictures are in black and white. Stark. Each one a spontaneous moment caught on the sly and preserved forever. Two girls hugging in front of the campfire, silhouetted by the soft-focus flames. The bare legs of someone playing tennis, white skirt flaring, exposing pale thighs. A girl swimming in Lake Midnight, the water up to her freckled shoulders, her hair as slick as a sea lion. Allison, I realize with a jolt. She's turned away from the camera, focused on something or someone just out of frame. Beads of water cling to her eyelashes.

The last photograph is of Vivian, a lit sparkler in her blurred hand, spelling her name in large slashes. Becca had set the exposure so the letters could be seen. Thin white streaks hanging in midair.

VIV

Fourth of July. Fifteen years ago. The night they vanished.

"My God," I say. "This could be—"

"The last picture ever taken of her? I think it is."

The realization makes me reach for the whiskey. The long gulp that follows creates a soft, numbing sensation that helps me ask, "What happened between you and Vivian? I know you stayed with them in Dogwood the year before I came to camp."

"The four of us have a complicated history."

Becca stops to correct herself. "**Had** a complicated history. Even outside of this place. We all went to school together. Which wasn't unusual. Sometimes it felt like half our class came here in the summer."

"Camp Rich Bitch," I say. "That's what it was called at my school."

"Mean," Becca says. "But accurate. Because most of them were indeed bitches. Vivian especially. She was the ruler. The queen bee. People loved her. People hated her. Vivian didn't care as long as she was the center of attention. But I got to see a different side of her."

"So you were friends."

"We were best friends. For a time, anyway. I like to think of Vivian as my rebellious phase. We were fourteen, pissed off at the world, sick of being girls and wanting so badly to be women. Viv especially. She was perfect at finding trouble. Rich boys who'd get her anything she wanted. Beer. Weed. Fake IDs she'd use to get us into all the clubs. Then it suddenly stopped."

"Why?"

"The short answer? Because Vivian wanted it to."

"And the long answer?"

"I'm not entirely sure," Becca says. "I think it was because she went through some fucked-up identity crisis after her sister died. She ever tell you about it?"

"Once," I say. "I got the sense she didn't like to talk about it."

"Probably because it was such a stupid death."

"She drowned, right?"

"She did." Becca takes another swig from the bottle before pressing it into my hands. "One night in the dead of winter, Katherine—that was her name, in case Viv never told you—decided to get shit-faced and go to Central Park. The reservoir was frozen over. Katherine walked out onto it. The ice broke, she fell in, never came back up."

I'm struck by the memory of Vivian pretending to be drowning. Her sister had to have crossed her mind as she flailed in the water and gurgled for help. All to get a boy's attention. What kind of person does that?

"Katherine's death absolutely crushed her," Becca says. "I remember running to her apartment right after it happened. She was crazed, Emma. Wailing, pounding the walls, shaking uncontrollably. I couldn't look away. It was ugly and beautiful at the same time. I wanted to take a picture of it, just so I'd never forget. Yeah, I know that's weird."

But it's not. At least not as weird as making the same three girls continually vanish beneath layers of paint.

"That was the beginning of the end of us," Becca continues. "I did the best-friend thing and went to the wake and the funeral and was by her side when she came back to school. But even then I knew she was pulling away from me and being drawn to them."

"Them?"

"Allison and Natalie. They were Katherine's best friends. All three were in the same class."

"I always thought they were the same age as Vivian," I say.

"She was a year younger. Although you couldn't tell from the way she acted."

Becca reaches over and takes the bottle from my lap. Choosing the particular poison she needs to get through the conversation. She takes a long gulp and swallows hard.

"They found comfort in one another. I assume that was the appeal. Honestly, before Katherine died, Viv wanted nothing to do with them. You should have heard the way she made fun of them whenever all five of us were at her apartment. We were like warring factions, even when playing something as innocuous as Truth or Dare."

"Two Truths and a Lie," I say. "That was Vivian's game of choice."

"Not when we were friends," Becca says. "I think she joined in because Katherine liked to play it. She idolized her sister. And when she died, I think she transferred those same feelings to Natalie and Allison. I wasn't surprised when I found out we'd all be bunking here together in the summer. I had already assumed it would happen. What I wasn't ready for was how much I'd be left out. Around them, Vivian acted like she hardly knew me. Natalie and Allison had consumed her attention. By the time camp was over, we were barely speaking to each other. It was the same way back at school. She had them, so there was no need for me. When summer came around again, I knew I wasn't going to be bunking with them. I'm sure Vivian saw to that. I was banished from Dogwood and shuffled to the cabin next door."

It's fully dark now. Night settles over us, as does a prolonged silence in which Becca and I simply pass the bottle back and forth. The whiskey's starting to hit me hard. When I look up at the stars, they're brighter than they should be. I hear the sound of girls coming back from the campfire. Footsteps, voices, a few peals of laughter echoing off the cabin walls.

"Why didn't you tell me all this the other morning?" I say. "Why lie?"

"Because I didn't want to go into it. And I was surprised **you** did. I mean, Vivian treated you the same way, right?"

I don't answer, choosing instead to take another gulp of whiskey.

"It wasn't that hard of a question," Becca says.

Oh, but it is. It doesn't take into account the way I had treated Vivian.

"No," I say. "It wasn't the same."

"I think we're past lying to each other, Em,"

Becca says. "I know what happened right before the three of them disappeared. I was in the cabin next to Dogwood, remember? The windows were open. I heard every word."

My heart falters in my chest, skipping like a scratched record.

"It was you, wasn't it? You painted the cabin door. And put the birds inside. And you've been watching me."

Becca jerks the bottle from my hands. I've been officially cut off.

"What the fuck are you talking about?"

"Someone's been toying with me ever since I got here," I say. "At first, I thought it was all in my head. But it's not. It's really happening. And you've been doing it."

"I didn't write on your door," Becca replies with a huff. "I have absolutely zero reason to mess with your head."

"Why should I believe you?"

"Because it's the truth. I'm not judging you for what you told Vivian that night. In fact, I wish I'd said some of it myself. She definitely had it coming."

I stand, feeling shockingly unbalanced. I look to the bottle still gripped in Becca's hand. Only a third of the whiskey is left. I have no idea how much of that is my doing.

"Just stay away from me for the rest of the summer." I start to walk away, trying hard to stay upright as I call over my shoulder, "And as for what I said to Vivian that night, it wasn't what it sounded like."

Only it was. Most of it. All that Becca's missing is context.

What she actually overheard that night.

Why it happened.

And how it was so much worse than she could ever imagine.

"Where's Viv?" I asked Natalie, who merely shrugged in response.

Allison did the same. "I don't know."

"She was just here."

"And now she's not," Natalie said. "She probably went back to the cabin."

But Vivian wasn't in Dogwood, either, which we discovered when we returned a few minutes later.

"I'm going to look for her," I announced.

"Maybe she doesn't want to be found," Natalie said as she scratched at a new round of mosquito bites.

I went anyway, heading to the latrine, which was the only logical place I thought she could be. When I tried the door, I found it locked. Strange. Especially at that late hour. I took a walk around the side of the building, pulled along by curiosity. When I reached the gap in the planks, I heard the sound of running water coming from inside.

The shower.

Humming just beneath it was another noise.

Moaning.

I should have left. I knew it even then. I should have simply turned around and gone back to Dogwood. Yet I couldn't resist taking a peek. That was something else Vivian had taught me. When you get an opportunity to look, you're a fool not to take it.

I leaned toward the gap. I looked.

What I saw was Vivian. Facing the shower wall, her palms flat against it, breasts pressing into the wood. Theo stood behind her. Hands over hers. Hips thrusting. Face buried against her neck and muffling his grunts.

The sight of the two of them, doing something I'd only heard whispered about, cleaved my heart in two. It hurt so much I could hear it breaking. A sick, cracking sound. Like wood shattered by an ax.

I wanted to run away, afraid that Vivian and Theo would be able to hear it, too. But when I turned around, there was Casey, a lit cigarette dangling from her lips.

"Emma?" Smoke pushed from her mouth with each syllable. "Is something wrong?"

I shook my head, even though tears had already started to leak from my eyes. The movement set them free, flinging them away from my face.

"You're upset," Casey said.

"I'm not," I lied. "I just—I need to be alone."

I slipped past her, running not to the cabin

but to the lake, where I stood so close that water lapped at my sneakers. Then I cried. I had no idea for how long. I just wept and wept, the tears falling directly from my eyes into the water, mixing with Lake Midnight.

After crying so much that my tears ran dry, I returned to Dogwood, finding Vivian, Natalie, and Allison all there. They sat in a circle on the floor, smack in the middle of a game of Two Truths and a Lie. In Vivian's hand was the flask she had told me about. Its existence truly wasn't a lie. Now she took a slow drink from it, as if to prove how foolish I had been to doubt her.

"There you are," she said, holding out the flask. "Want a swig?"

I stared at her damp ponytail, her pinkened skin, her stupid locket. And at that moment I despised her more than I had despised anyone in my life. I could feel the hatred boiling under my skin. It burned.

"No," I said.

Allison continued with the turn I had interrupted. Her choices were, as usual, either self-aggrandizing or stupid. "One: I met Sir Andrew Lloyd Webber. Two: I haven't consumed bread in a year. Three: I think Madonna's version of 'Don't Cry for Me Argentina' is better than Patti LuPone's."

"The second one," Vivian said, taking another hit of the flask. "Not that I care."

Allison flashed a chorus-girl smile, trying not to act hurt. "Correct. I had pancakes this morning, and my mother made me French toast the morning I left for camp."

"My turn," I announced. "One: My name is Emma Davis. Two: I am spending the summer at Camp Nightingale."

I paused, ready for the lie.

"Three: I didn't just see Vivian and Theo fucking in the latrine showers."

Natalie slapped a hand over her gaping mouth. Allison shrieked, "Oh my God, Viv! Is that true?"

Vivian remained calm, looking at me with a dark glint in her eyes. "Clearly that upsets you."

I turned away, unable to endure the hardness of her stare, and said nothing.

Vivian kept talking. "I'm the one who should be upset by this situation. Knowing that you were spying on me. Watching me have sex like some pervert. Is that what you are, Emma? A pervert?"

Her calmness was what ultimately got under my skin. The slow way she spoke. So deliberate, accented with just the right amount of disdain. I was sure she did it on purpose, lighting the fuse that would eventually make me explode.

I gave her what she wanted.

"You knew I liked him!" I screamed, the words raging forth, unstoppable. "You knew and couldn't

stand the thought of having someone pay more attention to me than to you. So you fucked him.
Because you could."

"Theo?" Vivian laughed. A single short, disbelieving burst. It was the cruelest sound I'd ever
heard. "You actually think Theo is interested in
you? Jesus, Em, you're just a baby."

"That's still better than being a bitch like you."

"I'm a bitch, but you're delusional. Truly fucking delusional."

Had any tears been left in my body, I'm certain
I would have started crying on the spot. But I'd
used them all up. All I could do was push past
her and crawl into bed. I laid on my side, my back
turned to them, knees pulled to my chest. I closed
my eyes and breathed deeply, trying to ignore the
horrible hollow feeling in my chest.

The three of them didn't say anything else after
that. They went to the latrine to do their gossiping, sparing me the humiliation of having to listen. I fell asleep not long after they left, my brain
and body deciding together that unconsciousness
was the best remedy for my misery.

When I woke, it was the middle of the night.
The creak of the floorboard was what roused me.
The sound jolted me awake and propelled me upright. Light from the full moon outside slanted
through the window in a gray-white beam. Each
girl passed through it, shimmering a moment on
their way out the door.

First Allison.

Then Natalie.

And finally Vivian, who froze when she saw me awake and watching.

"Where are you going?" I asked.

Vivian smiled, although no amusement could be found in that slight upturn of her lips. Instead, I sensed sadness, regret, the hint of an apology.

"You're too young for this, Em," she said.

She raised an index finger and pressed it to her lips. Shushing me. Conspiring with me. Requesting my silence.

I refused. I needed to have the last word.

Only after it was uttered, its sour echo lingering in the air, did Vivian leave the cabin, closing the door behind her, vanishing forever.

26

I'm drunk by the time I'm again walking among the cabins. Or, more accurately, stumbling. With each step, the mulch path seems to shift under my feet. I overcompensate by stomping, trying to pin it into place, which makes me lose my balance more often than not. The end result is dizziness. Or maybe that's just from the whiskey.

I try to sober up as I stumble along. Years of observing my mother has taught me a few tricks, and I utilize them all. I slap my cheeks. I shake my arms and take deep breaths. I widen my eyes, pretending there are invisible toothpicks holding up the lids.

Rather than head straight to Dogwood, I keep walking, pulled subconsciously in another direction. Past the cabins. To the latrine. But I don't go inside. Instead, I lean against it, momentarily lost. I close my eyes and wonder why I've come here in the first place.

I open them only when I feel a nearby presence,

alarmingly close and getting closer. On the edge of my vision, I see someone round the corner of the latrine. A shape. Dark and swift. My body tenses. I almost scream, somehow managing to stop it when the shape comes into focus.

Casey.

Checking to see who's there while sneaking a cigarette like a high school sophomore.

"You startled me," she says before a deep drag and a languid puff. "I thought you were Mindy."

I say nothing.

Casey drops the cigarette, stubs it out. "Are you okay?"

"I'm fine," I say, stifling a giggle even though my talk with Becca has left me feeling unbearably sad. "Just fine."

"My God, are you drunk?"

"I'm not," I say, sounding just like my mother, the words slurred into one. **Imnot.**

Casey shakes her head, part horrified, part amused. "You better not let Mindy see you like this. She'll totally freak out."

She leaves. I stay, roaming the perimeter of the building, an index finger sliding along the cedar shingles. Then I see the crack. That gap between planks now stuffed with clay. And I remember why I'm here—I'm retracing my steps. Going to the same spot I went after Vivian disappeared from the campfire. Fifteen years later, I can still see her and Theo together in the shower stall. I can still feel the heartache that caused. A muted memory pain.

I also feel something else. A shiver of awareness jumping along the skin of my arms, the back of my neck.

I look up, expecting to see Casey again. Or, worse, Mindy.

Instead, I see Vivian.

Not all of her. Just a glimpse as she rounds the corner of the latrine. A spray of blond hair. A slip of white dress scraping the cedar wall. Before disappearing completely, she turns and peers at me from around the edge of the building. I see her smooth forehead, her dark eyes, her tiny nose. It's the same Vivian I remember from camp. The same one who later haunted me.

I instinctively reach for my bracelet, finding instead only a patch of skin where it should have been wound around my wrist.

It's not there.

I check my left arm, just to be sure. It's bare. That bit of string keeping the bracelet together had given way. Now it's lying somewhere on the grounds of Camp Nightingale.

Which means it could be anywhere.

Which means it's gone.

I flick my gaze to the corner of the latrine. Vivian is still there, peering at me.

I'm not going crazy, I think. **I'm not.**

I rub the skin of my left wrist, as if that will somehow work the same magic as the bracelet. It doesn't help. Vivian remains where she's at. Staring. Not speaking. Yet I keep rubbing, the friction heating my flesh.

I'm not going crazy.

I want to tell her that she's not real, that she has no power over me, that I'm stronger than everyone realizes. But I can't. Not with my bracelet God knows where and Vivian right there and fear shooting like a bottle rocket up my spine.

So I run.

I'm not going crazy.

Away from the latrine.

I'm not going crazy.

Back to Dogwood.

I'm not.

My run is really an uneasy combination of swaying, tripping, and lurching that ultimately lands me at the cabin door. I fling it open, push inside, slam it shut. I collapse against the door, breathless and frightened and sad about the lost bracelet.

Sasha, Krystal, and Miranda sit on the floor, hunched over a book. My presence makes them look up in surprise. Miranda slams the book shut and tries to slide it under my bunk. But she's too slow, the gesture too obvious. I can clearly see what they were reading.

Vivian's diary.

"So all of you know," I say, still out of breath from my awkward trip.

It's not a question. The guilt burning in their eyes already tells me that they do.

"We googled you," Sasha says, a finger pointed Miranda's way. "It was her idea."

"I'm sorry," Miranda says. "You were acting so weird the past two days that we had to find out why."

"It's okay. Really, it's fine. I'm glad you know. You deserve to be aware of what happened in this cabin."

Exhaustion, whiskey, and sadness get the best of me, and I find myself listing to the side. Like a sailor on a rocking ship. Or my mother on Christmas Eve. I try to right myself, fail, plop down onto the lid of my hickory trunk.

"You probably have questions," I say.

Sasha's the first to ask one. Of course. Insatiably curious Sasha.

"What were they like?"

"Like the three of you but also very, very different."

"Where did they go?" Krystal asks.

"I don't know," I say.

Yet I would have gone with them. It's one of the few things I'm certain of. That, despite Vivian's hurtful betrayal with Theo, I still wanted her approval. And had she asked, I would have willingly followed, marching behind them into the darkness.

"But that's not the whole story," I say. "There's more. Things no one but me knows."

Seeing Vivian again has messed with my emotions. I want to laugh. I want to cry. I want to confess. Instead, I say, "Two Truths and a Lie. Let's play."

I slip off the trunk, joining them. It's a sudden, ungainly slump that makes the three of them recoil when I hit the floor. Even Miranda, who I thought was the bravest of the group.

"One: I have been to the Louvre. Twice. Two: Fifteen years ago, three of my friends left this cabin. No one saw them again."

I pause, hesitant to speak aloud something I've avoided saying for fifteen years. But no matter how much I want to stay silent, guilt compels me to keep talking.

"Three: Right before they left, I said something. Something I regret. Something that's haunted me ever since."

I hope you never come back.

The memory of that moment arrives without warning. It feels like a sharpened sword swooping toward me, slicing me open, exposing my cold heart.

"I told them I hoped they'd never come back," I say. "Right to Vivian's face. It was the last thing I ever said to her."

Tears burn the corners of my eyes—grief and guilt bubbling out of me.

"That doesn't mean what happened to them is your fault," Miranda says. "Those were words, Emma. You didn't make them disappear."

Sasha nods. "It's not your fault they didn't come back."

I stare at the floor, avoiding their sympathy. I don't deserve it. Not when there's still more to confess. Still more I've kept hidden from everyone.

"But they **did** come back." A tear slips out, rolls down my cheek. "Later that night. Only they couldn't get back into the cabin."

"Why?" Miranda asks.

I know I should stop. I've already said too much. But there's no turning back now. I'm tired of omitting things, which is practically the same as lying. I want to speak the truth. Maybe that's what might finally heal me.

"Because I locked the door behind them."

Miranda sucks in air. A muted gasp. Trying to hide her shock.

"You locked them out?"

I nod, another tear falling. It traces the path of the first, deviating only when it reaches my mouth. I taste it on my lips. Salty. Bitter.

"And I refused to let them back in. Even after they knocked. And jiggled the doorknob. And pleaded with me to let them in."

I look to the cabin door, picturing it the way it appeared that night. Pale in the darkness, dusted with moonlight, doorknob rattling back and forth. I hear the sharp rapping on the wood and someone calling my name on the other side.

Emma.

It was Vivian.

Come on, Em. Let me in.

I shrank into my bottom bunk, squeezing myself into the corner. I pulled the covers to my chin and huddled beneath them, trying to will away the sound coming from the other side of the door.

Emma, please.

I slid under the covers, lost in the darkness within, staying there until the knocking, the rattling, Vivian herself faded away.

"I could have let them in," I say. "I should have. But I didn't. Because I was young and stupid and angry. But if I **had** let them in, all three would still be here. And I wouldn't be carrying around this awful feeling that I killed them."

Two more tears follow the designated path. I wipe them away with the back of my hand.

"I paint them. All three of them. Every painting I've finished for years has included them. Only no one knows they're there. I cover them up. And I don't know why. I can't help myself. But I can't keep on painting them. It's crazy. **I'm** crazy. But now I think that if I can somehow find out what happened, then maybe I'll be able to stop paint-ing them. Which means that maybe I've finally forgiven myself."

I stop talking and look up from the floor. Sasha, Krystal, and Miranda stare at me, silent and mo-tionless. They look at me the same way children eye a stranger. Curious and skittish.

"I'm sorry," I say. "I'm not feeling well. I'll be fine in the morning."

I stand, woozy, swaying like a storm-battered tree. The girls slide out of my way and start to climb to their feet. I gesture for them to stay where they are.

"Don't let me spoil your night. Keep playing."

They do. Because they're nervous. Because they're scared. Because they don't know what else to do but to keep playing, appeasing me, wait-ing until I pass out, which likely will be any sec-ond now.

"One more round," Miranda says, her decisive-ness not quite masking her fear. "I'll go."

I close my eyes before crawling into bed. Rather, they close on their own, no matter how much I try to keep them open. I'm too tired. Too drunk. Too emotionally flattened by my confession. Tempo-rarily blinded, I feel my way into bed, reaching for the mattress, my pillow, the wall. I curl into a ball, my knees to my chest, back turned to the girls. My standard humiliation position.

"One: I once got sick after riding the Cyclone

at Coney Island." Miranda's voice slows, cautious, pausing to hear if I'm asleep yet. "Two: I read about a hundred books a year."

Sleep overwhelms me immediately. It's like a trapdoor, opening up beneath me. I willingly fall, plummeting into unconsciousness. As I tumble, I can still hear Miranda, her voice faint and fading fast.

"Three: I'm worried about Emma."

This is how it continues.
 You scream again.
 And again.
You do it even though you don't know why. Yet you also sort of do. Because no matter how much you try, you can't rid your mind of those too-terrible-to-think thoughts. Deep down, you know that one of them is true.

So you scream one more time, waking the rest of the camp. Even standing in the lake, ten feet from shore, you can sense a wave of energy pulsing toward you. It's a sudden jolt. A collective surprise. A heron on the shore senses it and spreads its long, elegant wings. It takes flight, rising high, riding the sound of your screams.

The first person you see is Franny. She bursts onto the back deck of the Lodge. The screams have already tipped her off that something is wrong. One quick glance at you in the water confirms it. She flies down the wooden steps, the hem of her white nightgown fluttering.

Chet is next, all sleepy eyes and bedhead. He stays on the deck, unnerved, his hands gripping the railing. After that comes Theo, not even pausing, racing down the steps. You see that he's clad only in a pair of boxer shorts, the sight of all that exposed skin obscene under the circumstances. You look away, queasy.

Others have gathered along the shore, campers and counselors alike, standing motionless in the mist. All of them scared and startled and curious. That above everything else. Their curiosity comes at you like a frigid wind. You hate them just then. You hate their eagerness to learn something you already know, no matter how terrible it may be.

Becca Schoenfeld stands among them. You hate her most of all because she actually has the gall to chronicle what's happening. She elbows her way to the front of the crowd, her camera raised. When she clicks off a few shots, the noise of the shutter skips across the lake like a flat stone.

But it's only Franny who comes forward. She stands at the edge of the lake, her bare toes this close from the water.

"Emma?" she says. "What are you doing out here? Are you hurt?"

You don't answer. You're unsure how.

"Em?" It's Theo, whom you still can't bear to look at. "Come out of the water."

"Go back to the Lodge," Franny snaps at him. "I can handle this."

She enters the lake. Not wading like you did. She marches. Knees lifting. Arms pumping. Nightgown darkening at the hem as it sucks up water. She stops a few feet from you, her head cocked in concern. Her voice is low, strained but calm.

"Emma, what's the matter?"

"They're gone," you say.

"Who's gone?"

"The other girls in the cabin."

Franny swallows, sending a ripple down the graceful curve of her throat. "All of them?"

When you nod, the light in her green eyes dims.

That's when you realize it's serious.

Things move quickly after that. Everyone spreads out across the camp, going to places you've already looked. The fire pit. The latrine. The cabin, where Theo opens each hickory trunk cautiously, as if the girls could be inside them, waiting to spring out like a jack-in-the-box.

The hunt turns up nothing, which is no surprise to you. You know what's going on. You knew it the moment you woke up in that empty and silent cabin.

A search party is organized. Just a small one—an attempt by all to pretend the situation isn't as dire as everyone fears it truly is. You insist on tagging along, even though you're in no condition to be roaming the woods, calling out the names of girls who may or may not be missing. You march behind Theo, trying hard to keep up, ignoring how the chill of the lake water lingers on your skin. It makes you shiver, despite the fact that the temperature has inched past ninety degrees and that your skin is coated with a thin sheen of sweat. You search the woods that flank the camp. First one side, then the other. While marching through the forest, you picture Buchanan Harris doing the very same thing a hundred years earlier. Blazing a trail, armed with just a machete and willful optimism. It's a strange thought. Silly, too. Yet it takes your mind off your tired feet and sore limbs and the fact that a trio of dead girls might be waiting for you just around the next bend.

No girls appear, alive or dead. There's no trace of them. It's as if they had never existed at all. Like they were a figment of the camp's imagination. A mass hallucination.

You return to Camp Nightingale during lunch, with all the remaining campers in the mess hall, picking at plates of sad, soggy pizza slices. Everyone looks up as you hobble inside. Various emotions swirl in their eyes. Hope. Fear. Blame. It's that last one you feel the most as you make your way to Franny's table. It heats the back of your neck like a sunburn.

"Anything?" Franny asks.

Theo shakes his head. A few of the campers begin to weep, their sobs breaking out all around you, disrupting the otherwise quiet of the mess hall. It makes you hate them all over again. Most of these crying girls barely knew the missing. You're the one who should be crying. But you look to Franny for guidance. She's not weeping. She's calm in the face of this unfathomable storm.

"I think it's time I call the police," she says.

A half hour later, you're still in the mess hall. It's been cleared of crying campers and their equally moist-eyed counselors. The kitchen staff has been shuffled outside. The whole place is empty except for you and a state police detective whose name you've already forgotten.

"Now then," he says, "how many girls seem to be missing?"

You notice his choice of words. Seem to be missing. Like you're making the whole thing up. Like he doesn't believe you.

"I thought Franny already told you everything."

"I'd like to hear it from you." He leans back in his chair, crosses his arms. "If you don't mind."

"Three," you say.

"All staying in the same cabin?"

"Yes."

"And you're sure you've looked everywhere for them?"

"Not the whole property," you say. "But the entire camp's been searched."

The detective sighs, reaches into his suit coat, and removes a pen and a notebook. "Let's start by telling me their names."

You hesitate, because to identify them is to make it real. Once you say their names, they'll be known to the world as missing persons. And you don't think you're ready for that. You bite the inside of your cheek, stalling. But the detective stares you down, getting peeved, his face pinkening ever so slightly.

"Miss Davis?"

"Right," you say. "Their names."

You take a deep breath. Your heart does several sad, little flips in your chest.

"Their names are Sasha, Krystal, and Miranda."

PART TWO

AND A LIE

27

The detective writes their names in his notebook, thus making the situation official. My heart completes another sorrowful flip-flop in my chest.

"Let's go back to the beginning," he says. "Back to the moment you realized the girls were missing from the cabin."

An awkward moment passes in which I'm not sure who he's talking about. **Which ones?** I almost say.

I can't help but feel like that thirteen-year-old cowering in the presence of a different detective asking me about a different set of missing girls. Everything is so similar. The empty mess hall and the slightly impatient lawman and my simmering panic. Other than my age and the new cast of missing persons, the only major difference is the mug of coffee sitting on the table in front of me. The first time around it was orange juice.

This isn't happening.

That's what I tell myself as I sit rigid in my plastic cafeteria chair, waiting for the mess hall walls and floor to melt away. Like a dream. A painting splashed with turpentine. And when it all slides away, I'll be somewhere else. Back in my loft, maybe. Awakening in front of an empty canvas.

But the walls and floor remain. As does the detective, whose name suddenly comes to me. Flynn. Detective Nathan Flynn.

This isn't happening. Not again.

Three girls go missing from the very same cabin at the very same camp where three other girls disappeared fifteen years earlier? The odds of that happening are astronomical. I'm sure Sasha, that tiny well of knowledge, would have a percentage at the ready.

Still, I can't believe it. Even as the floor and walls stubbornly refuse to evaporate and Detective Flynn keeps sitting there and I examine my hands to make sure they're the hands of a woman and not a thirteen-year-old girl.

This isn't happening.
I'm not going crazy.

"Miss Davis, I need you to focus, okay?" Flynn's voice slices through my thoughts. "I understand your shock. I really do. But every minute you spend not answering these questions means another minute goes by that those girls are still out there."

It's enough to shake off my lingering disbelief. At least for the moment. I look at him, fighting back tears, and say, "What was the question again?"

"When did you realize the girls were missing?"

"When I woke up."

"What time was this?"

I think back to the moment I awoke in the cabin. It was only hours ago yet feels like a lifetime.

"A little past five."

"You always such an early riser?"

"Not usually," I say. "But I am here."

Flynn makes a note of this. I'm not sure why.

"So you woke up and saw they were gone," he says. "Then what?"

"I went to look for them."

"Where?"

"All over the camp." I take a sip of the coffee. It's lukewarm, slightly bitter. "Latrine. Mess hall. Arts and crafts building. Even other cabins."

"And there was no sign of them?"

"No," I say, my voice cracking. "Nothing."

Flynn flips to a new page in his notebook even though what I've told him amounts to only a few measly sentences.

"Why did you go to the lake?"

Confusion rolls over me again. Does he mean now? Fifteen years ago?

"I don't understand the question," I say.

"Mrs. Harris-White told me they found you standing in the lake this morning. After you realized the girls in your cabin were missing. Did you think they'd be there?"

I barely remember that moment. I recall seeing

the sun rise over the lake. That first blush of daylight. It drew me to it.

Flynn persists. "Did you have some reason to think the girls had gone swimming?"

"They can't swim. At least, I don't think they can."

I remember one of them telling me that. Krystal? Or was it Sasha? Now that I think about it, I don't recall seeing any of them actually go into the water.

"I just thought they might be there," I say. "Standing in the lake."

"The way **you** were standing in the lake?"

"I don't know why I did that."

The sound of my voice makes me cringe. I sound so weak, so confused. Pain nudges my temples, making it hard to think.

"Mrs. Harris-White also said you were screaming."

That I remember. In fact, I can still hear my cries streaking across the water. I can still see that heron startled into flight.

"I was."

"Why?"

"Because I was scared," I say.

"Scared?"

"Wouldn't you be? If you woke up and everyone else in your cabin was gone?"

"I'd be worried," Flynn says. "I don't think I'd scream."

"Well, I did."

Because I knew what was going on. I was stupid enough to come back here, and now it's happening again.

Detective Flynn flips to a fresh page. "Is there a chance you screamed for another reason?"

"Such as?"

"I don't know. Maybe out of guilt."

I shift in my seat, discomfited by Flynn's tone. I detect slight mistrust, a sliver of suspicion.

"Guilt?" I say.

"You know, for losing them when they were under your care."

"I didn't **lose** them."

"But they **were** under your care, right? You were their camp counselor."

"Instructor," I say. "I told them when I first arrived that I was here to be a friend and not some authority figure."

"And were you?" Flynn says. "Friends, I mean."

"Yes."

"So you liked them?"

"Yes."

"And you had no issues with them? No disagreements or fights?"

"**No,**" I say, stressing the word. "I told you, I liked them."

Impatience nudges my ribs and shimmies down my legs. Why is he wasting all this time asking me questions when the girls are still out there, maybe hurt, definitely lost? Why doesn't anyone seem to be searching? I glance out the mess hall window and see a couple of police cruisers and a smattering of state troopers milling about outside.

"Is someone looking for them?" I ask. "There's going to be a search party, right?"

"There will be. We just need some more information from you."

"How much more?"

"Well, for starters, is there anything about the girls you think I should know? Something about them that might aid in the search?"

"Um, Krystal is spelled with a **K**," I say. "In case that helps."

"It certainly will."

Flynn doesn't elaborate, leaving me to picture each of them on the sides of milk cartons, a noble public service that's actually horrible when you think about it. Who wants to open their fridge and see the face of a missing child staring back at them?

"Anything else?" Flynn asks.

I close my eyes, rub my temples. My head is killing me.

"Let me think," I say. "Sasha. She's so smart. The downside is she knows so much it makes her a little scared. She's afraid of bears. And snakes."

It occurs to me that Sasha might be afraid right now, wherever she is. The others, too. It breaks my heart to think of them lost in the woods, terrified of their surroundings. I hope they're all together, so they can comfort one another. Please, God, let them be together.

I keep talking, overcome with the urge to tell the detective everything I know about the girls. "Miranda's the oldest. And the bravest. Her uncle is a cop, I think. Or maybe it was her dad. Although she lives with her grandmother. She never mentioned parents, come to think of it."

A realization pops into my head, coming at me like a thunderclap.

"She took her phone."

"Who did?"

"Miranda. I mean, I'm not certain she took it with her, but it wasn't among her things. Could that be used to find her?"

Flynn, who had been sagging in his chair while I prattled on, suddenly perks up. "Yes, it definitely could. All cell phones come with a GPS. Do you know the carrier?"

"I don't."

"I'll have someone contact her grandmother and ask," Flynn says. "Now let's talk about **why** you think the girls are gone."

"I don't know."

"There has to be a reason, don't you think? Like maybe they left because they were mad at you about something?"

"Nothing I can think of."

That's a lie. The latest in a long line of them.

Because there is something that would make them want to leave Dogwood.

Me.

The way I acted.

Drunk and crying and still touching my bare wrist, which now has a red streak on its side where my thumb kept rubbing the skin. I wasn't in my right mind last night, and it scared them. I saw it in their eyes.

"You think they ran away?" I ask.

"I'm saying that's the most logical reason. On average, more than two million youth run away each year. The vast majority are quickly located and returned home."

It sounds like another one of those statistics Sasha would have at the ready. But I don't believe for a second the three of them ran away. They gave no indication of unhappiness in their home lives.

"What if they didn't?" I say. "What would be another reason?"

"Foul play."

Flynn says it so quickly it makes me gasp. "Like kidnapping?"

"Is it a possibility? Yes. Is it likely? No. Less than one percent of all missing children are abducted by strangers."

"What if the kidnapper isn't a stranger?"

Flynn quickly flips to another page of his notebook, pen poised over paper. "Do you know of such a person?"

I do. Maybe.

"Has anyone talked to the kitchen staff?" I say. "The other day, I caught one of them staring at the campers on the beach. Not a good stare, either. It was creepy."

"Creepy?"

"Like he didn't think it was wrong to ogle a sixteen-year-old girl."

"So it was a male?"

I give a firm nod. "The tag on his apron said his name was Marvin. Two other kitchen workers were there. Women. They saw the whole thing."

"I'll be sure to ask around," Flynn says, writing down everything.

Seeing his pen scurry over the paper pleases me. It means I'm helping. Energized, I grab the coffee and take another bitter gulp.

"Let's talk about fifteen years ago," Flynn says. "I've been informed you were here when three other girls went missing. Is that correct?"

I stare at him, slightly uneasy. "I assume you already know that it is."

"You were staying in the same cabin, were you not?"

I detect more suspicion in his voice. Less subtle this time around.

"Yes," I say, buzzing with defensiveness. "None of them, by the way, were among the vast majority you claim to have been located and returned home."

"I'm aware of that."

"Then why are you asking me about it?"

Flynn pretends not to hear the question and plows ahead. "Back then, a fellow camper said she heard you and one of the girls who vanished fighting earlier that night."

Becca. Of course she told the police about what she'd heard. But I can't be too mad at her for that. I would have done the same thing if the roles had been reversed.

"It was an argument," I say weakly. "Not a fight."

"What was this argument about?"

"I honestly can't remember," I say, when of course I can. Me screaming at Vivian about Theo. Just a stupid girl fighting over a stupid boy.

"As you mentioned, none of those girls were seen or heard from again," Flynn says. "Why do you think that is?"

"I'm not an expert on disappearances."

"Yet you're hesitant to think this current set of missing girls ran away."

"Because I know them," I say. "They wouldn't do something like that."

"And what about the girls who went missing fifteen years ago? You knew them, too."

"I did."

"You knew them well enough to get angry at them."

"**One** of them."

I reach for the coffee and take another gulp, this time to steel myself.

"Maybe even violently angry."

Flynn catches me mid-sip. The coffee stops halfway down my throat, choking me. I let out a series of short, rough coughs. Coffee and spittle fling from my mouth.

"What are you implying?" I say between coughs.

"I'm just being thorough, Miss Davis."

"Maybe you should start searching for Miranda, Krystal, and Sasha instead. Be thorough with that."

I take another look out the window. The troopers are still there, milling outside the mess hall. It's as if they're guarding the place. Trying to keep someone out.

Or someone in.

A grim understanding settles over me. I now know the reason no one seems to be searching for the girls. Why Detective Flynn keeps focusing on my relationships with all of them. I should have seen it coming. I should have realized it the moment I woke up and Miranda, Sasha, and Krystal were gone.

I'm a suspect.

The **only** suspect.

"I didn't touch those girls. Then or now."

"You have to admit, it's an awfully big coincidence," Flynn says. "Fifteen years ago, all the girls from your cabin vanished in the night. All of them but you. Now here we are, with all the girls from your cabin once again vanishing in the night. All of them but you."

"I was thirteen the first time it happened. What kind of violence do you think a thirteen-year-old girl is capable of?"

"I have a daughter that age," Flynn says. "You'd be surprised."

"And what about now?" I say, wincing at both the hysterical pitch of my voice and the headache that accompanies it. "I'm an artist. I'm here to teach girls how to paint. I have absolutely no reason to hurt anyone."

In my head, a much cooler voice speaks to me. **Keep calm, Emma. Think clearly. Go over what you know.**

"I'm not the only one who was here back then," I say. "There are plenty of others."

Casey, for example, although I doubt she could swat a mosquito let alone hurt two sets of girls for no apparent reason. Then there's Becca, who definitely had a reason to hate Vivian, Natalie, and Allison.

I think about Theo. About seeing him with Vivian in the shower. About me pounding his chest. **Where are they? What did you do to them?**

But Theo had a sound alibi fifteen years ago. Franny is a different story entirely. Vivian's diary slides into my thoughts.

I'm close to finding out her dirty little secret.
I know the truth.
I'm scared.

"I think you should talk to Franny," I say.

"Why?"

"Vivian—she's one of the girls who vanished fifteen years ago—was poking around camp. Investigating."

"Investigating what?" Flynn asks, his impatience more pronounced.

God, I wish I knew. Although Vivian had left behind plenty of clues, there's nothing to pinpoint what, exactly, Franny might be hiding.

"Something Franny might have wanted to keep secret."

"Wait, are you saying you think Mrs. Harris-White did something to the girls in your cabin? Not just now, but also fifteen years ago?"

It sounds ridiculous. It **is** ridiculous. But it's the only reason I can think of to explain a situation that defies easy explanation. Everything I've learned since coming back to camp points to such a conclusion. Vivian was looking for something, possibly related to Peaceful Valley Asylum. She found it and enlisted the help of Natalie and Allison. All three promptly vanished. That can't be a coincidence. Now I'm back, looking for what Vivian was after, and Miranda, Krystal, and Sasha also go missing. Again, too strange to be a coincidence.

It's possible Vivian stumbled upon something Franny was desperate to keep hidden. Perhaps something worth killing over. Now maybe I'm on the verge of finding it out, too, and this is another warning from Franny.

Her story about the falcons shoots into my brain, breaking through all my other cluttered thoughts. Is that why she told it? To make me frightened enough to stop searching? Did she tell Vivian the same story after she'd been caught in the Lodge?

"It makes more sense than thinking I did it," I say.

"This is a good person you're talking about." Flynn puts down his notebook, pulls out a handkerchief, mops his brow. "Hell, she's the biggest taxpayer in this county. All this land? That's a lot of property taxes she pays each year. Yet she's never complained. Never tried to pay less. In fact, she gives just as much to charity. The main hospital in the county? Guess whose name is on the damn building?"

"All I know is that it wasn't me," I say. "It was never me."

"So you say. But no one knows what happened. We only have your word, which, if you'll excuse me, seems kind of suspect."

"Something strange is going on here."

The detective shoves the handkerchief back in his pocket and gives me an expectant look. "Would you care to elaborate?"

I'd been hoping it wouldn't reach this point. That Detective Flynn would accept my word as fact and start trying to find out what really happened to Miranda, Krystal, and Sasha. But now there's no choice. I have to tell him everything. Because maybe everything that happened—the shower, the birds, the person at the window—wasn't directed at me. Maybe it was meant for one of the girls.

"Someone's been watching me all week," I say. "I was spied on in the shower. Someone put birds in the cabin."

"Birds?" Flynn says, once again reaching for his notebook.

"Crows. Three of them. One morning, I woke up and saw someone standing at the window. They'd vandalized the outside of the cabin."

"When was this?"

"Two days ago."

"What was the vandalism?"

"Someone had painted the door." I hesitate before saying the rest. "They wrote the word **liar**."

Flynn's brows arch. Exactly the reaction I'm expecting. "Interesting word choice. Any reason behind it?"

"Yes," I say, annoyed. "Maybe to preemptively make sure no one believes me."

"Or maybe you did it to deflect suspicion from yourself."

"You think I **planned** to abduct those girls?"

"That makes about as much sense as everything else you've told me," Flynn says.

My headache flares—a fire at my temples.

This isn't happening.

I'm not going crazy.

"Someone was watching us," I say. "Someone was **there**."

"It's hard to believe you without any proof," Flynn says. "And right now, there's nothing to back up your story."

Another realization swerves into my head. One I was too upset to conjure until just now. One that will prove to Flynn he's wrong about me.

"There is," I say. "A camera. Pointed right at the cabin door."

28

The cabin glows green on the monitor, thanks to its night-vision feature. It's an ugly green. A queasy shade made worse by the camera's position. Instead of a straight shot from the back of one cabin to the front of Dogwood, it's been angled downward into a bird's-eye view that induces vertigo.

"The camera is motion sensitive," Chet explains. "It starts recording only when movement is detected. It stops when whatever it's recording also stops moving. Each time the camera records something, a digital file is automatically saved. For instance, this is a paused shot from the night it was installed."

On-screen, the cabin door is ajar. The motion that triggered the camera. In that sliver of darkness, I can make out a foot and a green-tinted glimpse of leg.

Chet moves to a second monitor—one of three that sit side by side in the Lodge's basement. While most of the space is filled with tidily stacked boxes and cobwebbed furniture, just as Mindy had predicted on my arrival-day tour, one corner has been outfitted with unpainted drywall and a floor of white linoleum. This is where the monitors reside, sitting on a metal desk with two PC towers slid together like books on a shelf.

Chet occupies a creaky office chair in front of the desk. The rest of us—Theo, Franny, Detective Flynn, and myself—stand behind him.

"This all seems pretty elaborate for one camera at one cabin," Flynn says.

"It's just a test camera," Chet replies. "We're going to install more throughout the camp. For security reasons. At least, that was the plan."

Behind him, Franny flinches. Like the rest of us, she knows there won't be a camp left unless Krystal, Sasha, and Miranda are found by the end of the day. This could very well end her dream of one last glorious summer.

"The camera can also be set to a constant live feed. That's what this is." Chet points to the third monitor, a daytime view of Dogwood. "Usually the live feed is turned off because there's no one to constantly monitor it. I turned it on while we're all down here, just in case the girls return."

I stare at the screen, hoping against hope I'll see Sasha, Krystal, or Miranda come into view, returning from an extended hike, oblivious to all the worry they've caused. Instead, I see Casey pass by, leading a group of crying girls to their cabins. Mindy appears next, bringing up the rear. She gives the camera a fleeting glance as she passes.

"The recordings are stored here," Chet says, using a mouse to open a file folder located on the center monitor. Inside are dozens of digital files identified only by a series of numbers. "The file names correspond to the day, hour, minute, and second each recording was made. So this file— 0630044833—means it was recorded on June thirtieth, thirty-three seconds after four forty-eight a.m."

He clicks once, and the image frozen on the first monitor jerks to life. The door opens wider, and I see myself slip out of the cabin and walk awkwardly out of the camera's view. I recall that moment well. Heading to the latrine at the break of dawn armed with a full bladder and a swarm of memories.

"What were you doing up at that hour?" Flynn asks.

"I was going to the bathroom," I say, bristling. "I assume that's still legal."

"Are there files from last night?" Flynn asks Chet, who uses the mouse to scroll down and check the folders.

"Several."

Flynn turns to me. "You said you realized the girls were gone at about five, right?"

"Yes," I say. "And they were there when I went to sleep last night."

"What time was this?"

I shake my head, unable to remember. I was too dazed—by whiskey, by memories—to keep track of the time.

"There's one file from between midnight and four," Chet announces. "Then there are three between four thirty and five thirty this morning."

"Let's see them," Flynn says.

"This is from a little after one."

Chet clicks the first file, and Dogwood appears. At first, there's no movement at all, making me wonder what triggered the camera. But then something appears—a green-white blur just on the edge of the screen. A mother deer and two fawns step into frame, their eyes giving off a chartreuse glow as they carefully cross in front of Dogwood. Twenty seconds tick by as they make their way past the cabin. Once the second fawn exits the frame, its white tail flicking, the camera shuts off.

"That's it for those hours," Chet says. "This one is about five minutes before five."

He clicks, and the first monitor lights up again. It's the same view as before, minus the deer but with the addition of the cabin door slowly opening.

Miranda is the first to emerge. She pokes her head outside, looking in both directions, making sure the coast is clear. Then she tiptoes out of the cabin, wearing her camp polo and cargo shorts. A pale rectangle is clenched in her hand. Her phone.

She's soon followed by Sasha and Krystal, sticking close together. Krystal carries a flashlight and a rolled-up comic book stuffed into the back pocket of her cargo shorts. I can make out the edge of Captain America's shield emblazoned on the cover. Sasha carries a water bottle, which she drops when closing the cabin door. It rolls along the ground, out of frame. Sasha runs after it, disappearing for a second. When she returns, the three of them confer in front of the cabin door, oblivious to the camera's presence. Eventually they go right, heading toward the heart of camp, vanishing one by one.

First Miranda, then Krystal, and finally Sasha.

I make a note of the order in which they depart, just in case I'll need to paint them one day. I hate myself for thinking this way.

"This is five minutes later," Chet says once the screen goes dark and he opens the next file.

I don't need to look at the monitor to know what it shows. Me emerging from the cabin in bare feet and the T-shirt and boxer shorts I wore to bed the night before. I pause outside the door, rubbing my arms to ward off the chill. Then I walk away in the opposite direction of the girls, toward the latrine. Even though I know what to expect, the footage is a gut punch.

Five minutes. That's how little time had passed between the girls leaving the cabin and my realizing they were gone.

Five fucking minutes.

I question every thought I had and every move I made this morning. If only I had awakened earlier. If only I hadn't wasted so much time thinking of reasons for why they'd be gone. If only I had gone to the mess hall instead of the latrine.

In any of those scenarios, I might have spotted the girls retreating to wherever it was they went to. I might have been able to stop them.

Even worse is how guilty it makes me look. Stepping outside mere minutes after the girls departed. While it was a complete coincidence, it doesn't appear that way. It looks intentional, like I was waiting to follow them at a discreet distance. It doesn't matter that I went in the opposite direction. Because the next video—the final one from that highly trafficked predawn hour—shows me walking past Dogwood during my wander around the cabins. I stare at my image on the monitor, noticing the hard set of my jaw and the blankness in my eyes. I know it's worry, but to others it might look like anger as I unwittingly followed the same path the girls had taken.

"I was looking for them," I say, preempting any questions from the others. "It was right after I woke up and realized they were gone. I searched the latrine first, then looked around the cabins before heading to the other side of camp."

"You've already mentioned that," Detective Flynn says. "But, again, there's no way to prove that. All this video does is confirm that you left the cabin not long after the girls did. And now no one can find them."

"I didn't do anything to those girls!"

I look to Chet, to Theo, to Franny, silently begging them to back me up, even though there's no reason they should. I'm not surprised when, instead of coming to my defense, Franny says, "Normally, I wouldn't feel comfortable sharing this. Everyone has a right to privacy, especially regarding incidents in their past. But under these circumstances, I feel I must. Emma, please forgive me."

She offers a look that's half-apology, half-pity. I don't want either. So I look away as Franny says, "Years ago, Miss Davis was under psychiatric care for an undisclosed mental illness."

While she talks, I stare at the third monitor. The live feed from outside the cabin. Currently, the area is empty. No campers. No Mindy or Casey. Just the front door of Dogwood at that Hitchcockian angle.

"We discovered this during a background check," Franny continues. "Against the advice of our attorneys, we invited her here for the summer. We didn't think she was a threat to herself or the campers. Nonetheless, precautions were taken."

Flynn, proving himself to be nobody's fool, says, "Hence the camera."

"Yes," Franny says. "I just thought you should know. To show we're doing everything we can to help in your search. I don't mean to imply in any way whatsoever that I think Emma had something to do with this disappearance."

Yet that's exactly what she's doing. I keep my gaze fixed on the monitor, unwilling to look away because it would mean facing Franny again. And I'm not sure I can do that.

On the screen, a girl edges into view, her back straight, her steps precise. She knows the camera is there. At first, I think it's a camper, maybe sneaking out of a neighboring cabin to get another peek of the state troopers milling around the mess hall.

Then I see the blond hair, the white dress, the locket around her neck.

It's Vivian.

Right there on the monitor.

I gasp in shock—a ragged, watery sound.

Chet's the first to notice and says, "Emma? What's wrong?"

My hand trembles as I point to the monitor. Vivian is still there. She looks directly into the camera and gives a coy smile. As if she knows I'm watching. She even waves to me.

"You see that, right?"

"See what?" It's Theo this time, his brow creasing with doctor-like concern.

"Her," I say. "In front of Dogwood."

All of them turn to the monitor, crowding around it, blocking my view.

"There's nothing there," Theo says.

"Did you see one of the missing girls?" Flynn says.

"Vivian. I saw Vivian."

I push between them, regaining my view of the live feed. On the monitor, all I see is that same angled view of Dogwood. Vivian's no longer there. Nor is anyone else.

I tell myself, **This isn't happening.**

I tell myself, **I'm not going crazy.**

It's no use. Panic and fear have already overtaken me, turning my body numb. A fuzzy blackness encroaches on the edge of my vision, pulsing across my eyes until I see nothing at all. My arm jabs forward, reaching for something to grab on to. Someone catches it. Theo. Or maybe Detective Flynn.

But it's too late.

My arm slips from their grasp, and I fall, crashing onto the cellar floor and fainting dead away.

The sweatshirt sat on a table in the arts and crafts building, sleeves spread wide. It was the same way my mother laid out clothes she wanted me to wear. The whole ensemble revealed, enticing me to put it on. Only this shirt was different. Rather than wear it, the police wanted me to identify it.

"Do you recognize it?" asked a female state trooper with a warm smile and a matronly bosom.

I stared at the sweatshirt—white with **Princeton** spelled across the front in proud Tiger Orange—and nodded. "It's Vivian's."

"Are you sure?"

"Yes."

She had worn it to one of the campfires. I remembered because I had joked that it made her look like a marshmallow. She said it kept the mosquitoes away, fashion be damned.

The trooper shot a glance at a colleague on the other side of the table. He nodded and quickly folded the sweatshirt. Latex gloves covered his hands. I had no idea why.

"Did you take that out of Dogwood?" I said.

The female trooper ignored the question. "Was Vivian wearing that sweatshirt when you saw her leave the cabin?"

"No."

"Give it some more thought. Take your time."

"I don't need more time. She wasn't wearing it."

If I seemed irritable, it was justified. The girls had been missing for more than a day, and everyone was running out of hope. I felt it all throughout camp. It was like a leak in a tub of water, the optimism draining away drop by precious drop. During that time, the arts and crafts building had been taken over by the police, who used it to organize search parties, sign in volunteers, and, in my case, informally interrogate thirteen-year-old girls.

I had spent an hour there the night before, being grilled by a pair of detectives who took turns asking me questions. An exhausting back-and-forth, my neck sore from swiveling between them. I answered most of their questions. When the girls had left. What they were wearing. What Vivian said before departing the cabin. As for what I'd told her as she slipped outside and how I prevented them from getting back in, well, that remained unspoken.

The shame was too great. The guilt was even worse.

Now I was being asked a new round of questions, although the female trooper displayed far more patience than the detectives. In fact, she looked like she wanted to hug me to her oversize chest and tell me that everything would be okay.

"I believe you," she said.

"Where did you find that sweatshirt?"

"I'm not at liberty to say."

I looked to the other side of the room, where the folded sweatshirt was being passed to yet another trooper. He also wore gloves. The skin of his hands shone white beneath the latex as he placed the sweatshirt into a cardboard evidence box. Dread flooded my heart.

"Did any of the girls have secrets they might have shared with you but not with others?" the trooper said.

"I don't know."

"But they did have secrets?"

"It's kind of hard to call something a secret if I don't know who else they told."

My teenage bitchiness was intentional. An attempt to wipe that pitying look off the trooper's face. I didn't deserve her pity. Instead, it only made her lean in closer, acting like the cool guidance counselor at school who was always telling us to think of her as a friend and not as an authority figure.

"Most times teenage girls run away, they do so because they're meeting someone," she said. "A boyfriend. Or a lover. It's usually someone others don't approve of. A forbidden romance. Did any of the girls mention anything like that?"

I wasn't sure how much I should say, mostly because I didn't know what was going on.

"The girls ran away? Is that what you think?"

"We don't know, honey. Maybe. That's why we need your help. Because sometimes girls run away to meet a boy who ends up hurting them. We don't want your friends to get hurt. We just want to find them. So if you know anything—anything at all—I'd really appreciate it if you told me."

I thought of **The Lovely Bones**. The teenager found dead in a field. The creepy neighbor who killed her.

"Vivian **was** seeing someone," I said.

The trooper's eyes momentarily brightened before she settled back down, forcing herself to keep playing it cool.

"Did she happen to tell you who it was?"

"Do you think he might have done something to her?"

"We won't know until we talk to him."

I took that as a yes. Which meant they thought Vivian, Natalie, and Allison were more than lost. They thought they were dead. Murdered. Just three sets of lovely bones on the forest floor.

"Emma," the trooper said. "If you know his name, you need to tell us."

I opened my mouth. My heart thundered so hard I felt it in my teeth.

"It's Theo," I said. "Theodore Harris-White."

I didn't believe it, not even as I said it. Yet I

wanted to. I wanted to think Theo had something
to do with the girls' disappearance, that he was
capable of hurting them. Because he already **had**
hurt someone.

Me.

He shattered my heart without even realizing it.

This was my chance to hurt him back.

"Are you sure?" the trooper said.

I tried to convince myself it wasn't bitter jealousy making me do this. That it made sense Theo
would be involved. Once Vivian, Natalie, and Allison returned to the locked cabin, the first thing
they would have done was find a counselor. They
didn't because they had been out after hours, not
to mention drinking. Both offenses would have
gotten them kicked out of camp. So they had gone
to the one person of authority they could trust—
Theo. Now they were missing, likely presumed
dead. That couldn't be a coincidence.

At least that's the lie I told myself.

"I'm certain," I said.

A few minutes later, I was allowed to return to
Dogwood. The area outside the arts and crafts
building hummed with activity as I left. There
were cops and reporters and the bray of bloodhounds in the distance. Troopers had already
started searching the camp pickup. I spotted them
as I passed, peering into the open cab doors and
rifling through the glove compartment.

When I turned away, I saw a search party just

returning from a trek through the woods. Most of them were townies, come to help any way they could. But I spotted a few familiar faces in the crowd. The kitchen worker who had piled my plate with pancakes on the Fourth of July, which suddenly felt like weeks ago. The handyman who always seemed to be fixing something around camp.

Then there was Theo, looking haggard in jeans and a T-shirt darkened by sweat. His hair was a shambles. A smudge of dirt stained his cheek.

I flung myself toward him, not quite knowing what I intended to do until I was right there in front of him. I was both mad at Vivian and terrified for her, furious at Theo and in love with him. So my hands curled into fists. I pounded his chest.

"Where are they?" I cried. "What did you do to them?"

Theo didn't move, didn't flinch.

Further proof in my confused mind that he had already steeled himself for a beating from my tiny hands.

That, deep down, he knew he deserved it.

29

This isn't happening.
I'm not going crazy.

The words crash into my brain the moment I regain consciousness, making me sit up with a start. My head slams into something hard above me. Pain pulses along my hairline, joining another, previously unnoticed pain at the back of my head.

"Whoa," someone says. "Easy."

A moment of pure confusion passes before I realize where I am. Camp Nightingale. Dogwood. Ensconced in a bunk bed, the top of which I just introduced to my forehead. The person who spoke is Theo. He sits on my hickory trunk with Sasha's copy of **National Geographic**, passing the time until I wake up.

I rub my head, my palm alternating between the two points of pain. The one in the front is already fading. The one in the back is the opposite. It grows in intensity.

"You took quite a tumble in the cellar," Theo

says. "I broke some of your fall, but you still banged your head pretty bad."

I slide out of bed and stand, gripping Miranda's bunk in case I need support. My legs are rubbery but strong enough to keep me upright. Small traces of the dark fuzziness that engulfed me in the Lodge remain. I blink until they're gone.

"You need to rest," Theo says.

That's impossible at the moment. Not with him here. Not when my limbs tingle with anxiety, aching and restless. I look around the cabin and see everything is the same as it was this morning. Sasha's bed is still meticulously made. Krystal's teddy bear remains a lump beneath the blankets.

"They're still missing, aren't they?"

Theo confirms it with a solemn nod. My legs start to quiver, begging me to lie down again. I tighten my grip on the edge of Miranda's bunk and remain standing.

"Detective Flynn broke the news to their families. He asked if any of them have been contacted by one of the girls. No one has. Miranda's grandmother didn't even know she had a cell phone, so there's still no word on what carrier she uses."

"Did Flynn talk to the kitchen staff?"

"He did. All of them live in the next town over. They're all cafeteria staff at the middle school there. Just happy to have a job for the summer. They carpool together every morning before breakfast and every evening after dinner. No one stayed behind last night, and no one came in early this morning. Not even Marvin."

All that information I had given Flynn—all my attempts to help—ended up being for nothing. Disappointment swells in my chest, tight against my rib cage.

Theo sets the magazine aside and says, "Do you want to talk about what happened back at the Lodge?"

"Not really."

"You said you saw Vivian."

My mouth goes dry, making it hard to speak. My tongue feels too sticky and heavy to form words. A bottle of water sits next to Theo. He gives it to me, and I swallow all but a few drops.

"I did," I say after clearing my throat. "On the live feed of the cabin."

"I looked, Emma. No one was there."

"Oh, I know. It was . . ."

I'm unable to adequately describe it. A hallucination? My imagination?

"Stress," Theo says. "You're under a tremendous amount."

"But I've seen her before. When I was much younger. It's why I was sent away. I thought she was gone. But she's not. I keep seeing her. Here. Now."

Theo cocks his head, looking at me the same way I'm sure he looks at his patients when he has to give them bad news.

"I had a conversation with my mother," he says. "We both agree it was wrong to invite you back here, even if it was with the best intentions. That doesn't mean we think any of this is your fault. It's ours. We underestimated the effect being here would have on you."

"Are you telling me to leave camp?"

"Yes," Theo says. "I think it's for the best."

"But what about the girls?"

"There's a search party looking for them right now. They've split into two groups. One is taking the woods to the right of camp and another is doing the same thing on the left."

"I need to join it," I say, making a move toward the door on unsteady legs. "I want to help."

Theo blocks my path. "You're in no condition to go trampling through the woods."

"But I need to find them."

"They'll be found," Theo says as he grips my arms, holding me in place. "I promise. The plan is to add more searchers tomorrow, if necessary. Within twenty-four hours, every square foot of this property will have been thoroughly searched."

I don't remind him that a similar search did little good fifteen years ago. Every square foot of land was covered then, too. All it yielded was a sweatshirt.

"I'm staying," I insist. "I'm not leaving until they're found."

A rumble sounds in the distance—a deep thudding that echoes across the valley like thunder. A helicopter joining the search. The sound is familiar to me. I heard it a lot fifteen years ago. The cabin rattles as the chopper roars overhead, low in the sky, practically skimming the trees. Theo grimaces as it passes.

"My mother doesn't trust you, Em," he says, raising his voice so it can compete with the helicopter. "I'm not sure I do, either."

I get louder, too. "I swear to you, I didn't hurt those girls."

"How can you be so sure? You were so messed up last night that I doubt you'd remember it if you did."

The helicopter retreats from the area, zooming out over the lake. Its departure leaves the cabin draped in silence. Lingering in the newfound quiet are Theo's words—and the accusation coiled within them.

"What are you talking about?"

"Flynn talked to the other instructors," Theo says. "All of them. Casey said she saw you by the latrine last night. She said you seemed drunk. When we talked to Becca, she admitted the two of you shared a bottle of whiskey while the rest of us were at the campfire."

"I'm sorry," I say, my voice so incredibly meek I'm surprised Theo can even hear it.

"So you were drinking last night?"

I nod.

"Jesus, Emma. One of the campers could have seen you."

"I'm sorry," I say again. "It was stupid and wrong and completely unlike me. But it doesn't mean I did something to those girls. You saw the camera footage. You saw I went looking for them."

"Or followed them. There's no way of knowing with any certainty."

"There is," I tell him. "Because you know me. And you know I wouldn't hurt those girls."

He has no good reason to believe me. Not after all the lies I've told. One word from Theo to the police could thrust me into the same situation I had put him in fifteen years earlier. The fact that our roles are reversed isn't lost on me.

I tilt my head and stare into his brown eyes, willing him to look back. I want him to see me. Truly see me. If he does, maybe he'll recognize the girl I used to be. Not the damaged twenty-eight-year-old who is very likely losing her grip on sanity but the thirteen-year-old who adored him.

"Please believe me," I whisper.

A moment passes. A quivering period of time that lasts only a second but feels like minutes. During it, I can almost feel my fate hanging in the balance. Then Theo whispers back.

"I do."

I nod, overwhelmingly grateful. I resist the urge to cry with relief.

Then I kiss him.

It's a surprise to both of us. Just like the last time I kissed him, only more forceful. This time, it's not boldness that makes me do it. It's desperation. The girls' disappearance has me feeling so utterly helpless that I now crave the distraction I avoided the other day. I need something to momentarily take my mind off what's happening. I ache for it.

Theo stays completely still, not reacting as I continue to press my lips to his. But soon he's kissing me back, upping the intensity.

I press against him, my palms on his chest. Not hitting this time. Caressing. Theo's arms snake around me, holding me tight, pulling me even closer. I know the deal. I'm as much a distraction for him as he is for me. I don't care. Not when his lips are on my neck and his hand is sliding under my shirt.

More thudding sounds erupt from outside the window. Another helicopter approaching. Or maybe it's the same one, making another pass. It swoops directly over Dogwood, so loud I can't hear anything but the thrum of its rotors. The window rattles.

Caught in that noise, Theo lifts me, carries me to my bunk, lowering me into it. He takes off his shirt, revealing more scars. A dozen at least. They crisscross his skin from shoulder to navel, looking like claw marks. I think of his accident—twisted metal, shattered glass, shards breaking skin and glancing off bone.

I caused those scars.

Every single one.

Now Theo's on top of me, heavy and safe and warm. But I can't let this go any further, distraction be damned.

"Theo, stop."

He pulls away from me, confusion skidding through his eyes. "What's wrong?"

"I can't do this." I slide out from under him and move to the other side of the cabin, where I'm less likely to reach out and touch his scars, my fingers tracing the length of each one. "Not until I tell you something."

Although the helicopter has moved on, I can still hear it thudding over the lake. I wait until the sound subsides before saying, "I know, Theo. About you and Vivian."

"There was no me and Vivian."

"You don't need to lie about it. Not anymore."

"I'm not lying. What are you talking about?"

"I saw you, Theo. You and Vivian. In the shower. I saw, and it broke my heart."

"When was this?" Theo says.

"The night they vanished."

I don't need to say anything else. Theo understands the rest. Why I accused him. How that accusation has followed him since. He sits up and rubs his jaw, his fingers cutting through the salt-and-pepper stubble.

I had always thought having the truth exposed

would make me feel better. That relief would flood my body from my head to the tips of my toes. Instead, I only feel guilty. And petty. And unbearably sad.

"I'm so, so sorry," I say. "I was young and stupid and worried about the girls and heartbroken because of you. So when that state trooper asked me if any of them had a boyfriend no one knew about, I told her that you were secretly seeing Vivian."

"But I wasn't," he replies.

"Theo, I **saw** you."

"You saw **someone**. Just not me. Yes, Vivian flirted and made it clear she'd be up for it. But I was never interested."

I replay that moment in my mind. Hearing the moans muffled by the rush of the shower. Peering through the space between the planks. Seeing Vivian shoved against the wall, her hair running down her neck in wet tendrils, twisting like snakes. Theo behind her. Pushing into her. Face buried against her neck.

His face.

I never actually saw it.

I had just assumed it was Theo because I had seen him in the shower before.

"It had to be you," I say. "There's no one else it could be. You were the only man in the entire camp."

Even as the words emerge, I know I'm wrong. There was someone else here close to Theo's age.

Someone who went unnoticed, simply doing his job, hiding in plain sight.

"The groundskeeper," I say.

"Ben," Theo says with a huff of disgust. "And if he did something like that back then, who knows what he's been up to now."

30

"Tell me about the girls," Detective Flynn says. "The ones who are missing. Did you have any interactions with them?"

"I might have seen them. Don't remember if I did or not, but probably."

"Did you have any interactions with **any** of the girls in camp?"

"Not on purpose. Maybe if I needed to get somewhere and they were in my way, I'd say excuse me. Other than that, I keep to myself."

He looks up at us from a chair built for someone half his age, his gaze resting a moment on each of our faces. First me. Then Theo. And finally Detective Flynn.

We're all in the arts and crafts building, the mess hall having been taken over by the remaining campers and instructors for dinner. I spotted them glumly filing inside as Theo and I headed next door. A few of the girls still wept. Most wore stunned, blank expressions that were occasionally punctuated by disbelief. I saw it in their eyes when they lifted their faces to the sky as the search helicopter made another deafening pass over camp.

So we ended up here, in a former horse stable painted to resemble a storybook forest, lit by fluorescent bulbs that buzz overhead. I stand next to Theo, keeping several feet of space between us. I still don't entirely trust him. I'm sure he feels the same way about me. But for now, we're uncomfortable allies, united in our suspicion of a man whose full name I've only recently learned.

Ben Schumacher.

The groundskeeper. The man who had sex with Vivian. The same man who might know where Miranda, Krystal, and Sasha are. I let Flynn do the talking, choosing to stay silent even though all I want is to pummel Ben Schumacher until he tells me where they are and what he's done to them.

He certainly appears capable of doing harm. He's got a hard look about him. He's spent much of his life working outdoors, and it shows in the calluses on his hands and the sunburned streak on the bridge of his nose. He's big, too. There's a noticeable bulk hidden beneath his flannel shirt and white tee.

"Where were you at five this morning?" Detective Flynn asks him.

"Probably in the kitchen. About to get ready for work."

Flynn nods toward the gold wedding band on Ben's left hand. "Can your wife confirm that?"

"I hope so, seeing how she was in the kitchen with me. Although she's awfully groggy before that first cup of coffee."

Ben chuckles. The rest of us don't. He leans back in his chair and says, "Why are you asking me this stuff?"

"What's your job here?" Flynn says, ignoring the question.

"Groundskeeper. I told you that already."

"I know, but what specifically do you do?"

"Whatever needs doing. Mowing the lawn. Working on the buildings."

"So, general maintenance?"

"Yeah." Ben gives a half smirk at the vaguely genteel job description. "General maintenance."

"And how long have you worked for Camp Nightingale?"

"I don't. I work for the family. Sometimes that means doing some things for the camp. Sometimes it doesn't."

"Then how long have you worked for the Harris-Whites?"

"About fifteen years."

"Which means the summer Camp Nightingale closed was your first summer here?"

"It was," Ben says.

Flynn makes a note of it in the same notebook he jotted down all my useless information. "How did you get the job?"

"I was a year out of high school, picking up the

odd job here and there around town. Barely scraping by. So when I got wind that Mrs. Harris-White
was looking for a groundskeeper, I jumped at the
chance. Been here ever since."

For confirmation, Flynn turns to Theo, who
says, "It's true."

"Fifteen years is a long time to be working the
same job," Flynn tells Ben. "Do you like working
for the Harris-Whites?"

"It's decent work. Pays well. Puts a roof over my
family's head and food in their stomachs. I got no
complaints."

"What about the family? Do you like them?"

Ben looks to Theo, his expression unreadable.
"Like I said, no complaints."

"Back to your interactions with the girls in
camp," Flynn says. "Are you certain there wasn't
any contact with them? Maybe you had to do
some work in their cabin."

"He installed the camera outside Dogwood,"
Theo says.

Flynn writes that down in his notebook. "As you
know, Mr. Schumacher, that's the cabin where the
missing girls were staying. Did you happen to see
them when you were putting up the camera?"

"No."

"What about the oldest one? Miranda. I've been
told other camp workers noticed her."

"Not me," Ben says. "I keep my head down.
None of this camp stuff is my business."

"What about fifteen years ago? Were you the same way back then?"

"Yes."

Flynn makes a move to write down the answer in his notebook. But he pauses, his pen tip a millimeter from the page. "I'm giving you another shot at the answer. Just so I don't have to waste time writing down something that might be a lie."

"Why do you think I'm lying?"

"One of the girls who disappeared back then was named Vivian Hawthorne. You probably remember her."

"I remember that she was never found."

"I was told you might have had a relationship with Miss Hawthorne. Which would be the complete opposite of minding your own business. So is it true? Was there a relationship between the two of you?"

I expect a denial. Ben gives us all a defiant look as that half smirk lifts the corner of his lips. But then he says, "Yeah. Although it wasn't much of what you'd call a relationship."

"It was strictly sexual in nature?" Flynn says.

"That's right. A one-and-done kind of deal."

Ben's smirk grows, on the verge of a leer. Again, I resist the urge to punch him. But I can't stop myself from saying, "She was only sixteen. You know that, right?"

"And I was only nineteen," Ben says. "That age difference didn't seem like such a big deal. Besides, it wasn't illegal. I got three daughters of my own now. So I know damn well what the statutory rape laws are."

"But you knew it was a bad idea," Flynn tells him. "Otherwise you would have told someone about it after Miss Hawthorne and two other girls from her cabin went missing."

"Because I knew the cops would think I had something to do with it. That's what this is about, right? You're all standing there thinking I had something to do with what happened to those poor girls."

"Did you?"

Ben stands suddenly, sending the chair skidding across the floor behind him. Veins bulge at his temples, and his hands curl into fists, as though he's about to take a swing at Flynn. He definitely looks like he wants to.

"I'm a father now. I'd be going crazy if my girls were missing. Makes me sick to my stomach just thinking about it. You should be out there looking for them instead of asking me about some dumb shit I did fifteen years ago."

He stops, out of breath. His chest heaves, and his fists unclench. Resigned exhaustion settles over him as he retrieves his too-small chair and sits back down.

"Keep on asking your goddamn questions," he says. "I'll answer them. I've got nothing to hide."

"Then let's go back to Vivian Hawthorne," Flynn says. "How did it start?"

"I don't know. It just kind of happened."

"Did you instigate it?"

"Hell no," Ben says. "Like I said, I wasn't looking for trouble. I mean, I saw her around camp. It was hard not to notice her."

"Did you find her attractive?" Flynn asks.

"Sure. She was hot, and she knew it. But there was something else about her. A confidence. It made her stand out from the other girls. She was different."

"Different how?"

"Most of those girls were stuck-up. Snooty. They'd look right past me like I wasn't even there. Like I didn't exist. Vivian wasn't like that. The very first day of camp she came up to me and introduced herself. **I don't remember you from last year.** That's what she said. She asked me about my job, how long I'd been here. Just friendly. It felt nice having someone like her pay attention to me."

That sounds like the Vivian I knew. A master at seduction. It didn't matter if you were the camp groundskeeper or a thirteen-year-old girl. She knew exactly what kind of attention you needed before you even knew it yourself.

"We hung out a few times those first days of camp. During lunch, she'd come find me working and talk for a few minutes. By then, I knew what she wanted. She wasn't shy about it."

Flynn, who's been steadily writing all this down in his notebook, pauses long enough to say, "How many times did the two of you engage in intercourse?"

"Once."

"Do you remember the date?"

"Only because it was the Fourth of July," Ben says. "I was working late that day, trying to milk the overtime money Mrs. Harris-White was offering. All the girls were at the campfire, and I was getting ready to go home when Vivian showed up. She didn't say anything. She just came right up to me and kissed me. Then she walked away, looking over her shoulder to make sure I followed."

He gives no further details. Not that I need them. I already know the rest.

What I don't know is why.

"That Fourth of July was the night Miss Hawthorne and the others disappeared," Flynn says.

Ben nods. "I know. I don't need a reminder."

"What did you do after it was over?"

"Vivian left before me. I remember she was in a hurry to get out of there. She said people would start to realize she was gone. So she got dressed and left."

"And was that the last time you saw her?"

"Yes, sir, it was." Ben pauses to scratch the back of his neck, giving the question more thought. "Sort of."

"So you did see her again after that?"

"Not her," Ben clarified. "Something she left behind."

"I don't follow," Flynn says, speaking for all of us.

"I left the latrine not long after Vivian did. On the drive home, I realized my keys were missing. The ones I use for camp."

"What do they access?"

"Camp buildings," Ben says. "The Lodge. Mess hall. The toolshed and latrine."

"The cabins?" Flynn asks.

Ben offers us another partial smirk. "I bet you wish it was that easy, but no. Not the cabins."

Flynn again looks to Theo for confirmation. He gives a slight nod and says, "He's telling the truth."

"I thought they might have fallen out of my pocket in the latrine," Ben continues. "Or maybe somewhere else. When I got to work the next morning, Vivian and the two others had already disappeared. At the time, no one seemed too worried. They'd only been gone a couple of hours, and everyone assumed they'd come back eventually. So I went looking for the keys. I ended up finding them at the toolshed behind the Lodge. The door was open. The keys were still in the lock."

"And you think Miss Hawthorne left them there?"

"I do. I think she took them out of my pocket when we were in the latrine."

"What was kept in the toolshed?" Flynn says.

"Equipment, mostly. The lawn mower. Chains for tires in winter. That kind of thing."

"Why would she need to go to the toolshed?"

The question elicits a shrug from Ben. "Damned if I know."

But I do. Vivian went there to retrieve a shovel. The same one she used to dig a hole that would eventually conceal her diary.

"You should have told us," Theo says. "About all of it. But you didn't, and now my family can never trust you again."

Ben gives him a hard stare. In his eyes burns what can only be described as barely concealed disgust.

"Don't you dare judge me, **Theodore**," he says, spitting out the name like something that's left a bad taste in his mouth. "You think you're better than me? Just because some rich woman plucked you out of an orphanage? That just means you're lucky."

The color drains from Theo's face. I can't tell if it's because of shock or anger. He opens his mouth to reply but is cut off by a noise rising suddenly from outside. Someone shouting. The voice echoes off the water.

"I see something!"

Theo turns to me, panicked. "That's Chet."

We rush out of the arts and crafts building, Detective Flynn in the lead, surprisingly quick on his feet. At the mess hall, a bunch of girls are pushing out of the door, clutching one another. Several of them cry out in distress, even though no one knows what's going on. No one but Chet, who stands at the lake's edge, pointing to something in the water.

A canoe.

Unmoored. Adrift.

It bobs a hundred yards from shore at a sideways angle, making it clear no one is guiding it.

I race into the lake, marching high-kneed until the water reaches my thighs. I then fall forward, swimming now, taking quick, forceful strokes toward the errant canoe. Behind me, others do the same thing. Theo and Chet. Glimpses of them flash over my shoulder whenever I pause to take a breath.

I'm first to the canoe, followed soon after by Chet, then Theo. We each grip the edge of the boat with one hand and start the swim ashore with the other. It's an awkward, labored trip. My wet fingers keep slipping from the canoe's edge and our strokes are out of sync, making the boat jerk from side to side as we swim.

Once in shallow water, the three of us stand and drag the canoe to shore. A crowd has gathered by then. Detective Flynn and Ben Schumacher. Most of the campers, kept at bay by counselors. At the Lodge, Franny, Lottie, and Mindy watch from the back deck. I risk a glance inside the canoe, and my legs grow weak.

The boat is empty.

No oars. No life vests. Certainly no people.

The only thing inside is a pair of glasses, twisted like a wrung-out washcloth, one of the lenses spiderwebbed with cracks.

Flynn uses a handkerchief to lift it from the canoe. "Does anyone recognize these?"

I stare at the red frames, somehow still standing, even though the sight of them should have sent me tumbling again into unconsciousness. I even manage to nod.

"Sasha," I say, my voice weak. "They belong to Sasha."

31

Back in Dogwood, I lay in the bottom bunk, trying to keep it together. So far, I'm doing a shitty job. After the canoe was found, I went to the latrine and threw up. I then spent a half hour crying in the shower before changing into dry clothes. Now I hold Krystal's matted-fur teddy bear as Detective Flynn graces me with another disbelieving stare.

"That's an interesting thing you did back there," he says. "Swimming out to the canoe like that."

"You would have preferred I let it float away?"

Flynn remains standing in the center of the room. Some kind of power play, I assume. Letting me know that he's fully in charge here.

"I would have preferred for you to leave it alone and let the police retrieve it. It's evidence. Now it's been tainted by three additional people."

"Sorry," I say, only because it's what he obviously wants to hear.

"Maybe you are, maybe you aren't. Or maybe

you did it on purpose. Covering up fingerprints or trace evidence you'd previously left behind."

Flynn pauses, waiting for I don't know what. A confession? A vehement denial? Instead, I say, "That's ridiculous."

"Is it? Then please explain this."

He reaches into his pocket and pulls out a clear plastic bag. Inside is a curl of silver chain on which hang three pewter birds.

My charm bracelet.

"I know it's yours," Flynn says. "Three people confirmed they saw you wearing it."

"Where did you find it?"

"In the canoe."

I tighten my grip on Krystal's teddy bear to stave off a sudden onslaught of nausea. The cabin spins. I feel like I'm going to throw up again. I tell myself for the fiftieth time today that this isn't really happening.

But it is.

It has.

"Would you like to explain how it got there?" Flynn asks. "I know it wasn't on your wrist when you swam out to that canoe."

"I-I lost it." Shock makes it a struggle to utter even the simplest words. "Yesterday."

"Lost it," Flynn says. "That's convenient."

"The clasp broke." I pause, take a breath, try to think of a way to not sound insane. "I fixed it. With string. But it fell off at some point."

"You don't remember when?"

"I didn't notice. Not until later."

I stop talking. Nothing I say will make sense to him. It certainly doesn't make sense to me. The bracelet was there. Until it wasn't. I don't know when or where it went from being on my wrist to being lost.

"So how do you think it got into the canoe?" Flynn says.

"Maybe one of the girls found it and picked it up, intending to return it to me later."

It's a stretch. Even I can see that. But it's the most logical chain of events. Miranda saw me twisting the bracelet during yesterday's painting lesson. I can easily picture her spotting it on the ground, scooping it up, dropping it into her pocket. The only other possible explanation is that it was found by the same person responsible for the girls' disappearance.

"What if I'm being framed?"

It's less a fully formed thought than a desperate attempt to get Flynn on my side. Yet the more I think about it, the more it starts to make sense.

"That bracelet fell off yesterday, **before** the girls vanished. And now it's in the same canoe as Sasha's broken glasses. Talk about convenient. What if whoever took the girls put it there on purpose to make me look guilty?"

"I think you're doing a pretty good job of that all by yourself."

"I didn't touch those girls! How many times do I have to say it before you believe me?"

"I'd love to believe you," Detective Flynn says. "But it turns out you're a difficult woman to believe, Miss Davis. Not with all that talk about seeing people who weren't really there. Or your conspiracy theories. This morning, you told me Francesca Harris-White had something to do with it. But less than an hour ago, you were certain it was the groundskeeper."

"Maybe it was."

Flynn shakes his head. "We talked to his wife. She confirmed he was in the kitchen at five a.m., right where he said he was. And then there's all those things you said fifteen years ago about Theo Harris-White. Didn't you accuse him of hurting your friends back then?"

A sharp heat burns my cheeks.

"Yes," I say.

"I'm assuming you don't believe it now."

I look at the floor. "No."

"It would be interesting to know when you stopped believing he was guilty and started thinking he was innocent," Flynn says. "Because you never retracted that accusation. Officially, Mr. Harris-White is still a suspect in that disappearance. I guess you two now have something in common."

My face gets hotter with anger. Some of it's directed at Detective Flynn. The rest is reserved for me and how horribly I acted back then. Either way, I know I can't listen to Flynn rehash my bad behavior for a minute longer.

"Are you going to charge with me something?"

"Not yet," Flynn replies. "The girls haven't been found, dead or alive. And a bracelet isn't enough to charge you. At least not unless a lab analysis finds some of their DNA on it."

"Then get the hell out of this cabin until you do."

I don't regret saying it, even though I know it makes me look even guiltier. It occurs to me that some cops would even take it as an admission of guilt. Flynn, however, merely raises his hands in a don't-blame-me gesture and moves to the door.

"We're done, for now," he says. "But I'll be watching you, Miss Davis."

He won't be the only one. Between the camera outside the cabin and Vivian at my window, I've gotten used to being watched.

When Detective Flynn leaves, his exit lets in the sound of police boats out on the lake. They arrived shortly after the discovery of the canoe. Meanwhile, the helicopter is still going, rattling the cabin with each pass.

I can't remember if the helicopter fifteen years ago showed up the first day or the second. The boats and volunteer search party were the first. That I definitely remember. All those people wearing flimsy orange vests and grim expressions as they marched into the woods. All those boats criss-crossing the lake, giving up once Vivian's sweat-shirt was found in the forest. That's when the dogs were brought in, on the second day. Each allowed to sniff a piece of clothing plucked from the girls' trunks to absorb their scents. By then, Franny had already decided to close the camp. So as the dogs were barking their way around the lake, hysteri-cal campers were hustled onto buses or pulled into SUVs with dazed parents behind the wheels.

I wasn't so lucky. I had to spend another day here, for investigative purposes, I was told. An-other twenty-four hours spent huddled in this very bunk, feeling pretty much the same way I do now.

The helicopter has just passed once again when I hear a knock on the cabin door.

"Come in," I say, too spent with worry to open it myself.

A second later, Becca pokes her head into the cabin. A surprise, considering the tone of last night's conversation. At first, I think she's here to offer condolences. I turn away when she enters, just so I can avoid the half-pity, half-sorry look I'm certain she'll give me. My gaze drifts instead to the camera in her hands.

"If you're here to take more pictures, you can leave right now," I say.

"Listen, I know you're pissed I told that cop we got drunk last night. I'm sorry. I got freaked out by the whole situation and told the truth, not thinking it would make you look suspicious. If it's any consolation, it makes me look suspicious, too."

"As far as I know, all the girls in your cabin are present and accounted for."

"I'm trying to help you, Emma."

"I don't need your help."

"I think you do," Becca says. "You should hear what they're saying about you out there. Everyone thinks you did it. That you snapped and made those girls disappear the same way Viv, Natalie, and Allison vanished."

"Even you?"

Becca gives me a pointed nod. "Even me. No use lying at this point, right? But then I started examining some of the photos I took around camp this morning. Looking to see if I accidentally captured any clues about what might have happened."

"I don't need you playing detective for me," I say.

"It's better than the job you've been doing," she remarks. "Which, by the way, everyone also knows about. You haven't exactly been subtle with your sneaking around camp and asking questions. Casey even told me she saw you slip into the Lodge yesterday."

Of course Camp Nightingale is just as gossipy now as it was fifteen years ago. Maybe even more so. God knows what the counselors and campers have been saying about me. Probably that I'm obsessive and crazy and make bad choices. Guilty as charged.

"I wasn't sneaking," I say. "And I'm assuming you found something interesting or you wouldn't be here."

Becca sits on the floor next to my bunk and holds up the camera so I can see it. On the display screen is an image of me standing dumbly in Lake Midnight and Franny wading in after me. Once again, I'm reminded of how great a photographer Becca is. She captured the moment in all its awful clarity, right down to the water seeping into the hem of Franny's nightgown.

Theo's in the middle of the photo, standing in his boxers between the lake and the Lodge. The pale patchwork of scars on his chest pop in the morning light, visible to all. Yet I had missed them completely. I had other things on my mind.

Beyond Theo is the Lodge itself, its back deck occupied by Chet and Mindy. He's in track shorts and a T-shirt. She's in a surprisingly sensible cotton nightgown.

"Now here's one from the reverse angle," Becca says.

The next photo shows the full crowd of campers drawn to the water's edge by my screams. The girls clutch one another, fear still etching itself onto their sleep-pinkened faces.

"I counted them," Becca says. "Seventy-five

campers, counselors, and instructors. Out of a potential eighty."

I do the math. Three of the five people absent from the photo are Sasha, Miranda, and Krystal, for obvious reasons. I'm another, because at that moment I was being led by Franny from the chilly water of Lake Midnight. The fifth missing person is Becca, the person taking the photo.

"I'm not sure what you're getting at."

"Only one person in the entire camp didn't come to see what was going on," Becca replies. "Don't you think that's strange?"

I snatch the camera from her hands and bring the display screen closer to my face, trying to identify who might be missing. I recognize nearly all the girls, either from the painting lessons or just roaming around camp. I spot Roberta and Paige, caught in the middle of exchanging worried looks. I see Kim, Danica, and the other three counselors. Each of them huddle with the girls from their respective cabins. Behind them is Casey, identifiable by her red hair.

I click to the previous photo, seeing me and Franny in the lake, Theo on the grass, Chet and Mindy up at the Lodge.

The only person missing is Lottie.

"Now you see it?" Becca says.

"Are you sure she's not there?" I scan the photo again, looking in vain for any sign of Lottie behind Chet and Mindy. There isn't one.

"Positive. Which begs this question: Why?"

Nothing I can think of makes sense. My screams were loud enough to bring the entire camp to the lakeshore, which makes it impossible for Lottie not to have heard them. Yes, there's a chance her absence is completely innocuous. Maybe she's a heavy sleeper. Or she was in the shower, its spray drowning out the sound of my screams.

But then I think about my bracelet. It feels like it's still wrapped around my left wrist. A phantom sensation. The last time I remember being aware of its presence was when I was in the Lodge, searching the study.

With Lottie.

Maybe it fell off. Or maybe she took it while I was engrossed by all those old photographs of Camp Nightingale.

I consider Vivian's diary, which by this point has become a kind of Rosetta Stone for trying to decipher what was happening fifteen years ago. Vivian mentioned Lottie, but only in passing. Just that one sentence about how Lottie caught her in the Lodge study and then told Franny about it. I didn't give it much attention, mostly because I had Franny's dirty little secret distracting me.

But now I wonder if that brief mention has greater meaning, especially in light of my own encounter with Lottie in the study. She spoke at length about her family's decades of service with the Harris-White clan. That suggests an unusual amount of devotion, passed down through generations. Just how devoted of an employee could Lottie be?

Enough to take action if she knew Vivian was close to learning what Franny's dark secret could be? Then do it again after realizing I'm on the verge of doing the same thing, only this time as some twisted kind of warning?

"Maybe," I say, "Lottie wasn't there because she already knew what was happening."

FIFTEEN YEARS AGO

After lashing out at Theo, I spent the rest of the day weeping in my bottom bunk. I cried so hard that by the time night fell, my pillow was soaked with tears. The pillowcase, salty and damp, stuck to my cheek when I looked up as the cabin door opened. It was Lottie, solemnly bearing a tray of food from the mess hall. Pizza. Side salad. Bottle of Snapple.

"You need to eat something, honey," she said.

"I'm not hungry," I told her, when in truth I was famished. Pain gnawed at my gut, reminding me that I'd barely eaten since the girls left the cabin.

"Starving yourself won't help anyone," Lottie said as she placed the tray on my hickory trunk. "You need a good meal to be ready for when your friends return."

"Do you really think they're coming back?"

"Of course they will."

"Then I won't eat until they do."

Lottie gave me a patient smile. "I'll leave the tray here in case you change your mind."

Once she was gone, I approached the tray, sniffing at the food like a feral cat. Ignoring the salad, I went straight for the pizza. I managed two bites before the pain in my gut worsened. It was sharper than hunger, shooting from my stomach into my heart.

Guilt.

That I'd said that horrible thing to Vivian right before she left.

That I'd locked the door before they returned.

That all day I'd told myself I simply provided an answer to that state trooper's innocent question. But deep down I knew the score. By saying Theo's name, I had accused him of harming Vivian, Natalie, and Allison. All because he picked Vivian over me.

Not that such an outcome had ever really been in doubt. I was a scrawny, flat-chested nothing. Of course Theo chose her. And now I assumed he and everyone else in camp hated me. I couldn't blame them. I hated myself more.

Which is why I was surprised when Franny came to Dogwood later in the night.

She had spent the previous night there. Not wanting me to be alone, she crept in with a sleeping bag, some snacks, and a pile of board games. When it was time to sleep, Franny unrolled the sleeping bag on the floor next to my bunk. That's where she slept, lulling me to sleep by singing Beatles songs in a soft, gentle voice.

Now she was back, the bag of snacks and games

in one hand and her rolled-up sleeping bag in the other.

"I just got off the phone with your parents," she announced. "They'll be here tomorrow morning to take you home. So let's make your last night here a restful one."

I stared at her from my tear-stained pillow, confused. "You're staying here tonight, too?"

"Of course, my dear. It's not good to be here all by yourself."

She dropped the sleeping bag onto the floor and began to unroll it.

"You don't have to sleep on the floor again."

"Oh, but I do," Franny said. "We must keep the beds free for when your friends return any minute now."

I imagined Vivian, Natalie, and Allison flinging open the door and tramping inside, dirty and exhausted but very much alive. **We got lost,** Vivian would say. **Because Allison here doesn't know how to read a compass.** It was such a comforting thought that I glanced at the door, expecting them to do just that. When they didn't, I started to cry again, adding a few more drops to the pillowcase.

"Hush now," Franny said, swooping to my side. "No more tears for today, Emma."

"They've been gone so long."

"I know, but we mustn't lose hope. Ever."

She rubbed my back until I settled down, her gliding palm tender and soothing. I tried to recall if my own mother had ever done such a thing when I was sick or upset. I couldn't think of a single instance, which made me savor Franny's gentle touch all the more.

"Emma, I need to know something," she said, her voice on the edge of a whisper. "You don't really think Theo hurt your friends, do you?"

I said nothing in return. Fear kept me silent. I couldn't take back what I'd told the police. Not then. Yes, Theo was in a lot of trouble. But I also knew I'd be in trouble, too, if I admitted my accusation was a lie.

And that I'd locked Vivian, Natalie, and Allison out of the cabin.

And that we'd fought right before they left.

So many lies. Each one felt like a rock on my chest, holding me down, so heavy I could barely breath. I could either admit them and set myself free or add another one and hope I'd eventually get accustomed to the weight.

"Emma?" Franny said, this time with more insistence. "Do you?"

I remained silent.

"I see."

Franny removed her hand from my back, but not before I felt a tremor stirring in her fingers. They drummed along my spine a moment, then were gone. A few seconds later, Franny was gone, too. She left without saying another word. I spent the rest of the night alone, wide-awake in my lower bunk, wondering just what kind of monster I'd become.

In the morning, it was Lottie who knocked on Dogwood's door to tell me my parents had arrived to take me home. Since I couldn't sleep, I'd packed hours earlier, transferring the contents of my hickory trunk into my suitcase as dawn broke over the lake.

I carried the suitcase out of the cabin and into a camp that had become a ghost town. Silence hung over the empty cabins and darkened buildings— an eerie hush broken only by the sound of my parents' Volvo idling near the mess hall. My mother got out of the car and opened the trunk. She then flashed Lottie an embarrassed smile, as if I had been sent home from a sleepover after wetting my sleeping bag.

"Franny apologizes for not being able to say good-bye," Lottie told me, pretending that neither of us knew it was a lie. "She wishes you a safe trip home."

In the distance, the front door to the Lodge opened up and Theo stepped outside, flanked by two of the detectives who had quickly become a common sight around camp. The firm grip they kept on Theo's elbows made it clear this wasn't a voluntary exit. I stood dumbly by the car and watched as they walked him to the arts and crafts building, likely for another interrogation. Theo caught sight of me and gave me a pleading look, silently begging me to intervene.

It was my last chance to tell the truth.

Instead, I climbed into the Volvo's back seat and said, "Please, Dad. Just go."

As my father started to drive away, the Lodge door gaped open yet again. This time, Chet ran out, his face tear-stained, legs a blur. He sprinted to the arts and crafts building, calling out Theo's name. Lottie rushed to intercept him and dragged him back to the Lodge, waving to my father to leave before we saw anything else.

Yet I continued to watch, turning around in my seat so I could look out the back window. I kept on looking as Lottie, Chet, and the quiet remains of Camp Nightingale faded from view.

32

When Becca leaves, I remain curled up in my bunk, Krystal's bear in my arms, trying to think of what to do about Lottie. Tell someone else, obviously. But my options are few. Detective Flynn doesn't trust me. I don't trust Franny. And even Theo would have a hard time believing my word over the word of the woman who's been with his family for decades.

I stare out the window, weighing my options while watching the evening sky succumb to thick darkness. The search crew in the helicopter has started using a spotlight, sweeping it across the water. When it rumbles overhead every fifteen minutes or so, the light brightens the trees outside the cabin window.

I'm watching the play of the light in the leaves when there's another knock on the door. It opens a second later, revealing Mindy bearing a tray from the cafeteria.

"I brought dinner," she announces.

What sits on the tray definitely isn't cafeteria food. This is dinner straight from the Lodge. Filet mignon still swirling with steam and roasted potatoes seasoned with rosemary. Their scents fill the cabin, making it smell like Thanksgiving.

"I'm not hungry," I say, even though under normal circumstances, I'd already be devouring the steak. Especially considering how stress and shitty cafeteria food have conspired to keep me from consuming, well, almost anything since I arrived. But I can't even look at the food, let alone eat it. Anxiety has knotted my stomach so tight I worry it might never unravel.

"I also brought wine," Mindy says, holding up a bottle of pinot noir.

"That I'll take."

"I get half," Mindy says. "I'm telling you, it's been a day. The campers are terrified, and the rest of us are at our wit's end trying to keep them calm and occupied."

She sets the tray on the hickory trunk that was once Allison's and is now Sasha's. Maybe. Or maybe it doesn't belong to anyone anymore. It's like Krystal's teddy bear—temporarily ownerless.

From the way Mindy simply plucks the cork from the wine, I can tell the bottle had been opened back in the Lodge. Probably to prevent me from having access to a corkscrew. On the tray, I see that the fork and knife are plastic. When Mindy pours the wine, it's into plastic cups. It brings back memories of the mental hospital, where no sharp objects were allowed.

"Cheers," Mindy says as she hands me a cup and taps it with her own. "Drink up."

That I do, draining the entire cup before coming up for air and asking, "Why the special treatment?"

Mindy sits on the edge of Krystal's bed, facing me. "It was Franny's idea. She said you deserved something nice, considering all the stress you've been under. It's been a hard day for all of us, but you especially."

"I'm assuming there's an ulterior motive."

"I think she also thought it might be a good idea for us to share this wine and get comfortable with each other, seeing how I've been ordered to spend the night here."

"Why?" I ask.

"To keep an eye on you, I guess."

There's no need for her to elaborate. No one trusts me. Not when Sasha, Krystal, and Miranda remain missing. I'm still under suspicion until they're found. **If** they're found. Hence the flimsy knife and plastic cup, into which I pour more wine. Mindy watches as I fill it to the brim.

"The way I see it, we have two choices here," I say. "We can either ignore each other and sit in silence. Or we could chat."

"The second one," Mindy says. "I hate too much quiet."

It's exactly the answer I expected. Which is the reason I gave her the choice—to make it feel like it was her idea to gossip.

"How's the mood in the Lodge?" I ask. "Is everyone handling it well?"

"Of course not. They're worried sick. Especially Franny."

"What about Lottie?" I say. "She always struck me as a cool customer. I bet that's good in a time of crisis."

"I don't know. She seems just as worried as the rest of us."

"That doesn't surprise me. I imagine she must be pretty devoted to Franny after working for her all these years."

"You'd think," Mindy says. "But I also get the sense that Lottie considers it just a job, you know? She gets to Franny's penthouse in the morning and leaves in the evening like any employee would do. She gets sick days. She has vacation time. I don't think she's too happy about having to spend the summer here. Neither am I, but here I am, doing my best to impress Franny."

"And how's that working out for you?"

Mindy pours herself some more wine, filling her cup as high as I did. After taking a hearty sip, she says, "You don't like me very much, do you?"

"You're keeping me here under house arrest. So that would be a definite no."

"Even before this. When you first got to camp. It's okay to admit it."

I say nothing. Which, in its own way, is an answer.

"I knew it. I could tell," Mindy says. "I knew girls like you in college. So artsy and open-minded but so quick to judge people like me. Let me guess: you probably took one look at me and thought I was some spoiled sorority girl who screwed her way into the Harris-White family."

"Aren't you?"

"A sorority girl? Yes. And proud of it. Just like I'm proud of the fact that I was pretty enough and charming enough to catch the attention of someone like Chet Harris-White."

"I'll agree that you're pretty," I say, shedding any pretense of civility. Maybe it's the wine. Or the spirit of Vivian lingering in the cabin, encouraging bitchiness.

"For the record, Chet pursued me. And it took a lot of convincing. I had no interest in dating the spoiled rich kid."

"But aren't you spoiled and rich?"

"Far from it," Mindy says. "I grew up on a farm. Bet you didn't see that coming."

I had assumed she was born privileged. The daughter of a Southern attorney, perhaps, or a prominent physician, like Natalie was.

"It was a dairy farm," she tells me. "In middle-of-nowhere Pennsylvania. Every morning from kindergarten to graduation I was up before dawn, feeding and milking the cows. I hated every minute of it. But I knew I was smart, and I knew I was pretty. Two things women need most to get ahead in this world. I studied hard and socialized and tried my best to pretend that my hands didn't always stink of raw milk and cow manure. And it paid off. Class president. Homecoming queen. Valedictorian. When I got to Yale, the pretending continued, even after I started dating Chet."

Mindy leans back on the bed, swirling the wine in her plastic cup. She crosses her legs, getting comfortable. I think she might already be drunk. I envy her.

"I was so nervous the first time Chet took me to meet Franny. I thought she'd see right through me. Especially when I got out of the car and saw their name on that building. And then the ride in the elevator, all the way up to the top floor. Franny was waiting for us in the greenhouse. Have you seen it?"

"I have. It's impressive."

"It's **insane**," Mindy says. "But the nerves went away when I learned the truth."

She takes a gulp of wine, leaving me hanging.

"About what?"

"That they're not nearly as rich as they look. At least, not anymore. Franny sold the Harris years ago. All she owns now is the penthouse and Lake Midnight.

"That still sounds pretty rich to me."

"Oh, it is," Mindy says. "But now it's only a few million and not, like, a billion."

"How'd Franny lose so much money?"

"Because of this place." Even though Mindy looks around Dogwood's tight confines, I know she's referring to what lies beyond it. The camp. The lake. The woods. The girls. "Restoring a bad reputation can get expensive. For Franny that meant settlements to the families of those missing girls. Chet told me it was at least ten million each. I guess Franny threw it at them like it was nothing. She did the same thing to a whole bunch of charities, trying to get back in people's good graces. And don't even get me started on Theo."

"The accident," I say. "Chet mentioned it."

"That car he wrecked was chump change compared to what Franny had to spend to get Harvard to take him back. They weren't too keen on inviting an accused killer onto campus. No offense."

I nod, grudgingly respecting Mindy for giving as good as she gets. "None taken."

"Chet told me Franny had to pay for a new lab building before they'd even consider letting Theo return. I think that's around the same time she sold the Harris. In my opinion, she should have sold this place instead. Chet said he tried talking to her about selling the land around Lake Midnight, but she wouldn't even consider it. So I guess the sale will have to wait—"

Mindy cuts herself off before she can let slip that Franny is dying. Even though I already know about the cancer, I admire her discretion. It's nice to see there are some family secrets she's not willing to spill.

"Anyway, that's their money situation," she says. "Between you and me, I'm relieved. The thought of all that money scared the hell out of me. Don't get me wrong, there's still plenty. More than my family ever had. But it's less intimidating. The more money there is, the more I feel the need to pretend. Which means I'll keep worrying that my hands still smell like a dairy farm."

Mindy looks down at her hands, turning them over to inspect them in the light of the nightstand lantern.

"I'm sorry for judging you," I say.

"I'm used to it. Just don't tell Chet or Franny or anyone else. Please."

"I won't."

"Thank you. And for the record, I don't think you did anything to those girls. I've seen the way you act around them. You all liked one another. I could tell."

The mention of Miranda, Sasha, and Krystal sends another wave of worry crashing over me. To combat it, I gulp down more wine.

"I hope they're okay," I say. "I need them to be."

"I do, too." Mindy drains her cup, sets it on the nightstand, and crawls under Krystal's lumpy covers. "Otherwise the Harris-White name is going to be dragged through the mud again. And I've got a feeling that this time it's going to stick."

33

After the bottle of wine has been emptied and the steak and potatoes have long gone cold, Mindy falls asleep.

I don't.

Worry, fear, and the prospect of another night-time visit from Vivian keep me awake. Whenever I close my eyes, I see Sasha's mangled glasses and think of her alone somewhere, stumbling blindly, possibly bleeding. So I keep them open and clutch Krystal's teddy bear to my chest while listening to Mindy snore on the other side of the room. Every so often, the sound is drowned out by the helicopter taking another pass over the camp. Each time its spotlight sweeps past the cabin means another update on the status of the search.

The girls are still missing.

It's almost midnight when my phone springs to life in the darkness. Marc is calling, the ringtone loud and insistent in the quiet cabin.

Mindy's snoring abruptly stops. "Too loud," she says, still half-asleep.

I silence the phone and whisper, "Sorry. Go back to sleep."

The phone vibrates in my hand. Marc's sent a text.

Found something. CALL ME!

I wait until Mindy's snoring returns before sliding out of bed and tiptoeing to the door. I grab the doorknob, on the verge of twisting it open, when I realize that I can't go outside. Not with a camera aimed directly at the door and one of Detective Flynn's minions surely sitting in the Lodge's cellar, monitoring the live feed.

Rather than risk raising all kinds of red flags, I go to the window. Carefully, I take the lantern off the nightstand and place it on Miranda's bed, where I won't trip over it on my way back inside. I then reach across the nightstand and gingerly lift the window first, then its screen.

I shoot a glance Mindy's way, making sure she's still asleep before climbing atop the nightstand and swinging my legs out the window. I twist, the sill pressing into my stomach as I lower myself to the ground.

To avoid the camera outside Dogwood completely, I have to cut behind the other cabins on my way to the latrine. I move in a half crouch, trying not to be noticed by anyone inside the cabins or roaming about outside.

The only real threat of being spotted comes from the helicopter and its stupid spotlight, which passes overhead within a minute of my being outside. I throw myself against the wall of the nearest cabin, my back flattened against it, arms at my sides. The spotlight's beam sweeps past me, oblivious to my presence.

I don't move until the helicopter skims over the lake. Then I run, sprinting to the latrine, my phone sliding around in my pocket. Inside, I turn on the lights and check each bathroom stall and shower. Just like during my search for the girls this morning, it's empty. Unlike then, I'm relieved to be alone.

I make my way to one of the stalls, closing the door and locking it for extra privacy. Then I pull out my phone and call Marc. The connection is weak. When he answers, static stutters into his words.

"Billy and . . . found . . . thing."

I check the phone. There's one bar of signal. Not good at all. I stand atop the toilet seat, holding the phone toward the ceiling, hoping for a better signal. It now shows two bars, the second one wavering and unsteady. I stay on the toilet, my body tilted, bent elbow jutting toward the ceiling. It works. The static is gone.

"What did you find?"

"Not much," Marc tells me. "Billy says it's hard to research something like a private asylum. Especially one so small and remote. He ended up looking everywhere. Books. Newspapers. Historical records. He had a friend search the library's photo archives and made a few calls to the library at Syracuse. I'm going to email everything he found. Some of it couldn't be scanned because it was too old or in bad condition. But I wrote those down."

The sound of rustling paper bursts from the phone, high-pitched and screechy.

"Billy found a few mentions of a Mr. C. Cutler of Peaceful Valley in the ledger of Hardiman Brothers, a wig company on the Lower East Side. Do any of those names sound familiar?"

"Charles Cutler," I say. "He was the owner. He sold his patients' hair to wigmakers."

"That's Dickensian," Marc says. "And it would explain why the Hardiman brothers paid him fifty dollars on three different occasions."

"When was this?"

"Once in 1901. Twice in 1902."

"That lines up with what I saw in the book Vivian found at the library. There was a picture of the place from 1898."

"Did the book mention when it closed?" Marc asks.

"No. Why?"

"Because something strange happened after that." There's more rustling on Marc's end, followed by more static, which makes me worry the signal is again getting worse. "Billy found a newspaper article from 1904. It's about a man named Helmut Schmidt of Yonkers. Does that ring a bell?"

"Never heard of him."

"Well, Helmut was a German immigrant who spent ten years out west. When he returned to New York, he sought out his sister, Anya."

That name **is** familiar to me. There was a photograph of someone named Anya tucked into the box I found in the Lodge. I even remember her hair color. Flaxen.

"Helmut described her as 'often confused and prone to nervous exasperation,'" Marc says. "We both know what that means."

All too well. Anya suffered from a mental ailment that probably didn't even have a name at the time.

"It appears that while Helmut was gone, Anya's condition worsened until she was committed to Blackwell's Island. He looked for her there and was told she had been put into the care of Dr. Cutler and taken to—"

"Peaceful Valley," I say.

"Bingo. Which is why Helmut Schmidt then traveled upstate to Peaceful Valley to retrieve his sister. Only he couldn't find it, which is why he spoke to the press about it."

"Are you saying it didn't exist?"

"No," Marc says. "I'm saying it vanished."

That word again. Vanished. I've grown to hate the sound of it.

"How does an insane asylum just disappear?"

"No one knew. Or, more likely, no one cared," Marc says. "Especially because the place was in the middle of nowhere. And those who lived even remotely nearby wanted nothing to do with it. All they knew was that it was run by a doctor and his wife and that the land had been sold a year earlier."

"And that's it?"

"I guess so. Billy couldn't find any follow-up articles about Helmut Schmidt and his sister." I hear the clatter of keys, followed by a single, sharp click. "I just emailed the files."

My phone vibrates in my hand. An email alert.

"Got them," I say.

"I hope it helps." Darkness creeps into Marc's voice. The telltale sound of concern. "I'm worried about you, Em. Promise me you'll be careful."

"I will."

"Pinkie swear?"

"Yes," I say, smiling in spite of all my fear, exhaustion, and worry. "Pinkie swear."

I end the call and check my email. The first item Marc sent is scans of two pages from the same book I found in the library. One contains the paragraphs mentioning Peaceful Valley, minus Vivian's pencil mark. The other is the photograph of Charles Cutler cockily standing in front of his asylum.

The next few files are all text—pages from psychology books, psychiatric journals, a master's thesis that makes a cursory mention of Peaceful Valley in a section about the history of asylums and progressive treatments. I assume they all served as sources for one another, because the information is almost identical.

The final file Marc sent holds an assortment of images scanned from various archives. The first picture is the now-familiar one of Charles Cutler outside his domain, although the caption accompanying the photo identifies it only as Peaceful Valley, as if it had been a spa and not an asylum. The second photo is a shot of just the asylum itself—that Gothic main building with turret and weathervane, the utilitarian wing jutting out from its side.

But it's the third picture that makes my heart thrum like I've just chugged a pot of black coffee. Identified merely as the entrance to Peaceful Valley, it shows a low stone wall broken by a wrought-iron gate and ornate archway.

They're the same gate and arch I passed through the other day in Theo's truck.

The very same ones that now grace Camp Nightingale.

The blood freezes in my veins.

Peaceful Valley Asylum was here. Right on this very piece of land. Which explains why Helmut Schmidt couldn't find it. By the time he came looking for his sister, Buchanan Harris had already turned the area into Lake Midnight.

That, I realize, is the information Vivian was looking for. It's why she snuck into the Lodge and went to the library. It's why she was so worried about her diary getting into the wrong hands that she rowed across the lake to hide it.

And it's why she was so scared.

Because she learned that there's a ring of truth to the stories surrounding Lake Midnight. Only it wasn't a deaf village or a leper colony that got buried beneath the water.

It was an insane asylum.

34

Despite the late hour, Camp Nightingale still crawls with cops. They linger in the arts and crafts building, visible through the lit windows. More stand outside, chatting as they sip coffee, smoke cigarettes, wait for bad news to arrive. One trooper has a sleepy bloodhound at his feet. Both man and dog lift their heads as I hurry to the Lodge.

"You need something, sweetheart?" the trooper asks.

"Not from you," I say, tacking on a sarcastic **"sweetheart."**

At the Lodge, I pound on the red front door, not even trying to be discreet about my arrival. I want the whole fucking place to know I'm here. The pounding continues for a full minute before the door swings away from my fist, revealing Chet. A lock of hair droops over his bloodshot eyes. He pushes it away and says, "You shouldn't be out of your cabin, Emma."

"I don't care."

"Where's Mindy?"

"Asleep. Where's your mother?"

Franny's voice drifts to the door. "In here, dear. Do you need something?"

I push past Chet into the entrance hall and then the living room. Franny is there, cocooned in her Navajo blanket. The antique weapons on the wall behind her take on new, sinister meaning. The rifles, the knives, the lone spear.

"This is certainly a pleasant surprise," Franny says with faked hospitality. "I suppose you can't sleep, either. Not with all this unpleasantness."

"We need to talk," I say.

Chet joins us in the living room. He touches my shoulder, trying to steer me back to the door. Franny gestures for him to stop.

"About what?" she says.

"Peaceful Valley Asylum. I know it was on this land. Vivian knew it, too."

It's easy to see why she went looking for it. She'd heard the story about Lake Midnight, possibly from Casey. Like me, she probably considered it nothing more than a campfire tale. But then she found that old box by the water's edge, filled with scissors that rattled like glass. She did some digging. Searching the Lodge. Sneaking off to the library. Eventually she realized the campfire tale was partially true.

And she needed to expose it. I suspect she felt a

kinship with those women from the asylum, all of them likely drowned, just like her sister.

Keeping that secret must have made Vivian so lonely and scared. She hinted at it in her diary when referring to Natalie and Allison.

The less they know the better.

Vivian wasn't able to save them. Just like her, they had learned too much after finding her diary. But she had managed to keep me safe. I understand that now. Her mistreatment of me wasn't an act of cruelty but one of mercy. It was her way of trying to protect me from any danger her discovery created. To save me, she forced me to hate her.

It worked.

"The only people she told were Natalie and Allison," I say. "Then all three of them disappeared. I doubt that was a coincidence."

A dainty china cup and saucer sit in front of Franny, the tea inside steaming. When she reaches for them, the cup rattles against the saucer so violently that she sets it down without taking a sip. "I don't know what you want me to say."

"You can tell me what happened to that asylum. Something bad, right? And all those poor girls there, they suffered, too."

Franny tries to pull the blanket tighter around her, the noticeable tremor still in her hands. Veins pulse under her paper-white skin. She loses her grip, and the blanket drifts to her sides. Chet rushes in and pulls it back over her shoulders.

"That's enough, Emma," he barks. "You need to go back to your cabin."

I ignore him. "I know those women existed. I saw their pictures."

I march to the study, heading straight for the desk and its bottom drawer. I yank it open and see the familiar wooden box right where I had left it. I carry it into the living room and slam it down on the coffee table.

"These girls right here." I open the box and grab a handful of photos, holding them up so Franny and Chet see their haunted faces. "Charles Cutler made them grow their hair. Then he chopped it off and sold it. And then they vanished."

Franny's expression softens, turning from fear to something that resembles pity. "Oh, Emma. You poor thing. Now I know why you've been so distressed."

"Just tell me what happened to them!"

"Nothing," Franny says. "Nothing at all."

I study her face, looking for hints that she's lying. I can't find any.

"I don't understand," I say.

"I think perhaps I should explain."

It's Lottie who says it. She emerges from the kitchen wearing a silk robe over a nightgown. A mug of coffee rests in her hands.

"I think that might be best," Franny says.

Lottie sits down next to her and reaches for the wooden box. "It just occurred to me, Emma, that you might not know my given name."

"It's not Lottie?"

"Dear me, no," Lottie says. "That's just a nickname Franny gave me when I was a little girl. My real name is Charlotte. I was named after my great-grandfather. Charles Cutler."

I falter a moment, buzzing with confusion.

"His mother was insane," Lottie says. "My great-great-grandmother. Charles saw what madness did to her and decided to devote his life to helping others who suffered the same way. First at an asylum in New York City. A terrible place. The women forced to endure horrible conditions. They didn't get better. They only suffered more. So he got the idea to create Peaceful Valley on a large parcel of land owned by my great-grandmother's family. A small private retreat for a dozen women. For his patients, Charles chose the worst cases he observed in that filthy, overcrowded asylum. Madwomen too poor to afford proper care. Alone. No friends. No families. He took them in."

Lottie rifles through the open box, smiling at the photographs as if they were pictures of old friends. She pulls one out and looks at it. On the back, I see the words **Juliet Irish Red.**

"From the very beginning, it was a struggle.

Even though he and my great-grandmother were the only employees, the asylum required so much money. The patients needed food, clothing, medicine. To make ends meet, he came up with the idea to sell the patients' hair—with their permission, of course. That kept things afloat for another year or so, but Charles knew Peaceful Valley would eventually have to close. His noble experiment had failed."

She pulls out two more photos. **Lucille Tawny** and **Henrietta Golden**.

"But he was a smart man, Emma," Lottie says. "In that failure, he saw opportunity. He knew an old friend was looking to buy a large parcel of land for a private retreat. A wealthy lumberman named Buchanan Harris. My great-grandfather offered the land at a discounted price if he was given a position in Mr. Harris's company. That was the start of a relationship between our families that continues today."

"But what happened to Peaceful Valley?"

"It stayed open while my grandfather went about building the dam that would create Lake Midnight," Franny says.

"During that time, Charles Cutler found new situations for the women in his care," Lottie adds. "None of them returned to those brutal asylums in the city. My great-grandfather made sure of it. He was a good man, Emma. He cared deeply about those women. Which is why I still have their photographs. They're my family's most prized possession."

I sway slightly, shocked my legs are still able to support me. They've gone numb, just like the rest of me. I had been so focused on learning Franny's dark secret that I never stopped to consider that Vivian was wrong.

"So it had nothing to do with what happened to Vivian and the others?"

"Not a thing," Franny says.

"Then why did you keep it a secret?"

"We didn't," Lottie says. "It's no secret. Just ancient history, which has been warped over the years."

"We know the stories campers tell about Lake Midnight," Franny adds. "All that hokum about curses, drowned villagers, and ghosts. People always prefer drama over the truth. If Vivian had wanted to know more about it, all she needed to do was ask."

I nod, feeling suddenly humiliated. It's just as bad as when Vivian cut me down right before she disappeared. Almost worse. Once again, I've accused someone in the Harris-White family of doing a terrible deed.

"I'm sorry," I say, knowing that a simple apology isn't nearly adequate. "I'm going to go now."

"Emma, wait," Franny says. "Please stay. Have some tea until you feel better."

I edge out of the room, unable to accept any more kindness from her. In the entrance hall, I break into a run, fleeing out the front door without closing it behind me. I keep running. Past the cops outside the arts and crafts building. Past the cluster of dark and quiet cabins. All the way to the latrine, where I plan to hop into a shower stall with my clothes still on and pretend I'm not crying tears of shame.

I stop when I notice a girl standing just outside the latrine. Her stillness catches my attention. That and her white dress aglow in the moonlight.

Vivian.

She stands in the woods that encroach upon the camp, just a few feet from the line where the trees end and the grass begins. She says nothing. She only stares.

I'm not surprised to see her. Not after the day I've had. In fact, I've been expecting it. I don't even reach for the bracelet that's no longer there.

This meeting was inevitable.

Rather than speak, Vivian merely turns and walks deeper into the forest, the hem of her white dress scraping the underbrush.

I start walking, too. Not away from the woods but toward it. Pulled along against my will by Vivian's reemergence. I cross the threshold separating camp from forest. The point of no return. Under my feet, leaves crunch and sticks snap. A twig from a nearby tree, as slim and gnarled as a witch's finger, grasps a lock of my hair and gives it a yank. Pain pricks my scalp. Yet I keep walking, telling myself it's what I need to do. That it's perfectly normal.

"I'm not going crazy," I whisper. "I'm not going crazy."

Oh, but I am.

Of course I am.

35

I follow Vivian to the sculpture garden, where she sits in the same chair Franny occupied days earlier. The statues around us watch with their blank eyes.

"Long time, no see, Em," Vivian says as I cautiously step between two of the statues. "Miss me?"

I find my voice. It's small and meek and skitters like a mouse across the clearing.

"You're not real. You have no power over me."

Vivian leans back in her chair and crosses her legs, her hands primly folded on her knee. Such a strangely ladylike gesture, especially coming from her. "Then why are you here? I didn't ask you to follow me. You're still trailing after me like a lost puppy."

"Why did you come back?" I say. "I was doing fine without you. For years."

"Oh, you mean painting us then covering us up? Is that the **fine** you're talking about? If so, I hate to break it to you, girlfriend, but that's not fine. I mean, honestly, vanishing once should have been enough for you. But, no, you had to make us do it over and over."

"I don't do that anymore. I've stopped."

"You've **paused**," Vivian says. "There's a difference."

"That's why you're here, isn't it? Because I stopped painting you."

It's how I have kept her at bay all these years. Painting her. Covering her up. Doing it again. Then again. Now that I've vowed not to do it anymore, she's returned, demanding my attention.

"This has nothing to do with me," Vivian says. "It's all you, sweetheart."

"Then why am I only seeing you and not—"

"Natalie and Allison?" Vivian lets out a knowing chuckle. "Come on, Em. We both know you don't really care about them."

"That's not true."

"You barely knew them."

Vivian stands, and for a quick, heart-halting moment, I think she's going to reach out and grab me. Instead, she begins to wind her way around the statues, caressing them like lovers. Fingers trickling up arms. Palms gliding across throats.

"I knew them as well as I knew you," I tell her.

"Really? Did you ever have a conversation with either of them? One on one?"

I did. I know I did. But when I scan my memory, no such recollections appear.

"Now that I think about it, I'm not sure you even talked to them when I wasn't around," Vivian says. "At least not about something other than me."

She's right. It's true.

"That's not my fault," I say. "You made sure it was that way."

Vivian never wasn't around. She ruled the cabin the same way a queen bee ruled the hive. The rest of us were just drones, buzzing around her, catering to her needs, her whims, her interests.

"That's why you're not seeing Natalie and Allison right now," Vivian says. "I'm the puzzle you're still trying to figure out."

"Will you go away if I do?"

Vivian pauses before a sculpture of a woman carrying a jug on her shoulder, her toga slanted across her chest. "That depends. Do you want me to go away?"

Yes. And I hope you never come back.

I don't say it. I can't. Not that. So I think it. A mental whisper that floats across the clearing, wispy as fog. But Vivian hears it. I know by the way her lips curl upward in cruel amusement.

"Now **that** brings back old times," she says. "You certainly got your wish, didn't you?"

I want to run away, but guilt holds me in place. It's a numbing sensation. A flash freeze. By now, I'm used to it. I've been feeling it on and off for the past fifteen years.

"I'm sorry for saying that."

Vivian shrugs. "Sure. Whatever. It still doesn't change things between us."

"I want to make it right."

"Oh, I know. That's why you came back here, right? Trying to find out what happened. Snooping around just like I did. As a result, look what happened to your new best friends."

Her mention of the new girls catches me off guard. I spend a millisecond wondering just how she knows about them. Then it dawns on me.

She's not real.

She has no power over me.

I'm stronger than everyone realizes.

Strong enough to understand that Vivian isn't a ghost haunting me. Nor is she a hallucination. She's **me**. A fragment of my distressed brain trying to help me figure out what's happening.

Which is why I stare her down and say, "You know where they are, don't you? You know where I can find them."

"I can't tell you that."

"Why not?"

"Because I'm not real," Vivian says. "That's your motto, right? I have no power over you?"

"Just tell me."

Vivian moves on to another statue, hugging it from behind, her chin resting on its delicate shoulder. "Let's play a game, Emma. Two Truths and a

Lie. One: Everything you need to know is already in your possession."

"Just tell me where they are."

She shifts to the statue's other shoulder, her head coyly tilted. "Two: The question isn't where to find them but where to find **us**. As in me and Natalie and Allison."

"Vivian, please."

"Three," she says. "As for where we are, that's not my place to say. But I can tell you this: **If** you find us, maybe—just maybe—I'll go away and never come back."

She slips behind the statue, temporarily eclipsed. I wait for her to pop into view again on the other side. When a minute passes and she doesn't appear, I take a few weak steps toward the statue.

"Vivian?" I say. "Viv?"

There's no answer. Nor is there any sign of her presence.

I continue my approach, picking up speed on my way to the statue. When I reach it, I peer around its marble shoulder.

Nothing is there.

Vivian is gone.

Yet her parting words remain, hovering in the middle of the clearing like moonlight. Those three statements. Two true, one a lie.

I have no idea about the first two. Like much of what Vivian said while she was alive, it's hard to tell the difference between what's true and what's false.

As for her third statement, I hope it isn't a lie.

I want it to be the truth.

Every word of it.

36

I return to Dogwood the same way I left—
zigzagging around the cabins to avoid being spotted. The helicopter seems to have packed it in for
the night. So, too, have the search boats. When
I get a glimpse of the lake, I see no activity on
the water. It's just an empty black mirror reflecting starlight. But the camera is a different story. I
know it remains, ever watchful, which is why I slip
to the back of the cabin and hoist myself inside
through the open window.

Mindy's snores tell me she's still asleep. Good.
I get to avoid having to explain both where I've
been and where I plan on going next.

To find the girls.

Both sets of them.

Vivian's words—my words—haunt me as I
crawl down from the nightstand.

**The question isn't where to find them but
where to find us.**

Something Miranda said comes back to me. I
heard the words as I was free-falling into sleep.

I'm worried about Emma.

That worry might have led her to action. Brash, confident Miranda. Mystery lover and future detective. Like Vivian, leading another set of girls into the woods for answers.

Then there's Vivian's toying suggestion that I might finally be rid of her if I find out what happened to the three of them. Maybe she's right. Maybe the only way to free myself from the grip of guilt is to learn the truth.

I hope you never come back.

Christ, I hate myself for saying that, even though I had no way of knowing it would come true. Natalie and Allison were already outside when I uttered those words. Vivian was right in that regard—I really didn't talk to them very much. Something else I regret. I should have paid more attention to them. Treated them as individuals and not just part of Vivian's entourage. All the same, I'm grateful they never heard what I said to Vivian. That those weren't my parting words to all of them.

I tiptoe across the cabin, careful to avoid that one creaky floorboard, the memory of something else Vivian said fresh in my mind.

Everything you need to know is already in your possession.

I know what she's referring to.

The map.

It's why they came back to the cabin, only to discover the door locked. Vivian needed her hand-drawn map to help her find the spot where her diary was hidden. She still thought there was something sinister behind the lake's creation and Peaceful Valley's end. I suspect she was planning to use it to expose whatever she thought she had found out about Franny and the Harris family.

I quietly open my trunk and remove my flashlight. Then I reach inside and feel around, searching for the map.

It's not there.

The girls must have taken it with them, bolstering my theory that they set off to find their predecessors.

More hope. That I'm right. That I'm not too late.

As Mindy keeps on snoring, I take another trip out the window. Soon I'm rushing headlong through a patch of trees to the edge of the lake. At the water, I make a left, hurrying along the lakeshore to the dock and canoe racks. Atop the slope of lawn, the Lodge rises heavy and dark. Only one window is illuminated. Second floor. Overlooking Lake Midnight.

Five minutes later, I'm out on the lake in a canoe. I row in strong, fast strokes, hoping the helicopter and search boats don't return until I reach the other side. My phone sits in my lap, set to the compass app. I glance at it every few seconds, keeping myself on track, making sure I'm cutting across the lake in a straight line.

I know I'm near the far shore when I start to hear eerie scraping along the bottom of the canoe. Underwater tree branches, making their presence known. Flicking on the flashlight, I'm greeted by dozens of dead trees rising from the lake. They're a ghostly gray in the flashlight's beam. The same color as bones.

I wedge the flashlight between my neck and shoulder, tilting my head to keep it in place. Then I resume rowing, using the oars to push myself away from the submerged trees or, when a collision is unavoidable, blunt the impact. Soon I'm past the trees and close to the other side of the lake. The flashlight's beam skims the shore, brightening the tall pines there. A pair of deer at the water's edge freeze in the light before stomping away. Gray specks flutter within the beam itself. Insects, drawn to the light.

I steer the boat to the left and row parallel to the shore, flashlight aimed to the land on my right. The beam catches more trees, more bugs, the flap of an owl's wings, blurred white. Finally, it illuminates a wooden structure rotted beyond repair.

The gazebo.

I guide the canoe onto shore and hop out while it's still running aground. I shove my phone back into my pocket and aim the flashlight toward the woods. I breathe deeply, trying to focus, rewinding to that earlier trip and how we got from here to the **X** marking Vivian's diary. I can't remember how deep into the woods we traveled or how, exactly, we found our way there.

I sweep the flashlight's beam back and forth over the ground, looking for any footprints we might have left behind. All I see is hard dirt, dead leaves, pine needles dried to splinters. But then the beam catches something that glows dull-white. Stepping closer, I see splashes of color—vibrant yellows, blues, and reds.

It's a page from a comic book. Captain America, in all his patriotic heroism, fighting his way through several panels of action. A small rock rests atop the page, keeping it in place.

The girls were here.

Just recently.

The page's placement is no accident. It's their trail of bread crumbs, marking the way back to the lake and their canoe.

I step over the paper, tighten my grip around the flashlight, and, like the girls before me, vanish into the woods.

37

The forest at night isn't silent. Far from it. It's alive with noise as I move deeper through the woods. Crickets screech and frogs belch, competing with the calls of night birds rustling the pines. I fear that other sounds are being drowned out. The footfall in the underbrush. The cracking twig signaling someone is near. Although there's no reason to believe I was followed here, I can't dismiss the idea. I've been watched too much not to be on alert.

My flashlight remains aimed at the ground a few feet ahead of me. I sweep it back and forth, looking for another page ripped from Krystal's comic book. I spot one where the ground begins to slant upward. It, too, sits beneath a rock. As does another one placed fifty yards ahead.

I pass five more pages as the incline sharpens. Captain America, leading me higher. Another page waits where the land flattens out at the top of the incline. It shows Captain America deflecting bullets with his raised shield. The dialogue bubble by his head reads, **I refuse to give up.**

I pause long enough to swing the flashlight in a circle, studying my surroundings. The beam brightens the birches around me, making them glow white. To my right are patches of starlight. I'm now atop the ridge, mere yards from the cliff that drops away into the lake. I turn left, approaching the line of boulders that punctuate yet another steep rise.

Captain America is there as well, placed atop several boulders, held in place with small rocks. I scramble among them until I reach the massive rock. The monolith. I aim the flashlight up the hill, angling for a better view of the path ahead.

There's still no sign of the girls. Not even more Captain America. Just more boulders, more trees, more leaf-strewn earth pitched sharply upward.

The forest around me continues to hum. I close my eyes, trying to tune out the noise and really listen.

That's when I hear something—a dull thud that sounds once, twice.

"Girls?" I shout out, the echo of my voice booming back at me. "Is that you?"

The forest noise ceases, save for the frightened scatter of some spooked animal fleeing to my left. In that blessed moment of silence, I hear a muted reply.

"Emma?"

Miranda. I'm sure of it. And she sounds close. So wonderfully, tantalizingly close.

"It's me," I call back. "Where are you?"

"The hobbit house."

"We're trapped," someone else says. Krystal, I think.

Miranda adds one more desperate word: **"Hurry."**

I rush onward, my flashlight gripped in my hand. I leap over tree roots. I dodge boulders. In my haste, I trip over a downed branch and fly forward, landing on my hands and knees. I stay that way and crawl up the incline, my fingers clawing the earth, feet flicking to propel me higher.

I don't slow down, not even when the crumbling stone foundation comes into view. Instead, I go faster, climbing back to my feet and running toward the root cellar cut into the earth. At the door, someone has pushed the ancient slide bolt into place, locking the girls inside. A knee-high boulder has been rolled in front of it for good measure.

Another thump arrives from inside the root cellar. The door shimmies. "Are you here yet?" Miranda calls. "We need to get the fuck out of here."

"In a second!"

I rap on the door, announcing my presence, before giving the slide bolt a mighty shove. It rasps past the door itself, allowing Miranda to open it a crack before being stopped by the boulder. A thick, sickly odor drifts out. A mix of damp earth, sweat, and urine that makes my stomach roil. Miranda presses her face to the crack. I see one bloodshot eye, a red-rimmed nostril, her parted lips sucking in fresh air.

"Help us," she says with a gasp, giving the door another desperate rattle. "Why aren't you opening it?"

"It's still blocked," I say. "I'm working on it. How are Krystal and Sasha?"

"Awful. We all are. Now **please** let us out."

"One more minute. I promise."

I crouch, place my palms flat on the boulder, and give it a push. It's so heavy I can barely move it. I try again, this time gritting my teeth and grunting with exertion. The boulder doesn't budge.

Using the flashlight, I scan the ground for anything that can help. I grab a rounded rock that had chipped off the crumbled wall nearby. Then I spot a fat branch on the ground that's almost as long as I am. It looks sturdy enough to be used as a lever. I hope.

I shove one end of the branch as far under the boulder as it can go and place the rock under it a few feet away before grasping the other end of the branch and pushing downward. It does the trick, setting the rock rolling the tiniest bit. I drop the branch and run to the boulder, pushing again, continuing the momentum until it's past the door.

"All clear!"

The door flies open, and the girls burst out. Sweaty and dirt-smeared, they suck in fresh air, stretch their limbs, give dazed looks to the sky. Without her glasses, Sasha is forced to squint. Her nose is swollen and colored a brutal shade of purple. Rust-colored flecks run from her nose all the way to her neck. Dried blood.

"Is it really night?" she says with almost clinical detachment. Shock, with a dash of hunger and dehydration thrown in for good measure.

Rather than hug her, I run my hands up and down her arms, checking for injuries. I feel stupid for not bringing food. Or water. Or a damn first-aid kit. All I can do is use the hem of my T-shirt to wipe some of the blood from Sasha's face.

"How long were we in there?" Miranda says as she spreads out on the ground, her arms and legs akimbo, panting with relief. "My phone died before noon."

"Almost a full day."

Hearing that makes Krystal's legs buckle. She staggers a moment before plopping down next to Miranda. "Damn."

"Tell me what happened," I say. "From the moment you left the cabin."

"We came here to look for your friends," Krystal says. "It was Miranda's idea."

Miranda sits up, too spent to be ashamed. "I only wanted to help. You were so upset last night. I could tell you needed to know what happened. And since this is where you found that diary, I thought there might be more clues here."

"Why didn't you say anything?"

"Because we knew you wouldn't have let us row here by ourselves."

I finish wiping Sasha's face. The dried blood leaves a dark-red stain on my shirt. "You came here and then what?"

"Someone jumped us," Miranda says, fear peeking through her exhaustion. Tears cling to the corners of her eyes.

"Who?"

"None of us got a good look."

"Miranda and Krystal went inside," Sasha says, nodding toward the root cellar. "I didn't want to, so I stayed out here. But then someone came out of nowhere."

She croaks out a sob. It's followed by more words that tumble forth in a rush, that clinical tone now long gone. "They punched me and my glasses fell off and I couldn't see who it was and then they shoved me inside and slammed the door."

Someone followed them here, attacked, trapped them rather than outright killing them. It makes no sense.

Unless whoever did it wanted them alive.

Which means they might be coming back any minute now.

Fear zips through me. I yank my phone from my pocket to see if I can call the police. There's no signal. Which explains why Miranda couldn't do the same right after they were trapped.

"We need to go," I tell the girls. "Right now. I know you're tired, but do you think you can run?"

Miranda climbs to her feet and shoots me a worried look. "Why do we need to run?"

"Because you're still in danger. We all are."

A beam of light hits my face. A flashlight. Bright enough to both silence and blind me. I put my hand over my eyes, shielding them from the glare. Behind the flashlight, I can make out a silhouette. Tall. Masculine.

The glare falls away. My vision blurs, eyes adjusting. When they come back into focus, I see Theo, flashlight in hand, taking a step toward us.

"Emma?" he says. "What are you doing here?"

38

Seeing Theo here feels like a minor earthquake. The ground under my feet trembles. Only it's me who's really trembling. A seismic shifting in my body I'm powerless to control.

Because his presence can't be an accident.

He's here for a reason.

"What's going on?" he says.

"I'd ask you the same thing," I say, a catch in my throat. "But I think I already know."

He's come back for the girls.

He attacked them, locked them away, waited until the dead of night to return. A chain of events I suspect happened fifteen years ago with a different trio.

My accusation, as misguided as it was, might have been correct. Truth disguised as a lie.

I hate thinking this way. Of everyone in camp, he's the only one I truly hoped was innocent. But the suspicion refuses to leave, as uncontrollable as my quaking, exhausted body.

I edge in front of the girls, shielding them from

Theo and whatever he might try to do next. I slip a trembling hand through my flashlight's wrist strap, securing it. Although not much of a weapon, it'll do in a pinch. If it comes to that. I desperately hope it doesn't.

"Miranda," I say with as much calm as I can muster, "there's a canoe on shore in the same place we landed the other day. Take Sasha and Krystal there as fast you can. If Sasha has trouble, you might need to carry her. Do you think you can do that?"

"Why?" Miranda says. "What's going on?"

"Just answer the question. Yes or no?"

Miranda's reply is streaked with fear. "Yes."

"Good. When you get to the canoe, row across the lake. Don't wait for me. Not even a second. Just row as fast as you can back to camp."

Theo aims his flashlight at my face again. "Emma, maybe you should step away from the girls. Let me see if they're hurt."

I ignore him. "Miranda, do you understand?"

"Yes," she says again, more forceful this time, steeling herself for the sprint.

"Good. Now go. **Hurry!**"

That last word—and the desperate way I say it—gets the girls moving. Miranda bolts away, all but dragging Sasha behind her. Krystal follows, slower but just as determined.

Theo makes a move to stop them, but I lunge forward, flashlight raised, threatening to strike.

He freezes when I'm two feet away and drops his flashlight. He raises his hands, palms open. I don't lower my flashlight. I need to keep him like this. Just long enough to give the girls a head start.

"Don't you dare go after them," I warn.

"Emma, I don't know what's going on."

"Stop lying!" I shout. "You know exactly what's happening. What did you plan to do with those girls?"

Theo's eyes go wide. "Me? What were **you** going to do with them? I followed you here, Em. I watched from the Lodge as you got into that canoe and rowed across the lake."

It's another lie. It has to be.

"If you thought I was guilty, why didn't you tell the police?"

"Because," Theo says, "I wanted to be wrong."

As did I. All that guilt I'd felt about accusing him. All that shame and remorse. It was for nothing.

"I need to know why you did it," I say. "Both now and back then."

"I didn't—"

I lift the flashlight higher. Theo flinches.

"Hey, let's talk about this," he says. "Without the flashlight."

"I think you had the hots for Vivian," I tell him. "You wanted her, and she rejected you. You got mad. You made her disappear. Natalie and Allison, too."

"You're wrong, Emma. About everything."

Theo takes a step toward me. I stay put, trying not to show my fear. Yet my hand trembles, the flashlight's beam quivering skyward.

"Since you got away with it once, I guess you thought you could do it again. Only this time you tried to make me look guilty. My bracelet in the canoe was insurance."

"You're troubled, Emma," he says, carefully choosing his words, making sure not to offend me. "You need help. So how about you drop the flashlight and come with me. I won't hurt you. I promise."

Theo risks another step closer. This time, I take a step back.

"I'm done being lied to by you," I say.

"It's not a lie. I want to help you."

We repeat our steps. Forward for him, backward for me.

"You could have helped me fifteen years ago by admitting what you did."

If Theo had turned himself in, then maybe I wouldn't have felt so guilty about what happened.

Maybe I wouldn't have hallucinated the girls.

Maybe I would have been normal.

"Instead, I spent fifteen years blaming myself for what happened to them," I say. "And I blamed myself for causing you pain."

Another step for Theo.

"I don't blame you, Emma," he says. "This isn't your fault. You're sick."

Another step for me.

"Stop saying that!"

"But it's true, Em. You know it is."

Instead of one step forward, Theo takes two. I move backward, first shuffling then turning around and running. Theo chases after me, catching up within seconds. He grabs my arm and jerks me toward him. I cry out, the sound streaking through the dark woods. I hear its echo as I raise the flashlight and swing it against Theo's skull.

It's a weak blow. Just enough to shock him into letting me go.

I give him a shove, knocking him off-balance. Then I run again, this time in the opposite direction. Back the way I came. Toward the lake.

"Emma!" Theo shouts at my back. "Don't!"

I keep running. Heart pounding. Pulse loud in my ears. Trees and rocks seem to lurch at me from all sides. I dodge some, slam into others. But I don't stop. I can't.

Because Theo's also up and running. His footfalls echo through the woods behind me, outpacing my own. He'll catch up sooner rather than later. Outrunning him isn't an option.

I need to hide.

Something suddenly looms before me in the darkness.

The monolith.

I run to it, swerving right until I'm at its north-western edge. I shine my light over the rock wall, seeing the fissure that opens up a foot from the ground.

The cave Miranda had crawled into.

I drop to my hands and knees in front of it and shine the flashlight inside. I see rock walls, dirt floor, a dark recess that runs at least a few feet into the ground. A shimmer of cool air wafts out of it, and I let out an involuntary shiver.

Theo's voice rings out from somewhere close. **Too** close.

"Emma? I know you're here. Come on out."

I flick off my light, drop to my stomach, and back into the cave, worried I might not even fit. I do. Barely. There's roughly six inches of space above me and slightly less on each side.

The sky outside the cave brightens. Theo's flashlight. He's reached the rock.

I will myself not to breathe as I slide back even more. The cave floor feels uneven, like I'm on a slant, edging downhill.

A flower of light blooms on the ground near the mouth of the cave. I hear the crunch of Theo's footsteps, the sound of his labored breaths.

"Emma?" he says. "Are you here?"

I move back even farther, wondering how deep the cave goes, hoping it's far enough to escape the beam of Theo's flashlight if he aims it inside.

"Emma, please come out."

Theo's right outside the cave now. I see his shoes, his toes pointed in the opposite direction.

I continue to slide backward, faster now, praying he can't hear me. I feel water dripping down the cave walls. Mud starts to squish beneath me, gurgling up between my fingers.

I'm still sliding, although now it's not by choice. It's because of the mud and the tunnel's slant, which turns sharply steeper. I dig my knees and the heels of my palms into the mud, hoping they'll act as brakes. It only sends me slipping even more.

Soon I'm sliding fast, out of control, my chin leaving a groove in the mud. When I flick on the flashlight still around my wrist, all I see are gray walls, brown mud, the shockingly long path I've just traveled.

Then the ground below me vanishes, and I'm suddenly in midair.

Dropping.

Helpless and flailing.

My screams swallowed by their echoes ringing through the cave as I plummet into nothingness.

39

Water breaks my fall.

I drop right into it, caught by surprise, unable to close my mouth before plunging under. Liquid pours in, choking me as I keep falling, somersaulting in the depths, the flashlight's beam streaking through the water, revealing dirt, algae, a darting fish.

When I finally do touch bottom, it's a gentle bump and not the life-ending crash against hard stone I expected. Still, it's a shock to my nervous system. I push off from the bottom as water continues to tickle the back of my throat. I gag, coughing air that bubbles past my face. Then I'm at the surface, my head emerging and water unplugging from my nostrils. I cough a few times, spitting up water. Then I breathe. Long and slow inhalations of dank, subterranean air.

With the flashlight miraculously still dangling from my arm, I paddle in place, trying to get a sense of my surroundings. I'm in a cavern roughly the same size as Camp Nightingale's mess hall. The beam of the flashlight stretches over black water, damp rock, a strip of dryish land surrounding the pool in a crescent shape. The water itself takes up about half the cave, no larger than a backyard swimming pool. When I aim the flashlight upward, I see a dome of rock above me dripping with stalactites. The cavern's shape makes me think of a stomach. I've tumbled into the belly of a beast.

A dark hollow sits in a corner where rock wall meets cave ceiling. The spot from which I fell. I sweep the flashlight up and down, trying to gauge how far I dropped. It looks to be about ten feet.

I swim forward, heading to the land that partially rings the water. The ground there is studded with pebbles, painted pale by the flashlight. I pull myself onto it and collapse, exhausted and aching.

I reach into my pocket and optimistically search for my phone. It's still there. Even better, it still works. Thank you, waterproof case.

The phone doesn't have any signal. Not that I was expecting one this far below ground. Still, I try calling 911 in case, by some small miracle, it actually goes through. It doesn't. I'm not surprised.

I remember what Detective Flynn said about tracking someone's location using the GPS on their phones. I can't help but wonder if that still applies when the missing person is underground. I doubt it. Even if it's possible, such a thing could take hours, maybe even days to pinpoint my location.

If I want to get out of here, I'll have to do it myself.

I aim the flashlight to the stretch of cave wall rising to the hole above me. It's steep. Not quite a ninety-degree angle, but mighty close. Before trying to climb it, I scan the rest of the cavern, looking for another way out. I aim the flashlight into every corner and dark cranny I can find, seeing nothing but more water, more rock, more dead ends.

Scaling that wall is my only option.

In desperation, I run to it, not pausing to look for places to grip. Instead, I leap onto the wall, clawing at rock, scrambling for outcroppings. I get about three feet before I lose my grip and fly backward, landing hard on the cave floor.

I try again, this time making it four feet off the ground before getting bucked off. This time I land directly on my tailbone. Sharp pain shoots up my back, momentarily paralyzing me.

Yet I make a third attempt, slowing down a bit, puzzling together the best places to grip and the right direction in which to climb. It works. I find myself rising higher. Six feet. Seven.

When I'm about a foot from the tunnel that leads back outside, I realize there's nothing left to grasp. I reach up with my right arm, my palm smacking smooth rock that's cold and slippery. My left arm and shoulder, bearing all that weight, start to give out.

My body droops.

For a second, I dangle against the cave wall. Then I plummet back to earth, landing feetfirst, my right ankle twisting beneath me before buckling. I think I hear something snap. Or maybe it's my imagination as I collapse into a pained heap.

I scream, hoping it will take the edge off. It doesn't. The pain continues. So does the screaming. I look at my ankle and my foot, bent in a way it shouldn't ever be. There'll be no more climbing for me.

That's when reality sets in.

I'm trapped here.

No one knows where I am.

I'm now as lost as Vivian, Natalie, and Allison.

40

The flashlight dies shortly after 4:00 a.m. I know the time because I check my phone as soon as the dying beam flickers into nothingness. I regret looking, even as I'm comforted by the blue-white glow of the screen. Time continues to pass at an agonizing pace. It's as if the minutes last longer down here, stretching themselves until a single hour feels like three.

Wanting to preserve as much battery as possible, I shut off the phone and return it to my pocket. Then I sit in darkness so complete it feels like death. Nothing but black emptiness.

I start to shiver, realizing how alarmingly cold it is down here. The pool of frigid water doesn't help. Ditto my wet clothes, which cling to my clammy skin. My body trembles. My teeth chatter.

Yet none of that keeps me from dozing off as I huddle against the side of the cave, my knees pulled to my chest. Each blink in the darkness somehow ends with me falling asleep only to bolt awake with a spasm of pain and a startled yelp.

I'm beyond exhausted, if such a thing exists. I can't remember the last time I slept. I guess it was this morning, when I woke up inside Dogwood. I turn on my phone and do another time check.

Four thirty.

Fuck.

I then look for a signal, once again finding none.

Double fuck.

I turn off the phone and count the passing seconds, saying them aloud in the echo chamber of the cavern.

"One. Two. Three."

When I blink, my eyes stay closed.

"Four. Five. Six."

I'm suddenly too tired to speak. But the counting continues, now in my thoughts.

Seven. Eight. Nine.

I sleep after that. For how long, I have no idea. When I awake, it's with another pain-filled jolt, me still counting, the number flying from my parched lips.

"Ten."

My eyes snap open, my sleep-blurred gaze landing on Vivian right in front of me. She reclines on the cave floor, her elbow bent, head propped up. It's how she liked to play Two Truths and a Lie. She claimed the relaxed position made it harder to tell when she was lying.

"You're awake," she says. "Finally."

"How long was I asleep?" I say, now long past

trying to cast her away through sheer force of will.

"An hour or so."

"Have you been here that whole time?"

"Off and on. I guess you thought you were rid of me."

"I certainly wanted to be."

There's no point in lying to her. She's not real.

"Well, you're not." Vivian spreads her arms wide in mock delight. "Surprise!"

"You must find this amusing," I say as I sit up and roll my neck until it cracks. "I'm a lost girl, too."

"You think you're going to die down here?"

"Probably."

"That sucks," Vivian says with a sigh. "Although I guess it makes us even, then."

"I wanted you to come back," I say. "I didn't mean it. And I'm sorry. Just like I'm sorry for locking the cabin door. It was a horrible thing to do, and I regret it every day. That's all truth. No lies."

"I probably would have done the same thing," Vivian admits. "That's why I liked you, Em. We were both bitches when we had to be."

"Does that mean we still would have been friends if you hadn't disappeared?"

Vivian twirls a lock of hair around her finger, giving it some thought. "Maybe. There would have been a lot of drama. Lots of driving each other crazy. But there would have been good times, too.

You being a bridesmaid at my wedding. Drinking with me after my inevitable divorce."

She smiles at me. Her kind smile. The one from the Vivian I thought of as a potential big sister. I miss that Vivian. I mourn her.

"Viv, what happened to you guys that night? Was it Theo?"

"I can't believe you haven't figured it out yet. I left you so many clues, Em."

"Why can't you just tell me?"

"Because this is something you have to figure out on your own," Vivian says. "Your problem is that you're blinded by the past. Everything you need to know is right there in front of you. All you need to do is look."

She points to the other side of the cavern, where a snake of light crawls along the rock wall. Several more surround it, undulating like waves, making the dome of the cavern feel like a disco.

Then it hits me. I can **see**.

The darkness is gone, replaced by a warm light radiating through the entire cave. It comes, quite improbably, from the pool in the middle of the cavern. The light is a rich gold tinged with pink that makes the water glow like a hotel swimming pool. I check my phone, seeing that it's now six. Sunrise.

The presence of light means one thing—there's another way out of the cave.

"Vivian, I think I can get out!"

She's no longer there. Not that she ever truly was. But this time there's no lingering presence, no sense she could return at any moment.

Vivian might be gone for good.

I stand and limp to the water's edge. The light seems brightest to my right. Its undiluted glow suggests a straight path from the cave to the outside world. Most likely an underwater tunnel connecting cave to lake.

I slide back into the pool and face the light. Through the water, I see a glowing circle roughly the same size as the tunnel I entered through. If it stays that same width across its entire length, I might be able to swim my way out of the cavern.

I do a few laps around the pool, loosening up while testing out my injured ankle. It hurts, of course. It's also swollen, which limits movement. I need to fight through both. I have no choice.

Properly warmed up, I line my body up with the tunnel entrance. I start shivering again, this time more from nerves than the chill of the water. I'm scared as hell and long for another way out of here. There isn't one. The only way out is through.

I take a deep breath. I slip under the water. I stare at that gold-and-pink light and start to swim toward it.

41

Swim.

That's all I need to do.

Swim and try not to think about how much my ankle hurts.

Or that the tunnel may slowly be closing in on me.

Or that I'm not even a quarter of the way through it yet.

I need to do nothing else but swim. As hard and as fast as I can. Straight toward the light like the little girl in that movie that gave me nightmares when I was nine.

Swim.

Don't think about that movie and its creepy clown and fizzing TV or how the silt from the lake water clouds my vision and stings my eyes.

Just swim.

Don't think about how the tunnel really is getting smaller or how my shoulders skim the walls, scraping away mossy blooms of algae that make it even harder to see.

Just fucking swim.

Don't think about the algae or the shrinking tunnel or how each flick of my right foot sends pain screaming through my ankle or how the pressure is building in my chest like a balloon that's about to pop.

I swim straight into the light, blinded by it, the glare forcing my eyes shut. My lungs scream. My ankle screams. I'm on the verge of screaming myself. But then the tunnel falls away, slipping from my shoulders like an unzipped dress. My eyes open to the sight of water everywhere. No cave. No walls. Just blessed open lake glowing yellow in the ever-brightening dawn.

I shoot to the surface and gasp, gulping down precious air until the ache in my lungs subsides. My ankle still hurts. As do my exhausted, limp-rag arms. Yet I have enough strength to stay afloat and keep my head above water. I might even be able to swim back to camp after some rest.

Hopefully it won't come to that. Hopefully people are looking for me.

Sure enough, I hear the hum of a motorboat in the distance. I rotate in the water until I can see it—a white skiff, one of two normally moored to Camp Nightingale's dock. Chet sits by the outboard motor, steering the boat across the lake.

I swing an arm out of the water, waving to him. With what little air I have in my lungs, I scream his name.

"Chet!"

He spots me, his face bright with surprise to see me floundering in the lake. He cuts the motor, grabs a wooden oar, and paddles my way.

"Emma? My God, we've been looking everywhere for you."

I resume swimming. He keeps paddling. Together we finally meet, and I latch on to the side of the boat. With Chet's help, I climb aboard and collapse inside, panting, too tired to move.

"Did you find the girls?" I ask, panting out the words, still catching my breath.

"Early this morning. They're dehydrated, hungry, and in shock, but they'll be fine. Last I heard, Theo was going to take them to the hospital."

I sit up, buzzing with alarm.

"Theo's back at camp?"

"Yes," Chet says. "He said he found you with the girls and that you attacked him before vanishing in the woods."

"He's lying."

"That's crazy, Emma. You know that, right?"

I keep talking. Setting the crazy free. "He hurt those girls, Chet. He can't be near them. We have to call the police."

I reach for my phone, amazingly still in my pocket and in working order. There's even a bit of battery left. I start to dial 911 but am halted by a shadow crossing the screen.

Chet's reflection, as warped as a funhouse mirror.

Gripped in his hand is the oar. I see that reflection, too. A faint glimpse of wood swiping across my screen right before Chet swings it into the back of my head.

For a slice of a second, everything stops. My heart. My brain. My lungs and ears and eyes. As if my body needs a moment to figure out how to react.

In that thin sliver of time, I assume that this is what death must feel like. Not a drift into deep slumber or a slow edge toward a warm light. Just a sudden halt.

But then the pain arrives. A screaming, nerve-jolting pain that floods every part of me, telling me I'm still alive.

The dead don't feel this kind of pain.

It hurts so much I envy them.

Anguish takes over, rendering me helpless. My vision blurs. My head rings. I belch out a grunt of surprise as the phone springs from my hands, and I collapse to the bottom of the boat.

42

I come to on the floor of the boat. I feel the scruff of fiberglass against my cheek, smell the fish stench, hear the echo of the water below.

The boat is moving now. The outboard motor hums like white noise. Occasional sprays of lake water mist my face.

I've landed on my side, my left arm pinned beneath me, my right one twitching slightly. My left eye is closed, smushed as it is against the floor. The lid of my right eye keeps blinking, the sky and clouds above flickering like an old movie. Rather than breath, I hyperventilate—short, gasping breaths that huff out air as quickly as I take it in.

I'm still in pain, but it's no longer all-consuming. A steady drumbeat instead of a clash of cymbals. I'm surprised to learn that I can move, if I really put my mind to it. That twitching right arm bends. Both legs stretch. I wiggle my fingers, marveling at the accomplishment.

The clarity of my thoughts is another surprise. I know what's going on. I'm not struck dumb or deaf or blind. I assume Chet pulled back on the swing of that oar right before striking me. Or else I'm just very lucky. Either way, I'll take it.

When the sound of the motor ceases and the boat slows, I'm able to flip onto my back, pleased to learn that my left eye also works. I see Chet standing over me. The oar is back in his hands, although he switches between holding it too tightly and almost letting it fall from his grip.

"I can't believe you had the nerve to come back here, Emma," he says. "Even though it was my idea, it still surprised me. Don't get me wrong. I'm glad you came back. I just didn't think you'd be that stupid."

"Why . . ." I pause to take a dry-mouthed swallow, hoping it will help get the words out. Each syllable is a struggle. "Why ask me back?"

"Because I thought it would be fun," Chet says. "I knew you were crazy. Theo told me all about that. And I wanted to see just how crazy you'd get. You know, trap a few birds and put them in the cabin. A little paint on the door and an appearance at the window. A little peek in the shower."

Chet pauses to give me a wink that makes my stomach roil.

"I totally didn't expect you to run with it, though. I thought it would take a lot more work to make you look guilty. But all that talk about seeing Vivian? That alone made everyone think you'd snapped."

"But **why**?"

"Because of the real reason I wanted you back here. Girls from your cabin go missing, and to put you at the scene of the crime, I drop something of yours into an empty canoe with a broken pair of glasses and set it adrift. That bracelet of yours worked wonders, by the way. When I snapped it off your wrist outside the Lodge, I knew it would be perfect."

He flashes me a twisted smile. It's the grin of a madman. Someone far more insane than I ever was.

"After that, all I needed to do was delete any surveillance video of me near your cabin and change the file name of the one showing you leaving Dogwood yesterday morning. I'll let you in on a little secret, Em. The girls didn't sneak out five minutes before you woke up. They'd been gone at least an hour."

I sit up, using my elbows for support. I tremble a moment before locking my arms and steadying myself. That small movement wakes me up a bit, gives me some lift. I hear the newfound strength in my voice as I say, "All that effort. I don't understand."

"Because you almost ruined our lives," Chet says with a snarl. "Especially Theo's. So much that he tried to kill himself. That's how much you fucked him up, Emma. When you destroyed his reputation, you destroyed ours as well. When I got to Yale, half the school wouldn't even talk to me. They saw me as the kid whose brother got away with murder because we're filthy rich. And we're not. Not anymore. All we have left is my mother's apartment and this godforsaken lake."

Even though my skull is stormy with pain, I finally understand.

This is his revenge.

An attempt to make me look as guilty as I had made Theo look. He wants me to live under the same cloud of suspicion. To lose everything.

"I didn't want to kill you, Emma," he says. "I would have much rather watched you suffer for the next fifteen years. But the plan has changed. You made sure of that when you freed those girls. Now I have no choice but to make you disappear."

Chet grabs me by the shirt collar and hoists me off the floor. I don't struggle. I can't. All I can do is wobble precariously as he plops me onto the edge of the boat. The motion jars still more energy into me.

Now that I'm off the floor, I can see we're in a part of the lake I don't recognize. A cove of sorts. Trees crowd the shore, ringing the water like walls of a fortress. Muted light seeps through them, doing little to burn away the fog that rolls across the water.

Something sits in the mist, jutting out of the water a few feet from the boat.

A rooster weathervane.

It's the same weathervane I've seen in pictures, perched atop Peaceful Valley Asylum. Only now it's edged with rust and crusted with barnacles. And the asylum it sits upon rests deep beneath Lake Midnight. I peer into the water, getting shimmery glimpses of its mud-caked roof.

It's still here. Right where it's always been. Only now covered by the lake. That part of Casey's story is true.

"I had a feeling you'd recognize it," Chet says. "You knowing about this place was another surprise. Little nosy Emma has really been doing her homework."

Judging from the ring of dried mud along the shore, I suspect the lake is usually high enough to completely cover the weathervane. It can be seen now only because of the current drought.

"I found it when I was a teenager," Chet says. "No one else knows it's still here. Not my mom. Not Lottie. I guess they think old Buchanan Harris razed it when he bought the land. Instead, he just left it here and flooded the place. And now no one will know to look for you here."

My heart gallops. Blood pumps to my brain, making me more alert as well as more afraid. Rather than silence me, the fear sparks my voice. "Don't do this, Chet. It's not too late."

"I think it is, Em."

"The girls didn't see you. They told me so. If you want me to tell the cops I did it, I will."

Words are my only defense. I have no strength to fight him off. Even if I did, I'd be no match against another swing of the oar.

"No one will know you did it," I say. "Just you and me. And I'm not going to tell anyone. I'll take the blame. I'll plead guilty."

Chet transfers the oar from one hand to the other. I think I'm getting through to him.

"You want to see me suffer, right? Then imagine me in prison. Think how much I'll suffer then."

I'm hit by a flash of memory. Me leaving Camp Nightingale fifteen years ago. Chet was there, calling after his brother, his face tear-streaked. Maybe that was the moment he decided he needed to get revenge. If so, I need to remind him of the boy he was before that.

"You're not a killer," I tell him. "You're too good of a person for that. I'm the one who did something bad. Don't be like me. Don't become someone you're not."

Chet raises the oar, ready to bring it down once more. I lurch forward before he can do it, slamming myself into him. The strength comes out of nowhere. A coiled energy ignited by terror and desperation. It sends Chet stumbling against one of the boat's seats. His legs catch on it, and he tumbles backward. The oar leaves his hands, clatters to the floor. I reach for it, but Chet's faster. He grabs the oar with one hand and slaps me with the back of the other.

Spikes of pain sting my cheek. But the blow also zaps one last bit of adrenaline into me. Enough to let me scramble to the front of the boat and crawl onto the bow.

Behind me, Chet's on his feet, oar in hand.

He lifts it.

He swings.

I close my eyes, screaming, waiting for the blow to connect with my skull.

Instead, a shot rings out, the sound careening across the cove. My eyes fly open in time to see the oar explode into a thousand splinters. I shut them again as wood sprays my face. I duck, trying to avoid it.

The boat tips.

I tip with it, tumbling backward, over the side of the boat and into Lake Midnight.

43

My fall through the water is brief. Just a quick, disorienting drop before I slam into something a few feet from the surface. Wood, I think. Slick with moss and algae and a hundred years of lake water rising and falling.

A roof.

As I'm realizing this, the wood beneath me buckles, giving way. Soon I'm falling again. Still underwater but now also surrounded by walls, encased within them.

Peaceful Valley Asylum.

I'm inside it, dropping from the ceiling to the floor below. I brace myself for another smash through it. It never comes. Instead, I bounce off the floor and drift upward.

Faint light trickles through algae-streaked windows. It's enough brightness for me to see an empty room taken over by mud. Everything is tilted—walls, ceiling, doorframe. The door itself has come off its hinges and now sits askew, revealing a short hall, stairs, more light. I swim toward them, struggling to make it through the doorway, across the hall, down the steps.

At the bottom, the front door gapes open. The door itself sits on the floor, all but blending in with the lake bottom. To my left is a sitting room. There's a hole in the wall where bricks and floorboards and scraps of wallpaper have tumbled out. A striped bass circles the room. I swim out the open door, passing from inside to outside, even though it's all part of the same watery landscape.

Pain pulses through my body. My lungs burn. I need air. I need sleep. I start to swim upward, heading to the surface, when something catches my eye.

A skull.

Bleached white.

Jaw missing.

Eye sockets aimed at the sky.

Scattered around it are more bones. A dozen, at least. I glimpse the arch of ribs, the curl of fingers, a second skull a few yards from the first.

The girls.

I know because nestled among the bones, shining faintly in the muck, is a length of gold chain and a locket in the shape of a heart. A tiny emerald sits in its center.

Something enters the water behind me. I feel it more than see it—a shuddering of the lake. An arm reaches out and wraps around my waist. Then I'm tugged upward, away from the girls, toward the water's surface.

Soon we're breaking through Lake Midnight. I see sky, trees, the camp's other motorboat bobbing on the water a few yards away. Within it stands Detective Flynn, his gun trained on Chet, who drops the decimated oar.

And I see Theo. Swimming next to me. Arm still around my waist. Lake water sloshing against his chin.

"Are you okay?" he says.

I think of Vivian, Natalie, and Allison lying directly below us.

I think of all the years they spent down there, waiting for me to find them.

So when Theo asks again if I'm okay, I can only nod, choke out a sob, and let the tears flow.

44

I sit in the front seat of Detective Flynn's police-issued sedan, the hospital a distant memory in the rearview mirror. I ended up being more bruised and battered than I initially thought. The doctor's diagnosis was startling. A concussion from the oar. A sprained ankle from the fall. Lacerations, dehydration, a persistent headache.

I ended up spending two days in the hospital. The girls were there for one of them. I shared a room with Miranda, and we spent that time complaining about our sorry states, giggling over the ridiculousness of it all and gossiping about the handsome male nurse who worked the morning shift.

Visitors streamed in and out. Sasha and Krystal from the room next door. Miranda's grandmother—a whirling dervish of Catholic guilt and smothering hugs. Becca dropped by with a book of Ansel Adams photographs, and Casey brought apologies for ever thinking I had tried to hurt the girls of Dogwood. Marc arrived with a stack of gossip mags and the news that he's back together with Billy the librarian. Even my parents flew in from Florida, a gesture that touched me more than I expected.

We plan to head back to Manhattan later this afternoon. Marc is going to tag along. It'll be an interesting drive for all parties involved.

For now, though, I have unfinished business to attend to, as Detective Flynn reminds me.

"Here's what probably happened," he says. "Based on what she wrote in her diary, Vivian, like you, assumed the worst about Peaceful Valley, Charles Cutler, and Buchanan Harris. She found the location of the asylum and took Allison and Natalie with her to get proof of its existence. From the way you described it, it's probably very easy to get disoriented down there. They went into the water, swam around the wreckage, never came back up. Accidental drowning."

Just because I had assumed exactly that doesn't make dealing with it any easier. Not when I now know that Vivian died the same way her sister did. It's too tragic to comprehend.

"So there's nothing to suggest Chet killed them?" I say, knowing it's impossible.

Flynn shakes his head. "He swears he didn't do it. I have no reason to doubt him. He was only ten at the time. Besides, there's still quite a few bones at the bottom of that lake. It'll take a while to find them all. Until then, we won't know for certain it's your friends down there."

But I already know. It was Vivian, Natalie, and Allison I saw in the depths of the lake. The locket was all the proof I need. Now just thinking about it causes grief to balloon in my chest. A common occurrence over the past two days.

"As for the second group of girls from Dogwood, Chet said he had no plans to hurt them," Flynn says. "Seems to me like he didn't know what he was going to do. He was just running on anger, not thinking about the consequences."

"Where is he now?"

"County jail for the time being. He plans to plead guilty to all charges tomorrow. From there, he'll probably be transferred to a mental-health facility for an unknown amount of time."

I'm relieved to hear it. I want Chet to get the help he needs. Because I know a thing or two about seeking vengeance. Like Chet, I've felt the desire for revenge burn inside me. It's singed both of us.

But I've healed. Not completely, but definitely getting there.

"And I guess I owe you an apology," Flynn says. "For not believing you."

"You were only doing your job."

"But I should have listened to you more. I was so quick to think you did it because it was the easiest explanation. For that, I'm sorry."

"Apology accepted."

We ride in silence until we reach the wrought-iron gate of Camp Nightingale. When I straighten in my seat, Flynn looks my way and says, "Nervous to be back?"

"Not as much as I thought I'd be," I tell him.

Seeing the outskirts of camp brings a tumble of emotions. Sadness and regret, love and disgust. And brutal relief. The kind you feel when you learn the whole truth about something. The cheating spouse exposed. An official diagnosis. Having the truth revealed means you can finally start to unburden yourself of it.

Flynn steers the car into the heart of camp. It feels as empty and silent as the morning I woke to find the girls missing from Dogwood. This time, with good reason. All the campers, counselors, and instructors have been sent home. Camp Nightingale has closed early. This time for good.

As sad as it is, I know it's for the best. There's too much tragedy associated with the place. Besides, Franny has enough to deal with.

Lottie is outside waiting for me when the sedan pulls up to the Lodge. Because I'm loopy from painkillers and my ankle is wrapped with a mile of ACE bandage, she needs to help me from the car. Before letting go of my hand, she gives it an extra squeeze. A signal that she has no hard feelings about what I've said. I'm grateful for her forgiveness.

Flynn honks the horn and gives me a wave. Then he's off, steering the sedan out of camp as Lottie guides me to the Lodge. Inside, there's no sign of Mindy. I'm not surprised. When visiting me in the hospital, Casey mentioned that she was returning to the family farm. She said it with relish, as if Mindy got exactly what she deserved. If that means something better than being with Chet, then I'm inclined to agree.

"I'm afraid there's not much time," Lottie says. "Franny only has a few minutes before we need to go. The people at the jail are sticklers about visiting hours."

"I understand."

I'm led to the back deck, where Franny rests in an Adirondack chair tilted to face the sun. She greets me warmly, clasping my hand and smiling as if the years of accusations and misdeeds between us mean nothing. Maybe now they don't. Maybe now we're even.

"Dear Emma. How nice to see you up and about again." She gestures to the floor next to her chair, where my suitcase and box of painting supplies have been placed. "It's all there. I made sure Lottie packed everything. The only things missing are Vivian's diary, which the police took, and the photograph she removed from the Lodge. That deserves to stay with Lottie, don't you think?"

"I couldn't agree more."

"Are you sure you don't want to have one last

look around Dogwood?" Franny asks. "In case we missed something?"

"No," I say. "I'm fine."

Dogwood is the last place I want to be. It's too full of memories, both good and bad. With all that's happened—and all I now know—I'm not ready to face them. The sight of those names carved into hickory and the sound of that creaking third floorboard would probably break me.

Franny gives me a knowing look, like she understands completely. "I'm sorry I didn't visit you in the hospital. Under the circumstances, I thought it best to stay away."

"You have nothing to feel sorry about," I tell her, meaning every word.

"But I do. What Chet did is inexcusable. I'm truly, deeply sorry for whatever pain he caused. To you and the other girls in Dogwood. And please believe me when I say that I didn't know what he had planned. If I had, I never would have asked you back."

"I believe you," I say. "And I forgive you. Not that you did anything wrong. You've been nothing but kind to me, Franny. It's me who should be begging for your forgiveness."

"I already gave it. Long, long ago."

"But I didn't deserve it."

"You did," Franny says. "Because I saw goodness in you, even if you never knew it was there yourself. And speaking of forgiveness, I think there's someone else who has a thing or two to say about that."

She stretches out her hand, seeking help in getting out of her chair. I oblige and gently lift her to her feet. We lean against each other, wobbling in tandem to the deck's railing. Below is Lake Midnight, as beautiful as always. And sitting on the lawn, staring out at the water, is Theo.

"Go on," Franny urges. "You two have a lot to talk about."

At first, I say nothing to Theo. I simply join him on the lawn, my eyes on the lake. Theo is silent in return, for obvious reasons. I've now accused him twice. If anyone deserves the silent treatment, it's me.

I glance at his profile, studying the scar on his cheek and a new mark on his forehead—a deep-purple bruise where I had struck him with the flashlight. I've caused him so much pain. Chet's actions aside, he has every right to hate me.

Yet Theo still made sure I made it out of the lake alive. Detective Flynn talked at length about how quick Theo was to dive into the water after me. Zero hesitation. That's how he described it. It's a debt I'll never be able to properly repay. I could sit here and thank Theo for hours, beg for his forgiveness, or apologize so many times I lose count. But I don't. Instead, I hold out my hand and say, "Hi, I'm Emma."

Theo at last acknowledges my presence with a turn of his head. Shaking my hand, he replies, "I'm Theo. Nice to meet you."

It's all he needs to say.

Theo shifts beside me and pulls something out of his pocket, which he drops into my hand. I don't need to look to know it's my charm bracelet. I can feel the chain curled against my palm, the weight of the three pewter birds.

"I thought you'd like it back," Theo says, adding with a grin, "even though we've only just met."

I cup the bracelet in my hand. I've had it for such a long time. It's been my devoted companion for more than half my life. But it's time to say good-bye. Now that I know the truth, I won't be needing it anymore.

"Thank you," I say. "But . . ."

"But what?"

"I think I've outgrown it. Besides, I know a better place for it."

Without a second thought, I toss the bracelet into the air, the three birds taking flight at last. I close my eyes before it lands. I don't want the memory of seeing it vanish from view. Instead, I listen, reaching for Theo's hand as the bracelet drops with a light splash into the depths of Lake Midnight.

This is how it ends.

Franny passes away on a muggy evening in late September. She dies not at the lake but in the bedroom of her penthouse at the Harris. Theo and Lottie are with her. According to Theo, her last words are, "I'm ready."

A week later, you attend her funeral on a Monday that's been kissed by Indian summer. You think Franny would have appreciated that. After the service, you and Theo go for a walk in Central Park. You haven't seen him since leaving Camp Nightingale. With everything that was going on, both of you agreed that space and time were necessary.

Now a host of unspoken emotions hangs over the reunion. There's grief, of course. And happiness at seeing each other. And another, stranger feeling—trepidation. You don't know what kind of relationship the two of you will have going forward. Especially when halfway into your walk, Theo says, "I'm going away next week."

You come to a sudden stop. "Where?"

"Africa," Theo says. "I signed on for another tour with Doctors Without Borders. One year. I think it'll be good for me to get away. I need time to sort things out."

You understand. You think it sounds like a fine idea. You wish him well.

"When I get back, I'd love to have dinner," Theo says.

"You mean like a date?"

"It could just be a casual meal between two friends who have a habit of accusing each other of doing terrible things," Theo replies. "But I kind of like the date idea better."

"I do, too," you say.

That night, you begin to paint again. It strikes you after hours spent lying awake thinking about changing seasons and the passing of time. You get out of bed, stand before a blank canvas, and realize what you need to do—paint not what you see but what you saw.

You paint the girls in the same order. Always.

Vivian first.

Then Natalie.

Then Allison.

You cover them with sinuous shapes in various shades of blue and green and brown. Moss and cobalt, pewter and pine. You fill the canvas with algae, pondweed, underwater trees with branches twisting toward the surface. You paint a weathervane-topped building submerged in the chilly depths, dark and empty, waiting for someone to find it.

When that canvas is complete, you paint another. Then another. And another. Bold paintings of walls and foundations hidden underwater, engulfed by plant life, lost to time. Each time you paint over the girls feels like a burial, a funeral. You paint nonstop for weeks. Your wrist aches. Your fingers don't uncurl even when there's not a brush in them. When you sleep, you dream of colors.

Your therapist tells you that what you're doing is healthy. You're sorting through your feelings, dealing with your grief.

By January, you have completed twenty-one paintings. Your underwater series.

You show them to Randall, who's ecstatic. He gasps at each canvas. Marvels at how you've outdone yourself.

A new gallery show is planned, hastily put together by Randall to capitalize on all the publicity surrounding Lake Midnight. It's set for March. Buzz steadily builds. You're profiled in The New Yorker. Your parents plan to attend.

The morning of the opening, you get a phone call from Detective Nathan Flynn. He tells you what you've known all along—the bones discovered in the water belong to Natalie and Allison.

"What about Vivian?" you ask.

"That's a very good question," Flynn says.

He tells you that none of the bones are a match.

He tells you that both Natalie's and Allison's skulls were fractured in a way that suggests they were struck in the head, possibly with a shovel found near the bones.

He tells you that chains and bricks had also been discovered, indicating both bodies might have been weighed down.

He tells you the strand of hair in the plastic baggie you found buried with Vivian's diary is actually processed polyester used mostly in the making of wigs.

He tells you that same baggie also contained traces of a laminate and adhesive that were once common in the production of fake IDs.

"What are you suggesting?" you ask.

"Exactly what you're thinking," he says.

What you're thinking about are Vivian's last words to you, when she knocked on Dogwood's locked door.

Come on, Em. Let me in.

Me.

That's what she had said.

Not us.

Meaning that she was alone.

You hang up the phone with a queasy feeling in your gut. The conversation leaves you so stunned that you almost opt out of attending that night's opening. Only Marc keeps you from backing out. He nudges you through the motions of getting ready. Shower. Slinky blue dress. Black heels with red soles.

At the gallery, you see that Randall has once again pulled out all the stops. You sip wine and watch shrimp canapés float by on silver trays as you talk to the guy from Christie's, the lady from the Times, the television actress who helped set your career in motion. Sasha, Krystal, and Miranda attend. Marc takes a picture of the four of you standing in front of your largest painting, No. 6, which seems as massive as Lake Midnight itself.

Later that night, you're at that very same work when a woman comes up beside you.

"This is lovely," she says, her eyes on the painting. "So beautifully strange. Are you the artist?"

"I am."

You glance her way, getting a glimpse of red hair, a striking frame, regal bearing. Her clothes are effortlessly cool. Black dress. Black gloves. Floppy black hat and a Burberry trench. You think she might be a model.

Then you recognize her pert nose and cruel smile, and your legs buckle.

"Vivian?"

She continues to stare at the painting, speaking in a calm whisper only the two of you can hear.

"Two Truths and a Lie, Emma," she says. "You ready to play?"

You want to say no. You have to say yes.

"One: Allison and Natalie were with my sister the night she died," she says. "They dared her to go out on that ice. They saw her fall in and drown. Yet they told no one. But I had my suspicions. I knew Katherine wouldn't do something so dangerous unless she'd been coerced. So I befriended them, earned their trust, pretended to trust them in return. It's how I learned the truth, teasing it out of them on the Fourth of July. They swore they tried to help Katherine. I knew they were lying. After all, I pretended to drown in front of everyone. As I flailed in that water, only Theo made a move to help me. Natalie and Allison did nothing. They simply watched, just as they had watched Katherine drown."

You think about the day you came back to the cabin and found the girls fighting. You realize now that you had walked into their confession. And contrary to how friendly they had seemed afterward, nothing between them was fine.

"Two: Since I already suspected what Natalie

and Allison had done, I spent a year researching and planning. I learned about the history
of Lake Midnight. I found a place no one knew
about—a flooded insane asylum. I placed a
sweatshirt in the woods to confuse searchers.
I fucked the groundskeeper and stole the key
to his toolshed. Then I led Allison and Natalie
to that secret spot on the lake where no one
would ever look. I did to them what they had
done to my sister."

Now you understand that you misinterpreted
her diary. She didn't look for Peaceful Valley to
expose its existence. She sought it out because
it was the best place to hide her crime.

You think about the shovel stolen from the
toolshed. You think about fractured skulls
resting on the lake bed. You think about the
locket, which you now know Vivian dropped
into the water because just like you and your
bracelet, she no longer needed it.

"Three: Vivian is dead."

Your mouth is so dry with shock you're not
sure you can speak. But you do, managing to
croak out, "The third one."

"Wrong," she says. "Vivian died fifteen years
ago. Let her rest in peace, Em."

She leaves the gallery quickly, her boots
clicking against the floor. You follow her, much
slower, your legs wobbly from shock. Out on
the street, you see a town car streak away from

the curb. Tinted windows deny you a good look. No one else is on the block. It's just you and your palpitating heart.

Back in the gallery, you murmur your good-byes to Marc, Randall, all the others. You say you're not feeling well. You blame it on the shrimp you haven't even touched.

At home in your studio, you paint all night and into the dawn. You paint until garbage trucks rumble by and the sun peeks over the buildings on the other side of the street. When you stop, you stand before the finished canvas.

It's a portrait of Vivian.

Not how she looked back then but how she looks now. Her nose. Her chin. Her eyes, which you've painted midnight blue. She stares back at you with a coy smile playing across her lips.

It's the last time you'll ever paint her. You know that with bone-deep certainty.

In a few hours, when the post office opens, you'll ship the painting to Detective Flynn. You'll include a note telling him that Vivian is alive and was last seen in Manhattan. You'll ask that the painting be released to the media, who can use it any way they want.

You will expose who she is, how she looks, what she's done.

You won't hide her beneath layers of paint.

You will refuse to cover her up.

The time for lies is over.

ACKNOWLEDGMENTS

I need to thank the many people who helped with the writing and publication of this book, starting with my fabulous US editor, Maya Ziv, whose gentle encouragement helped me transform it from an ungainly caterpillar into something that resembles a butterfly. Thanks are also due to Madeline Newquist, for keeping things on track; Andrea Monagle, for her eagle eye; and the publicity and marketing dream team of Emily Canders, Abigail Endler, and Elina Vaysbeyn.

In the UK, I must thank my dream team across the pond: Gillian Green, Stephenie Naulls, and Joanna Bennett. (With special well wishes to Emily Yau.)

Additional thanks go to everyone at Aevitas Creative Management, especially my agent, Michelle Brower, who has stuck with me all these years, and Chelsey Heller, who continues to do stellar work on the international front.

Other necessary thanks go to Stephen King, for his generosity; Taylor Swift, whose lyrics from **Sad Beautiful Tragic** I shamelessly cribbed; Joan

Lindsay and Peter Weir, whose **Picnic at Hanging Rock** initially inspired this book; Sarah Dutton, for being a great reader and an even better friend; and the Ritter and Livio families, for being so proud of me.

Finally, I could thank Mike Livio until the end of time and it still wouldn't be enough. I truly couldn't do this without his patience, calmness, and steady hand.

ABOUT THE AUTHOR

The Last Time I Lied is the second thriller from **Riley Sager**, the pseudonym of an author who lives in Princeton, New Jersey. Riley's first novel, **Final Girls,** was a national and international best-seller that has been published in more than two dozen countries.